PHILLIP MARGOLIN OMNIBUS

The Associate

The Last Innocent Man

PHILLIP MARGOLIN OMNIBUS

The Associate
The Last Innocent Man

PHILLIP MARGOLIN

timewarner
paperbacks

A *Time Warner* Paperback

This omnibus edition first published in Great Britain by
Time Warner Paperbacks in 2004
Phillip Margolin Omnibus Copyright © Phillip Margolin 2004

Previously published separately:
The Associate first published in the United States in 2001
by HarperCollins Publishers Inc.
First published in Great Britain in 2001 by
Little, Brown and Company
Published by Time Warner Paperbacks in 2002
Copyright © 2001 by Phillip Margolin

The Last Innocent Man first published in the United States in 1981
by Little, Brown and Company
Published by Bantam Books in 1995
Published by Warner Books in 1997
Reprinted 1999
Copyright © 1981 by Phillip Margolin

The moral right of the author has been asserted.

A CIP catalogue record for this book
is available from the British Library.

ISBN 0 7515 3649 0

Printed and bound in Great Britain by
Clays Ltd, St Ives plc

Time Warner Paperbacks
An imprint of
Time Warner Books UK
Brettenham House
Lancaster Place
London WC2E 7EN

www.TimeWarnerBooks.co.uk

The Associate

For Daniel and Chris

*My son and his new wife—two terrific people
on the threshold of a terrific life together*

ACKNOWLEDGMENTS

I owe a debt of gratitude to the many people who volunteered their time and ideas to help me write this book. Since science has never been my strong point, I am tremendously grateful to Dr. Lynn Loriaux, who invented the fictional drug Insufort for me and answered many other science questions. Dr. John Lundy and Dr. Karen Gunson, the Oregon State Medical Examiner, taught me how human remains are identified. Ed Pritchard was my computer guru.

I received invaluable information about the life of an associate at a major law firm from Alison Brody, an associate at Portland's Miller, Nash law firm, and Scott Crawford, Mike Jacobs, Melissa Robertson, Bryan Geon, Sharon Hill, Richard Vangelisti, Maria Gorecki, associates at the Stoel, Rives law firm in Portland. I also want to thank Stoel, Rives partners, Randy Foster and Barnes Ellis. I want to make sure that my readers understand that the Reed, Briggs firm in *The Associate* is an invention and that the partners and associates in it are not based on any real person.

Mike Williams and Jonathan Hoffman are exceptional

attorneys who are regularly involved in the high-stakes civil litigation that forms the backdrop for this book. I am very grateful to them for walking me through the steps the plaintiffs' and defendants' attorneys take in a product liability case.

I also received invaluable technical assistance from Mike Shinn, Dan Bronson, Mark Anderson, Chip Horner, Steve Millen of Riverview Cemetery, Dr. Nathan Selden, Detective Sergeant Jon F. Rhodes of the Portland Police Bureau, Sergeant Mary Lindstrand of the Multnomah County Sheriff's Office, and my good friend Vince Kohler.

Thanks also to my fantastic children, Ami and Daniel; Johnathan Hoffman and Richard Vangelisti; as well as Joe, Eleonore, Jerry and Judy Margolin, and Norman and Helen Stamm for their valuable comments on my first draft.

I have to thank Dan Conaway, my intrepid editor for his insights. I am truly lucky to work with him. I am also very lucky to have Jean Naggar and everyone at her agency on my side.

People are always asking me where I get my ideas. In the case of *The Associate* there is an easy answer. Doreen, my incredible wife of more than thirty years, dreamed up the plot device that is at the heart of this book. I can't tell you what it is, because I don't want to ruin any surprises, but it's pretty clever, as is she.

PROLOGUE

An icy wind whipped down Mercer Street, rattling awnings, scattering paper scraps and raking Gene Arnold's cheeks raw. He turned up his coat collar and ducked his head to avoid the arctic chill. This wasn't the Arizona lawyer's first visit to New York City, but it was his first winter visit and he was unprepared for the biting cold.

Arnold was an unremarkable man, someone you could sit opposite for an hour and not remember five minutes later. He was of average height, tortoiseshell glasses magnified his brown eyes, and his small, bald head was partially ringed by a fringe of dull gray hair. Arnold's private life was as placid as his personality. He was unmarried, read a lot, and the most exciting thing he did was play golf. Nothing that had happened to him had even registered as a blip on the world's radar screen except for a tragedy he had endured seven years before.

Arnold's law practice was as tedious as his life, business transactions mostly. He was in New York to secure financing for Martin Alvarez, the king of the Arizona used car market, who wanted to expand into New Mexico.

Arnold's successful meeting with a potential investor had ended sooner than expected, leaving him time to wander around SoHo in search of a painting he could add to his small collection of art.

Arnold's eyes teared and his nose started to run as he looked around desperately for shelter from the wind. An art gallery on the corner of Mercer and Spring streets was open and he ducked into it, sighing with relief when a blast of warm air greeted him. A thin young woman dressed in black was leaning on a counter near the front of the store. She looked up from the catalog she was reading.

"Can I help you?" she asked, flashing him a practiced smile.

"Just looking," Arnold answered self-consciously.

The art hanging on the white walls of the gallery did not fit into one category. Arnold glanced briefly at a series of collages with a feminist theme before stopping to admire some paintings that were more his style. Back home he owned several western scenes, brown and red mesas at sunset, cowboys on the trail, that sort of thing. These landscapes were of New England, seascapes really. Dories on a raging ocean, waves breaking on a deserted beach, a cottage scarred by the sea's salt spray. Very nice.

Arnold wandered over to a group of black-and-white photographs entitled *Couples*. The first grainy shot showed two teenagers holding hands in a park. They were viewed from behind, leaning into each other, their heads almost touching. The photographer had captured their intimate moment perfectly. The picture made Arnold sad.

He would have given anything to be that boy with that girl. Being alone was the hardest thing.

The next photo showed a black couple sitting in a café. They were laughing, his head thrown back, mouth open, she smiling shyly, delighted that she was the source of such joy.

Arnold studied the photo. It wasn't the type of art that he usually purchased, but there was something about the photograph that drew him to it. He checked the information on the small, white rectangle next to the photo and learned that the photographer was Claude Bernier and the price was within his means.

Arnold moved to the third photograph in the series. It showed a man and a woman dressed for the rain striding across a square in the center of some city. They were angry, faces tight. The woman's eyes blazed, the man's mouth was a grim line.

"Oh, my God," Arnold said. He fell forward, bracing himself against the wall.

"Sir?" The young woman was staring at him, alarmed by his ashen pallor and his inability to stand upright. Arnold stared back, panicky, light-headed.

"Are you okay?"

Arnold nodded, but the woman was unconvinced. She hurried forward and slipped a hand under his elbow.

"Is there someplace I can sit down?" he asked weakly.

The woman led him up front to a chair behind the counter. Arnold sagged onto it and put his hand to his forehead.

"Can I get you some water?" she asked anxiously.

Arnold saw that she was trying to hold it together. He

imagined that she was thinking "heart attack" and wondering what it would be like to sit with a corpse while she waited for the police.

"Water would be good. I'm okay, really. Nothing to worry about," he said, trying to reassure her. "I'm just a little dizzy."

By the time the woman returned with the water Arnold had regained his composure. He took two sips and breathed deeply. When he looked up the woman was watching him and worrying her hands.

"I'm much better." He gave her a weak smile. "I'm just not used to this cold."

"Please, sit here as long as you want."

"Thanks." He paused, then pointed toward the exhibit. "The photographer, Bernier, does he live near here?"

"Claude? Sure. He's got a walk-up in Chelsea."

"I want to buy one of his pictures."

Arnold stood up slowly, steadier now, and led the woman to the photograph of the angry couple. As he crossed the room doubts assailed him, but they melted away as he drew closer to the scene that Bernier had captured.

"Do you think he'd see me today?" Arnold asked as he produced a credit card without moving his eyes from the photo.

The woman looked worried. "Do you feel up to it?"

Arnold nodded. She seemed on the verge of trying to change his mind. Then she carried the photograph to the front to ring up the purchase. As she waited for clearance from the credit-card company she used the phone. Arnold sat down again. His initial shock had abated and had been replaced by a sense of urgency and purpose.

"Claude can see you anytime," the woman told him as she handed Arnold his purchase and stationery from the gallery bearing the photographer's address and phone number. He memorized the address and placed the paper in his jacket pocket.

"Thank you. You've been very kind," he told the sales-clerk before stepping into the street. A frigid wind greet-ed him, but Gene Arnold was too distracted to notice.

Part I

❧

Monkey Etiquette

ONE

The headlight beams of Dr. Sergey Kaidanov's battered SAAB bounced off a stand of Douglas firs then came to rest on the unpainted wall of a one-story, cinderblock building buried in the woods several miles from downtown Portland. As soon as Kaidanov unlocked the front door of the building the rhesus monkeys started making that half-cooing, half-barking sound that set his nerves on edge. The volume of noise increased when Kaidanov flipped on the lights.

Most of the monkeys were housed in two rooms at the back of the building. Kaidanov walked down a narrow hall and stood in front of a thick metal door that sealed off one of the rooms. He slid back a metal sheet and studied the animals through the window it concealed. There were sixteen rhesus monkeys in each room. Each monkey was in its own steel mesh cage. The cages were stacked two high and two across on a flatcar with rollers. Kaidanov hated everything about the monkeys—their sour, unwashed smell, the noises they made, the unnerving way they followed his every move.

As soon as Kaidanov's face was framed in the window,

the monkey two from the door in the top cage leaped toward him and stared him down. Its fur was brownish gray and it gripped the mesh with hands containing opposable thumbs on both arms and legs. This was the dominant monkey in the room and it had established its dominance within three weeks even though there was no way it could get at the others.

Rhesus monkeys were very aggressive, very nervous, and always alert. It was bad etiquette to look one in the eye, but Kaidanov did it just to show the little bastard who was the boss. The monkey didn't blink. It stretched its doglike muzzle through the mesh as far as it could, baring a set of vicious canines. At two feet tall and forty pounds, the monkey didn't look like it could do much damage to a one-hundred-and-ninety-pound, five-foot-eight male human, but it was much stronger than it looked.

Kaidanov checked his watch. It was three in the morning. He couldn't imagine what was so important that he had to meet here at this hour, but the person whose call had dragged him from a deep sleep paid Kaidanov to do as he was told, no questions asked.

Kaidanov needed caffeine. He was about to go to his office to brew a pot of coffee when he noticed that the padlock on the dominant monkey's cage was open. He must have forgotten to close it after the last feeding. The scientist started to open the door but stopped when he remembered that the key to the monkey rooms was in his office.

Kaidanov returned to the front of the building. His office was twelve by fifteen and stuffed with lab equipment. A small desk on casters stood just inside the door. It was covered by a phone book, articles from research journals, and printouts of contractions that the monkeys experienced during pregnancy. Behind the table was a cheap office chair. Along the walls were metal filing cabinets, a sink, and a paper towel dispenser.

Kaidanov walked around the desk. The coffeepot was sitting on a table alongside a centrifuge, scales, a rack of test tubes, and a Pokémon mug filled with Magic Markers, pens, and pencils. Above the table was a television screen attached to a security camera that showed the front of the building.

The pot of coffee was almost brewed when Kaidanov heard a car pull up and a door slam. On the television a figure in a hooded windbreaker ran toward the lab. Kaidanov left his office and opened the front door. The scientist peered at the hooded face and saw two cold eyes staring at him through the slits in a ski mask. Before he could speak, a gun butt struck his forehead, blinding him with pain. Kaidanov collapsed to the floor. The muzzle of a gun ground into his neck.

"Move," a muffled voice commanded. He scrambled to his knees and a booted foot shoved him forward. The pain in his face brought tears to his eyes as he crawled the short distance to his office.

"The keys to the monkey rooms."

Kaidanov pointed toward a hook on the wall. Seconds later a blow to the back of his head knocked him unconscious.

Kaidanov had no idea how long he had been out. The first thing he heard when he came to were the hysterical shrieks of terrified monkeys and the sound of cages crashing together. The scientist felt like a nail had been driven into his skull, but he managed to struggle into a sitting position. Around him filing cabinets had been opened and overturned. The floor was littered with gasoline-drenched paper, but that was not the only object doused in gasoline—his clothing, face, and hands reeked of it. Then the acrid smell of smoke assailed his nostrils and his stomach turned when he saw the shadow of flames dancing on the wall outside his office.

Fear dragged Kaidanov to his knees just as his assailant reentered the office holding the gun and a five-gallon can of gas. Kaidanov scurried back against the wall, much the way the more docile monkeys skittered to the back of their cages whenever he entered the monkey room. The gas can hit the desk with a metallic thud and Kaidanov's assailant pulled out a lighter. Kaidanov tried to speak, but terror made him mute. Just as the lid of the lighter flipped open, an insane shriek issued from the doorway. An apparition, engulfed in flame, eyes wide with panic and pain, filled the entrance to the office. The dominant monkey, Kaidanov thought. It had been able to force open its cage door because Kaidanov had forgotten to secure the padlock.

The term "monkey etiquette" flashed through Kaidanov's mind. He ducked his head and assumed a submissive position then watched out of the corner of his eye as his assailant turned and stared. The human and the primate locked eyes seconds before forty pounds of adrenaline-fueled, flame-tortured muscle launched itself through the air with a terrifying scream. Kaidanov saw the rhesus land on its prey and sink its fangs into his attacker's shoulder. As the pair toppled to the floor, Kaidanov staggered out the door and ran toward the woods. Moments later two shots rang out.

TWO

"Ready to rock-and-roll?" Joe Molinari asked as he ambled into Daniel Ames's tiny office.

"Not today," Daniel answered regretfully, pointing at the papers on his desk. "Briggs just laid this on me."

"We're talking happy hour, compadre," Molinari said as he slid his angular body onto one of Daniel's two client chairs.

The litigation associates at Reed, Briggs, Stephens, Stottlemeyer and Compton met for happy hour once a week at a popular steak house to bitch and moan about how hard they worked and how unappreciated they were—and to make fun of other lawyers who were not among those chosen to work at Portland, Oregon's largest and most prestigious law firm. Daniel enjoyed the camaraderie, but he knew that it would be impossible to drag himself back to the office after sharing a pitcher of margaritas with the gang.

"Briggs needs my memo tomorrow morning."

Molinari shook his head ruefully. "When are you going to learn to say no, Ames? I've got a picture of strikers outside an auto plant. I put it on my door when I'm full up. I can make you a copy."

Daniel smiled. "Thanks, Joe. I may take you up on that, but I've got to get this done."

"Hey, man, you've got to stand up for yourself. Lincoln freed the slaves."

"The Thirteenth Amendment doesn't apply to associates at Reed, Briggs."

"You're hopeless"—Molinari laughed as he levered himself out of the chair—"but you know where we are if you come to your senses."

Molinari disappeared down the corridor and Daniel sighed. He envied his friend. If the situation had been reversed Joe wouldn't have hesitated to go for a drink. He could afford to give the finger to people like Arthur Briggs and he would never understand that someone in Daniel's position could not.

Molinari's father was a high muck-a-muck in a Los Angeles ad agency. Joe had gone to an elite prep school, an Ivy League college, and got his law degree at Georgetown. With his connections, he could have gotten a job anywhere, but he liked white-water rafting and mountain climbing, so he had condescended to offer his services to Reed, Briggs. Daniel, on the other hand, thanked God every day for his job.

On one wall of Daniel's narrow office were his diplomas and his certificate of membership in the Oregon State Bar. Joe and some of the other associates took their education and profession for granted, but Daniel had made it through Portland State and the U. of O. law school the hard way, earning every cent of his tuition and knowing that there was no safety net to catch him if he failed. He took pride in earning a spot in Oregon's best law firm without Ivy League credentials or family connections, but he could not shake the feeling that his hold on success was tenuous.

Daniel's office wasn't much, but no one in his family had ever even worked in an office. His mother waitressed when she was sober and serviced long-haul drivers when she was too drunk to hold a job. He phoned her on her birthday and Christmas when he knew where she was living. He'd had six "fathers" to the best of his recollection. The nice ones had ignored him, the bad ones had left him with night sweats and scars.

Uncle Jack, father number four, had been the best of the lot because he owned a house with a yard. It was the first time Daniel had lived in a house. Most of the time he and his mother stayed in trailers or dark, evil-smelling rooms in transient hotels. Daniel had been eight when they moved in with Uncle Jack. He'd had his own room and thought this was what heaven was like. Four months later he was standing half-asleep on the sidewalk at four in the morning listening to his mother's drunken screams as she pounded her hands bloody on Uncle Jack's bolted front door.

Daniel had run away from home several times, but he'd left for good at seventeen, living on the streets until he could not stand it, then joining the army. The army had saved Daniel's life. It was the first stable environment in which he had ever lived and it was the first time his intelligence had been recognized.

Daniel's dark jacket was hanging from a hook behind his door, his paycheck sticking out of the inside pocket. *Ninety thousand dollars!* The size of his salary still amazed him and he felt incredibly lucky to have been chosen by the powers at Reed, Briggs. Every day he half expected to be told that his hiring had been a cruel practical joke.

Daniel had talked with the recruiting partner who visited the law school only to practice his interviewing technique. His invitation to a second interview at the firm had come as a shock, as had the offer of employment. Reed, Briggs's hires were graduates of Andover and Exeter; they attended Yale and Berkeley as undergraduates and went to Harvard and NYU for law school. Daniel was no dummy—his undergraduate degree in biology was with honors and he had made the *Law Review*—but there were still times when he felt out of his league.

Daniel swiveled his chair toward the window and watched the darkness gather over the Willamette River. When was the last time he had left these offices when it was still light out? Molinari was right. He did have to learn to say no, to relax a little, but he worried that he would earn a reputation as a slacker if he turned down work. Just last night he had awakened, drenched in sweat, from a dream in which he cringed in the dark at the bottom of an elevator shaft as a car descended slowly, but inexorably, toward him. You didn't have to be Sigmund Freud to dope out the meaning of that one.

At 6:45, Daniel finished rereading a draft of his memo. He stretched and rubbed his eyes. When he pulled his hands away he saw Susan Webster smiling at him from the doorway. He couldn't decide what was more shocking—that she was smiling or that she'd deigned to pay him a visit.

"Hi," he said casually, consciously keeping his eyes off of her runway-model figure.

"Hi yourself," she answered as she perched gracefully on the arm of one of Daniel's chairs. She glanced at the papers spread across his desk.

"If you're not at happy hour you must be working on a case of monumental importance. Is that a brief for the United States Supreme Court or a letter to the president?"

Susan looked and dressed like a cover girl, but her degree from Harvard was in physics and she'd been in the top ten at Stanford Law. Because of their science backgrounds, Susan and Daniel had been chosen as part of a team that was defending Geller Pharmaceuticals against a claim that one of its products caused birth defects. During the six months that they had worked together she had never asked Daniel's opinion on anything and rarely addressed him, so he was surprised that she was talking to him now.

"This is a memo for Mr. Briggs," Daniel said finally.

"Oh? Anything interesting?"

"It's another one of Aaron Flynn's cases," Daniel replied.

"Flynn again, huh? He sure has his fingers in a lot of pies."

"I'll say."

"Which of our clients is he suing, this time?" Susan asked.

"Oregon Mutual. They insure Dr. April Fairweather for malpractice."

"The therapist?"

"Yeah. How did you know?"

"Arthur had me do some work on the case, too. It's really weird. Do you know the facts?" Susan asked.

"No," Daniel answered. "I'm just working on an evidence issue."

"This college student went to Fairweather because she was depressed and having trouble sleeping. She's alleging that Fairweather hypnotized her and caused her to develop false memories that her folks were in a satanic cult that did all sorts of stuff to her when she was a kid."

"What sorts of stuff?"

"Weird sex, torture."

"Sounds kinky. Is any of it true?"

"I doubt it."

"I met Dr. Fairweather once when she was with Mr. Briggs," Daniel said. "She seemed normal enough."

"Do you have a lot more work to do on the memo?"

"No. I just have to proof it once more."

"So you're almost done?" Susan asked.

"Pretty much."

Daniel didn't really imagine that Susan was going to suggest a drink or dinner—he pictured Susan's dates as rich, GQ-model types who drove exotic sports cars and owned homes in the West Hills with fabulous views of the mountains—but for just a second he fantasized that she'd been won over by his curly black hair, his blue eyes, and his engaging smile.

Susan leaned forward and spoke in an inviting whisper.

"Since you're finished with your work"—she paused dramatically—"could you do me a huge favor?"

Daniel had no idea where this was going, so he waited for Susan to continue.

"Coincidentally, it involves another one of Flynn's cases, Geller Pharmaceuticals," Susan said. "You know he made that request for production weeks ago?"

Daniel nodded.

"As usual, Geller took forever to get the documents to us. They're supposed to be delivered to Flynn by eight in the morning."

Susan paused.

"Renee has it in for me," she said. Renee Gilchrist was Arthur Briggs's secretary. "She knew I had important plans tonight, but she told Brock Newbauer that I could review the documents this evening. She claims that she forgot, but I know she did it on purpose." Susan leaned closer and spoke conspiratorially. "She is jealous of any woman Arthur works with. That is a fact. Anyway, since you're done, I was wondering if you could finish the document review?"

Daniel was exhausted and hungry. He'd been looking forward to going home.

"Gee, I don't know. I still have some more work on this memo and I'm pretty beat."

"I'll make it up to you, I promise. And there's not that much to do. Just a couple of boxes and you'd only have to give the papers a cursory review. You know, check for attorney work product or privileged stuff. It would mean a lot to me."

Susan looked desperate. He was almost done, and there wasn't anything he was going to do tonight. Maybe finish a book he'd been reading, if he wasn't too tired, or watch some TV. What the hell, it never hurt to do a good deed.

"Okay." He sighed. "I'll save you."

Susan reached across the desk and laid her hand on top of his.

"Thank you, Daniel. I owe you."

"Big time," he said, already feeling like a sucker. "Now go and have fun."

Susan stood up. "The boxes are in the small conference room near the copying machine. Make sure they get to Flynn's office by eight in the morning. And thanks again."

Susan was gone so quickly her disappearance seemed magical. Daniel stood and stretched. He was going to take a break anyway, so he decided to see what he'd let himself in for. He walked down the hall to the conference room and turned on the light. Five banker's boxes covered the table. He opened one. It was packed with paperwork. Daniel did a quick calculation and came up with a ballpark figure of three to five thousand pages per box. This would take all night, if he was lucky. This was impossible. He'd never get home.

Daniel hurried into the hall to see if he could catch Susan, but she was gone.

THREE

The Insufort case had started with the Moffitts. Lillian Moffitt worked as a dental hygienist and her husband, Alan, was an officer in the loan department of a bank. The day they found out that Lillian was pregnant was one of the happiest days of their lives. But Toby Moffitt was born with severe birth defects and their happiness turned to heartache. Alan and Lillian tried to convince themselves that Toby's bad fortune was part of God's mysterious plan, but they wondered what part of this plan could include heaping such misery on their little boy. All became clear to Lillian on the day she went to her neighborhood grocery store and saw a headline in a supermarket tabloid about Insufort, which called it the "Son of Thalidomide."

Thalidomide was one of the great horror stories of the mid-twentieth century. Women who used it during pregnancy bore babies with dolphinlike flippers instead of normal limbs. The article in the tabloid claimed that Insufort was as harmful as Thalidomide and that women who took the drug were giving birth to monsters. While she was pregnant Lillian had taken Insufort.

The night that the Moffitts read the article about

Insufort they prayed for guidance. The next morning they called Aaron Flynn. The Moffitts had seen Aaron Flynn's television ads and they had read about the flamboyant Irishman's multimillion-dollar judgments against a major auto company and the manufacturer of a defective birth control device. "Could Mr. Flynn help Toby?" they asked. "You bet," he told them.

Soon after the Moffitts hired him, Flynn ran newspaper and television ads informing other mothers who had used Insufort that he was there to help them. Then he posted information about his case on corporate protest sites on the Internet. He also alerted friends in the media that Toby Moffitt's case was the tip of a product liability iceberg. This strategy brought in more clients.

One of the first things that Flynn did after filing *Moffitt* v. *Geller Pharmaceuticals* was to serve requests for discovery on Geller through its law firm, Reed, Briggs, Stephens, Stottlemeyer and Compton. Flynn asked for every document Geller had regarding the testing and analysis of Insufort, the warnings that had been provided to physicians dispensing the drug, copies of other lawsuits that had been filed, reports from physicians and others telling of problems with Insufort, data about the manufacturing process—and any other information that would help him discover the connection between Insufort and Toby Moffitt's terrible deformity. The boxes of paper that Susan Webster had conned Daniel into reviewing were only a few of the boxes of discovery that had flowed through the offices of Reed, Briggs to the law offices of Aaron Flynn since the Geller Pharmaceutical litigation had commenced.

*

Daniel was furious with Susan, but he took every task seriously, no matter how routine. At first he tried to read each page of each document, but his attention to detail waned after a few hours, as did his energy. By three in the morning he was barely aware of what was on each page. That's when he went to a small room on the twenty-eighth floor with a bed, an alarm clock, and a washroom with a narrow shower that was used by associates who were pulling all-nighters.

When the alarm went off at six, Daniel showered and shaved and, coffee in hand, attacked the remaining documents. There were still two boxes to go and an eight o'clock deadline to meet. Daniel remembered Susan saying that he only had to give the documents a cursory review. He hated doing anything halfway, but there wasn't much more he could do in the time remaining. At 7:30, Daniel began stuffing the remaining papers back in their boxes. He was almost through when Renee Gilchrist walked in, immediately noticing the boxes spread over the conference table and Daniel's obvious exhaustion.

Arthur Briggs's secretary was in her early thirties. At five nine, she was almost as tall as Daniel and she had the sleek, muscular build of an aerobics instructor. Renee's dark hair was cut short. It framed wide blue eyes, a straight nose, and full lips that were pursed in an angry frown.

"Is that the Geller discovery?" she asked.

"All one billion pages of it," Daniel answered groggily.

"Susan Webster was supposed to review that."

Daniel shrugged, a little embarrassed that Renee had found out that he'd been duped into doing Susan's work.

"She had plans for last night and I wasn't doing anything."

Renee started to leave, then she stopped.

"You shouldn't let her do that to you."

"It's no big thing. Like I said, she was busy and I wasn't."

Renee shook her head. "You're too nice a guy, Daniel."

Wheeling a dolly loaded with cardboard boxes across the lobby of Aaron Flynn's law office gave Daniel the same queasy feeling he would have if he saw someone running keys along the side of a Rolls-Royce Silver Cloud. The exterior of Flynn's pre-World War I office building gave no hint of the grandeur Daniel encountered when he stepped out of the elevator on the seventh floor into a huge lobby that soared upward two stories. The lobby floor was made of shiny black marble and the space was decorated in rich dark woods and bronzed metals. Several columns of lapis-colored marble supported the ceiling. A balcony containing the library ran along three sides of the upper story. Carved into the middle of the lobby floor was a medallion displaying blind Justice holding her scales. Written around the rim in gold leaf were the words JUSTICE FOR ALL.

A young woman sat at the far side of the lobby on a high dais that looked more like a bench for a judge than a desk for a receptionist. Daniel was asking the woman where to leave his load when the man himself strode through a door that led to the inner sanctum. Aaron Flynn was talking quietly to another man with the shoulders and neck of a serious bodybuilder and the craggy, weather-beaten face of an outdoorsman.

"Let me know as soon as you find out where the card was used," Flynn said.

"I'll get on it," his companion answered. Then he walked past Daniel and out of the office.

On television, Aaron Flynn's deep voice asked viewers if they needed a champion to help them take on the mighty corporations that had wronged them. "You are not alone," he promised, his face at once sober and compassionate. "Together we will fight for justice, and we will prevail."

Flynn was equally impressive in person. He was tall and broad-shouldered with red hair and a face that radiated self-confidence and sincerity. His clients saw Flynn as a savior, but Daniel didn't trust him. Part of Daniel's duties on the team defending Geller Pharmaceuticals was to review the animal and human studies conducted on Insufort. They showed it to be a safe product. Daniel was convinced that Flynn's claim that the drug caused birth defects had no factual basis. It would not be the first time Flynn had tried to make millions by creating causes out of whole cloth.

Five years ago one of the networks had broadcast a horrifying story about a six-year-old boy who was killed in his driveway. His mother swore that her sports utility vehicle had surged forward suddenly when she stepped on the brake, driving her son through the garage door. Other victims of "sudden acceleration" surfaced. They claimed that their SUVs would surge forward when the brake was applied and could not be stopped.

Aaron Flynn had just opened his practice in Portland, but he had the good fortune to represent the plaintiff in the first "sudden acceleration" case. His million-dollar judgment against the manufacturer of the SUV made his reputation. In the end, the explanation for "sudden acceleration" proved simple. It was not caused by a mechanical malfunction but by human error: drivers were stepping on the gas instead of the brake. By the time the truth came out, the manufacturer had paid millions in damages and settlements, and attorneys like Flynn had made out like bandits.

Daniel had been introduced to Flynn when the lawyer visited the Reed, Briggs offices for a deposition, but the introduction was quick and Flynn had barely glanced his way during the proceedings. That was why Daniel was surprised when Flynn smiled and addressed him by name.

"Daniel Ames, isn't it?"

"Yes, Mr. Flynn."

"From the way you look, I'd guess you've not had much sleep."

"No, sir," Daniel answered cautiously.

Flynn nodded sympathetically. "Lisa can bring you to our coffee room for a mug of java and a muffin."

"Thanks, Mr. Flynn, but I've got to get back," Daniel answered, unwilling to accept gifts from the enemy even though the idea of coffee and a muffin sounded like heaven.

Flynn smiled to show he understood. Then he turned his attention to the stack of boxes on the dolly.

"So Arthur's got you slaving away doing document review. Not what you expected, I'll bet, when you were studying the opinions of Holmes and Cardozo at Yale."

"Actually, it was the U. of O."

Flynn grinned. "Then you must be one of the really bright lights if you were able to squeeze in between the lads and lassies of the Ivy League. I'm a graduate of the law school at the University of Arizona myself. Middle of the class."

He looked at the boxes of discovery again and sighed.

"You know, when I filed *Moffitt* v. *Geller Pharmaceuticals* this firm consisted of two partners and six associates. But since your client has been kind enough to answer my requests for discovery with such thoroughness, I've had to lease another floor and hire five new associates, ten paralegals, and eight support staff people to work on my little set-to with Geller."

"You're keeping me employed, too, Mr. Flynn," Daniel said, making a nervous joke to keep the conversation going. There was something about Flynn that made Daniel want to prolong their meeting. "It seems like you cross swords with Reed, Briggs pretty often."

"So I do," Flynn answered with a laugh. "If you ever grow tired of toiling away for evil corporate interests and decide you want to engage in some honest labor, give me a call. We state school boys should stick together. It was good seeing you again."

Flynn stuck out his hand. As they shook, the elevator door opened, attracting Flynn's attention.

"Before you go, I'd like you to meet someone."

Flynn released Daniel's hand and led him toward the office entrance. A haggard-looking woman in her late twenties was propping open the door with her shoulder and pushing a stroller into the lobby. In the stroller was a baby boy about six months old. His head was down and Daniel could not see his face. Flynn greeted them both.

"Alice, how are you? And how is Patrick doing?"

At the sound of his name, the little boy looked up. He had a mop of blond hair the color of new-mown hay and sky-blue eyes, but below his eyes something had gone terribly wrong. Where his lip should have been was a raw and gaping hole so wide that Daniel could see the saliva that moistened the back of the baby's throat. Patrick's left nostril was normal, but his deformed lip had pushed into the right side of the baby's nose, stretching it wide like Silly Putty. Patrick should have been adorable, but his cleft palate made him look like a horror-movie monster.

Flynn knelt next to the stroller and ruffled Patrick's hair. The baby made a whistling, hissing sound that bore no relation to the cute cooing sounds made by normal babies. Daniel fought with every ounce of his energy to hide his revulsion, then felt guilty for being repelled by the child.

"Daniel, this is Patrick Cummings," Flynn said pleasantly as he watched the reaction of the young associate. "And this is Alice Cummings, Patrick's mother. She had the misfortune to take Insufort during her pregnancy."

"Nice meeting you, Mrs. Cummings," Daniel said, managing somehow to keep his tone light. Patrick's mother was not fooled. She could see that her son's looks repulsed Daniel and she could not hide her sadness.

Daniel felt awful. He wanted to get out of Flynn's office as fast as possible, but he forced himself to say good-bye and to walk to the elevator slowly so Patrick's mother would not think that he was fleeing from her son.

When the elevator doors closed Daniel sagged against the wall. Up until now the children in the Geller case had only been names on a pleading, but Patrick Cummings was flesh and blood. As the car descended Daniel tried to imagine the life Patrick would lead. Would he ever have friends? Would he find a woman who would love him? Was his life over before it had started?

There was one other question that needed an answer: Was Insufort responsible for the fate of Patrick Cummings?

FOUR

Irene Kendall had let the john pick her up in the bar at the Mirage a little before eight in the evening. He'd had a good run at the craps table and was high on his good fortune. She'd listened attentively while he bragged about his gambling prowess. When he started to feel his drinks Irene hinted that she might be amenable to a sexual adventure. It was only after she was sure the john was panting for it that she explained that she was a working girl and told him her rates. The john laughed and told her that the bell captain had pointed her out to him. He said he preferred sex with whores.

The john had paid up front and tipped her afterward, and he hadn't roughed her up or asked for anything exotic. The only downside to the evening was the motel, a by-the-hour fuck pad in a run-down part of town. A lot of Irene's clientele stayed in the classy rooms at the Mirage or the other upscale casinos on the Strip and the motel was definitely a comedown. Still, the room was clean and the john was satisfied with a quick in-and-out, so she didn't have to work hard for her money. When Irene got ready to go, the john surprised her by telling her that she could stay in the room because he had to catch an early flight. She accepted the offer and immediately fell into a deep sleep.

Irene never heard the door being jimmied and had no idea that there was someone else in the room until a gloved hand clamped across her mouth. Her eyes sprang open and she tried to sit up, but the muzzle of a gun pressed hard into the flesh of her forehead and forced her head deep into her pillow.

"Scream and die. Answer my questions and live. Nod slowly if you understand me."

The feeble light cast by the flashing neon sign on the bar next door revealed that the speaker wore a ski mask. Irene nodded slowly and the gloved hand withdrew, leaving the sour taste of leather in her mouth.

"Where is he?"

"Gone," she gasped in a voice hoarse with fear.

"Say good-bye, bitch," the intruder whispered. Irene heard the gun cock.

"Please," she begged. "I'm not his friend, I'm a pro. He was a pickup at the Mirage. He fucked me, he paid me, and he left. He said I could use the room for the night because he had an early flight. I swear that's all I know."

"How long ago did he leave?"

The prostitute's eyes shifted to the clock radio on the nightstand.

"Fifteen minutes. He just left."

Two cruel eyes studied Irene for what seemed an eternity. Then the gun withdrew.

"Stay."

The intruder vanished though the door. Irene did not move for five minutes. Then she raced into the bathroom and threw up.

Part II

The Smoking Gun

FIVE

The main entrance to Reed, Briggs, Stephens, Stottlemeyer and Compton was on the thirtieth floor of a modern, thirty-story office building in the middle of downtown Portland, but Reed, Briggs leased several other floors. A week after delivering the boxes of discovery to Aaron Flynn's office, Daniel stepped out of the elevator on the twenty-seventh floor at 7:30 in the morning. This floor, where Daniel had his office, could only be entered by tapping in a code on a keypad that was attached to the wall next to one of two narrow glass panels that bracketed a locked door. Daniel started to reach for the keypad when he noticed what appeared to be some kind of microphone affixed to the wall above the keypad. Taped next to it was a sign that said:

REED, BRIGGS'S KEY ENTRY SYSTEM IS NOW VOICE-ACTIVATED. CLEARLY AND LOUDLY SAY YOUR NAME, THEN STATE "OPEN DOOR NOW."

On closer inspection Daniel could see that the "microphone" was really a round, metal cap from a juice bottle that had been taped to a small, plastic pencil sharpener. Both had been painted black. Daniel shook his head and tapped in his number. The lock clicked and he opened the door. As he expected, Joe Molinari was lurking behind a partition staring through the glass panel that gave him a view of the keypad.

"You're an asshole," Daniel said.

Molinari jerked him behind the partition just as Miranda Baker, a nineteen-year-old from the mailroom, approached the door.

"Watch this," Molinari said.

Baker started to tap in her code when she noticed the sign. She hesitated, then said, "Miranda Baker. Open door now." She tried the door, but it would not open. She looked puzzled. Molinari doubled over with laughter.

"That's not funny, Joe. She's a good kid."

"Wait," Molinari insisted, trying to stifle his laughter for fear that Baker would hear him. She repeated her name and the command. Molinari had tears in his eyes.

"I'm going to let her in," Daniel said just as Kate Ross, one of Reed, Briggs's in-house investigators, got out of the elevator. Kate walked up to Miranda as she was saying her name for the third time and yanking on the doorknob. Kate took one look at the sign and ripped it, the pencil sharpener, and the bottle cap off of the wall.

"Shit," Joe swore.

Kate said something to the young woman. They looked through the glass and stared coldly at Joe and Daniel. Miranda tapped in her code and opened the door. She flashed the two associates an angry look as she brushed past them.

Kate Ross was twenty-eight, five-foot-seven, and looked fit in tight jeans, an oxford blue shirt, and a navy-blue blazer. Kate stopped in front of the associates and held out the sign, bottle cap, and pencil sharpener. Her dark complexion, large brown eyes, and curly black, shoulder-length hair made Daniel think of those tough Israeli soldiers he'd seen on the evening news. The hard look she cast at Joe and Daniel made him glad that she wasn't carrying an Uzi.

"I believe these are yours."

Joe looked sheepish. Kate turned her attention to Daniel.

"Don't you have better things to do with your time?" she asked sternly.

"Hey, I had nothing to do with this," Daniel answered.

Kate looked skeptical. She dropped the bottle cap, pencil sharpener, and wadded-up sign into a garbage can and walked off.

"What a spoilsport," Molinari said when Kate was out of earshot.

Daniel hurried after Kate and caught up with her just as she was entering an office she shared with another investigator.

"I really didn't have anything to do with that," he said from the doorway.

Kate looked up from her mail. "Why should I care how you preppies amuse yourselves?" she asked angrily.

Daniel reddened. "Don't confuse me with Joe Molinari. I wasn't born with a silver spoon in my mouth. I'm a working stiff, just like you. I didn't like Joe's practical joke any more than you did. I was going to let Miranda in when you showed up."

"It didn't look that way to me," Kate answered defensively.

"Believe what you want to believe, but I don't lie," Daniel said angrily as he turned on his heel and walked down the hall to his office.

Reed, Briggs used a large wood-paneled room on the twenty-ninth floor for important depositions. As Daniel hurried toward it he narrowly missed running into Renee Gilchrist.

"'Morning, Renee," Daniel said as he stepped aside to let her pass.

Renee took a few steps, then turned around.

"Daniel."

"Yeah?"

"Mr. Briggs thought you did a good job on the Fairweather memo."

"Oh? He didn't say anything to me about it."

"He wouldn't."

The partners never told Daniel what they thought about his work and the only way he could tell if they believed it was any good was by the volume of work they gave him. It dawned on Daniel that Briggs had been loading him up for the past month.

"Thanks for telling me."

Renee smiled. "You'd better get in there. They're about to start the deposition."

At one end of the conference room, a wide picture window offered a view of the Willamette River and, beyond it, Mount Hood and Mount St. Helens. On another wall, a large oil painting of the Columbia Gorge hung over an oak credenza. On the credenza, silver urns filled with coffee and hot water stood next to a matching platter loaded down with croissants and muffins and a bowl filled with fruit.

Dr. Kurt Schroeder, a Geller Pharmaceuticals executive who was about to be deposed, sat at the end of a huge, cherrywood conference table, with his back to the window. Schroeder's thin lips were set in a rigid line and it was obvious that he did not enjoy his position on the hot seat.

To Schroeder's right sat Aaron Flynn and three associates. To Schroeder's left sat Arthur Briggs, a reed-thin, chain-smoker who always seemed to be on edge. Briggs's jet-black hair was swept back revealing a sharp widow's peak and his eyes were always moving as if he expected an attack from behind. In addition to being one of the most feared attorneys in Oregon, Briggs was a mover and shaker of the first magnitude with a heavy hand in politics, civic affairs, and almost every conservative cause of note. Daniel thought that Briggs was probably a sociopath who had channeled his energy into law instead of serial murder.

To Briggs's left was Brock Newbauer, a junior partner with a sunny smile and whitish-blond hair. Brock would never have made the cut at Reed, Briggs if his father's construction company had not been one of the firm's biggest clients.

Daniel took the chair next to Susan Webster. Arthur Briggs shot him an annoyed glance, but said nothing. Susan scribbled, *You're late,* on her notepad and moved it slightly in Daniel's direction.

"Good morning, Dr. Schroeder," Aaron Flynn said

with a welcoming smile. Daniel placed a legal pad on the table and started taking notes.

"Good morning," Schroeder answered without returning the smile.

"Why don't we start by having you tell everyone your occupation."

Schroeder cleared his throat. "I'm a board-certified pediatrician by training and am currently a senior vice-president and chief medical adviser to Geller Pharmaceuticals."

"Could you tell us a little bit about your educational background?"

"I graduated from Lehigh University with a chemistry major and biology minor. My medical degree is from Oregon Health Sciences University."

"What did you do after medical school?"

"I had an internship in pediatrics at the State University of New York, Kings County Hospital Center, in Brooklyn. Then I was assistant chief resident at the Children's Hospital of Philadelphia as a pediatric resident."

"What did you do after your residency?"

"I spent several years in private practice in Oregon before joining Geller Pharmaceuticals."

"When you joined Geller did it have any particular focus on pediatric drugs?"

"Yes, it did."

"Could you describe for us your job history after joining Geller?"

"I began in the clinical research and development division and rose through the ranks in various different positions of responsibility until I was appointed vice-president for medical affairs and later was promoted to senior vice-president. For the past eight years I've had responsibility for the development of, and gaining approval for, products we've discovered."

"And that would include Insufort?"

"Yes."

"Thank you. Now, Dr. Schroeder, I'd like to discuss with you the normal process for drug development and marketing and just sort of walk through the steps so that I'll have an understanding of what's involved in bringing a drug onto the market. And am I correct that the first step is identifying something that might have some pharmacological value?"

"Yes."

"And then you conduct preclinical studies, studies that are not done with humans."

"Yes."

"And the preclinical studies involve animals."

"Not necessarily. Prior to animal studies, you might conduct studies in tissues or cells. Maybe you would do a computer simulation."

"Okay, but at some point you get to the stage where you do what are called preclinical studies to assess both safety and effectiveness?"

"Yes."

"And when you do preclinical studies, the results of those studies are submitted to the Federal Drug Administration, or FDA, for review in what's called an investigational new drug application or IND, is that correct?"

"Yes."

"What is an IND?"

"It's a request for an exemption from the regulations which preclude physicians or companies from giving a substance which has not been approved by the FDA to humans in a clinical situation. If the FDA approves the IND, you are permitted to conduct clinical studies of the drug with humans."

"Can I assume that you, as chief medical adviser to Geller Pharmaceuticals, were familiar with the results of the preclinical and clinical studies conducted to determine if Insufort was a safe and effective product?"

"Well, I certainly reviewed the studies."

Flynn smiled at Schroeder. "Can I take it that is a yes?"

"Objection," Briggs said, asserting himself for the first time. "Dr. Schroeder did not say that he read each and every study and all of the documents involved."

"That's true," Schroeder said.

"Well, Geller Pharmaceuticals conducted extensive preclinical rodent studies, did it not?"

"Yes."

"You were aware of the results?"

"Yes."

"And there were studies of primates, pregnant monkeys?"

"Yes."

"And you were aware of those results?"

"Yes, I was."

"And there were phase-one clinical studies of human beings?"

"Yes."

"And you know about those results?"

"Yes."

"Tell me, Dr. Schroeder, did any of the clinical or pre-clinical studies show that Insufort can cause birth defects?"

"No, sir. They did not."

Flynn looked surprised. "None of them?" he asked.

"None of them."

Flynn turned to the young woman on his right. She handed him a one-page document. He scanned it for a moment, then returned his attention to Dr. Schroeder.

"What about the study conducted by Dr. Sergey Kaidanov?" Flynn asked.

Schroeder looked puzzled.

"Do you have a scientist in your employ named Dr. Sergey Kaidanov?"

"Dr. Kaidanov? Yes, he works for the company."

"In research and development?"

"I believe so."

Flynn nodded and the associate to his right pushed copies of the document that Flynn was holding across the conference table as Flynn handed a copy to the witness.

"I'd like this marked Plaintiff's Exhibit 234. I've given copies to counsel and Dr. Schroeder."

"Where did you get this?" Briggs demanded as soon as he'd skimmed the page.

Flynn smiled and gestured toward Daniel.

"I received it as part of the discovery that young man over there delivered to my office a few days ago."

Every eye in the room focused on Daniel, but he did not notice because he was reading Plaintiff's Exhibit 234, which appeared to be a cover letter for a report that Dr.

Sergey Kaidanov had sent to George Fournet, the in-house counsel for Geller Pharmaceuticals.

> *Dear Mr. Fournet,*
>
> *I have great concerns about thalglitazone (trade name, Insufort) based on the results emerging from our congenital anomaly study in pregnant primates. We have to date studied the effects of an oral dose of one hundred micrograms per kilogram, given for ten days beginning on the thirtieth day of conception, on the fetus in forty pregnant rhesus monkeys. The early results are striking—eighteen of the forty neonate primates (45 percent) were born with maxillofacial abnormalities, in some cases severe, the most severe being complete cleft lip and palate. It is unclear to me how this could have been missed in the rodent studies, but as we all know this does happen from time to time.*
>
> *The purpose of this letter and the enclosed preliminary results is to alert you to my findings, as I believe it will have important implications for our current phase II and III studies in human beings. I will forward a detailed anatomical and biochemical analysis when my study is completed.*

Daniel was stunned. Kaidanov's letter was the smoking gun that could destroy Geller Pharmaceuticals' case, and Aaron Flynn had just told Arthur Briggs that Daniel had placed the lethal weapon in his hands.

SIX

While Daniel read the letter in shocked silence, Susan Webster's fingers flew across the keys of her laptop.

"I have a few questions about this document, Dr. Schroeder," Aaron Flynn said in a cordial tone.

Susan slipped beside Arthur Briggs and gestured at a case she had called up on her computer. She whispered hurriedly in his ear and Briggs shouted, "Objection! This is a confidential communication between Dr. Kaidanov and his attorney that has been inadvertently turned over to you. You had an ethical obligation to refrain from reading the letter once you saw that it was an attorney/client communication."

Flynn chuckled. "Arthur, this is a report of the results of a preclincal test on rhesus monkeys. Your client, probably at your suggestion, has been instructing its scientists to send all their test results to in-house counsel, so you can raise this silly objection to our discovery requests, but it's too transparent to take seriously."

"You'll take this damn seriously when I report you to the bar disciplinary committee."

Flynn smiled. "Take any steps you think you must, Arthur."

Flynn nodded and one of his associates sped several copies of a legal document across the polished wood table.

"I want the record to reflect that I have just served Dr. Schroeder and his counsel a request for production of Dr. Kaidanov's study and all supporting documentation, as well as a notice of deposition for Dr. Kaidanov and Mr. Fournet."

Flynn turned back to the witness. "Now, Dr. Schroeder, I'd like to ask you a few questions about the Kaidanov study."

"Don't you say a thing," Briggs shouted at the witness.

"Arthur, Dr. Schroeder is under oath and we're in the middle of his deposition."

Flynn's tone was calm and condescending, and it raised Briggs's blood pressure another notch.

"I want Judge Norris on the phone." A blood vessel in Briggs's temple looked like it was about to burst. "I want a ruling on this before I'll let Dr. Schroeder give you the time of day."

Flynn shrugged. "Call the judge."

Daniel barely heard what Briggs and Flynn said. All he could think about was the steps he'd taken when he reviewed the discovery. How could he have missed Kaidanov's letter? He had skim-read many of the documents, but he was specifically looking for privileged information. A letter to an attorney would have raised a red flag. It didn't seem possible that it could slip by, but it had. Daniel was devastated. No one was perfect, but to be responsible for an error of these proportions . . .

As soon as Judge Norris was connected to the conference room, Flynn and Briggs took turns explaining the legal arguments supporting their position in the Kaidanov matter. The judge was too busy to deal with a matter of this complexity over the phone. He told the attorneys to stop questioning Schroeder until he ruled and he ordered Briggs and Flynn to submit briefs on their positions by the end of the week.

As soon as Flynn and his minions cleared the conference room, Briggs waved Kaidanov's letter in Schroeder's face.

"What is this, Kurt?"

"I've got no idea, Arthur." The Geller executive looked as upset as his attorney. "I've never seen the damn thing in my life."

"But you know this guy Kaidanov?"

"I know who he is. He works in R and D. I don't know him personally."

"And he's working with these monkeys?"

"No. Not to my knowledge."

"What does 'not to my knowledge' mean? You're not holding out on me, are you? This letter could cost your company millions, if you're lucky, and it could sink Geller if you're not."

Schroeder was sweating. "I swear, Arthur, I've never heard of a single study that we've conducted that came back with results like these. What kind of company do you think we run? If I got wind of a study of Insufort with those results, do you think I'd okay human trials?"

"I want to speak to Kaidanov and Fournet immediately, this afternoon," Briggs said.

"I'll phone my office and set it up."

When Schroeder walked over to the credenza and

punched in the number of his office, Briggs turned toward Daniel, who had tried to remain as inconspicuous as possible. Briggs held out his copy of the Kaidanov letter, which had sustained serious damage.

"Explain this, Ames," he demanded in a soft tone that was more frightening than the screams he'd expected.

"I . . . uh, Mr. Briggs . . . I've never seen it."

"Never seen it," Briggs repeated. "Was Flynn lying when he said that you gave it to him?"

Daniel glanced at Susan. She averted her eyes, but her body language revealed her anxiety. Daniel looked back at Briggs.

"Well?" Briggs asked, his voice slightly louder.

"He didn't mean that literally, Mr. Briggs. I was told to review five large boxes of documents that Geller produced in response to a demand for discovery." Daniel was the only one who saw Susan release her pent-up breath. "I was told to deliver the discovery first thing in the morning, eight A.M. I didn't see the boxes until eight the night before. There were roughly twenty thousand pages. I stayed at the office all evening. I even slept here. There were too many pages for me to review every one of them in that time."

"And that's your excuse?"

"It's not an excuse. Nobody could have gone through every page in those boxes in the time I had."

"You're not a 'nobody,' Ames. You're a Reed, Briggs associate. If we wanted nobodies we'd pay minimum wage and hire graduates of unaccredited, correspondence law schools."

"Mr. Briggs. I'm sorry, but—"

"My secretary will set up the meetings," Schroeder said as he hung up the phone. To Daniel's great relief, Schroeder's statement distracted Briggs.

Schroeder reread Kaidanov's letter. When he was done he held it up. He looked grim.

"I think this is a fraud. We never conducted a study with these results," he declared emphatically. "I'm certain of it."

"You'd better be right," Briggs said. "If Judge Norris rules that this letter is admissible in court, and we can't prove it's a fake, you, and everyone else at Geller Pharmaceuticals, will be selling pencils on street corners."

Briggs started to lead Newbauer and Schroeder out of the room. Daniel hung back, hoping to escape Briggs's notice, but the senior partner stopped at the door and cast a scathing look at him.

"I'll talk with you, later," Briggs said.

The door closed and Daniel was left alone in the conference room.

SEVEN

Daniel spent the afternoon waiting for the ax to fall. Around two, he dialed Susan's extension to find out what was going on, but her secretary told him that she was at Geller Pharmaceuticals with Arthur Briggs. An hour later, when he realized that he'd never get any work done, Daniel went home to his one-bedroom walk-up on the third floor of an old brick apartment house in northwest Portland. His place was small and sparsely furnished with things Daniel had transported from his law-school apartment in Eugene. Its most attractive feature was its location near Northwest Twenty-first and Twenty-third streets with their restaurants, shops, and crowds. But today the apartment could have been in the heart of Paris and Daniel would not have noticed. Arthur Briggs was going to fire him. He was sure of it. Everything he had worked for was going to be destroyed because of a single sheet of paper.

Something else troubled Daniel. He had been so worried about being fired that it was not until he was in bed, eyes closed, that the true importance of Dr. Sergey Kaidanov's letter dawned on him. Until he read the letter,

Daniel had been convinced that there was no merit to the lawsuit Aaron Flynn had brought on behalf of Toby Moffitt, Patrick Cummings, and the other children allegedly affected by Insufort. What if he was wrong? What if Geller Pharmaceuticals knew that it was selling a product that could deform innocent babies? Daniel was part of a team representing Geller. If the company was knowingly responsible for the horror that had been visited upon Patrick Cummings and Daniel continued to defend Geller, he would be aiding and abetting a terrible enterprise.

Daniel tossed and turned all night and was exhausted when his alarm went off. By the time he arrived at Reed, Briggs the next morning, he was certain that everyone in the firm knew about his blunder. Daniel managed to get from the elevator to his office without meeting anyone, but he was barely settled behind his desk when Joe Molinari walked in and his day started to go downhill.

"What the fuck did you do?" Molinari asked in a hushed voice as soon as he shut the door.

"What do you mean?" Daniel asked nervously.

"The word is that Briggs has a hair up his ass the size of a redwood and you put it there."

"Shit."

"So it's true."

Daniel felt utterly defeated.

"What happened?"

"I don't want to talk about it."

"Look, compadre, I'm here for you."

"I appreciate the support. I'd just rather be alone now."

"Okay," Molinari said reluctantly. He stood up. "Just remember what I said. If there's something I can do, ask."

Molinari left. Daniel felt exhausted and the day had just started. It suddenly dawned on him that he had never gotten around to discussing with Susan her role in the discovery fiasco. If Susan went to Briggs and told him that she was partly to blame, it might help, and from what Molinari said, he could use all the help he could get. Daniel walked down the hall to Susan's office. She was wearing a cream-colored blouse and a gray pantsuit and looked as fresh and untroubled as a woman who had slept for twenty-four hours.

"Susan?"

"Oh, hi," she answered with a smile.

"Got a minute?"

Daniel started toward a chair.

"Actually, I don't." Daniel stopped in his tracks. "Arthur needs this yesterday."

"We really have to talk."

"Now is not a good time," she said firmly. Her smile was starting to look a little strained.

"I was hoping that you'd tell Arthur that you were supposed to review the discovery and that I helped you out."

Susan looked surprised, as if the idea had never occurred to her.

"Why would I do that?"

"So he'd know how big the job was and that I didn't get started until the last minute," Daniel answered, trying to rein in his temper.

"Even if I was supposed to review the discovery, you're the one who did," Susan answered defensively. "If I tell Arthur, it won't help. All that will accomplish is getting me in trouble, too."

"If Briggs knew that we were both to blame it would take some of the pressure off of me."

Susan looked nervous. "*I* didn't go through the discovery. *You're* the one who missed that letter."

"You'd have missed it, too. Briggs would have missed it."

"You're right," Susan agreed quickly. "Look, you'll be okay. Arthur gets angry easily, but he'll be distracted by this mess and forget you delivered the letter."

"Fat chance."

"Or he'll see that you're right. That the letter was a needle in a haystack that no one could have found unless they were incredibly lucky. You don't have to worry."

"You're the one who doesn't have to worry," Daniel said with a trace of bitterness. "He'd never fire you."

Susan looked very uncomfortable. "I really do have to finish this assignment. It's research on the admissibility of Kaidanov's letter. Can we talk about this later?"

"When, after I'm unemployed?" Daniel shot back.

"I mean it, Daniel. I'll buzz you as soon as I get some free time."

Daniel could not concentrate on the pleading he was drafting because his thoughts kept drifting to the Insufort case. He could not believe that Geller Pharmaceuticals would intentionally sell a product that produced the horrible results he'd seen in Aaron Flynn's office. He had met many of the Geller executives. They weren't monsters. The results that Sergey Kaidanov wrote about had to be an anomaly.

Daniel set aside the pleading and opened a large folder

that held all of the Insufort studies. He started with the earliest and worked his way through them looking for anything that would help. By the time he had finished his review it was almost one. Daniel suddenly remembered Susan's promise to call him when she was through with her work. He dialed Susan's extension and her secretary told him that she had left for the day. Daniel wasn't surprised. Deep down he knew that Susan was not going to help him. If he wanted to stay at Reed, Briggs, he was going to have to save himself, but how?

Suddenly he laughed. The answer was obvious. Sergey Kaidanov wrote the report that was about to torpedo Geller's defense. Kaidanov's study had to be flawed. If he could find out why Kaidanov had erred he would save the litigation and, maybe, his job.

Daniel dialed Geller Pharmaceuticals and was connected to the receptionist in research and development.

"Dr. Kaidanov isn't in," she told him.

"When will he be in?"

"I couldn't say."

"I'm an attorney at Reed, Briggs, Stephens, Stottlemeyer and Compton, the law firm that represents Geller Pharmaceuticals, and I need to speak with Dr. Kaidanov about a matter of importance to a suit that was brought against your company."

"I'm supposed to refer all inquiries about Dr. Kaidanov to Dr. Schroeder. May I transfer you to his office?"

"I don't want to bother Dr. Schroeder. I know how busy he is. I'd rather just speak to Dr. Kaidanov myself."

"Well, you can't. He's not in and he hasn't been in for more than a week."

"Is he on vacation?"

"I don't have that information. You'll have to talk to Dr. Schroeder. Do you want me to connect you?"

"Uh, no. That's okay. Thanks."

Daniel dialed information and discovered that Sergey Kaidanov had an unlisted phone number. He thought for a moment then phoned personnel at Geller Pharmaceuticals.

"I need an address and phone number for Dr. Sergey Kaidanov," he said to the clerk who answered. "He works in research and development."

"I can't give out that information over the phone."

Daniel was desperate. He had to get to Kaidanov.

"Listen," he said forcefully, "this is George Fournet in legal. We just received a subpoena for Kaidanov. He's out of the office and I've got to get in touch with him ASAP. If he doesn't show up for his deposition we're going to be held in contempt by the judge. I have a messenger waiting to hand-deliver the subpoena, but he's all dressed up with no place to go."

"I'm not sure . . ."

"What's your name?"

"Bea Twiley."

"Did you get mine, Ms. Twiley; George Fournet? I am the head of the legal department and I don't waste my time on frivolous calls. Do you want to go to court and explain to United States District Court Judge Ivan Norris why you're there instead of Dr. Kaidanov?"

EIGHT

It was a little after three when Daniel found Sergey Kaidanov's drab, gray bungalow in a run-down neighborhood on the east side of the Willamette. The paint was peeling and the front lawn had not been mowed in a while. It was not the type of home in which Daniel expected to find a research scientist who worked for a prosperous pharmaceutical company.

The weather had turned nasty and there was no one on the street. Daniel parked down the block and watched the house. The shades in the front windows were drawn and the old newspapers lying on the lawn told Daniel that no one was home. He hunched his shoulders to ward off the wind and shivered as he walked up the path to Kaidanov's front door. After ringing the bell three times, he gave up. Daniel raised the metal flap of the mail slot and peeked inside the house. Mail was scattered across the floor.

Daniel followed a slate path that ran along the side of the bungalow to the back of the house. A low chain-link fence ran around the edge of a small, unkempt yard. Daniel opened the gate and went to the back door. The shades on the kitchen window were drawn. He knocked a few times, then tried the knob. The door opened. Daniel was about to call out Kaidanov's name when he saw the chaos in the kitchen. Cabinets and drawers were open and their contents littered the floor. Daniel took a slow survey of the room. There was a layer of dust on the counters. The sink was full of dirty dishes. Daniel stepped gingerly over broken glass and shattered plates and opened the refrigerator. He was hit by the sour smell of decay. Greenish-gray mold covered a piece of cheese. Daniel uncapped a bottle of spoiled milk and wrinkled his nose.

A small living room opened off of the kitchen. Except for an expensive stereo that had been ripped out of its cabinet, most of the other furnishings looked secondhand. CDs were strewn around the floor. Daniel saw a lot of classical music and some jazz.

A bookshelf took up one wall, but the books it used to hold had been thrown around the room. Many of the books were about scientific subjects like chemistry and microbiology. Daniel spotted a few popular novels and several books on gambling and mathematics.

The contents of a liquor cabinet were lying among the books and CDs on the hardwood floor. Most of the bottles contained Scotch and many of them were empty. On top of the liquor cabinet was more dust and a framed photograph of a slightly overweight man in his early forties dressed in sports clothes. Standing next to him was an attractive woman in a revealing sundress. They were smiling at the camera. The picture looked like it had been taken in front of a Las Vegas casino.

Daniel turned slowly, taking in the room again. This couldn't be a coincidence. Kaidanov's disappearance, the search of his home, and the primate study had to be connected.

A short hall led to the bedroom. Daniel edged into it, half expecting to find a mutilated corpse. Blankets and sheets were heaped on the floor, the mattress of a queen-size bed had been dislodged, drawers in a chest had been pulled out, and shirts, underwear, and socks had been strewn around the room. The doors to a clothes closet were open and it had obviously been searched.

Across the hall was a small office. More books had been pulled out of a bookshelf, but Daniel's attention was drawn to a monitor on Kaidanov's desktop. It looked odd sitting where it was supposed to be when everything else in the room had been tossed about. Daniel sat down and turned on the computer. As soon as it booted up, he tried to gain entry, but he needed a password. If Kaidanov had information about his study in the house it would be on his computer, but how could he access it?

Daniel turned off the computer and pulled the CPU tower out from under Kaidanov's desk. Using the screw-driver on his Swiss army knife, Daniel removed the sheet-metal cover of the computer's case, popped the cover, and pulled it off. He placed the computer on its side so he could see the motherboard, which held all of its electronics. Next to the motherboard was the hard-drive bay, a rack that held the hard drive in the computer. The hard drive was connected to the motherboard by a ribbon cable and a power cable. Daniel unplugged the cables from their connectors and unscrewed two more screws on the bay. He then flipped the CPU tower upright and took out two more screws on the other side. When all the screws were out Daniel gently slid the hard drive out of its bay. It consisted of a green circuit board encased in heavy black metal and was about the size of a paperback book. Daniel wrapped it in his handkerchief and placed it in his jacket pocket.

Daniel put the CPU tower back together and was sliding it under the desk when he froze at the distinctive sound of a bottle rolling across a wood floor. Daniel remembered that the liquor bottles were in the living room, which meant that he was trapped, because he would have to go through the living room to get out the front or back doors.

A shadow appeared on the corridor wall. Daniel could make out the bill of a baseball cap, but the shadow was too indistinct to tell him much more. He edged the door almost shut. The shadow flowed toward him along the wall. Daniel held his breath. If the intruder went into the bedroom he—Daniel—might be able to slip down the hall. If he went into the office first . . . Daniel opened the large blade on his knife.

Through the narrow gap in the door Daniel saw a figure in jeans and a leather jacket stop between the two rooms, facing away from him. The intruder hesitated, then the office door slammed into Daniel with enough force to stun him. Before he could recover, his wrist was bent back and his feet were kicked out from under him. The knife flew from his grasp.

Daniel crashed to the floor and lashed out with a punch that brought a gasp from his attacker. The grip on his arm loosened and he broke it, then struggled to his knees. A knee smashed into his face. Daniel grabbed his attacker's leg, surged to his feet, and twisted. His assailant went down with Daniel on top, his head pressed against the leather jacket. A blow glanced off Daniel's ear. He worked himself into a position to punch back, then reared up. As soon as he saw his attacker's face he checked his punch and gaped in astonishment.

"Kate?"

Kate Ross stared at Daniel. If she was relieved to discover that her foe was not a psychopath, she didn't show it.

"What the hell are you doing here?" she demanded angrily.

"I could ask you the same question," Daniel snapped.

"I'm working on a case for Arthur Briggs."

"If you're looking for Kaidanov he's not here."

Kate hit Daniel in the shoulder, none too gently.

"Get off me."

Daniel stood up and Kate got to her feet.

"How did you know I was behind the door?" he asked.

"I saw you push it shut."

"Oh."

"Did you make this mess?" Kate asked as she surveyed the chaos in the office.

"It was like this when I got here."

Kate walked into the hall and stared into the bedroom. Then she said, "Let's get out of here before someone calls 911."

Kate and Daniel agreed to meet downtown at the Starbucks on Pioneer Square, an open, brick-paved block in the center of the city. Daniel parked and found a table next to a window. When Kate walked in he was nursing a cup of coffee and watching a group of teenage boys, oblivious to the cold, playing hacky-sack in the square.

"I got this for you," Daniel said, pointing to a cup of coffee he'd put at Kate's place.

"You want to explain the B and E?" Kate asked without looking at Daniel's peace offering.

"Yeah, right after you explain the assault and battery," Daniel answered, peeved by Kate's offhand manner.

"When someone pulls a knife on you it's called self-defense, not assault."

Daniel flexed his still aching wrist. "Where did you learn that judo stuff?"

"I was a Portland cop before I went to work for Reed, Briggs." Daniel's eyebrows went up in surprise. "I still know the person who's in charge of burglary. Right now I'm undecided about whether to call him."

"Why, are you going to turn yourself in? I didn't hear anyone invite you into Kaidanov's house."

"Nice try, but Geller Pharmaceuticals is a Reed, Briggs client. Kurt Schroeder authorized the entry to look for Geller's property. So, let's start over. What were you doing at Kaidanov's house?"

"Did you hear what happened at the deposition in the Geller case?" Daniel asked with a mixture of nervousness and embarrassment.

"Dan, everyone in the firm knows about your screwup. It was the main topic of conversation yesterday."

"Do you know exactly what happened, why I'm in trouble?"

Kate shook her head. "I heard something about a

document that you turned over to Aaron Flynn, but I don't know the details."

"Are you familiar with the Insufort litigation?"

"Only a little. I told Briggs that I wouldn't work on it."

"Why?"

Kate's tough demeanor cracked for a second. "My sister's kid was born with birth defects. She and her husband have gone through hell caring for her."

Kate took a sip of coffee. When she looked up she had regained her composure.

"Do you mind if I give you some background on the case?" Daniel asked.

"Go ahead."

"Insulin is a protein hormone secreted by the pancreas that helps the body use sugar in the form of glucose. Insulin becomes less effective in metabolizing glucose during pregnancy, which can cause some pregnant women to become diabetic. Insulin resistance during pregnancy must be treated because high sugar levels are toxic to a fetus and can cause birth defects. Geller Pharmaceuticals addressed the problem of insulin resistance during pregnancy by developing thalglitazone, which has the trade name Insufort. Insufort reverses the body's insulin resistance and prevents diabetes and its complications."

"But there are problems, right? Birth defects?" Kate said. "And isn't there a connection between Insufort and the Thalidomide scare from the late 1950s?"

"Yes and no. One tabloid called Insufort the 'Son of Thalidomide,' and there is a connection. A drug called troglitazone helped pregnant women solve the insulin resistance problem, but it also may have caused liver failure. Geller's scientists combined a glitazone with the thalido ring from Thalidomide and created a harmless product that helps pregnant women overcome diabetes during pregnancy."

"So why are women who take the pill giving birth to deformed babies?"

"It's either a compliance problem or coincidence."

Kate looked at him with disgust.

"No, it's true," Daniel insisted. "Many of the women who claim that Insufort caused their child's birth defect probably didn't take the pill as prescribed. Maybe they took it occasionally or irregularly or only a few times and their glucose rose to dangerous levels."

"So we're blaming the victim."

"Look, Kate, most women give birth to healthy babies, but some women give birth to babies who have problems. Sometimes we know why. Some anticonvulsant drugs cause cleft palate. Babies of older mothers are more prone to have birth defects. Maternal infections can also cause them. Then there's alcohol, tobacco, and drugs. But the causes of most birth defects are medical mysteries. The difficulty is that Americans have been taught that there is an answer to every problem." Daniel leaned forward and looked at Kate. "Americans can't accept the fact that shit happens. You get cancer, so you blame overhead power lines; you run someone over, so you blame your car. Are you familiar with the Bendictin cases?"

Kate shook her head.

"'Morning sickness' is a problem for many pregnant women. For most it's unpleasant, but it can be deadly. You've heard of Charlotte Brontë?"

"The author of *Jane Eyre*."

Daniel nodded. "Hyperemesis gravida—'morning sickness'—killed her. In 1956, the FDA approved Bendictin, which was developed by Merrill Pharmaceuticals as a therapy for women with severe morning sickness. In 1979, the *National Enquirer* announced that Bendictin was the cause of thousands of defects in infants.

"The best way to determine if there is a cause-and-effect relationship between a drug and a problem is to conduct an epidemiological study. If a control group that hasn't taken the product has as many, or more, problems as the group that's taken the drug, you can conclude that there's probably not a casual connection between the drug and the problem. All of the epidemiological studies of Bendictin concluded that there was no statistical difference in the incidence of births of babies with defects in the two groups. That didn't stop lawyers from convincing women to sue."

"The plaintiffs' attorneys must have had some evidence of a causal connection between the drug and the defects."

"They used experts who altered the results of studies or conducted studies without proper controls or inaccurately reported doses. The plaintiffs lost almost every case because they couldn't show that Bendictin was to blame for any defects, but it cost Merrill Pharmaceuticals a hundred million dollars to defend all of the cases. In the end, a perfectly safe product was taken off the market because of all the bad publicity and other drug companies were scared to produce a drug that would help women counteract morning sickness. In 1990, the *Journal of the American Medical Association* reported a twofold increase in hospitalizations caused by severe nausea and vomiting in pregnancy since the disappearance of Bendictin. So who suffered? Only the innocent."

"Did all of the Insufort studies show that it's safe?" Kate asked.

"All but one," Daniel answered hesitantly.

Kate cocked her head to one side and watched Daniel carefully as she waited for him to continue.

"I'm in trouble because I missed a letter from Dr. Sergey Kaidanov when I reviewed some discovery that was turned over to Aaron Flynn. The letter discusses a primate study involving Insufort."

"And?"

A vision of Patrick Cummings flashed through Daniel's mind.

"The study showed a high incidence of birth defects in rhesus monkeys that had been given the drug during pregnancy," he answered quietly.

"Did Geller tell you about this study before the deposition?"

"No. Geller's chief medical adviser swears that he's never heard of it."

"I see." Kate sounded skeptical.

"The Kaidanov letter doesn't make sense, Kate. The percentage of defects was very high, in the forty-percent range. It's so out of line with the other study results that there's got to be something wrong."

"Maybe there's something wrong with Geller's other studies."

"No, I've never seen any evidence in any study of a link between Insufort and birth defects."

"Maybe you've never seen any evidence because Geller is hiding it. Remember the asbestos cases? The asbestos industry covered up studies that showed increased cancer in animals. It wasn't until a lawsuit was brought that it came out that they'd known about the problem for decades. The lead-paint industry continued to defend its product even though lead poisoning was one of the most common health problems in children under six and there was scientific documentation of the dangers of lead poisoning as early as 1897. And let's not forget the tobacco industry."

"Jesus, Kate, whose side are you on? Geller is our client."

"Our client is in the drug business to make a buck and it wouldn't surprise me if Geller covered up the Kaidanov study if the results are as devastating as you say they are. Do you think Geller markets Insufort to help women? Companies whose executives are men make a lot of these defective products that are used by women. There's Thalidomide, DES—the synthetic estrogen that was supposed to prevent miscarriages and caused vaginal cancer—and the Dalkon Shield."

"Plaintiffs' attorneys play on this sympathy for women to gouge money out of corporations with frivolous lawsuits so they can rake in millions," Daniel answered angrily. "They don't care about their clients or whether they really have a case. The Bendictin lawyers were hoping that jurors would be so appalled by the birth defects they saw that they'd forget that there was no evidence that Bendictin caused them. The breast implant cases used sympathy for women to sway public opinion even though there's no evidence of a connection between defects in silicone gel implants and connective tissue diseases like systemic lupus erythematosus and rheumatoid arthritis."

Kate looked fed up. "I have a good friend who's sterile because she used the Dalkon Shield. I worked on her lawsuit and I learned a lot about the way corporate America works. By the time the public discovers that a product is defective, the company has made so much money it can afford to buy off the victims. Tobacco is so flush it can make multibillion-dollar settlements and still keep trucking.

"And don't come down so hard on plaintiffs' attorneys. They can make millions when they win a case, but they don't make a penny if they lose."

"You think Aaron Flynn is a humanitarian?" Daniel asked, but his heart was not completely in tune with his words. As he spoke them he remembered Flynn ruffling Patrick Cummings's hair.

"Who else is going to represent the poor?" Kate asked. "'Cause it sure ain't Reed, Briggs. If lawyers like Flynn didn't take cases for a contingent fee no one but the rich could afford to sue. And they risk their own money on expenses, which they don't recover if they don't win. A good, decent lawyer can lose everything if he doesn't prevail. The lawyer who sued when my friend became sterile did it to pressure the company into taking a dangerous device off of the market. He cared about Jill. If Insufort is disfiguring children the only way to make Geller stop marketing it is to expose the problem, and one of the best ways to do that is in the courts."

Daniel expelled the breath he'd been holding.

"You're right. Sorry. I'm just scared that I'm gonna lose my job because I missed that damn letter. And I'm certain there's something wrong with Kaidanov's study. It doesn't make sense that he could get those results with Insufort. That's why I was trying to find him. You know he hasn't been at work for a while?"

Kate nodded.

"When I went to Kaidanov's house I didn't plan on going in, but I saw that the house had been searched and I thought he might be hurt or worse. And I did find something that might help."

Daniel pulled his handkerchief out of his pocket and laid the hard drive on the table. Kate stared at it.

"If the study exists, and Kaidanov wrote up his results, it may be on here."

Kate laughed. "You stole Kaidanov's hard drive?"

"I didn't steal it. I was trying to protect Geller. Isn't that why you were there, to protect Geller's property?"

Kate hesitated and Daniel remembered something about her.

"Wait a minute. Aren't you the investigator who got into the hard drive in that wrongful termination case when we needed to recover E-mail that an employee erased?"

Kate smiled ever so slightly.

"Could you look at this? I tried at Kaidanov's house, but you need a password to log on."

"Why should I?"

"I told you before that I wasn't born with a silver spoon like Joe Molinari. Well, the truth is that I wasn't born with any kind of spoon. This job is all I've got. Briggs will need a scapegoat if Kaidanov's letter sinks the Insufort case, and I'm it. I know there's something wrong with Kaidanov's study. If I can prove it I can save the case, and I might save my job."

"What if the study is the real thing?"

Daniel sighed and shook his head. "Then I'm toast."

Kate made a decision. She held out her hand.

"Give me that," she said, flicking her fingers toward the hard drive. "We'll take it to my house and see what we can see."

NINE

Daniel followed Kate Ross into the West Hills along winding roads. At first, the streets were lined with houses, then forest began to predominate and the houses appeared farther apart. Kate lived at the end of a cul-de-sac separated from her neighbors on either side by a quarter acre of woods. Her modern glass-and-steel ranch perched on a hill overlooking downtown Portland.

Daniel followed Kate along a slate path through a small flower garden to the front door. A staircase next to the entryway led up to Kate's bedroom. She walked past it and through a living-room and dining-room area. The outer wall was all glass. Daniel glanced quickly at her expensive-looking furnishings. The abstract painting on the living-room wall was an original oil, and so was a smaller French country landscape. The chairs and sofa were covered in leather and the dining-room table was polished oak and looked antique.

Kate walked down another staircase across from the kitchen to a workroom lit by fluorescent lights. Scattered around the basement room were several workbenches covered with monitors, wires, motherboards, and computer innards. A desk was affixed to one wall and ran its length. Over the desk was a bookshelf filled with computer manuals and books on computer science and other scientific subjects.

"Do you run a computer repair business in your spare time?" Daniel joked.

"Something like that," Kate replied as she removed Kaidanov's hard drive from her jacket pocket. She tossed the jacket over a chair, brushed her hair back, and seated herself at the wall-length desk. In front of her was a removable hard-drive rack into which Kate inserted Kaidanov's hard drive before snapping the rack into one of her computers.

"How are you going to get around the password?" Daniel asked nervously.

"No problem. I've written some software that has yet to meet a password it couldn't break."

"Where did you learn to do that?"

"Cal Tech."

Kate saw Daniel's eyes widen. She laughed.

"I was recruited into the computer crimes unit of the Portland Police Bureau out of college. It seemed a hell of a lot more exciting than sitting on my ass in some high-tech company. Now I do my own thing on the side. It pays well."

Kate turned back to the monitor and started tapping in commands on her keyboard. A minute later she smiled and shook her head.

"It's amazing. They all do this. I would have expected more from a scientist. His password's six numbers—probably his birthday."

"You're in?"

She nodded. "First thing I'm gonna do is make a magnetic copy of this little devil, just in case something goes wrong."

Kate's fingers flashed across the keyboard and lines of text began to appear on the screen.

"This should be finished in a minute."

"How come you quit the cops to go to work for Reed, Briggs?" Daniel asked to make conversation.

"That's none of your business, Ames," Kate snapped before swiveling her chair so her back was to him. Daniel was so surprised by her outburst that he was speechless.

"The copy is complete," she said a minute later, all business now. "Let's bring up Kaidanov's files."

Kate tapped in some commands. "The stuff that's still on here isn't about Insufort. If Kaidanov did have files about his monkeys, they've probably been erased."

"Shit."

"Not to worry. Unless special software was used, the files aren't really deleted. They'll still be on the hard drive. I just happen to have written a voodoo program that will raise the dead," Kate said as she tapped the keyboard. More text appeared on the screen. She stood up and waved Daniel in for a closer look.

"There appears to be a big block of files that was erased on March fourth. Sit down at the keyboard and hit 'page down' until you find what you want and we'll print it out."

Daniel took Kate's chair and stared at the monitor.

"There's a lot of stuff here."

"Give me some key words. I've got search software installed."

Daniel thought for a moment. "Try Insufort, rhesus monkeys, primates."

Kate leaned over his shoulder and tapped in some commands. Her hair brushed against his cheek. She smelled nice.

Suddenly the letter from Kaidanov to George Fournet appeared on the screen.

"That's it," Daniel said excitedly, but his excitement diminished as he scrolled through the files that followed the letter. When he stopped reading he looked grim.

"What's the matter?" Kate asked.

"Remember I didn't believe what I read in Kaidanov's letter?"

Kate nodded.

"Well, the deleted files are the supporting documents for Kaidanov's study. I've just skimmed them, but they appear to confirm his conclusions about the frequency of birth defects in the monkeys that were given Insufort."

"So the results of the study are real?"

Daniel nodded. "Which means I've just made my situation worse."

"But you may have helped get Insufort off the market."

"At the cost of my job."

"Do you really want to help Geller if it's marketing a product that destroys children's lives."

Daniel didn't answer.

"Here's something else to think about," Kate said. "Who deleted Kaidanov's files and trashed Kaidanov's house? Who wouldn't want Kaidanov's research to be made public?"

Daniel still didn't answer.

"Geller Pharmaceuticals fits that profile."

"I don't know."

"Can you think of anyone else with a motive, Dan?"

"No, you're right. It has to be someone from Geller."

He remembered Patrick Cummings again.

"This is bad."

"And it may be worse. Where do you think Kaidanov is?"

"That's a stretch, Kate. Geller's people are business-men, not killers." Daniel protested without much conviction.

"Wake up. We're talking about billions of dollars in losses if Geller has to take Insufort off of the market. And don't forget the lawsuit. How much do you think the plaintiffs will recover if Aaron Flynn proves that Geller intentionally marketed a dangerous product? After one successful lawsuit, every woman who's ever had a problem with Insufort will line up at Flynn's door and Geller will be swept away in a tidal wave of litigation."

Kate turned back to the computer and used the search program again while Daniel tried to figure out what he would do next.

"Yes!" Kate exclaimed a moment later as she pointed at the screen.

"Monkeys have to eat. That's an order for a crate of Purina monkey chow and there's an address. That must be the location of the lab."

Kate walked over to another computer. "I can get directions and a map on the Internet."

While she worked Daniel took a closer look at Kaidanov's study. The more he looked the more depressed he felt. Five minutes later Kate showed Daniel a map with directions to the lab from her town house.

"I dug up something else," Kate said. "After I got the map I found the assessment and taxation information on the property. The land is owned by Geller Pharmaceuticals."

TEN

Twenty minutes later Daniel was driving in the country on a narrow road with Kate beside him. The sun was setting and they had been quiet since leaving the highway. Kate was staring ahead and Daniel chanced an occasional glance at the investigator. Daniel had consulted with Kate at work a few times and she'd impressed him with her intelligence, but he had not been attracted to her. Now he noticed that she was good-looking in a rugged sort of way. Not model beautiful like Susan Webster, but interesting to look at. And she was certainly intriguing. He didn't know any other woman who wrote voodoo software programs and had been a cop.

"This is it," Kate said.

Daniel turned onto a logging road ignoring a "No Trespassing" sign. The shock absorbers on his secondhand Ford were not in the best of shape and Kate swore a lot after they left the pavement. She was registering another complaint when the road curved and a one-story building appeared. Just as they got out of the car the wind shifted and a strange odor made Kate's nostrils flare.

"What's that smell?" Daniel asked.

"It's a little like barbecue," Kate answered.

Pieces of glass covered the ground under a window that had blown out and the front door was charred and had buckled. Daniel peeked through the window cautiously, then jerked his head back. His face was drained of color.

"What is it?" Kate asked.

"There's a body on the floor. There's no skin. It's like a skeleton."

Kate extended a hand toward the door tentatively, worried that it might be hot. She touched her fingers to the metal. It was cold. Kate pushed and the door swung inward. She looked for a light switch and found one, but it didn't work.

"Do you have a flashlight?" Kate asked. Daniel got one from the car and Kate started inside. He tried to follow, but she stopped him.

"This is a crime scene. Just stay here and keep the door open so I can have a little more light."

Daniel propped open the door but did not go any farther. He was secretly grateful not to have to view the body.

Kate walked slowly toward the room she had seen through the window and stood in the doorway. Part of the roof had collapsed and a ray of fading sunlight illuminated a section of the room. Charred wooden beams had crushed a table and what had once been a video monitor. Near the monitor was a rack of plastic test tubes that had been melted by intense heat.

Kate edged around a burn-scarred desk that was tipped on its side. She noticed another roof beam resting on the top of two filing cabinets whose drawers had all been pulled out. The paint on the cabinets had blistered off. The metal was charred and scarred but intact. A breeze gusted through the broken window and drifted down through the gaps in the roof. It blew blackened scraps of paper around the room. The source of the paper was a pile of ashes in the center of the floor that Kate guessed had once been the contents of the filing cabinets.

Kate's eyes stayed on the pile for a moment more before being drawn, almost against her will, to the two bodies sprawled in the center of the room. One was human, its skull charred and its clothes seared to ash. Kate's stomach heaved, but she closed her eyes for a second and kept it together. When she opened her eyes they shifted to the second corpse. For a moment Kate was confused. The body was too small even for a child, unless it was an extremely young one. She braced herself and stepped closer. That's when she saw the tail. Kate backed out of the room.

"What's in there?" Daniel asked when she stepped outside.

"A human corpse and a dead monkey. I'm going to look down the hall."

"We should get out of here," Daniel said nervously.

"In a minute."

"No one's alive. We would have heard them."

"Just give me a second."

The light from the doorway barely reached the end of the hall, so Kate had to use the flashlight. She spotted two open doors but had no idea what was inside. The smell of burned flesh grew more intense as she neared the rooms.

Kate held her breath and cast the beam inside. The first room was filled with cages, each containing a monkey, and every monkey was pressing against the wire mesh as if it had been trying to claw through the wire when it died.

ELEVEN

A uniformed officer was taking Kate and Daniel's statements when an unmarked car parked behind the van from the medical examiner's office. Homicide detective Billie Brewster, a slender black woman in a navy-blue windbreaker and jeans, got out of the car. Her partner, Zeke Forbus, a heavyset white man with thinning brown hair, spotted Kate at the same time she spotted him.

"What's Annie Oakley doing here?" Forbus asked Brewster.

"Shut the fuck up," the black woman snapped angrily at her partner. Then she walked up to Kate and gave her a hug.

"How you doing, Kate?" Brewster asked with genuine concern.

"I'm doing fine, Billie," Kate answered without conviction. "How about you?"

The black woman shot her thumb over her shoulder toward her partner.

"I was doing great until they partnered me up with this redneck."

"Zeke," Kate said with a nod.

"Long time, Kate," Zeke Forbus answered without warmth. Then he turned his back to her and addressed the uniformed officer.

"What have we got here, Ron?"

"Crispy critters," the officer answered with a sly smile. "If you ain't had dinner, I'll get you a bucket of KFM."

"KFM?"

"Kentucky Fried Monkey," the cop answered, cackling at his joke. "We've got a passel of 'em inside."

"Why am I investigating monkey murders?" Forbus asked. "Don't we have animal control for that?"

"One of the crispy critters ain't a monkey, that's why," the uniform answered.

"I understand you called this in," Billie said to Kate. "Why were you out here at night in the middle of nowhere?"

"This is Daniel Ames, an associate at Reed, Briggs, the firm I work for. One of our clients, Geller Pharmaceuticals, is in the middle of a lawsuit over one of its products. Up until last week all of the tests of the product came out favorable to Geller, but a scientist named Sergey Kaidanov reported negative results in a study of rhesus monkeys."

"The same type of monkeys we've got in there?" Billie asked with a nod toward the lab.

"Exactly. Everyone wants to talk to Kaidanov because the study could have a huge impact on the lawsuit, but he disappeared about a week ago."

"Anyone fixed the time of this fire?" Billie asked the uniform.

"Not yet, but it's not recent."

"Go on," Billie told Kate.

"Dan and I went to Kaidanov's house to interview him. He wasn't there, but someone had taken the house apart."

"What's that mean?" Forbus asked.

"Someone searched it and left a mess. We did a little investigating and found an address for the lab. We came out here hoping that we'd find Kaidanov and it looks like we have."

"You think the dead guy is your scientist?"

"I think there's a good chance he is."

"Let's take a look," Billie said to Forbus as she started inside. Kate took a step toward the door, but Forbus held out an arm and barred her way.

"No civilians allowed in the crime scene."

"Oh, for Christ's sake," Billie responded, glaring at her partner.

"Forget it. He's right. I'm not a cop anymore," Kate said, trying to sound unconcerned, but Daniel saw her shoulders slump.

"What was all that about?" Daniel asked as soon as the detectives were out of earshot.

"Old business."

"Thanks for covering for me."

Kate looked puzzled.

"You know, about my breaking into Kaidanov's house."

Kate shrugged. "You didn't think I'd burn you, did you?"

A deputy medical examiner was videotaping the office while a tech from the crime lab snapped 35mm photographs, then digital shots that could be fed into a computer and E-mailed if necessary. Billie took in the scene from the doorway. A corpse lay on its stomach near the center of the room. The flesh on its side and back had been burned off and the heat from the fire had turned the bones grayish blue in color.

"Any ID?" Billie asked the medical examiner.

"Can't even tell the sex," he answered.

"Is it a murder?"

"Best guess, yes. Deutsch says it's definitely arson," he replied, referring to the arson investigator. "And look at the skull."

The detective took a few steps into the room so she could get a better look at the corpse. The back of the skull had shattered. An exiting bullet or a blunt instrument could have caused the damage. She would leave that determination to the ME.

Billie moved nearer to the corpse and squatted. The floor was concrete, so they might get lucky. From other arson murders she had investigated, Billie knew that fragments of clothing and flesh on the front of the body might have escaped the blaze. Where the body pressed against the floor there would be less oxygen for the fire to feed on and some protection for flesh and fibers.

Billie turned her attention to a tiny corpse a few feet from the human. All of its hair and flesh was gone. Its skull had also been shattered. She stared dispassionately at the monkey for a few minutes then stood up.

"If you want to see more monkeys, there are two rooms filled with them down the hall," the medical examiner said.

"I'll pass," Forbus said, stifling a yawn.

Billie wasn't surprised that the bizarre crime scene bored her partner. He was a good old boy hanging on long enough to collect his pension so he could fish 365 days a year. The only time she'd seen him show any interest in a case was last week when they'd investigated a murder at a strip joint. Billie, on the other hand, was fascinated by anything out of the ordinary, and this crime scene was the most unusual she'd encountered in some time.

Billie wandered down the hall. The doors to the monkey rooms were open and Billie stood quietly, surveying the scene. The monkeys had died hard and she pitied the poor bastards. Death by fire was the worst way to go. She shivered and turned away.

TWELVE

The offices of the Oregon State Medical Examiner were on Knott Street in a two-story, red-brick building that had once been a Scandinavian funeral home. Arbor vitae, split-leaf maples, and a variety of other shrubs partially hid a front porch whose overhang was supported by white pillars. Kate parked in the adjacent lot and walked up the front steps to the porch. Billie Brewster was waiting for her in the reception area.

"Thanks for letting me come," Kate said.

"You're lucky Zeke is still in court. There's no way I could swing this if he was here."

"Like I said, thanks."

Kate followed Billie toward the back of the building. When they entered the autopsy room they found Dr. Sally Grace, an assistant ME, and Dr. Jack Forester, a forensic anthropologist, standing on either side of a gurney that had been wheeled between the two stainless-steel autopsy tables that stood on either side of the room. The body from the primate lab lay on top of the gurney. Just before Billie had left the crime scene, the deputy medical examiner and several firefighters wearing latex gloves had used the few scraps of clothing that had escaped destruction to lift up the corpse and place it in a body bag. The area around the body had been searched for skull fragments and they had been taken to the ME's office along with the body. The corpse of the monkey found in the room with the human remains had also been brought to the ME's office, along with skull fragments found near it. The monkey's corpse was lying on a second gurney.

"Hi, Billie," Dr. Grace said. "You're a little late. We're almost done."

"Sorry, I was tied up in court."

"Who's your friend?" the coroner asked.

Billie made the introductions. "Kate's ex-PPB and an investigator with the Reed, Briggs law firm. The dead man may have been an important witness in a civil case her firm is defending. She's been very helpful."

"Well, the more the merrier," Dr. Grace said cheerfully as she turned back to the corpse.

Forester and Grace were wearing blue, water-impermeable gowns, masks, goggles, and heavy, black rubber aprons. Kate and Brewster donned similar outfits before joining them at the gurney.

"We found out some interesting stuff," Forester said. "The monkey is a rhesus. Most research labs use them. We found some blood and flesh on its teeth and we're going to do a DNA match with the other corpse to see if that's where it came from. The surprise is the way the monkey died."

"Which was?"

"Gunshot," Dr. Grace answered. "We found a shell for

a forty-five at the crime scene and the skull reconstruction shows an exit wound."

"Is that how this one got it?" Billie asked, motioning toward the remains on the gurney.

"That was my first thought, what with the skull blown out and all," Dr. Grace answered, "but we have a different cause of death with John Doe."

"Then it's a man?" Kate asked.

"We doped that out pretty easily," Dr. Grace said.

"Men's bones are larger because of the greater muscle attachment," Forester said, "so we either had an average-to below-average-size male or a woman who pumped iron."

Forester pointed at the skeleton's crotch. All of the flesh had been burned from the bones in this area.

"The human pelvis provides the most reliable means of determining the sex of skeletal remains. The female pelvis is designed to offer optimal space for the birth canal and has a notch in it. A male pelvis is curved. This is definitely the pelvis of a male."

"And there were no ovaries and no uterus," Dr. Grace added with a smile. "That was a big clue."

Billie laughed. "So, how was John Doe killed?"

"First, you need to know that he was dead before he was set on fire," the ME said. "There was still some blood in his heart. It was deep purple instead of red or pink, so I guessed that carbon monoxide was not present. The test confirmed my guess. If he was alive when he burned I would have found carbon monoxide in his blood.

"His airways were also free of soot, which he

would have breathed in if he was breathing when the fire started."

Dr. Grace bent over the corpse. "See these marks?" she asked, pointing to several notches that scarred one of the ribs. "They were made by a knife. The rib is in close proximity to the heart. Luckily, he was lying on a concrete floor, so his front was protected to a certain degree and the heart was preserved. It showed stab wounds and there was blood in the left chest and pericardial sac, which you'd expect with a stabbing."

"What about the skull? The monkey was shot. It looks like Doe's skull was blown out the same way," Billie said.

"Come over here," Dr. Grace said as she led the group over to a table covered by a white sheet that stood in front of a stainless-steel counter and sink. On the sheet were the fragments of Doe's skull that had been gathered at the crime scene. They had been painstakingly pieced together.

"Gunshots cause linear fractures that radiate out from the hole caused by the exit or entrance of the bullet. We didn't find linear fractures and you can see that there's no hole formed by the skull fragments.

"If the skull had been fractured by blunt force trauma from a club or baseball bat or something like that, we would have found sections of bone showing a depression from the blow."

"So what's the explanation?" Billie asked.

"The brain is blood-intensive. When the fire heated the blood it generated steam that blew out the back of John Doe's skull."

The detective grimaced.

"Was he stabbed to death at the lab?" Kate asked.

"I can't tell you that. We did find some fibers that were crushed into the fabric of his clothing and survived the fire. I'm having the lab test them. If they're the type of fibers you find in a car trunk, we can guess that he was transported to the lab, but that would only be a guess."

"What about time of death?" Billie asked. "Can you tell how many days he's been dead?"

"I can't do much for you there." Dr. Grace pointed to a sieve resting in a metal pot on one of the autopsy tables. "That's his last meal," she said, indicating pieces of steak, baked potato skin, lettuce, and tomato. "He was killed within an hour of eating, but how long ago I can't say."

Billie turned to Jack Forester. "Can you tell me enough about him for me to match him with a missing person report?"

"Well, we've got the teeth, of course. The guy has had dental work done. Brubaker's out of town," Forester said, referring to Dr. Harry Brubaker, the forensic dentist who was normally present at autopsies. "We'll get these over to him when he comes back from vacation. But he won't be much help until we have someone to whom he can match the dental work."

"Can you tell anything from the teeth?" asked Kate, who had read a few books in Forester's field.

"They do give us some idea of Doe's age," he answered. "We know a person is eighteen or younger if his wisdom teeth have not erupted, so this guy is definitely over eighteen. The degeneration of the skeleton also helps us with his age. Now this is very subjective, but the changes in this guy's spine tell me that he's probably older than thirty.

"The last thing I did was check out the configuration of the pelvis. Where the two halves of the pelvis meet in front is called the pubic symphysis and it wears with age. A guy named T. Wingate Todd made casts of the pelvis of a wide range of corpses whose ages were known. He found that the wear pattern on the pelvis is pretty consistent at different ages."

Forester pointed to a large Tupperware box that was sitting near the door. The lid was open and Billie could see several casts lying in foam.

"I matched the Todd casts to Doe. Taking all the other factors into account, I can give you a very subjective estimate of forty-five to fifty-five for our friend."

Forester pointed to the skeleton's nose.

"Now, I also know that we've got a Caucasian. An Asian's nasal aperture is oval, a black's is wide and short. This guy's is tall and narrow. Ergo, a Caucasian.

"You can also tell from the eye sockets. Whites' are the shape of aviator glasses, blacks' are squarer, and Asians' more rounded."

"Any way to tell eye color?" Billie asked.

Forester shook his head. "Not with a burn victim. The eyes burn out. But I can tell you the guy's height. He was between five eight and five ten. I got that from measuring his tibia and femur," Forester said, pointing to the corpse's shinbone and thighbone, "and comparing them to tables that were developed by measuring the lengths of the long bones of American casualties from the Second World War and the Korean War."

"So we've probably got a white male, five eight to five ten, of average build, and forty-five to fifty-five years of age," Billie summarized.

"Yup," Forester answered. "Get a possible and his dental records and Brubaker can give you a positive ID."

THIRTEEN

After dropping Kate at her house, Daniel drove home and fell into bed. Visions of a flaming laboratory jammed with screaming monkeys and deformed children haunted his dreams and he jerked awake more than once during the night. When he arrived at work the next morning, Daniel was pale and there were dark circles under his bloodshot eyes. He checked his voice mail and found a message from Renee Gilchrist telling him that he was expected in Arthur Briggs's office at eleven. This is it, Daniel thought. He slumped in his chair and looked around his office. A lump formed in his throat. He had worked so hard to get here and everything he'd earned was going to be snatched away because of a one-page letter.

At 10:54, Daniel pushed himself to his feet, checked his tie, and walked the last mile to Arthur Briggs's office. Renee announced Daniel's presence, then flashed him a sympathetic smile.

"Go on in. And good luck."

"Thanks, Renee."

Daniel straightened his shoulders and walked into the lion's den, an incredible corner office that was obviously the creation of an expensive interior decorator. With diplomas from Duke University and the University of Chicago law school, and framed tributes to its occupant, the room was a testament to the greatness of Arthur Briggs.

"Have a seat, Ames," he said without making eye contact.

The senior partner was reading a letter and he paid no attention to Daniel for a full minute. When Briggs finally signed his name and placed the letter in his out-box, he looked across his desk at the young associate with unforgiving eyes.

"Do you have any idea how much damage your incompetence has caused?"

Daniel knew that no answer was expected and he gave none.

"The partners met yesterday to discuss your situation," Briggs continued. "It has been decided that you should no longer work for this firm."

Though he had been expecting this, the words still stunned Daniel.

"You will be paid six months' salary and you can keep your health insurance for a year. That's very generous considering that your blunder could cost one of our best clients billions of dollars."

He'd been fired. At first Daniel felt shame, then his shame turned to anger and he stiffened.

"This is a crock and you know it, Mr. Briggs." His sharp words startled Daniel as much as they amazed Briggs. "You're firing me because you need a scapegoat now that Aaron Flynn knows about the Kaidanov study. But finding out about that study might help Reed, Briggs avoid aiding and abetting a client this firm should stop representing."

Briggs leaned back in his chair and made a steeple of his fingers but said nothing. Daniel pushed on.

"I think Geller Pharmaceuticals is covering up Kaidanov's results. Did you know that the police are investigating an arson fire at a primate lab located on land owned by Geller? It's where Kaidanov conducted his study. All of his monkeys are dead. And it looks like Kaidanov is dead, too—murdered. Quite a coincidence, wouldn't you say?"

Daniel paused, but Briggs just continued to stare at him as if he were some mildly interesting insect. Briggs's lack of reaction at hearing Geller linked to murder and arson surprised Daniel. But Briggs had made a fortune by perfecting a poker face, so Daniel forged on.

"Kaidanov has been missing for over a week. His home has been searched." Daniel thought he saw Briggs twitch. "Mr. Briggs, I've examined Dr. Kaidanov's hard drive. Someone tried to delete the primate study, but I've seen it." Now he definitely had Briggs's attention. "The results support the conclusions in Kaidanov's letter. I think there's a good possibility that Insufort is very dangerous and that someone connected to Geller tried to cover up Kaidanov's report."

"How do you know that Dr. Kaidanov's home was searched?"

Daniel swallowed hard. "I went over there," he said, suddenly remembering that searching the house and taking the hard drive were felonies.

"Is that where you examined Dr. Kaidanov's hard drive?"

Daniel felt like a laser beam had pierced him and he appreciated the terror witnesses experienced during one of Briggs's infamous cross-examinations.

"I'd rather not say," he answered.

"Is that right."

Daniel did not answer.

"Taking the Fifth, are we, Ames?" A terrible smile creased Briggs's lips. Daniel felt trapped. "Obviously I can't force you to answer my questions, but the police can. What do you think will happen if they discover that someone has stolen the hard drive from Dr. Kaidanov's home computer and I tell them that you've confessed to me that you were at his house and examined the hard drive?"

"I . . . I was acting on behalf of our client."

Even as he said the words Daniel knew that the excuse sounded pathetic.

"It's good that you've remembered that there is an attorney/client relationship between you and Geller, even though you no longer work for this firm. If you know that, then you know that any information about Insufort on Dr. Kaidanov's hard drive is the property of our client."

Briggs's smile disappeared. "I want the hard drive by five o'clock today, Ames."

"Mr. Briggs . . ."

"If it's not here by five, you will lose your health benefits, your severance pay, and you will be arrested. Is that clear?"

"What are you planning to do about Insufort?"

"My plans are none of your business since you no longer work for this firm."

"But Insufort is hurting babies. Someone at Geller may have committed murder to cover up the truth. The firm could be an accessory to—"

Briggs stood suddenly. "This meeting is over," he said, pointing toward the door. "Get out!"

Daniel hesitated, then walked to the door. As he crossed the room anger built in the pit of his stomach. He opened the door halfway, then turned and faced Briggs one more time.

"I've been scared and depressed about losing this job ever since the deposition, because working for Reed, Briggs really meant something to me. But maybe this is for the best. I don't think I want to work for a firm that would cover up the crimes Geller is committing. We're talking about little children, Mr. Briggs. I don't know how you can look in the mirror."

"You listen to me," Briggs shouted. "If you breathe one word of what you've told me to anyone, you'll be sued for slander and you will go to jail. How many people are going to hire a destitute, disbarred lawyer with a felony conviction? Now get the hell out!"

It wasn't until Daniel slammed the door to Briggs's office that he saw that he'd had an audience. Renee Gilchrist and a plain, middle-aged woman Daniel recognized as Dr. April Fairweather were both staring, openmouthed. Daniel's anger turned to embarrassment. He mumbled an apology and rushed toward his office.

Daniel was almost there when it dawned on him that Kate had the hard drive. He was about to go to her office when he saw a security guard standing in front of his door. He hurried the rest of the way. As soon as the guard spotted Daniel, he blocked the entrance.

"I work here," Daniel said. "What's going on?"

"I'm sorry, Mr. Ames," the guard said firmly but politely, "but you can't go in until we're through."

Daniel looked over the guard's shoulder. A second guard was emptying his files into a box.

"What about my things, my personal items like my diplomas?"

"You can have them as soon as we're through." The guard held out his hand. "I'll need your keys."

Daniel was thoroughly humiliated. He wanted to fight, to protest, to scream that he had rights, but he knew that there was nothing he could do, so he meekly handed over his office keys.

"How much longer will this take? I'd like to get out of here."

"We'll be done soon," the guard answered.

A crowd was starting to gather. Joe Molinari placed his hand on Daniel's shoulder.

"What's going on, Ames?"

"Briggs sacked me."

"Ah, shit."

"It wasn't a surprise. I've seen this coming since the deposition."

"Is there anything I can do?" Joe asked.

"Thanks, but it's over. Briggs needed a scapegoat and I'm it."

Molinari squeezed Daniel's shoulder supportively.

"Look, I know people. I'm going to ask around. Maybe I can line up something for you."

"I appreciate the offer, but who's going to hire me? What kind of letter of recommendation do you think Briggs is going to write?"

"Don't think like that. Briggs doesn't control every law firm in Portland. You're good, amigo. Any firm would be lucky to get you."

"I don't know if I want to keep practicing law, Joe."

"Don't be a defeatist asshole. This is like riding a polo pony. When you get thrown you don't just lie on the ground feeling sorry for yourself. You get your ass back in the saddle and play on. I'll give you a day to mope, then we're going to figure out how to get you back working horrible hours and taking abuse from intellectual inferiors."

Daniel couldn't help smiling. Then he remembered Kate.

"Can I use your phone? They won't let me into my office."

"Sure."

"Thanks, Joe. For everything."

"Aw shucks, you're making me blush."

Daniel shook his head. "You're still a jerk."

Joe laughed and they started walking toward Molinari's office. When they reached his door, Daniel turned toward his friend.

"This is a private call, okay?"

"Say no more."

Daniel closed the door and dialed Kate's extension. Joe stood guard outside.

"It's Daniel," he said as soon as she picked up. "Are you alone?"

"Yeah, why?"

"Briggs fired me."

"Oh, Daniel. I'm so sorry."

"I can't say I didn't expect it."

"You should fight this."

"I'm not sure I'd want my job back even if I could get it. Really, being fired might have been the best thing."

"How can you say that?"

"I told Briggs that Geller might be covering up the fact that Insufort causes birth defects in little children. He threatened to have me arrested, to sue me. He wasn't the least bit concerned that Geller is ruining the lives of all those kids and their parents. So I guess the question is, would I have accepted Reed, Briggs's job offer if I knew I'd be using my legal education to protect a company that destroys lives for profit?

"But that's not why I called. I wasn't thinking straight after Briggs told me I was fired and I told him that I had Kaidanov's hard drive. He wants it by five today or he's going after me."

"You didn't . . . ?"

"No. I didn't mention you. He has no idea that you have it and I want to make certain that he doesn't find out. Can you get it to me? Briggs says he'll have me arrested if I don't give it to him and I'm in enough trouble already. And we have a copy, anyway."

"What are you going to do with the information?"

"I don't know, Kate, and I'm too mixed up now to make decisions."

"I'll get you the hard drive before one."

"Thanks."

There was dead air for a moment. Then Kate said, "You're a good person, Dan, and good people land on their feet. You'll come out of this okay."

Daniel appreciated the sentiment, but he wasn't sure that was the way things happened in the real world.

FOURTEEN

As soon as she left the medical examiner's office, Billie Brewster drove west along the Sunset Highway. Twenty minutes later the detective took one of the Hillsboro exits and found herself in open country where rolling green hills and a sweeping blue sky formed a backdrop for the three interconnected, black-glass-and-polished-granite buildings in the Geller Pharmaceuticals complex.

The main attraction in Building A was an atrium with a three-story waterfall that started just under a tinted-glass roof and occupied one corner of the spacious lobby. Billie learned the location of Kurt Schroeder's office at reception and walked up a staircase near the atrium that led to the second floor. A glass-encased sky bridge connected the main building to Building B, which housed research and development.

Moments after Billie flashed her badge at Schroeder's secretary she found herself seated across from Geller's chief medical adviser.

"Dr. Schroeder, I'm Detective Brewster with Portland homicide."

"Homicide?" Schroeder said nervously.

"Yesterday evening I was at a building that was destroyed in an arson fire. There were approximately twenty dead rhesus monkeys inside. They were set on fire in their cages."

"That's terrible, but what does this have to do with me or Geller Pharmaceuticals?"

"The records show that Geller owns the property where the building is located. We think it's a primate lab."

Schroeder's brow furrowed. "All of our research is conducted in this building. We do own property apart from this campus for expansion, but it's undeveloped. If you found a lab, it wasn't Geller's."

"A body was discovered in the lab, Dr. Schroeder. The corpse was badly burned, but we can tell it's a forty-five-to fifty-five-year-old white male, and we think it might be Dr. Sergey Kaidanov."

"Kaidanov! My God! He disappeared more than a week ago. We've been looking for him. This is terrible."

"Was Dr. Kaidanov involved in primate research?"

"That's where the problem comes in. The plaintiffs in a lawsuit we're defending produced what purports to be a letter from Kaidanov in which he claims to be conducting a primate study for our company, but we have no record of his being assigned to conduct such a study."

"A lawyer from the Reed, Briggs firm told me about that. That's where we got the idea that the victim might be Kaidanov."

Schroeder shivered. "God, I hope not."

"You can help with the identification by sending me Dr. Kaidanov's personnel file. His dental records would be very useful."

"I'll do what I can," he answered, apparently shaken by what he had learned.

Brewster handed Schroeder a paper with the location of the destroyed building.

"Can you check to see if your company has a lab on the property?"

"Certainly. I should have an answer for you in a day or so."

Brewster stood. "Thank you for your cooperation, Dr. Schroeder."

"Of course." He paused. "I hope you're wrong about Kaidanov."

"I hope so, too."

There were several phone messages waiting for Billie when she got back to the Justice Center. Halfway down the pile was a message from missing persons. Even though she was pretty certain of the identity of the body at the lab, Brewster had phoned them from the medical examiner's office and asked for a list of men who matched the description that Forester had given her. She dialed the extension for missing persons.

"Hey, Billie," Detective Aaron Davies said, "I got a live one for you. A guy named Gene Arnold. He's a lawyer from Arizona. His partner, Benjamin Kellogg, reported him missing right around the time you're interested in. He disappeared while staying at the Benson Hotel. I'll give you Kellogg's number."

Billie dialed the Arizona number. The receptionist at the firm connected her with Benjamin Kellogg and she identified herself.

"Have you found Gene?" Kellogg asked anxiously.

"No, but I wanted to get some information from you so I can follow up on your report. Can you tell me why you think Mr. Arnold is missing?"

"I know he's missing and I'm certain that something is wrong. We're all very worried about him."

"Why is that?"

"He went to New York on business, Sunday, February twenty-seventh. He was supposed to come straight back. I had his flight number and everything, but he wasn't on the plane. Then he called from Portland on Wednesday, March first. He asked for me, but I was in court, so he spoke with Maria Suarez, our secretary."

"You weren't expecting him to go to Oregon?"

"No. I've worked with Gene for six years, Maria even longer. We can't remember him ever mentioning any contacts, business or social, in Oregon."

"Okay, what did he tell Ms. Suarez?"

"He wanted me to know that he would be away for a few days on personal business. Maria said he asked about his mail and messages, and then he gave her his room number at the Benson Hotel and said he'd keep in touch. The hotel called on Tuesday, March seventh and said that Gene had reserved the room through Monday but had not checked out. They wanted to know if he still wanted it. I had no idea. The security chief said that he was putting Gene's belongings in storage. That's when I got scared that something was wrong and I contacted your missing persons bureau."

"And no one's heard from him since?"

"Not a word."

"Is Mr. Arnold married?"

"He's a widower. His wife died about a year before I started working here."

"Do you have a photograph of Mr. Arnold that you could send me?"

"I can find one."

"Good. I also need the name and phone number of Mr. Arnold's dentist."

Billie heard an intake of breath.

"You think he's dead?"

"I have no reason to believe that."

"You're homicide, right?"

Billie did not want to alarm Arnold's partner, but it was obvious that he was already upset.

"Yes."

"I'm not naive, Detective. I've handled some criminal cases. I know why a homicide detective needs dental records. You've got an unidentified body that might be Gene."

"I do have a body, but I'm pretty certain I know who it is."

"Then why call me?"

"I've been known to make mistakes. But I don't think I have in this case."

There was dead air for a moment. Finally Kellogg spoke.

"Gene's dentist is Ralph Hughes. If you give me your address I'll have him send you Gene's dental records."

Part III

The Cult

FIFTEEN

After Daniel traded the hard drive from Kaidanov's computer for a cardboard box with his personal belongings, he left his former employer's domain with hunched shoulders and a crimson face. Even though he had no reason to be ashamed, he was grateful that no one he knew had been in the waiting room or the elevator.

That evening, Daniel's phone rang several times. A few happy-hour companions had made condolence calls and promised to keep in touch. Joe Molinari invited him out to a bar. When Daniel said he was not in the mood to party Joe urged him to keep the faith. Daniel would not have minded talking to Kate Ross, but she did not call.

Daniel slept late on Saturday then treated himself to an extravagant lunch at Wildwood. He knew it was foolish to spend so much money when he was heavily in debt with no prospects for employment and almost no savings, but the gesture felt important: he'd been fired, but not defeated. After lunch, Daniel wandered around the neighborhood, but it was hard being in a crowd of happy people. He envied them too much. The army had given him his first taste of self-confidence and the inkling of an idea that he could have a future. His college diploma was more than a piece of paper. It was proof that he could be somebody. The job with Reed, Briggs was beyond his wildest dreams. Now the job was gone, and with it his reputation. Daniel believed that he would always be known as the associate whose incompetence destroyed Geller Pharmaceuticals.

Sunday was hard to take. Since Reed, Briggs had hired him Daniel had spent most of his time, even weekends, in the office or thinking about things that he had to do at the office. Now there was nothing to dwell on except his failure. He killed the day by going for a long run and watching football. Shortly after six, he was preparing dinner when the telephone rang. The news was on but Daniel was not paying much attention to it.

"Dan, it's Kate."

"Oh, hi," Daniel answered, involuntarily breaking into a smile.

"Sorry I didn't call yesterday. I was in Astoria investigating an oil spill the coast guard claims is from a ship one of our clients insures. Did everything go okay after I saw you?"

"I gave the hard drive back and the cops didn't break in my door, so I guess so."

"Well, cheer up. I may have something for you. Natalie Tasman, one of the paralegals at Jaffe, Katz, Lehane and Brindisi, is a friend. She told me that they're going to be looking for an associate soon, so I talked to Amanda Jaffe about you. You should give them a call tomorrow."

"Isn't Amanda Jaffe the lawyer who represented that doctor who was charged with those serial murders?"

"The same. The firm is small—there are only seven or eight lawyers—but everyone is top-notch. They practice criminal defense and plaintiff's litigation. I think you'll fit in over there a hell of a lot better than you fit in at Reed, Briggs."

"Thanks, Kate. You're a good friend."

"You're a good lawyer."

Daniel was about to reply when something on the television caught his eye.

"Hold on, Kate. There's something on TV about the fire."

On the screen, a reporter from one of the local television stations was standing in front of the burned-out shell of the primate lab.

"There is a bizarre twist in the multimillion-dollar litigation against Geller Pharmaceuticals, manufacturer of the pregnancy drug Insufort," the reporter said.

"Kate, turn on Channel Four, quick."

"Late yesterday," the reporter continued, "this station received copies of a study alleged to have been made on rhesus monkeys that were burned to death in the building behind me. According to the study, a significant percentage of the monkeys that were given Insufort during pregnancy gave birth to babies with birth defects.

"Eyewitness News has learned that Dr. Sergey Kaidanov, the scientist alleged to have authored the study and an employee of Geller Pharmaceuticals, has disappeared. We have also learned that the remains of an unidentified male were found in this building, which was destroyed by arson. According to the police, the man was murdered."

The picture changed and Aaron Flynn's face appeared on the screen.

"Earlier today, reporter Angela Graham talked with Aaron Flynn, the lead counsel for the plaintiffs in the Insufort litigation."

"Mr. Flynn, what is your reaction to this new information about Insufort?"

"Angela, I haven't had time to digest it all. I did learn recently that Dr. Kaidanov conducted this study, but I have not seen the study, so I can't comment. But the news that Dr. Kaidanov may have been murdered is shocking and raises the possibility of a cover-up.

"I must say that I am stunned by the possibility that evidence of the horrible effects of Insufort may have been intentionally destroyed."

The reporters moved to another story.

"Did you see that?" Daniel asked Kate.

"Yeah, and I just switched channels. The story was on the national news on Channel Six, too. Dan, I've got to ask: Did you leak the story?"

"Of course not. Briggs said he'd have me arrested if I told anyone what was on the hard drive." Daniel paused as what he'd just said sank in. "Oh, man. If Briggs thinks I leaked the study I'm screwed."

Kate and Daniel were silent for a moment. Then Kate asked the question they both wanted to ask.

"If you didn't tell the media and I didn't, who did?"

SIXTEEN

Billie Brewster sneaked a peek at the clock over the guard's station at the end of the visitors' room at the state penitentiary. Her brother noticed and he flashed her a tolerant smile.

"You got to go, sis?"

Billie was embarrassed at being caught. She'd never been able to put one over on Sherman.

"Duty calls, little brother."

"That's okay. Ain't no one wants to stay here longer than they have to."

"You remember that," Billie said as she squeezed his hand.

"You don't have to worry about me. I'm bein' good."

They stood and he hugged her tight. Billie hugged him back. She hated visiting her brother in this place, but she hated leaving him more. Every time the iron doors clanged shut behind her, she left a piece of her heart in the prison.

"Go on now," Sherman told her, flashing an innocent, toothy smile that almost made her forget that he was kept here by a trap of his own design.

*

Outside, a sleeting rain was falling, cold and unpleasant, like Billie's mood. As she walked along the sidewalk toward the prison parking lot, the detective hunched her shoulders. Her visits to her brother were always hard on her. After their father walked out, their mother had been forced to work two jobs. Billie was the only one around to raise Sherman. She was sixteen—still a child herself—but she'd tried the best she could to keep her brother straight. Her mother had told her repeatedly that it was not her fault that Sherman was at the penitentiary. She never really believed it.

This was Sherman's third fall, but his first since she'd joined the police force. He used to get nervous when she visited, afraid that someone would find out his sister was a cop. A high-school friend who was a guard at the penitentiary kept her up-to-date on Sherman. She knew he was in a gang. Since he'd joined and made a rep he'd loosened up. Billie hated what he was doing, but she wanted him safe. Life was loaded with trade-offs.

Billie kept herself from thinking about her brother on the trip back to Portland by listening to loud music and reviewing her cases. When she passed the Wilsonville exit, she phoned in for messages and was glad there was one from Dr. Brubaker, the forensic dentist. The murder at the lab was her most interesting case.

She got Brubaker on her cell phone. "Hi, Harry, what have you got for me?"

"An identification on the body at the primate lab."

"Don't keep me in suspense."

"It's the lawyer from Arizona."

"You're kidding."

"There's no question about it. The dental records of Gene Arnold match perfectly."

Completed in 1912, the thirteen-story Benson Hotel was listed in the National Register of Historic Places and was the hotel where presidents stayed when they visited Portland. Billie entered a luxurious lobby paneled in rich walnut, floored with Italian marble and lit by several crystal chandeliers, and found Kate waiting for her.

"Thanks for letting me tag along," Kate said as they headed for the reception desk.

"You've been straight with me about your information. It's the least I can do."

"I can't believe the body wasn't Kaidanov."

"I'd have lost a bundle myself if I was a betting woman."

Billie flashed her badge at a bright-eyed, Japanese woman and asked for Antonio Sedgwick, the hotel's chief of security. The woman went through a door behind the desk and returned a few minutes later with a muscular African-American in a conservative business suit. When the ex-Seattle cop spotted the homicide detective he flashed a big grin.

"Hey, Billie, haven't seen you in a while. You over here to scam a free lunch?"

"No such luck," Billie answered with a smile.

"Who's your friend?" Sedgwick asked.

"Kate Ross. She's an investigator with the Reed, Briggs firm."

Billie turned to Kate and pointed at the security chief. "You have my permission to shoot this man if he comes on to you. He's a notorious womanizer."

Sedgwick laughed.

"I ain't lyin'," Billie said with mock seriousness. "Shoot to kill."

"Besides ruining my love life, what brings you to the Benson?"

"One of your guests checked in on February twenty-ninth and disappeared by March seventh. Now he's turned up dead and I'd like to see his belongings."

Sedgwick snapped his fingers. "The guy from Arizona."

Billie nodded. "His name was Gene Arnold. What do you remember about him?"

"I never met him. He didn't check out on time, so we sent a bellman up to his room. There was a 'Do Not Disturb' sign on the door. We usually wait when we see that. At the end of the day I let myself in. It looked like he planned on coming back. All his stuff was there: toiletries on the sink, clothes hung up in the closet and neatly placed in the drawers. If I remember, there was even a book open on the end table, American history or something.

"We called his contact number to see if he was going to stay another day. They didn't know anything about it. We didn't need the room right away, so I left everything there for one more day. Then I had his stuff packed up and put it in the checkroom. If you want to take it I'll need a court order, but I can let you see it."

"That'll be fine for now."

The checkroom was to the right of the concierge desk. It was a narrow room with a high vaulted ceiling decorated with ornate molding that had been the hotel's original entrance. Its glory had faded over the years. Half the floor was marble but the other half was plywood and there were exposed pipes to the right of the door. Two bare sixty-watt bulbs produced the light that had once been provided by a crystal chandelier.

Arnold's valise was on a shelf to the left of the door. Sedgwick carried it to a small, unobstructed area near the front of the checkroom and opened it. Billie took out each item, inspected it, then placed it in a neat pile while Kate watched. When she was done she replaced the items carefully.

"Suits are over here," Sedgwick said, pointing at two suits on a pole that spanned the room.

Billie's inspection of the first suit revealed nothing, but she found a slip of paper written on the stationery of a SoHo art gallery in the inside pocket of the second suit jacket. It contained a name, Claude Bernier, a street address, and a Manhattan phone number. Billie and Kate wrote the information in their notebooks and Billie replaced the paper in the suit pocket.

"Mr. Bernier?"

"Yes."

"My name is Billie Brewster," the detective said as Kate listened on an extension in Sedgwick's office. "I'm with the Portland Police Bureau."

"Maine?"

"Oregon."

"I haven't been there for a while. What's this about?"

"I'm investigating a homicide and your name came up."

"You're kidding?"

"Do you know Gene Arnold, an attorney from Arizona? He was in New York in late February."

"Late February?" Bernier sounded puzzled. "Wait a minute. Is this guy bald, maybe forty-five? Glasses?"

"That's him," Billie answered after consulting the photograph that Benjamin Kellogg had sent her.

"Okay, now I've got him. Arnold, yeah. He was at my apartment. You say he was murdered?"

"Yes, sir. What can you tell me about the meeting?"

"Arnold bought one of my photographs from the Pitzer-Kraft Gallery. Fran works there. She called and told me that Arnold almost fainted while he was looking at it. She thought he was having a heart attack. Then he insisted on seeing me."

"What did he want?"

"He wanted to know everything about the couple in the photograph. That was the subject of the show, couples. This one was from Portland."

"What did you tell him?"

"Nothing much. They're all candid shots. I'd see a couple and snap them without them knowing I'd done it. I never got any names."

"Can you describe the couple in the shot that Arnold purchased?"

"It was a man and woman walking across that big open square you've got in the middle of the city."

"Pioneer Square?"

"That's it."

"Anything else you can tell me about them?"

"Arnold was pretty upset about that picture. He got more upset when I couldn't help him."

"Can you send me a print?"

"I think so. I'll have to look for the negative. I moved recently and everything's still a mess."

"Try hard, Mr. Bernier. That picture may show the person who murdered Gene Arnold."

SEVENTEEN

"Brock wanted you to know that everyone is in the conference room," Renee Gilchrist said.

Arthur Briggs's mouth was set in a grim line and Renee noticed dark circles under his eyes. "Tell Brock I'll be right down," he said.

One of the lines on his phone rang. Renee headed for the phone, but Briggs waved her away.

"Briggs," the senior partner answered absently. Then he straightened up. "Put him through."

Briggs turned to Renee. "I want my calls held. Tell Newbauer and the others to go ahead without me. Shut the door on your way out."

Renee crossed the room as Briggs turned back to the phone.

"Dr. Kaidanov, there are a lot of people who are very anxious to speak with you," she heard Briggs say as she pulled the door shut.

Thirty minutes later Arthur Briggs entered a small conference room. Brock Newbauer and Susan Webster were seated on one side of a polished oak table. Facing them were

Isaac Geller, the chairman of the board of Geller Pharmaceuticals, and Byron McFall, the company's president.

Geller was a medical-school dropout in his late forties who had made a fortune in commercial real estate when he met McFall, a powerfully built man ten years his junior, at a golf resort. The men hit it off immediately. By the time Geller was ready to return to Chicago and McFall to his investment firm in Seattle, they had agreed to talk about a possible investment by Geller in a financially troubled Oregon pharmaceutical company that was doing some interesting research. Both men had made millions as the result of their chance meeting.

"How bad is this thing, Arthur?" Geller asked as Briggs took his place at the head of the table.

"What's your take, Brock?" Briggs asked, addressing his junior partner.

Newbauer was surprised to be called on since Briggs was rarely interested in his opinion.

"Well, we've all heard the news. They're saying that man was set on fire and the monkeys, too," Newbauer said, stumbling. "It's terrible publicity. *The Oregonian* had an editorial this morning." Newbauer glanced across the table at Geller and McFall, then looked away quickly. "They're implying that the company had something to do with the murder."

"Which is utter hogwash," McFall said. "I want you to look into suing that rag for libel. And I want to find out who leaked that report to the press."

"I'm already on top of it, Byron," Briggs assured the irate executive. "What should we advise Geller Pharmaceuticals to do about the lawsuit, Brock?"

"I don't think we have a choice. Susan tells me there's a good chance that Judge Norris will let the Kaidanov letter in, and now it looks like Flynn has a copy of the study, too. If a jury hears evidence about the murder and the dead monkeys . . ." He shook his head despondently. "I think we have to seriously consider making a settlement offer."

Briggs nodded in a manner that made it appear that he valued Newbauer's advice before focusing his attention on Susan Webster.

"What do you think we should do?" he asked.

"I agree with Brock," Susan said firmly. "My research leads me to believe that Judge Norris will let Flynn use the Kaidanov documents at trial. If he convinces a jury that Geller Pharmaceuticals covered up Kaidanov's study, we'll lose the case and the damages will be astronomical. If Flynn convinces the jury that someone connected with Geller murdered Kaidanov and set fire to those monkeys, we'll need the world's biggest computer to figure the damages."

"This is bullshit, Arthur," McFall exploded. "I've talked with all our top people. No one knows anything about that damn lab or those fucking monkeys."

"Susan isn't suggesting you do. She's talking about a hypothetical situation so we can try to decide our best course of action."

"Which is?" Geller asked.

"I'd rather not say just yet," Briggs replied.

"Well, I insist that you do," McFall ordered angrily. "I'm the president of a company that pays your firm several million dollars a year. This is the biggest challenge

Geller Pharmaceuticals has ever faced and we need your advice."

During McFall's tirade, Isaac Geller had been coolly appraising his corporate counsel. Briggs was calm and composed, completely unruffled by a verbal assault under which Geller had seen many strong men and women wilt.

"You're onto something, aren't you, Arthur?"

Briggs smiled noncommittally.

Geller turned to McFall. "Maybe we shouldn't press Arthur," Geller suggested quietly. "His representation has always been top-notch. I'm certain that there must be something very important afoot if he is playing his cards so close to the vest."

"I still don't appreciate our attorney keeping secrets from us, Isaac," McFall insisted to save face.

"I respect Arthur's judgment."

"Very well," McFall grumbled, "but this better be good."

Briggs stood. "Thank you, gentlemen. I'll be in contact shortly, and I don't think you'll be disappointed."

EIGHTEEN

As soon as he got up, Daniel called Amanda Jaffe's office, but Amanda was in Washington County for three days handling pretrial motions in a murder case. After breakfast, Daniel went downtown and spent the day job hunting. He returned to his apartment, tired and discouraged, to find the light on his answering machine blinking. He pressed the play button, hoping that the caller was Kate or Amanda Jaffe.

"Ames, this is Arthur Briggs. I was wrong about you and I need your help. There's been a development in the Insufort case and you are the only one I can trust. Meet me tonight at eight."

The rest of the message told him how to get to a country cottage near the Columbia Gorge. Daniel's first reaction was that the message was a hoax engineered by Joe Molinari, but Daniel had heard Briggs's voice enough to know that it was his ex-boss on the phone. Only the message did not make sense. Briggs hated him, and even if he didn't, why would he need his help? He had partners, associates, and investigators galore. Daniel was a disgraced, disgruntled ex-employee—not exactly the person Briggs would be expected to call in an emergency. And why would Briggs want to meet miles out of town instead of in his office?

Daniel decided that there was only one way to discover if the call was genuine. He dialed Briggs's office.

"Renee, it's Daniel Ames."

"Oh, Daniel, I am so sorry. Are you okay?"

"I'm fine, thanks. Is Mr. Briggs in?"

"No. He's gone for the day. He'll be here in the morning."

Daniel thought for a moment.

"Mr. Briggs left a message on my answering machine. He said there was a new development in the Insufort case. He wanted to talk to me about it tonight. I'm supposed to meet him at a cottage off I-84 on the Columbia Gorge. Do you have any idea why he wants to see me or why he wants me to meet him at this cottage instead of his office?"

"No, but Arthur was excited about something today. This is a good sign, isn't it? Maybe he's going to rehire you."

"Yeah, maybe," Daniel answered thoughtfully. "Look, if Mr. Briggs phones in would you ask him to call me?"

"Sure."

"Thanks."

Daniel hung up and called Kate, but she was not in. He leaned back and stared at the wall. What would he do if Briggs offered him his job back? He'd convinced himself that he didn't want to work at the firm anymore, but did he really mean it? Working for Reed, Briggs had been his dream job.

Daniel made a decision. He wasn't certain that he wanted his job back, but he did want to hear what Arthur Briggs had to say. And he was very curious about the new development in the Insufort case that Briggs had mentioned. Maybe he had convinced Briggs that there was something wrong with the drug and Briggs was now on his side. The only way to find out was to meet with the man who had just fired him.

NINETEEN

Dr. Sergey Kaidanov huddled like a hunted animal in a copse of cottonwoods and watched the cottage as daylight faded. Kaidanov had not had a decent sleep since fleeing from the lab. A damp, uncombed beard covered the lower half of his face and his clothes looked a size too big on his emaciated frame. The woods were damp and the cruel wind blowing off the Gorge chilled the fugitive, but running for his life had inured Kaidanov to hardship and made him cunning and cautious. He was also desperate.

The newspapers said that someone had died in the lab. If it hadn't been for the monkey, the police would have found two bodies. Then there was his escape in Las Vegas. His car had been parked in the shadows of the motel lot. He had been about to start it when another car driven by the same person who'd attacked him in the lab pulled into the space in front of his motel room. Kaidanov had watched until his pursuer was inside. He had only been a few blocks from the motel when he figured out that he must have been traced through his credit card. It took another moment to remember that he'd told the whore that he was taking an early flight. Kaidanov had skipped his flight and used his credit cards sparingly since Vegas, living on fast food and sleeping in his car. He smelled and he was unshaven, but he was still alive. After tonight, he might even be safe.

Headlights lit up the cottage. Moments later a Mercedes parked out front. Kaidanov checked his watch. It was 7:29. Arthur Briggs had arranged to meet him at 7:30 so they would have time to talk before Briggs's associate arrived.

The lights went on in the cottage. Kaidanov scurried across the road. He'd checked out the cottage earlier and he knew that there was a back door. He made a wide circle around the house. There was a farm next to the cottage, but the land directly behind the house was heavily wooded. Kaidanov raced from the cover of a stand of trees and knocked on the back door. A moment later Arthur Briggs let him into a small kitchen.

"Dr. Kaidanov?" he asked.

The scientist nodded. "Do you have something to eat?" he asked. "I haven't had any food since breakfast."

"Certainly. There's not much, but I can make you a sandwich."

"Anything. A drink would help."

Briggs motioned toward a kitchen table and started toward the refrigerator. As he passed the kitchen door Briggs saw someone enter the front room. He stopped, puzzled, then walked out of the kitchen. Kaidanov stood, tense as a startled deer. He heard Briggs say, "What are you doing here?" He was out of the back door before Briggs screamed, "Run!" and shots rang out.

Kaidanov plunged into the woods as the kitchen door slammed open. He had planned his escape route earlier and he never slowed. He could hear branches snap and the underbrush crackle behind him. He made a sharp turn and circled back toward his car, pausing briefly before racing on to make sure his pursuer kept going straight ahead. Through a gap in the trees, Kaidanov saw someone of average height dressed in a black windbreaker. A hood concealed the killer's face, but there was no doubt in the Russian's mind that this was the same person who tried to kill him at the lab.

Kaidanov had parked his car half a mile up a side road where it could not be seen from the street that ran in front of the cottage and could not be discovered without a thorough search. The engine started right away. Kaidanov left the headlights off until he was on the highway headed east. He had no idea where he was going. All he cared about was that he was still breathing.

TWENTY

I-84 runs along the Columbia Gorge and is one of the most scenic highways in the United States, but Daniel could barely see the magnificent vista created by the Columbia River and the high cliffs on either side of it because the sun had nearly set. Twenty minutes after leaving the city, he took an off-ramp and found himself on a two-lane road in sparsely populated countryside. After he had traveled two miles, he began to look for Starlight Road. The high beams of a speeding car blinded Daniel for a moment and he almost missed the street sign. Three-quarters of a mile later he spotted a modest cottage that was set back from the road.

A Mercedes, similar to one that Daniel had seen Arthur Briggs drive, was parked on the gravel driveway near the front door, but the house was dark. Daniel wondered why. He remembered the speeding car. Had it come from Starlight Road? He couldn't remember. Daniel parked his car facing the road in case he had to get away in a hurry. He left the motor running and walked toward the cottage.

Daniel paused on the doorstep and listened, but he heard no sounds inside. The night air was cool and a wind whipped through the trees. Daniel hunched his shoulders against the chill and rapped on the front door. It swung open slightly.

"Mr. Briggs," Daniel called into the dark interior. All he heard was the sigh of the wind. Daniel pushed the door open and was about to call out again when he saw someone stretched out on the floor. He knelt beside the body. It was Arthur Briggs. Blood had pooled around his ex-boss and Daniel was careful to avoid getting any of it on him. There was a bullet hole in Briggs's forehead and two more entry wounds in his torso.

Daniel started to reach out for Briggs to check for a pulse when he heard a car driving toward the house and headlights lit up the front room. Daniel leaped to his feet and raced out of the house. The headlights swung in his direction, illuminating his face. Daniel flung up his arm to block the driver's view and dove into his car, then he floored the accelerator and drove away like a madman.

TWENTY-ONE

Arthur Briggs was not the first murdered man Daniel had seen, but it had been years since his first encounter with violent death. Daniel was fifteen when he ran away from home for the second time. After two evenings of sleeping in doorways, he had spent his third night with two other runaways under the Broadway Bridge in an encampment created by the homeless. The sounds made by traffic passing overhead and the voices of the river were impossible to shut out, but most disturbing were the unfamiliar noises of the camp. Drunks wept softly and the insane raged at things others could not see. Daniel feared being beaten and robbed or worse, so he tried to stay awake. When he did nod off, the slightest noise near his bedroll would jerk him into full consciousness, knife in hand.

Around two in the morning Daniel had passed out from exhaustion only to be awakened by the sounds of two men fighting over a bottle of screw-top wine. He had looked on wide-eyed as the men struck each other with insane energy. When the fight was over the winner was covered in blood and the loser lay curled in a ball, moaning in pain. The wine bottle had been destroyed early in the struggle and the liquid victory prize had seeped into the dirt of the battlefield.

Daniel lay in his sleeping bag, stunned by the violence and paralyzed with fright. By the time he was able to move, the prostrate man had ceased to moan. Daniel had not slept for the rest of the night. In the morning, after he packed his gear, he had walked over to the dead man. The image of his first corpse was still a vivid memory and Arthur Briggs resembled him in many ways. His eyes were sightless, his skin waxy, and his incredible energy had drained away.

Halfway back to Portland the adrenaline that had fueled his mad escape began to wear off and reality set in. Briggs was dead and a witness had seen him running from the cottage. Did the driver get a good enough look to identify him? It was dark, but the headlights had caught him before he could cover his face. Daniel felt sick. He had been jailed as a teenager and he had hated the experience. If he went to jail now it would be for murder.

As soon as Daniel was back in his apartment he ran into the bathroom and examined himself in the mirror. He could see no blood, but to be safe, he changed his clothes and put them in the washing machine in the basement. When he returned to his apartment, he tried to think of ways the police could connect him to the murder. He was pretty sure that he hadn't left fingerprints in the cottage, but the witness may have gotten a good look at him. Then there was Renee Gilchrist. He'd told her that Briggs wanted to meet him that night at the cottage. If she told the cops he was dead.

Suddenly Daniel remembered the recording of Briggs's

call on his answering machine. The message would place him at the Starlight Road cottage at the time of the murder. Daniel had just finished erasing the tape when his phone rang. He waited. It rang again. Daniel picked up the receiver.

"Mr. Ames?"

"Yes."

"This is Detective Brewster of the Portland Police Bureau." Daniel's gut did a back flip. "We met the other night."

"Oh, right."

"I'm downstairs with another detective and some uniformed police officers. We'd like to talk with you."

"About what?" Daniel asked as he went to the window. Brewster was talking on a cell phone. Zeke Forbus was standing next to her. A uniformed officer was looking up at his window. Daniel pulled back.

"I'd rather not discuss the matter over the phone," Billie said. "Would you be willing to come downstairs?"

Daniel went through his options. He could stay in the apartment and the police would kick in the door and drag him out or he could go downstairs voluntarily. Either way he was going to be arrested; it was just a matter of how.

"Okay," Daniel said, "I'll be down in a minute."

Daniel looked around the apartment. His clothes were in the washing machine in the basement. The police would search his apartment, but they might not look downstairs. He started to leave when it dawned on him that he might be locked up. He needed to tell someone, but who? Daniel hesitated, then dialed Kate Ross. Her answering machine took the call.

"Kate, this is Daniel. The police are downstairs. I don't know what's going on," he said to protect both of them, "but check on me. If I'm not home I might be in jail."

Daniel hung up and locked the apartment. When he got to the ground floor he could see Brewster and Forbus waiting outside the door. He guessed that the uniforms would be on either side of it to grab him in case he had a gun. To avoid being roughed up, Daniel opened the door with one hand and held the other hand where it could be seen. As soon as he walked outside the two uniforms converged on him. One had his gun drawn. Daniel expected this, but it scared the hell out of him just the same.

"Please stand with your hands against the wall, Mr. Ames, and spread your legs," Zeke Forbus said.

"I'm not armed."

"Then there won't be a problem."

The frisk was fast and thorough. During the pat-down, the officer emptied Daniel's pockets and took his key ring.

"What is this about?" Daniel asked.

"We're investigating the murder of Arthur Briggs," Billie answered.

"Why are you talking to me?" Daniel asked. He immediately regretted saying anything when it occurred to him that most people would have expressed shock at the violent death of someone they knew.

"We have a witness who saw you driving away from the scene of the murder," Forbus said.

"We're here so you can explain why you were there," Billie told him. "If you have any information that can help us find Mr. Briggs's killer, we'd appreciate the help."

Daniel's mouth was dry. The only way the police could

have found him this quickly was if the witness recognized him.

"I'd like to talk to an attorney before I say anything else."

"You seem like a nice enough person, Mr. Ames," Billie said. "If you have any explanation for what happened I'll try to help you."

Billie seemed so sincere that Daniel almost fell for her line, but he'd had run-ins with the police when he was on the street and he knew the game she was playing.

"Thank you, Detective, but I'd rather wait until I've talked to a lawyer."

Billie nodded. "We'll respect your wishes. Please turn around and put your hands behind you."

"Why?"

"I'm placing you under arrest for the murder of Arthur Briggs."

Daniel rode in the back of a patrol car with his hands cuffed behind him. He spent the first few minutes of the trip to the Justice Center trying to get comfortable and the rest of it with his thoughts, because no one spoke to him during the ride. By the time the car parked in the police garage, Daniel was sick with worry.

The Justice Center was a modern, sixteen-story building in downtown Portland that was home to the Multnomah County jail, two circuit and two district courts, state parole and probation, the state crime lab, and the Portland police central precinct. Brewster and Forbus drove behind the car transporting Daniel and escorted him up to the detective division. Neither detective spoke to him except to tell him what to do.

The detective division was a wide-open space that stretched along one side of the thirteenth floor. Each detective had his own cubicle separated from the others by a chest-high divider. As soon as he was brought into the office, Daniel's cuffs were taken off and he was placed in a small, cinderblock holding cell. Light was provided by a harsh fluorescent fixture that was recessed in the ceiling. The only place to sit in the tiny room was a hard wooden bench that ran along the back wall. There were no other furnishings.

Forbus sat with Daniel for a few minutes. He explained that Daniel would be held in the cell for a while and told him that he could knock on the door if he wanted to use the rest room or needed a glass of water. Then he closed the door and drew a metal sheet across a small, tinted-glass window in the door, cutting off all contact with the world outside the cell. Daniel stretched out on the bench, placed an arm across his eyes to shield them from the light, and tried to relax.

Twenty minutes later Forbus reentered the room with a photographer who took several photographs of Daniel. As soon as the photographer left, Forbus gave the prisoner a flimsy, white, one-piece, disposable Tyvex jumpsuit made of paper that zipped up the front and felt slick and odd against his skin. The detective explained that Daniel would wear this suit until he was given a uniform in the jail.

When Daniel was dressed, Forbus led his prisoner across the hallway into a small interrogation room furnished with several, heavy wooden chairs and a table that was affixed to the wall. Daniel noticed a box of tissues on the table and wondered how many men had wept in this room.

Forbus made no attempt to question Daniel about the murder and Daniel had to fight an urge to open the subject. The detective asked Daniel's age, date of birth, and other statistical information for his custody report. He was tempted to refuse to answer the detective's questions, but he wanted to put off returning to the cell as long as possible. When Forbus had the information he needed he put Daniel back in the holding cell. His watch had been taken from him and he could only guess how long he stayed in the lockup, but it seemed like hours before he heard a key in the lock again and Billie Brewster came in.

"I'm going to take you over to the jail now," she said as she cuffed Daniel's hands behind his back. Brewster led him down a carpeted hall to an elevator that took them to the ground floor. After a short walk through Central Precinct and the garage, Daniel found himself standing on a red dot in front of a blue metal door in the reception area of the jail. The detective passed a custody report through a slot to a sheriff's deputy in a green uniform who was stationed behind a plate of thick glass.

"If you want to talk with me about what happened at the cottage, tell one of the deputies," Brewster said in a kind voice. Then she surprised Daniel by putting a hand on his shoulder and saying, "Good luck, Daniel."

As soon as Brewster left, the door behind Daniel snapped open and he was ordered into a narrow concrete chute about six feet long and seven feet wide. Another handcuffed prisoner was stretched out on a bench that ran along the wall. Daniel was afraid to ask him to move, so he stayed standing. A few minutes later a door at the other end of the room opened and Daniel was taken out by a deputy who patted him down before leading him over to a brightly illuminated area where his picture was taken again. After that, Daniel was escorted to a window that opened into a small medical facility. A woman on the other side of the window asked Daniel for a medical history then turned him over to another deputy for finger-printing. Finally, he was led down a hall along a concrete floor and heard what sounded like a dog howling. The guard prodded Daniel around a corner and the howling turned to screams. They were coming from one of sever-al single cells that lined the wall of a large holding area. Blue metal doors fronted all the cells. Toward the top third of the doors were narrow glass windows. A female deputy was talking through a grille beneath one of the windows in a firm voice. Daniel realized that the inhuman screams and moans he had heard were coming from this cell.

"This isn't doing you any good, Mr. Packard," the woman deputy was saying, but Mr. Packard was unaffect-ed by her attempts to calm him and continued to howl.

The guard unlocked Daniel's cuffs and placed him in a cell enclosed by chain-link fencing that stood in the center of the holding area. Another prisoner in street clothes was lying on a concrete bench. Daniel took a closer look at his cellmate, who was sleeping through Mr. Packard's insane lament. The man was stripped to the waist, revealing a torso covered with tattoos. It took an effort not to stare. To make it easier, Daniel turned away and looked at his surroundings through the grille. It dawned on him that no other prisoner was making any noise. He could see into some of the other holding cells through the slit windows and what he saw were men pacing, locked in with their own thoughts as Daniel was locked in with his.

At first Daniel tried to remember all he could about his other jail experiences so he could prepare himself to survive. He knew that being in jail was like being back in high school in a class made up of bullies, liars, and lunatics. Most criminals were irresponsible, angry men who were unable to succeed in the world and took out their frustrations on those who could. Daniel resolved to tell no one that he had graduated high school, let alone college and law school.

There was a second bench in the cell and Daniel stretched out on it. He had not slept and it had to be early morning by now. He closed his eyes, but the bright lights in the holding area, the hard surface, and the constant, unfamiliar noises made sleep impossible. Daniel tossed and turned for a while until his thoughts turned to the question he would have asked himself earlier if he had not been shell-shocked by the discovery of the dead man and the shame and terror of his arrest: "Who had killed Arthur Briggs and why?"

Daniel knew almost nothing about Briggs's private life, except that he was married and had two grown children. The only times he had been in Briggs's presence socially were at firm functions. From experience, Daniel knew that Briggs was a rude, abrasive man who was extremely aggressive in court, but he had no idea if Briggs had enemies—or friends, for that matter. It soon became obvious to Daniel that he lacked the information to make even a rudimentary guess about the identity of Briggs's killer, so he turned to motive.

In the message Briggs had left on Daniel's answering machine he had said that he needed to talk to Daniel about a new development in the Insufort case. He'd also said that he knew that he was wrong about Daniel and that Daniel was the only person he could trust. Suddenly it occurred to him: the Kaidanov report!

Daniel sat up. The new development in the Geller case must have involved the report, because that was the only aspect of the case of any importance that involved Daniel. It was the reason he was fired. What had Briggs talked about during their last meeting? He'd gotten furious when Daniel told him that Geller was covering up the results of Kaidanov's study. Of course! Briggs must have found out that Geller was involved in a cover-up. That would explain why he thought Daniel was the only person he could trust. The firm would lose Geller Pharmaceuticals as a client, and its hefty retainer, if Briggs exposed a plot to cover up Kaidanov's study, so he would not have been able to trust anyone at Geller or anyone in his own firm. But he could trust Daniel because Daniel had urged Briggs to expose the cover-up. The only problem with his theory was that he could more easily imagine Arthur Briggs involved in a conspiracy with Geller than exposing a cover-up by a client that brought millions to the firm.

But what if he was wrong about Briggs? He'd known so little about the senior partner. Maybe Briggs had spoken to the wrong people at Geller and they had silenced him. Daniel had to tell someone what he had figured out, but who? And what proof did he have? A wave of despair swept over him and all of his energy and excitement drained away. No one would believe him if he started talking about cover-ups and conspiracies. They would think he was a crazy, disgruntled employee. Just the type of maniac who would murder the person who had fired him.

An hour later a deputy brought Daniel and his comatose cellmate a brown-bag breakfast. The tattooed man continued to sleep. Daniel opened his bag and took out a baloney sandwich on pasty white bread, an orange, and a small carton of milk. He had no appetite and the sandwich looked repulsive, but Daniel knew he had to eat to keep up his strength. He finished his meal shortly before a guard handcuffed him and led him out of the holding cell. The jail had a receipt for Daniel's possessions, which included his wallet. For a dollar fifty he was allowed to purchase a hygiene kit containing shampoo, toothpaste, and a toothbrush.

The guard took Daniel upstairs to the seventh floor. After a short walk from the elevator, Daniel was led through a sally port into a two-story-high, open area. At one end of the floor was a glassed-in rec room with a television. Along the walls were two tiers of cells. Daniel was told to strip. The guard took his Tyvex suit and gave him plastic shower slippers, a set of pink dyed underwear and socks, a pair of blue cotton pants with an elastic waist, and a blue, pullover, V-neck shirt. Then the guard told him to enter cell 7C.

The cell had a two-tiered bunk bed. A muscular Hispanic was stretched out on the lower bunk. He turned on his side and stared at Daniel with little interest. Along the wall was a concrete slab. Daniel saw that his cellmate's toiletries were at one end of the slab and he placed his on the other end. Behind the bunk was a narrow window that stretched the length of the cell and looked out at the new federal courthouse.

As soon as the guard closed the door, Daniel addressed his cellmate.

"How you doin'?"

"Okay," the man answered. Then he asked, "Whatchoo in for?" in a thick accent.

"Nothing much."

Daniel knew better than to talk about his case. Every cellmate was a potential state's witness.

"Me, too," the man answered with a sly smile. "Name's Pedro."

"Daniel. I'm gonna sack out."

"Yeah sure."

Daniel remembered something he had learned the last time he was in jail. He grabbed his toothbrush before climbing into his upper bunk. He did not sleep, but he did spend several hours using the concrete wall to sharpen the end of the toothbrush into a sharp point in case his cellmate turned out to be less friendly than he seemed.

TWENTY-TWO

"Ames, your attorney's here."

Daniel was still groggy from a sleepless night and it took him a minute to process the fact that the guard was talking to him.

"What attorney?" he asked.

"How should I know? Get a move on."

As Daniel climbed down from his bunk he wondered if the court had already assigned him a public defender. The guard led him into the common area and through the sally port into a long corridor lined with noncontact visiting rooms where prisoners and visitors sat on either side of a thick glass window and conversed by telephone. A metal door at the end of the corridor led into a shorter hallway. On one side were two contact visiting rooms. Daniel could see into the closest room through a window that took up half the wall. It was furnished with a round table that was bolted to the floor and two molded plastic chairs. An attractive woman with shoulder-length black hair was seated in one of the chairs. When Daniel stepped into the room the guard closed the door and the woman stood up. Daniel was five eleven. The woman was almost as tall and had the broad shoulders and solid build of an athlete. She wore a conservative business suit.

"Hi, Daniel," she said, extending her hand. "I'm Amanda Jaffe."

Daniel colored. His jail-issue clothes were a size too big, his hair was uncombed, and he had a day's growth of beard. He also smelled.

Amanda smiled. "I bet this wasn't what you expected when you called for a job interview."

"What are you doing here?"

"Kate Ross phoned me after she tracked you to the jail. Why don't we sit down," Amanda said as she returned to her seat. Daniel remained standing.

"Look, Ms. Jaffe . . ."

"Amanda," she corrected.

"I can't afford to hire you. Kate must have told you that I just lost my job, my savings probably won't cover the cost of this consultation, and my job prospects have just plummeted to minus zero."

"Don't worry about the fee."

"I've got to worry about it. No matter what you charge, there's no way I can pay it."

"Daniel, please sit down. I'm getting a crick in my neck."

Daniel sat reluctantly on the other chair.

"Kate thinks very highly of you. She doesn't believe that you murdered Arthur Briggs."

"I didn't."

"Good. Then try to relax so I can get the information I need to get you out of here."

"But your money . . ."

"I'm taking the case pro bono and Kate is covering my expenses."

"I can't let you two do that."

Amanda's smile disappeared and she looked deadly serious.

"You're in big trouble, Daniel. You've been charged with murder. If you're convicted you're looking at life in prison or a death sentence. This is not the time to be proud. Accept our help. You need it."

Amanda's words had a sobering effect. Life in prison or execution. What was happening to him?

"Before coming here, I talked to Mike Greene, the prosecutor who's handling your case. He claims to have a witness who saw you running from the crime scene. She also says that she heard you have an angry argument with Arthur Briggs on Friday."

"Who's the witness?"

"Dr. April Fairweather."

"Fairweather! Are you kidding?"

"You know her?"

"She's a Reed, Briggs client, but she had nothing to do with the Insufort litigation."

"The lawsuit involving the pregnancy pill? What's that got to do with Arthur Briggs's murder?"

"That's why I was at the cottage. Briggs left a message on my answering machine telling me there was a new development in the case. He said he needed my help, which surprised the hell out of me since he'd just fired me for screwing up the case."

"I'm not following this. Maybe you should start at the beginning."

Daniel explained the Geller Pharmaceuticals case, the discovery of Dr. Sergey Kaidanov's letter, his search of Kaidanov's house, the discovery of the murdered man at the lab, and the leak of the study to the press. Then he told Amanda about being fired, his argument with Briggs, and what happened at the cottage.

"Now I know how the police figured out that I was there so fast," Daniel concluded. "Dr. Fairweather was in Mr. Briggs's waiting area when he fired me. She saw us argue. What I can't figure out is what she was doing at the cottage. Her case had nothing to do with the Geller case. It doesn't make sense that Briggs would have wanted her there if he was going to talk about Insufort."

Amanda was quiet for a moment. Daniel thought that she looked worried and he began to get nervous. Then she brightened and Daniel leaned forward expectantly.

"You have a motive to murder Briggs because Briggs fired you and threatened you, but the message on your answering machine shows that he changed his opinion about you for some reason. There's a chance I might be able to persuade Mike to hold off on an indictment if he hears the tape."

Daniel's face fell. "I erased it."

"What?"

"I panicked and I erased the answering machine tape just before the police came. It was proof that I was at Starlight Road when the murder occurred."

Amanda failed to conceal her disappointment and Daniel knew he'd screwed up.

"How long do I have to stay in jail?" he asked nervously.

"You're not going to get out quickly. Bail isn't

automatic in a murder charge. I have to ask for a bail hearing and they're hard to win. If you had to stay in jail for a week or more, do you think you could handle it?"

Daniel felt sick, but he nodded.

"I've been in jail before."

Amanda tensed. "Tell me about that."

Daniel looked down at the tabletop. "My . . . my home life wasn't good. When I was a kid I ran away a lot." He shrugged. "When you're living on the streets there are a lot of opportunities to get in trouble."

"What kind of trouble were you in?"

"Burglary, assault. The cases never stuck, but I was arrested twice and I stayed in jail both times."

Daniel told her the approximate dates of his arrests and Amanda made some notes on her pad. Then she asked him several other background questions. When she was finished, she put her pad in her attaché case.

"I'm going back to my office to meet with my investigator. You'll make your first appearance in court at two this afternoon and I'll be there. This appearance will be over quickly. The judge will read the formal charges against you and make sure you have counsel. I'll ask him to set a date for a bail hearing and we'll request a preliminary hearing. Then we'll go from there. Do you have any questions?"

"No, not now. I'm too numb."

"I don't blame you. If I were in your position I'd be scared to death. But you have one thing going for you that gives me hope." Daniel looked up expectantly. "You've told me you're innocent and I do believe that the truth will come out."

Daniel should have found Amanda's words reassuring, but he remembered an editorial about the death penalty he had read recently. It had called for a moratorium on executions because of all the innocent people who were languishing on death row.

Kate Ross was waiting in the public reception area. She stood up the moment Amanda got out of the jail elevator.

"How is Daniel?" she asked anxiously.

"He's holding up okay. I get the impression that he's pretty tough. If I can't get him out on bail before the trial I don't think being in jail will break him."

"Will you be able to get him out?"

"I don't know, Kate. Mike Greene told me a little about the state's case. It's not airtight, but it's strong."

"What have they got?"

"Briggs fired Daniel and they argued in front of witnesses, so Daniel had a reason to shoot Briggs. They haven't recovered the murder weapon and they didn't find it when they searched Daniel's apartment, but Mike Greene will just argue that he threw the gun away. The really bad news is that an eyewitness saw Daniel running from the scene of the murder."

"Who is it? Give me the name. If there's evidence that the witness is lying, I'll find it."

"I appreciate the offer, but I'm afraid you're not going to be able to work on Daniel's case."

"Why not?"

"Conflict of interest. The eyewitness is Dr. April Fairweather, a Reed, Briggs client."

Kate's mouth dropped open. "You're kidding?"

"Daniel had the same reaction. She was supposed to meet with Briggs at eight-fifteen at the cottage where he was killed. She says she saw Daniel run out and drive away."

"You can't take Fairweather's word for anything, Amanda. She's—" Kate stopped suddenly. "Damn."

"What?"

"You're right. There is a conflict."

"Do you know something about Dr. Fairweather that I should know?"

Kate nodded. "But I can't talk about it. I learned it while working on her case. All I can tell you to do is dig deep."

"For what?"

"I'm sorry, Amanda. I'll have to talk to one of the partners before I can say anything. I suspect the partner is going to tell me that Fairweather will have to give her okay before I can talk to you, and I doubt she'll do it."

"Daniel will understand why you can't get involved. He knows you're helping him with expenses and he's very grateful."

"I wish there was something else I could do."

"Well, there isn't, for now, but don't worry. Herb Cross will conduct the investigation, and you know how good he is. If you want to show your support, be in court at two for Daniel's arraignment."

"I plan to be."

The offices of Jaffe, Katz, Lehane and Brindisi, one of Oregon's premier law firms, took up the eighth floor of the Stockman Building in downtown Portland. Amanda's father, Frank Jaffe, and two law-school classmates had started their practice as soon as they passed the bar. Amanda had joined the firm six years ago after graduating with honors from New York University School of Law and serving a two-year clerkship at the Ninth Circuit Court of Appeals. As a reward for solving the Cardoni serial murder case, the firm's members had voted to make her a partner. Six months ago she had moved from one of the small offices used by the associates to a larger office with a view of the West Hills. Amanda had decorated her new office with two abstracts she'd purchased at a gallery near her condominium in the Pearl District and several photographs of Broadway that had been taken shortly after the First World War around the time that the Stockman Building had been constructed.

As soon as she returned from her meeting with Daniel, Amanda started making notes about her new client. She liked Daniel and she hoped that he was innocent, but she had been practicing criminal law long enough to know that you never took your client's word for anything, no matter how sincere they seemed. Daniel had a strong motive to murder his ex-boss, he had admitted being at the scene of the crime, and he had destroyed the answering-machine tape—the evidence that Daniel claimed would have proved his relationship with Arthur Briggs had changed.

Amanda leaned back and tapped her pen against her palm. What did Kate know that would help her cast doubt on the eyewitness identification made by April Fairweather? What difference would impeachment evidence make, anyway? Daniel was at the cottage. He'd told her so. That meant that Daniel could not testify, because he would have to admit that Fairweather had seen him. She sighed. This was not going to be easy. She was going to have to work very hard and be very lucky if she was going to keep Daniel Ames off of death row.

TWENTY-THREE

At Daniel's arraignment, Amanda Jaffe asked for a bail hearing and the judge set it for Friday. Daniel made a plan for getting through the week. It involved staying in his cell as much as possible and being as inconspicuous as possible when he was in the presence of other prisoners.

Every morning at ten o'clock the guards unlocked the bottom tier of cells and let the prisoners watch television, talk, and walk around in the glassed-in recreation area. This was the most frightening time for Daniel. He had found a corner of the room from which the television was not visible and he had stayed there until it was time to return to his cell. On Thursday morning Daniel made for his corner only to find a wiry white man with a shaved head and swastika tattoo on his muscled biceps headed the same way. Daniel tried to avoid him, but he did not move fast enough and they collided. Daniel's stomach clenched.

"Sorry," he mumbled.

The man glared. When Daniel did not look away fast enough, he moved close to him.

"What are you lookin' at, pussy?"

"Nothing," Daniel answered, praying that he could avoid a fight.

"You sayin' I'm nothing?"

Daniel had been a civilized human being for many years, but the next second he was back on the street, he was fifteen, and he was listening to George, an ex-con who had been kind to him until Daniel rebuffed his sexual advances with a broken bottle. George had tried to seduce Daniel with tales of life in the Joint that had been filled with survival tips. The tips had come in handy on the other occasions he'd spent time in jail and Daniel flashed on them now.

"I . . . I said I'm sorry," Daniel apologized again in a voice intentionally meek and subservient. The prisoner took a step forward.

"That ain't good enough," he was saying when Daniel stomped hard on his foot. When the inmate bent forward reflexively Daniel snapped a hard elbow into his face. Blood sprayed from the man's nose. Before he could get his bearings Daniel struck him again, this time in the throat. The inmate went down hard and his head made a hollow sound as it bounced off the concrete floor.

Daniel turned to see if anyone else was going to come for him. Most of the inmates gave the fallen man and his assailant a wide berth, but two prisoners with shaved heads started across the room. One man was slightly shorter than Daniel and had a weight lifter's build. His biceps expanded and contracted as he flexed his fists. The other man was tall and flabby, but he had pit bull eyes and huge hands.

Daniel knew there was no way he could take out two

men, but he was poised to go at the weight lifter when the skinheads stopped abruptly. That's when Daniel noticed the four Hispanics who stood beside him. One was his cellmate.

"Whas up, bro?" Pedro asked the weight lifter.

"Get out of the way, monkey," he answered.

Pedro smiled, but he did not move. The weight lifter started forward.

"Break it up," a guard shouted from the door to the rec room. Three guards armed with truncheons backed him up.

"We ain't through with you, fucker," the fat skinhead said to Daniel, spitting on the floor between them. Then he touched the weight lifter on the arm and the two men backed into the crowd.

One of the guards knelt to check the unconscious man, who was covered with blood from his broken nose.

"Who did this?" he demanded. No one answered.

"All right, that's it. No more rec time. Get back in your cells."

The room cleared quickly.

"Thanks, man," Daniel said when he and Pedro were locked up. "I'd have been dead if you hadn't stepped in."

Pedro shrugged. "I don' like those skinhead mother-fuckers."

"Well, it's appreciated."

Pedro smiled. "I didn' figure you for no fighter, but you clocked that Nazi good."

"Lucky punch."

Pedro's smile widened. "Sucker punch."

They both laughed. Then Pedro's smile fell away abruptly and he wagged a warning finger at Daniel.

"You watch your back. Those are bad people. They gonna hurt you if they get the chance."

Daniel nodded. Then he climbed onto his upper bunk. As soon as he was certain that Pedro could not see him, he let go of his self-control and started to shake.

TWENTY-FOUR

Herb Cross, a slender African-American in his late thirties, led Amanda Jaffe up a narrow stairway to the second-floor office of Dr. April Fairweather. Fairweather worked over a hardware store in a low-rent building on Stark. The stairwell was dingy and poorly lit, as was the hall in front of the doctor's office.

Herb had briefed Amanda on what little he had discovered about the therapist during the ride from their law office. Fairweather did not have a criminal record. She had a single credit card and never let the charges get too high. Fairweather advertised herself as a consulting therapist and claimed to have a doctorate, but she was not licensed by any state agency. Then again she didn't have to be to practice her kind of New Age therapy. Fairweather lived in a cheap garden apartment in Beaverton, and Herb had talked to a few of her neighbors, but all he'd learned was that she never said more than an occasional hello.

The investigator opened a wooden door with a frosted-glass window. On the other side was a small reception room. As Amanda closed the door, a short, mousy woman in a frayed gray business suit walked out of the interior office. Amanda noticed that Dr. Fairweather had not done much with her light brown hair. She didn't see any jewelry, either. The lawyer concluded that the psychologist was not someone who gave a lot of thought to her looks.

"Can I help you?" Fairweather asked as she eyed the investigator warily. She seemed frightened, so Amanda stepped forward and smiled.

"I'm Amanda Jaffe, the attorney representing Daniel Ames. This is my associate, Herb Cross. If you have a few minutes we'd like to talk to you."

Fairweather grew rigid. "No, I can't do that."

"I'm going to have a chance to talk to you in court, Dr. Fairweather," Amanda pressed. "I might be able to save some time if we clear up a few things here."

"I'm not supposed to talk to you," Fairweather answered. Her shoulders hunched and her gaze drifted toward the floor.

"Did the district attorney tell you that? Because you have the right to talk to anyone you want to. Talking to me would be the right thing to do."

"I don't want to do that and I'd like you to go."

"Okay." Amanda held out her card and Fairweather took it reluctantly. "If you change your mind please call me."

"That is one uptight lady," Herb Cross said as soon as the door closed behind them.

"Yes, she is," Amanda mused, "and I'd love to know why."

On the way back to the office, Amanda and Cross brainstormed about ways to get through Fairweather's armor.

When they walked into the firm's waiting room, the receptionist handed Amanda a small box wrapped in brown paper. FOR AMES BAIL HEARING was written on the paper in block letters with a Magic Marker. There was no return address.

"This isn't how the DA's office sends discovery," Amanda said as she stripped away the wrapping paper. "Who brought it over?"

"A messenger," the receptionist answered.

"Did he say who sent it?"

"No."

The box was cardboard without any markings. Amanda lifted the lid. There was no note inside, but there was a videocassette. Moments later Herb Cross and Amanda Jaffe were sitting in the conference room in front of a VCR. A title informed the lawyer and the private investigator that they were going to see a speech that Dr. April Fairweather had given at a conference devoted to abuse survivors three years before. On the screen, a distinguished gentleman stepped behind a podium and introduced Dr. Fairweather in glowing terms. After the introduction Dr. Fairweather took the man's place at the podium and began to speak. A few minutes into the tape, the investigator and the attorney turned to each other.

"Is this for real?" Cross asked.

"I certainly hope so," Amanda answered.

TWENTY-FIVE

Daniel barely slept Thursday evening worrying about what would happen the next day in the rec room. Fortunately, his bail hearing was set for Friday and early the next morning he was placed in chains and transported two blocks to the Multnomah County Courthouse, where he was lodged in a large open cell in the courthouse jail with other prisoners awaiting court appearances. At 9:45, two sheriff's deputies gave Daniel a suit that Amanda's investigator had brought to the jail for the hearing. As soon as he was dressed the deputies escorted him from the seventh-floor holding area to the courtroom where his case was to be heard.

The Multnomah County Courthouse is a blunt, functional building constructed of gray concrete whose exterior makes no pretensions to art. The interiors are another matter. The Honorable Gerald Opton's fifth-floor courtroom had grand, high ceilings, ornate molding, marble Corinthian columns, and a polished wood dais. The spectator section consisted of several rows of hard wooden benches set back behind a low wooden fence that separated the public from those having business before the court.

The benches were packed because of the publicity Daniel's case had received, but Daniel spotted Kate Ross easily. She smiled at him. Daniel was embarrassed to have her see him in chains and all he could manage was a restrained nod.

Several partners from Reed, Briggs occupied the front row of the courtroom. Daniel wondered if the DA was going to use them as witnesses. Seated behind the partners with two other associates was Joe Molinari. He gave Daniel a thumbs-up, which made Daniel smile. The other associates nodded at him and he was relieved to see that some of his friends from the firm were still standing by him. Susan Webster was conspicuously absent.

Daniel scanned the crowd for other familiar faces and was surprised to see a young black man in a charcoal-gray business suit, armed with a pen and a legal pad, whom he recognized as one of the associates Aaron Flynn had brought to Kurt Schroeder's deposition.

When his guards brought Daniel into the courtroom Amanda Jaffe was talking to Deputy District Attorney Mike Greene, a large man who looked like a football or basketball player. Looks were deceiving. Greene was a gentle soul who played competitive chess and the saxophone instead of sports. The defense attorney and the DA had faced each other in court several times and they had started dating after the violent resolution of the Cardoni case.

Amanda heard one of the deputies unlock Daniel's handcuffs and hurried to her client. With his suit on, Daniel looked like any other young attorney, but three days in jail had taken their toll. As soon as his manacles were removed, Amanda led him to the defense table, where they conferred in whispers.

"Are you okay?" she asked.

Daniel shook his head. "You've got to get me out of jail. I've been in a fight and the guy has friends. They're going to come after me as soon as I'm back at the Justice Center. What are my chances of making bail?"

Amanda was about to answer when the bailiff rapped his gavel. She touched Daniel on the forearm.

"You're going to be okay."

The Honorable Gerald Opton entered the courtroom and everyone stood. Jerry Opton was one of three judges in the homicide rotation. These judges heard murder cases exclusively for one or two years so they could develop an expertise in this area of law. Assignment to the homicide rotation was usually reserved for experienced judges. Opton had only been on the bench for five years, but he had been a homicide specialist in the Multnomah County District Attorney's Office for ten years. He was a stocky, balding man whose features bore a faint resemblance to the actor Jack Nicholson. Despite being a career prosecutor before his elevation to the bench, Opton was a favorite of defense attorneys and prosecutors alike. He was scrupulously fair, well versed in the law, and ran his court with a firm hand that was softened by a wry sense of humor.

"Are we ready to go?" the judge asked the attorneys.

"Ready for Mr. Ames," Amanda said.

"Ready for the state," Greene intoned.

"Bailiff, please call the case."

The bailiff read the name and number of Daniel's case

into the record. For purposes of the bail hearing, the parties had entered into a stipulation that Arthur Briggs had been shot with a .45-caliber bullet and a person other than Briggs had intentionally caused the death. This helped speed up the hearing because the prosecutor did not have to call the medical examiner as a witness. The parties had further stipulated that Daniel worked at Reed, Briggs until the week before the murder when Briggs had fired him. After reading the stipulation into the record, Mike Greene called his first witness.

In response to Greene's questions, Zeke Forbus told the judge that he had been summoned to the crime scene at Starlight Road and had interviewed Dr. April Fairweather. Dr. Fairweather had given him the name and description of a man she had seen leaving the crime scene and the car in which he had driven away. Forbus testified that he ran a check on the car owned by the man Dr. Fairweather named and he discovered that the car was the make and color that Dr. Fairweather had described. Finally, Forbus described Daniel's arrest.

"Good morning, Detective Forbus," Amanda said when the witness was turned over to her for cross-examination. Forbus did not answer. He distrusted defense attorneys and he especially disliked women lawyers.

"Were you present during the arrest of Mr. Ames and the search of his apartment?"

"Yes, ma'am."

"Did Mr. Ames make any incriminating statements to you or any other police officer or detective following his arrest?"

"He asked for an attorney, right away."

"Can I take it that means that Mr. Ames did not make any statement that incriminated himself in the murder of Mr. Briggs?"

"That is correct."

"Have Mr. Ames's fingerprints been found at the crime scene?"

"Not to my knowledge."

"When Mr. Briggs was found he was lying in a pool of blood, was he not?"

"Yes."

"Did you find any blood on Mr. Ames or his clothing?"

"Mr. Ames washed his clothes. We found them in a washing machine in the basement."

"Your Honor, would you please instruct Detective Forbus to answer my questions?"

Judge Opton smiled. "Come on, Detective. You're not going to score any points this way. Do everyone a favor. Listen to the question and answer it, okay?"

"Sorry, Judge," Forbus answered. "No blood was found on Mr. Ames or his clothing."

"Did you find the murder weapon on Mr. Ames or in his apartment?"

"No."

"You searched his car?"

"Yes."

"Find any blood or guns?"

"No."

"Would it be fair to say that the only evidence you have connecting Daniel Ames with the scene of the crime is the statement of Dr. Fairweather?"

"Yes."

"Thank you. No further questions."

"Mr. Greene?" Judge Opton said.

"We call Dr. April Fairweather to the stand."

Daniel turned sideways and watched Fairweather walk down the aisle toward the witness box. Whenever he saw her he got an impression of a person in hiding. Fairweather kept her eyes front and avoided looking at Daniel. When she took the oath she continued to look away from him.

"Dr. Fairweather," Mike Greene began as soon as the witness was sworn, "what is your profession?"

Fairweather sat erect with her hands folded in her lap and her eyes glued on the deputy district attorney. Her response was so soft that Daniel strained to hear her. The judge asked her to raise her voice and repeat her answer.

"I am a counselor."

"Is that what your doctorate is in?"

"Yes, and my master's degree."

"Is it as a result of your practice that you came to be a client of Arthur Briggs?"

"Yes, sir. A patient sued me. My insurance company employed Mr. Briggs to represent them in cases of this sort."

"Did you ever meet with Mr. Briggs at his office to discuss your case?"

"We met on several occasions."

"While at the office, did you ever meet the defendant, Daniel Ames?"

"Yes. Mr. Briggs introduced me to him. He told me his name and we shook hands."

Daniel remembered that Dr. Fairweather had also

refused to meet his eye when Arthur Briggs had introduced them. When he'd shaken her hand it had been damp and cold, and she'd jerked it away as if she was afraid Daniel would trap it.

"Did you see Mr. Ames a second time at the Reed, Briggs offices?"

"Yes."

"When was that?"

"The Friday before Mr. Briggs was killed."

"Please describe that occasion for the judge."

"I was sitting in the waiting area in front of Mr. Briggs's office when the door opened. Mr. Ames stood in the doorway with his back to me speaking to Mr. Briggs."

"Can you remember anything he said?"

"No, but I could tell that he was angry."

"How do you know that he was angry with Mr. Briggs?"

"I could hear Mr. Briggs shouting at him, then Mr. Ames slammed the door. When he turned around he looked furious. Then he saw me and Mr. Briggs's secretary and he rushed away."

"Did you have a third occasion to encounter Mr. Ames?"

"Yes, sir."

"When was that?"

"The night of the murder."

"Where were you?"

"At a cottage on Starlight Road."

"What time was it?"

"A little after eight."

"How do you know that?"

"Mr. Briggs's secretary called me earlier in the day and told me that there had been a development in my case and

Mr. Briggs needed to meet with me at the Starlight Road address at eight-fifteen that evening. I'm always punctual and I checked the clock on my dashboard when I turned into Starlight Road."

"What did you see as you approached the cottage?"

"I saw Mr. Ames. He was running and he looked upset. When he saw my car, he threw his arm in front of his face. Then he dashed to his own car and drove away at a high rate of speed."

"How can you be sure that it was Mr. Ames you saw at the cottage?"

"As I said, I'd met him before and he ran right into my headlight beams. It was like watching someone on a stage standing in a spotlight."

"And there is no doubt in your mind that it was Daniel Ames, the defendant, whom you saw running from the cottage on Starlight Road?"

"None."

"For the record, do you see Mr. Ames in court today?"

"Yes."

"Please point him out for the judge."

Fairweather shifted in her seat and pointed her finger at Daniel, but she still would not look him in the eye.

"After Mr. Ames drove away, what did you do?"

Fairweather paused before answering the prosecutor's question in the same soft monotone in which she had spoken during all of Greene's direct examination.

"I parked my car and entered the house. The lights were off and it took a moment for my eyes to adjust. Then I saw Mr. Briggs lying on the floor. I walked over to him and I knew at once that he was dead."

"How did you know that?"

"He was lying in a pool of blood. I knelt down and felt for a pulse, but there was none."

"What did you do next?"

"I left the house and used my cell phone to call 911."

"Thank you, Dr. Fairweather. Your witness, Ms. Jaffe."

"What is your date of birth, Dr. Fairweather?" Amanda asked in a friendly tone.

"July twenty-ninth, 1957," Fairweather answered, averting her eyes.

"And where were you born?"

"Crawford, Idaho."

"What is your father's name?"

Daniel thought he saw Fairweather flinch.

"Herman Garlock," she answered, her voice dropping again.

"And your mother?"

"Linda Garlock."

"If your parents are both named Garlock, why are you named Fairweather?"

"I changed my name legally five years ago."

"What was your given name?"

"Florence Garlock."

"When is the last time you spoke to either of your parents?"

"I don't know the exact date. It would have been around 1978."

"You haven't had any contact with them for more than twenty years?"

"That's correct."

"Can you tell me why?"

"I did not wish to contact them."

"Wouldn't you agree it's rather unusual for a daughter to have no contact with her parents for twenty years?"

"Objection, relevance," Mike Greene said.

"Is the witness's relationship to her parents relevant to this case, Ms. Jaffe?" Judge Opton asked.

"It is, Your Honor, but I'll withdraw the question for now."

Amanda turned her attention back to the witness.

"Do you have any siblings?"

"I have a younger sister, Dorothy."

"Has your sister maintained a relationship with your parents?"

"Yes."

Amanda made a few notes, then switched to another subject.

"I'd like to talk to you about your educational background. What school or schools awarded you your master's and Ph.D.?"

"Templeton University."

"Where did you receive your undergraduate degree?"

"I don't have one."

Amanda looked surprised. "I'm a little confused," she said. "Before you can get a master's and a doctorate, don't you have to graduate from college?"

"That was not a requirement at Templeton."

"Is Templeton University a regular school with a campus and a football team?"

"Templeton is a correspondence university. I attended by mail."

"How long did it take you to get a master's degree and a Ph.D. by mail?"

"About three years."

"Each?"

"Total."

Amanda had Judge Opton's attention and Daniel noticed that Mike Greene was starting to look nervous.

"What major are your degrees in?"

"Theocentric counseling."

"I don't believe I've heard of that. Could you explain theocentric counseling to Judge Opton?"

"Theocentric is God-centered. There's no specific religious connection," Fairweather said without turning to the judge. Daniel had the impression that she was not speaking to anyone in particular, as if she was distancing herself from what was happening in the courtroom.

"Dr. Fairweather, is Templeton an accredited university like Oregon State?"

"I don't believe so."

"And you're not licensed by any state agency, are you?"

"No."

"Let's go back to your parents. Was your father abusive to you when you were a child?"

"Objection. This is totally irrelevant."

Amanda stood. "To the contrary, Your Honor. If you will give me a little leeway here, you will see that this line of questioning goes directly to the issue of this witness's credibility and competence."

Judge Opton took a moment to decide what to do. He did not look happy.

"I'm going to let you continue based solely on your

assertion that you can prove relevance. If I'm not convinced pretty quickly, I'll uphold Mr. Greene's objection."

"Thank you, Your Honor. Dr. Fairweather, was your father abusive?"

"Yes."

"In what way?"

"Sexually, physically, and emotionally."

"Since what age?"

"I don't know exactly. My earliest memory would be somewhere around four or five."

"When you say 'physical abuse' what do you mean?"

"Hitting, choking, being locked in closets," she answered in a flat, emotionless tone that reminded Daniel of the way he might describe something he saw on the evening news.

"And 'sexual abuse'?"

"Touching, intercourse."

"He had intercourse with you at four?"

"Yes."

"Anything else?"

"Sodomy, oral sex. He . . . he used objects. Bottles, other things."

"How long did this go on?"

"Until I left the family."

"How old were you then?"

"Twenty-one."

"So this went on for 17 years?"

"Yes."

"Every year?"

"Every week."

"Did you report this physical and sexual abuse to anyone?"

"I . . . I may have tried to report it to my teachers. I can't remember."

"Would it surprise you to learn that my investigator has spoken to several of your teachers and they have no memory of your making any such complaint?"

"Like I said, I can't remember if I did or not."

"Did your mother know what was going on?"

"She participated."

"How?"

"She performed oral sex on me, inserted objects in my vagina, my rectal area."

"What kind of objects?"

"A broom handle, a gun."

"A gun?"

"Yes."

"What kind of gun?"

"I don't know."

"Was it a rifle or a pistol?"

"I can't remember."

"Was your sister also molested?"

"I think so."

"Did she ever complain about this abuse?"

"She has no memory of it."

"But you think she was abused sexually?"

"We shared a bedroom from six to seventeen or eighteen and I believe my father came into the bedroom and had sex with my sister."

"How often?"

"Two to three times a week."

"And she doesn't remember this?"

"She denies it."

"Ms. Jaffe," Judge Opton interrupted. He was obviously upset. "Where are you going with this?"

"A few more questions and it will all be clear, Your Honor. I promise."

"It better be, because I am this close to ending this examination."

Amanda turned her full attention to the witness and went for the kill.

"Other than your parents, were you ever sexually abused by anyone else?"

"Yes."

"How many people molested you?"

"I'm not exactly certain."

"Can you give the judge a ballpark figure?"

"Maybe fifteen. Maybe as many as thirty-five."

Judge Opton frowned.

"Can you identify any of the other people who sexually molested you, these fifteen to thirty-five people?"

"No."

"Were they men or women?"

"It's hard to say."

"Why is that?"

"They were wearing robes with hoods. They wore masks."

The judge leaned forward.

"Can you describe these costumes?"

"They were black-hooded robes, they reached the floor. When I was little it seemed to me that the people could fly, that they floated instead of walking. Now I realize that it just seemed that way because the robes covered their feet."

"Can you remember anything else about the costumes?"

"They had circular medallions."

"Did the medallions symbolize something?"

"They symbolized the fact that these people worshiped Satan."

"So you were molested by Satan worshipers?"

"Yes."

Amanda now had the judge's full attention. Mike Greene struggled to appear nonchalant, as if mass molestations by devil worshipers were a commonplace occurrence in his life.

"Where did these attacks take place?"

"Sometimes in a barn. I also remember the basement of a church."

"Can you give the judge some idea of what happened at these meetings? For instance, why don't you tell him the worst experience you can remember."

"One time I was taken to the barn and tied down to a table and an abortion was performed on me . . ."

"An abortion? You were pregnant?"

"Yes."

"How old were you?"

"Thirteen."

"And they aborted you?"

"Yes. And then I was forced to eat the fetus of my . . . my child."

Judge Opton struggled to maintain his judicial composure.

"How often were you taken to these satanic group meetings?"

"About once a month."

"And how old were you the last time you went?"

"I believe I was eighteen or nineteen."

"Was your sister also taken to these ceremonies?"

"Yes, but she denies it. She says she has no memory of them."

"Were other people's children at these meetings?"

"I remember two or three."

"Was anything done to these other children?"

"They were put in boxes with insects," Dr. Fairweather answered in the same monotone she'd used to answer all of Amanda's questions. "Snakes were made to crawl on them, electric shock was used, they were made to eat parts of animals, photographs were made of them having sex with adults."

"Were there animal sacrifices at these meetings?"

"Yes. I remember cats, dogs. Once there was a sheep."

"What did they do?"

"They cut the belly of the animal open. Sometimes they hung it from the ceiling, cut open the belly, the organs would fall on the people, or the children were forced to eat it."

"Were there human sacrifices?"

"Yes."

"Where were they?"

"In a barn."

"Do you know where the barn was?"

"It was in the country, way out. There were high trees all around and the only light was in the barn from lanterns. Inside, there were blackout curtains to keep out sunlight or to prevent people from seeing in."

"What happened in the barn on the first occasion when you saw a human sacrifice?"

"This man was tied up from the rafters with his hands above his head."

"Was he clothed?"

"No, he was naked."

"Was he screaming or fighting?"

"Yes."

"What happened to this man?"

"The people took knives and flayed his skin off."

"Was he alive when this happened?"

"Yes."

"How many people were involved?"

"I can't remember. More than fifteen."

"And they all were involved in skinning this man alive?"

"Some were chanting and playing drums and calling on demons."

"Do you know why the victims were selected for the ritual?"

"They were selected because they were Christians."

"What happened to the body after it was taken down?"

"There was a ceremony in which the blood was drunk from a chalice, people had sex, that kind of behavior."

"What did the blood represent?"

"Whoever drank the blood of a Christian got that person's power."

"What were these satanic cult members hoping to achieve by following Satan?"

"They wanted to live with Satan for eternity and have

everything they wanted, and when Satan overcame the world, you would be a chosen one."

"How were the victims found?"

"The way I understand it, there were people in the cult who were programmed to capture Christians for these ceremonies."

"Were they captured at random off of the street?"

"That's how I understood it."

"Flaying someone alive is murder, isn't it, Dr. Fairweather?"

"Yes."

"And these people probably had families who would worry about them?"

"I suppose."

"Did you ever tell the police about these horrible things that happened to you and these other people?"

"No, I couldn't."

"Why is that?"

"I was terrified and scared for my life."

"Well, you left the cult at twenty-one and you're in your forties now. So you've been away from your parents and these people for twenty years. Didn't it ever occur to you to tell anyone about this after you broke away?"

"I wasn't able to tell anyone."

"Why is that?"

"I was led to believe from the time I was very young that there were members of the cult who could read my mind and that I was constantly being watched and . . ."

"Yes?"

"I believe there were some medical mind-control

experiments performed on me by doctors who were members of the cult."

"What was the purpose of these experiments?"

"To make me behave and do what they wanted."

"What were these experiments?"

"I remember having electrical shock. I remember people giving me certain words or codes or phrases and then telling me what I needed to do when I heard them."

"Where did this happen?"

"In a place that was like an operating room. There were bright lights over my head. I was naked and strapped down. They attached electrodes to my head. That's all I remember."

"How did these experiments work? What did they do to you?"

"There was a phrase said and they would say, 'When you hear this phrase you will do thus and such. Do you understand?' And no matter what I said, they would say, 'We don't believe you,' and I would get more shocks. And at some point they would stop. I guess when they thought I was under control."

"Were you ever given these codes or phrases?"

"Yes."

"How?"

"On the phone or someone in the street would give me a sign. They might say the phrase and I would have to do what I was told."

"What types of things were you told?"

"If I saw red I was supposed to try and kill myself, but not succeed."

"Fake a suicide?"

"Yes."

"Were you ever ordered to do this?"

"Yes, several times."

"How did you attempt suicide?"

"I cut my wrists."

"How many times?"

"I can't say for sure."

"Were you ever hospitalized for this?"

"Twice. I was sent for psychiatric treatment."

Amanda Jaffe was about to ask another question when Mike Greene stood and buttoned his suit jacket.

"Your Honor, I think this might be a good time for a recess."

"I agree, Mr. Greene. We'll recess for fifteen minutes. Dr. Fairweather, you can step down, but you'll have to be back in court when we reconvene. I'll see counsel in chambers."

The judge left the courtroom through a door behind the dais. Daniel turned to Amanda and looked at her wide-eyed.

"She's nuts," he said.

"Yes, she is," Amanda answered with a comforting smile. "And we are sitting in the catbird seat. You hang tight while I talk to the judge. Hopefully, I'll have good news when I come out."

"How did you know about that Satan stuff?"

"I'll tell you later."

Amanda and Mike Greene left the courtroom and Joe Molinari walked up to the bar of the court. One of the guards told Joe they could talk across the low fence but could not touch or exchange anything.

"Thanks for coming," Daniel said.

"Hey, dude, this is the best show in town, and your lawyer kicks ass. You and me are going to be at happy hour this afternoon."

Daniel knew better than to get his hopes up, so he just smiled.

"What is going on here?" Judge Opton asked Mike Greene as soon as the judge and the two attorneys were seated in his chambers.

"Believe me, I had no idea she was going to say that stuff."

Opton shook his head. "Just when you thought you've seen it all. Well, Mike, what are we going to do?"

Greene exhaled. "Fairweather and Forbus are my only witnesses. You've heard everything I've got."

"Are you going to argue that you've proved by clear and convincing evidence that Mr. Ames murdered Arthur Briggs? Because you've got to do that before I'll deny bail."

"She still saw what she saw, Judge," Greene answered halfheartedly.

"Your witness sees a lot of things. What's your position, Amanda?"

"The only evidence connecting Daniel to the murder is the testimony of Dr. Fairweather and I don't believe she's a credible witness."

"You don't have to be diplomatic. We're not on the record. The woman is a total fruitcake. Fucking electrodes. Jesus, Mike, where did you dig her up?"

Greene didn't answer.

"Okay, here's what we'll do when we go back outside," Opton said. "You'll end your cross, Amanda, and you'll rest, Mike. You can argue against bail, but I'm going to grant it, understood?"

Greene nodded. Opton turned to Amanda.

"What can your client afford?"

"Daniel's on his own and he's almost broke, Judge. As you heard, Reed, Briggs just fired him. His mother doesn't have a dime and he doesn't know where his father is. He worked his way through college and law school, so he's up to his nose in debt and he doesn't have much in savings. I'm taking the case pro bono."

Opton's eyebrows raised. Amanda ignored his surprise and continued.

"I think you should release him on his own recognizance. Daniel swears he's innocent and there isn't any credible evidence that links him to the murder. Even if you believed Dr. Fairweather, the best you have is Daniel running from the scene, but no evidence that he had a murder weapon or shot Briggs."

"Mike?"

Greene looked defeated. "I'll go on the record against recog, but I can't make a great argument against it, right now."

"Okay. I'll let you protect your office. You can make an impassioned plea. Just don't go on too long." Opton stood up. "Let's get this over with."

Mike Greene looked grim when he emerged from the judge's chambers and Amanda Jaffe's face betrayed no emotion. As soon as Amanda sat down she turned to Daniel.

"Judge Opton decided that Fairweather is nuts. He can't take her word for the ID, so Mike has no evidence connecting you to the scene of the crime. You'll be out of jail by noon."

"It's over? I'm free?"

"Don't get too excited. You're still charged with murder, but the judge is going to release you on your own word. You're going to be recogged, so you won't have to post bail."

"Thank you," Daniel said. "You're amazing."

"I am good," Amanda replied, "but we wouldn't have won without your guardian angel."

"Did you have any idea this was going to happen?" Mike Greene asked Zeke Forbus. "Because I love to have a little advance notice whenever I'm going to make a total fool out of myself in court. It gives me time to buy a disguise so I can make a quick escape."

Greene rarely got upset and Forbus was rarely embarrassed, but today had not been a normal day.

"Believe me, Mike, I was as surprised as you are. Fairweather seemed a little uptight when I talked to her, but I had no idea she was crazy."

Greene turned his chair toward the window in his office so he would not have to look at the homicide detective. A chessboard on his credenza displayed a position in the Queen's Gambit Declined that the prosecutor was studying. He stared at it for a moment in hopes of distancing himself from his real-life problems, but it was no use. He swung his chair back so he was face-to-face with Forbus.

"Where do we go from here, Zeke?"

"I still think he did it, so I'm going to try and find a way to prove Ames was really at the cottage."

"Any idea how you're going to do that?"

Forbus shook his head.

"Well think, damn it. We've got to move. The preliminary hearing is set for next week. Normally, I'd bypass it by getting a secret indictment out of the grand jury, but I've got nothing to show them. I'm going to have to dismiss the charges against Ames if we don't come up with something fast."

TWENTY-SIX

Daniel was so stunned at the speed with which his bail hearing ended that he barely heard the legal arguments. As soon as the judge ruled, the guards took him back to jail, where he waited to be processed out. Daniel had spent the past week tamping down his emotions, but he finally let himself believe that he would soon be out of jail. When the numbness wore off he became euphoric and he stayed high until it dawned on him that he was still the defendant in a murder case. He had been freed because there was no corroboration for April Fairweather's testimony, but what would happen when the police talked to Renee Gilchrist? Would she tell them about his phone call on the afternoon of the murder? Was that enough evidence to change the judge's mind about bail? By the time Daniel's property was returned, depression had set in.

Amanda had arranged to have the jail release Daniel through the garage so he could avoid the press. She told him that someone would be waiting for him. Daniel expected to see Amanda's investigator, but Kate Ross was standing in the shadows of the garage when he walked out of the jail. She flashed a big smile and Daniel's depression evaporated as soon as she hugged him.

"You don't smell too bad," Kate joked after she let him go.

Daniel's face split with a huge grin. "Neither do you."

"Come on. Let's get something to eat," Kate said. Daniel had not thought about food all day, but he was suddenly famished.

"You up for baloney on white or something a little more exotic?" Kate asked.

"I'm up for anything that is not baloney on white."

Kate's car was parked a block away. As they walked to it Daniel savored the heat of the sun, the brush of the breeze on his face, and the knowledge that he could walk to Kate's car or not, as he chose.

"How are you feeling?" Kate asked when they were on the road.

"Okay. I sort of shut down when I was in jail. It's going to take me a while to believe I'm really out."

"Amanda's good," Kate reassured him. "She'll keep you out."

"I'll say she's good." Then Daniel remembered Amanda's cryptic remark. "When I thanked her for winning the bail hearing Amanda said that I have a guardian angel. Do you know what she meant?"

Kate's smile disappeared. "Yeah, I do. We talked about it this morning. Amanda destroyed Fairweather because she received a videotape of a speech Fairweather gave a few years ago. She was talking to a group of so-called satanic ritual abuse survivors and she told them that she had been a victim of a satanic cult. Most of what Amanda used in her cross was in Fairweather's speech."

"Who gave Amanda the tape?"

"It was sent anonymously. She thought that I sent it."

"But you didn't?"

"I've seen the tape. It was in Fairweather's case file at the office," Kate said in obvious distress. "I wanted to tell Amanda about it, but I couldn't for the same reason I couldn't investigate Fairweather for Amanda."

"Hey, you've done more for me than anyone could," Daniel reassured her. "I'd still be in jail if you didn't ask Amanda to take my case."

"Then you understand? Fairweather is a client. There's a conflict."

"I would have thought less of you if you'd violated your trust."

Kate looked relieved.

"Does Amanda have any idea who sent the tape?" Daniel asked.

"No, but everyone at the conference knew about it. So did everyone at Reed, Briggs who was working on the case and anyone they told. Then there's Aaron Flynn and the people in his firm. I don't know if they were aware of the tape before the hearing, but Flynn's investigators are good."

"Boy, you've certainly narrowed the number of suspects."

Kate smiled, relieved that Daniel was not mad at her.

Daniel became quiet.

"What are you thinking?" Kate asked.

"That this isn't the first anonymous message someone has sent recently."

"You're talking about the Kaidanov study."

Daniel nodded.

"I thought about that," Kate said. "We don't know that the same person sent both packages. Is there a connection between the Insufort case and Fairweather's?"

"I can think of two. Briggs was the defense attorney in both cases. He told Fairweather to come to the cottage at eight-fifteen and he wanted me there at eight, which means he wanted us there at the same time."

"What's the other connection between Fairweather and the Insufort litigation?"

"Aaron Flynn. He represents the plaintiffs in both cases."

Daniel suddenly noticed that they were almost at Kate's house.

"I thought we were going to lunch."

"We are. Amanda didn't want you out in public, so we're eating at my place. You're staying with me, too. Your place is a mess. The cops trashed it when they searched. I didn't think you'd want to spend your first day of freedom with a mop and dustpan. I've got a nice guest room and Herb Cross brought over a valise with clothes and other things. You'll even be able to use your own toothbrush."

Kate pulled into her driveway and parked.

"You're a good friend," Daniel said warmly.

"That I am, and you'll need a few if we're going to get you out of this mess."

Daniel showered and changed into a clean pair of jeans and a baggy sweatshirt. When he opened the bathroom door he smelled brewing coffee. He followed the aroma into the kitchen and found Kate reading the afternoon edition of the newspaper. She looked up and smiled.

"Can I fix you some eggs and toast?"

"Yeah, thanks."

Kate walked to the stove. "How do you like your bacon?"

"On a plate," Daniel cracked. Kate's laugh brought Daniel an unexpected degree of pleasure.

Kate took three thick strips and laid them in a pan. Daniel sat at the kitchen table and read the story about his case in the late edition of the paper.

"I thought *The Oregonian* was fair," Kate said as she scrambled the eggs. "They wrote that Amanda cast serious doubts on Fairweather's identification and they pointed out that there wasn't any other evidence connecting you to the murder."

That should have made Daniel happy, but it didn't. He was waiting for the other shoe to drop when the police interviewed Renee.

Kate placed a plate piled high with eggs, bacon, and toast in front of Daniel, then brought him a cup of coffee.

"I'd never guess that you had this domestic streak," Daniel joked.

"Don't get used to it," Kate answered, tossing a set of keys next to Daniel's plate. "You're on your own after tonight."

"What are these?"

"A spare set of keys to my house. I'm going to be away for a few days and you'll need them."

"Where are you going?"

"To Arizona."

Daniel looked confused.

"While you were getting yourself arrested the cops found out the identity of the dead man at the lab. It wasn't Dr. Kaidanov."

"Who was it?"

"An Arizona lawyer named Gene Arnold."

"What was he doing at the lab?"

"No one knows. His partner doesn't even know what he was doing in Oregon. Arnold went to New York on business, saw a photograph in an art gallery of two people walking across Pioneer Square, and flew here. He checked into the Benson and disappeared. Now we know where he went, but not why. I'm betting the answer is in Arizona."

TWENTY-SEVEN

Kate rented a car at the airport and drove to Desert Grove under a vast blue sky along a desolate highway surrounded by desert and red-rock mesas. She appreciated the stark beauty of the scenery, but for someone who had spent her life in the Pacific Northwest there was too much sun and too little green. Shortly before one, Kate parked in front of a flat, modern, one-story building on the outskirts of town ARNOLD & KELLOGG, ATTORNEYS-AT-LAW was stenciled in gold on a plate-glass window that fronted the street.

Benjamin Kellogg, a big-boned Scandinavian in his early thirties with wheat-colored hair, ushered her down the hall to his office.

"Thank you for meeting with me on a Saturday," Kate said when they were seated.

"Gene wasn't just my law partner, Ms. Ross. I'd appreciate hearing anything you can tell me that will help me understand what happened."

"Quite frankly, no one—the police, my firm, no one—has any clue to why your partner died where he did. That's why I'm here."

"I'll help if I can," Kellogg assured her.

"My firm is defending Geller Pharmaceuticals in a lawsuit that questions the safety of Insufort, one of its products. Information about a study allegedly conducted by our client surfaced during a deposition. The results of the study supported the plaintiff's claim that the drug is harmful. Soon after the existence of the report was discovered, the lab where the study was conducted was destroyed in an arson fire. Your partner's body was found in the ruins. Was Gene Arnold or your firm connected in any way with this litigation?"

"No."

"Can you think of any reason for Mr. Arnold to come to Oregon?"

Kellogg looked completely baffled. "I'm sorry, Ms. Ross, but I have no idea why Gene was in Oregon. We don't have any cases there."

"Has Mr. Arnold ever mentioned friends or business acquaintants who live in Oregon?"

"No, but Gene hired me six years ago, fresh out of law school. I only made partner last year. I don't know much about things that happened here before I moved from Phoenix, except for the murders, of course. They were news statewide."

"What murders?"

"Gene's wife and the wife of our biggest client were kidnapped and murdered. It probably wasn't a big deal out of state, but it was major news in Arizona." Kellogg shook his head. "It was really horrible. First, Martin's wife was killed, then Gene's. Neither one of them ever really got over it."

Kate leaned forward. "This is the first I've heard about these murders. Can you fill me in?"

"I don't know much more than what I read. Like I said, this was before I moved to Desert Grove, about seven years ago. I didn't know Gene then, or Martin Alvarez."

"Who is Martin Alvarez?"

"He's the wealthiest man in Laurel County. A year or so before I got here his wife was murdered during a bungled kidnapping attempt. Paul McCann, a local guy, was arrested. Then Gene's wife was kidnapped and murdered. For a while Gene was a suspect in his wife's murder, but they dropped the charges. It was a horrible time for Gene. He was still a mess during the first year I worked here."

"Did they ever catch Mrs. Arnold's killer?"

"No."

"Can you give me any more details?"

"Not really. It was all over by the time I started working for Gene and he never talked about it."

"Who would know more about the murders?"

Kellogg hesitated. "There's Martin, but I'm not certain he'll see you."

"Why is that?"

"Martin worshiped his wife. He was devastated by her death. From what I hear he was very gregarious before she was killed. Everyone says that he threw the best parties; he was very active in the community and a great contributor to local charities. That all changed after his wife died. He's very reclusive now. He rarely leaves his hacienda, even to conduct business."

TWENTY-EIGHT

The Alvarez ranch was several miles out of town. There was no marker on the highway and Kate would have missed the turn onto the dirt track that led to the hacienda if Benjamin Kellogg had not given her precise directions. Kate drove on through a swirl of dust, but there was no sign of civilization. On both sides of the road clumps of desert plants clung to the arid and rocky ground and giant cacti stretched their arms toward a blue sky marred only by occasional wisps of clean white cloud. Kate was beginning to wonder if she'd made the right turn when an expanse of brown adobe walls materialized in the distance.

A guard inspected Kate's identification before directing her to a parking area in front of a massive whitewashed Spanish-style house with a red tile roof. She noticed another armed guard as she walked up a flagstone path to a front door of carved oak, which opened before she could knock.

"Miss Ross?" asked a slender, light-boned woman of middle age dressed in a plain dress and comfortable shoes.

"Yes, ma'am."

The woman smiled. "I'm Anna Cordova, Mr. Alvarez's assistant. He's out at the pool."

Cordova inquired politely about Kate's plane trip as she led the investigator across a tiled entryway, down four wide hardwood steps, and across a sunken living room. A blanket with an intricate American Indian design decorated one wall and an oil painting of a cattle drive decorated another; a glass case in a corner displayed pre-Columbian art. Kate walked by a stone fireplace and a painting that looked like a Georgia O'Keeffe.

Outside, into the heat again. But this time there was shade from a roof that overhung a wide patio of brownish-red Spanish tile. At the end of the patio was a pool wide enough for six lap lanes and deep enough at one end for a diving board. An armed guard stood in the shadows created by the high wall that surrounded the compound. His eyes followed Kate as she crossed the veranda, but Kate lost interest in him quickly. Her attention was drawn to a heavyset man in white cotton pants and a loose-fitting short-sleeve shirt who was seated under an umbrella at a circular glass table, staring toward the pool.

Martin Alvarez stood when he heard the women approach. Kate guessed that he was six two. A black eye patch covered his right eye and a scar ran across his temple, reddish white against his dark, pockmarked skin. There were streaks of gray in his jet-black hair. A bushy mustache covered his upper lip. Alvarez's shoulders were thick and his forearms were heavily muscled. The investigator's immediate impression was that he was a hard, unforgiving man.

"Martin, Miss Ross is here," Anna Cordova said.

Alvarez crossed the pool deck with a determined stride.

"Gene is dead?" he asked without preliminaries.

Kate nodded.

"There is no mistake?" Alvarez asked. His face betrayed no emotions.

"No."

"The details, please. And do not spare my feelings. I am hardened to violence. Nothing you tell me will be worse than what I've already experienced."

"Mr. Arnold was killed with a sharp instrument, probably a knife. He didn't suffer. His death would have been quick."

"Why did it take you so long to identify him? Kellogg reported him missing weeks ago."

"His body was found in the ruins of a laboratory in the woods, several miles from downtown Portland. Mr. Arnold's body had to be identified through dental records because the body burned with the building."

There was a quick intake of breath.

"He was dead before the fire was set," Kate added quickly to put Alvarez's mind at ease.

"Why don't you continue your conversation by the pool." Cordova pointed to the glass-topped table. "I'll have Miguel bring you some refreshments. Would you like an iced tea?" she asked Kate.

"That would be fine, thank you."

Alvarez walked back to the table. Kate sat across from him under the shade of a large umbrella.

"Do you have any suspects?" Alvarez asked.

"No. The police don't even know what Mr. Arnold was doing in Oregon."

"I don't either. Gene was in New York to obtain financing for one of my business ventures. I expected him back as soon as he was finished."

"So he wasn't supposed to go to Portland after he was through in New York?"

"No."

"Have you ever had any dealings with the Geller Pharmaceutical Company?"

"No."

"Can you think of any reason why Mr. Arnold would be interested in primate research?"

"No. Why do you ask?"

Kate gave Alvarez a brief explanation of the Insufort case. Alvarez blanched when she mentioned Aaron Flynn's name.

"Is something wrong?" Kate asked.

"Seven years ago a man named Paul McCann murdered my wife. Aaron Flynn was his attorney."

"Was Flynn a big man with red hair?"

"Yes."

Kate told Alvarez about the Bernier photograph.

"My best guess is that Mr. Arnold came to Oregon to talk to one of the people in the picture. Maybe Flynn is in it. Do you know why that would have been such a shock?"

Alvarez's brow furrowed and Kate thought that he looked genuinely perplexed.

"I can only guess that seeing Flynn brought back memories of his wife's murder," Alvarez answered after some thought.

"Were the murders of your wife and Mr. Arnold's related?"

"Yes."

Kate let that rest for a moment.

"How did Mr. Arnold get along with Flynn when they were living in Desert Grove?"

"I don't think they saw much of each other outside of professional meetings," Alvarez answered stiffly. Then he paused, lost in thought, before shaking his head. "None of this makes sense."

"It might help me to make sense of it if I knew more about what happened here, seven years ago."

Alvarez hesitated. Kate could only guess at how painful his memories must be. After a moment he fingered his scar.

"If you think it would help . . . ?"

"I don't know if it will, but we have nothing to go on now."

"I've spent seven years thinking about the murder of my wife, trying to piece together what happened. I'll tell you what I know and what I learned from others if it will help you catch the person who murdered Gene." He pointed at his sightless eye. "He may be the same person who did this to me."

Part IV

Death in the Desert

TWENTY-NINE

1

It was morning in the desert. As Patty Alvarez rode Conquistador toward the red-rock canyons to the east, a crimson tinge appeared along the horizon. Then the sun began to grow huge, displaying thick waves of red-hot gas and yellow flares so bright that she couldn't gaze directly at them.

Patty liked to ride first thing in the morning because it was still cool. In an hour rivulets of sweat would be running between her breasts and her blouse would stick to her hot skin. That's when she would turn for home.

Conquistador was a King-bred quarter horse, a reddish-brown bay with a black mane and tail who had once been a champion. Martin Alvarez had presented Conquistador to his wife on her thirty-second birthday and he was Patty's favorite. As they raced across the narrow valley, she felt the muscular bay moving between her legs, reminding her of the things Martin had done to her that morning before she left the hacienda. There were two stallions in her life. Patty smiled at the thought.

One way to cut the heat was to race through the gaps between the stone monuments that spread out before her. In the canyons, the narrow rock walls shot up to the sky and cast cooling shadows over the trail. Conquistador knew the route of their morning run by heart, so Patty could concentrate on the view. Patty believed that the mesas had been painted by nature and sculpted by God. She never tired of looking at them. They were red or brown or yellow, depending on the light, and she imagined that she saw the faces of Indians or the bodies of muscular warriors in the rock.

The land in front of the canyon was flat and the huge boulders that marked both sides of the entrance were big enough for a man to hide behind. Conquistador was drawing alongside the massive stone pile on the right when two men appeared abruptly from behind the boulders to the left. They wore navy-blue ski masks, jeans, and jackets that were zipped to the neck, a bizarre outfit to wear in a land where the heat of the day was over one hundred degrees. As the man in front raised his hand toward Patty, palm outstretched, the other man leveled a rifle at her horse.

Patty knew instantly what was happening. Martin was rich, very rich, and he loved Patty past caring. Everyone knew this, and Patty was certain that these men knew it, too. They would use Martin's love to make him pay a fortune in ransom for her. And once he paid she was certain that she would die.

Patty dropped her body forward, hugging Conquistador as she kicked her heels into his flanks. The bay sprang forward. Wind like a freight train barreled past the quarter horse. Hooves beat against the parched ground, dust flew. The men jumped aside. Patty saw a swirl of light and shadow in the canyon, and freedom. Then a shot rang out in the still desert air.

2

There were seventy thousand people living in Laurel County, Arizona, but there was no debate over who among them was the richest and most powerful. Martin Alvarez was a bear of a man with a broad flat face the color of tanned leather. He wore his hair in a ponytail, had diamond studs in his ears, and wore buckskin jackets, hand-tooled cowboy boots, and bolo ties. Martin had started with one used-car lot on the outskirts of town and now owned car dealerships all over the state, as well as a statewide chain of retail stores and profitable land holdings. But Martin's proudest possession was his wife, the redheaded, green-eyed former Miss Laurel County.

Patty Alvarez was fifteen years Martin's junior. When the most powerful man in Laurel County started courting her she had been scared to death, but she knew that marrying Martin meant security. And there was the prestige of being Mrs. Martin Alvarez. She would go from being a name scratched into the stalls in the high-school boys' room to the top of Laurel County society. So she had said yes when Martin proposed and had been happily surprised to find that she had grown to love the husband who doted on her.

The Martin Alvarez seated behind the large oak desk in the hacienda's home office was a man on the verge of violence. The only thing keeping him civilized was the absence of a target. Seated on the other side of the desk were FBI Agent Thomas Chandler, Detective Norman Chisholm of the Laurel County Sheriff's Office, and Ramon Quiroz, the Laurel County district attorney. Several other law enforcement officers were also crowded into the room. Two FBI technicians were working on Martin's phone.

"I know you've told Mr. Quiroz and several others what happened today, but I'd like to hear it firsthand, if you don't mind," Chandler said.

Martin looked ready to explode. He was tired of talking, he wanted action, but he restrained himself and recounted the day's events to the FBI agent.

"Patty rides every morning. Sometimes we ride together, but I had a conference call at seven, so she rode alone. She usually takes the same route and she's usually back between eight and nine. When she didn't return by ten I grew worried. I brought one of the men and we went looking for her."

Martin paused. Chandler watched him control his anguish and anger.

"We found Conquistador near the entrance to a canyon roughly four miles east of here."

"Conquistador is her horse?"

"Was. He's dead," Martin replied bitterly.

"And your wife was missing?"

Martin nodded. "But there was blood on the rocks where Conquistador fell."

"I've got my forensic people out there now," Chandler said. "They'll analyze the blood to see if it's from the horse."

He did not mention the other, obvious possibility.

"What did you do after you found Conquistador?"

"I called Ramon from my cell phone. Then we waited by the horse."

"Tell me about the call from the kidnappers."

"As soon as Norm arrived he told me to go home. He was worried it was a kidnapping and they'd call while I was out. They did, about two hours ago. They said no cops, but Ramon and Norm insisted that I bring you in."

"That was a very smart move."

"Unless they kill Patty," Martin said, turning his steady eyes on Chandler.

"These people want money, Mr. Alvarez. That's what this is all about. There won't be any money if they kill your wife."

Chandler waited a beat, hoping that Martin would relax a little. He didn't.

"Please tell me, word for word, as best you remember, what was said during the call."

"It was a man but he disguised his voice. He said, 'We've got your wife. If you want her to live it will cost you one million dollars. We want it in unmarked bills. Nothing larger than hundreds.' I told him it would take a day to get the money. He said he would call back with instructions. I asked to speak to Patty. He hung up. That's everything. The call didn't take long."

"Okay," the FBI agent said.

"I want honesty, Chandler," Martin demanded. "Total honesty. What are my wife's chances?"

Chandler looked grim. He shook his head.

"I have no idea what your wife's chances are. There are too many variables. So I'm not going to guess or give you a best-case scenario. The honest truth is that I don't know. All I can promise is that we will do everything in our power to get your wife back."

3

The kidnappers told Martin to leave the ransom money under a log that crossed over Rattlesnake Creek in the mountains several hours' drive from Desert Grove. Martin's banker had the money ready, but on Chandler's instructions, Martin told the kidnappers that it would take two more hours for the bank to put the ransom together. Martin drove to the bank to pick up a large duffel bag stuffed with money while Chandler used the darkness to infiltrate a heavily armed team into the woods near the stream.

Thomas Chandler had been raised in Philadelphia, educated in Boston, and trained for his job in Quantico, Virginia. Nothing in his childhood, his schooling, or his FBI training had prepared him for lying for hours in a cold, damp forest on sharp, stony ground. Chandler had only been able to remain motionless for a little while. Soon he was shifting his body every few minutes, doing the best a city boy could to move quietly.

Scanning the area around the creek only took his mind

off his discomfort for a little while. The wide stream twist-ed through the woods, the water deep and clear as it boiled over several boulders that changed the course of the creek. Through night-vision glasses the area looked like a neon video game.

Chandler was turning his collar up as protection against the cold mountain air when a noise made him freeze. He checked his watch. It was after ten, just about the time Alvarez would be arriving. A twig cracked and the agent saw a flashlight beam light up a stretch of the trail that wound through the woods to Rattlesnake Creek. Chandler focused his night vision-glasses on the spot where a tree felled by lightning lay across the waterway. Moments later Martin Alvarez came into view carrying a large duffel bag across his broad shoulders. Chandler watched Alvarez wedge the bag under the log. When he stood up, Alvarez cast a quick look around before return-ing the way he had come.

As soon as Martin disappeared up the trail Chandler trained his glasses on the duffel bag, but nothing happened. The bag lay under the log, the stream ran swiftly between its banks, and the stillness of the forest lay over the agent like a blanket. Chandler found it impossible to watch the duffel bag continuously. Besides, he knew that the snipers hiding in blinds throughout the forest and the other agents in the capture team were on alert. He shifted for comfort and closed his eyes. He was starting to nod off when fear of falling asleep jerked him back to his duty. Chandler chided himself, slapped his face to stir his adrenaline, and refocused his glasses on the log just as a man dressed entirely in black rose out of the creek and grabbed the duffel.

Chandler unholstered his weapon. "FBI! Freeze!"

Automatic fire sprayed through the woods from somewhere on the other side of the creek. Chandler hit the ground. The man with the duffel fled down the stream using the burst as cover. Chandler heard the other agents return fire. He got to his feet and raced into the frigid water. The fleeing man suddenly darted out of the stream and into the forest with Chandler in pursuit. It was hard to move in the dense underbrush. The agent tripped over a root and stumbled forward just as another burst of automatic fire shredded the foliage above his head, showering him with leaves.

As soon as the gunfire stopped Chandler regained his footing. He heard ragged breathing and the sound of someone smashing through the bushes. Then a shot rang out, followed by a sharp grunt, and one of the snipers yelled, "He's hit."

Chandler raced ahead until he burst into a clearing, nearly running into a large man wearing a ski mask and bleeding badly from a leg wound. The man tried to pivot on his injured leg and stumbled. Chandler drove into him, taking him to the ground. Moments later a chokehold ended the brief fight. By that time several other agents assisted in subduing the captive.

"Where's the other one?" Chandler demanded as soon as he caught his breath.

"They're after him," one of the agents answered.

Chandler remembered the duffel bag. He turned in a circle, then asked for a flashlight. He shined the light over the area where he'd just fought. Then he asked the handcuffed prisoner, "Where's the ransom money?"

An agent pulled off the ski mask. The man he confronted was six feet tall. His face had the ruddy complexion of someone who worked outdoors and his red hair was plastered across his forehead.

"Where is Patty Alvarez?" Chandler demanded.

The man looked beat, but he did not look beaten.

"I want a lawyer," he answered. "I ain't sayin' nothin' before I talk to a lawyer."

Chandler knelt next to the man, gripped his chin, and forced his head up so they were eye to eye.

"If Patty Alvarez is dead, you're facing the death penalty," Chandler whispered so only the man could hear what he said. "If you cooperate right now we can deal. Keep asking for a lawyer and I'll be smiling at you when they pull the switch."

Chandler released the man's chin. The man broke eye contact. Two winded agents burst into the clearing. They started to speak, but Chandler held up his hand and led them out of earshot of the prisoner.

"There's a deer trail a half mile up the creek," one of the agents said. "We followed it for a mile. It crosses a deserted logging road that wasn't on any of our maps. There were fresh tire tracks in the dirt."

Chandler swore. The prisoner's accomplice must have grabbed the duffel bag while the two of them were out of his sight. Chandler pushed past the other agents and walked up to the prisoner.

"Your partner has the money and he's gone. That means you are going down for every charge I can think of unless you help us, right now. You have one minute to make up your mind."

4

Martin Alvarez focused intently on the testimony of Lester Dobbs, who had cut a deal shortly after his arrest near Rattlesnake Creek, then led the FBI agents to the shallow grave where Patty Alvarez was buried. However, someone other than Dobbs had captured the attention of Paul McCann, the man who was on trial for Patty's murder.

Melissa Arnold was the court reporter for the Laurel County Circuit Court during the trial of *State* v. *McCann*. Every day while court was in session, she sat in front of the dais from which Judge Melvin Schrieber presided typing every word that was spoken in court onto her stenograph machine with amazing accuracy. The ability to type with accuracy was not the only amazing thing about Melissa Arnold. She had long, honey-blond hair that hung to her shoulders, pale blue eyes, and full lips. The consensus around the courthouse was that she had the most beautiful legs anyone had ever seen. The rest of Melissa's body was also outstanding. So outstanding, in fact, that Paul McCann could not keep his eyes off her, even though Lester Dobbs was giving testimony that could send him to death row.

Paul McCann was addicted to women, so it was not surprising that his attention was riveted on the most stunning woman in the room. Women were also addicted to Paul. He was a big man who dressed in loud clothes and sported gaudy jewelry. He wore his styled hair a little long, left his mustache a trifle bushy, and exposed his curly black chest hair whenever possible. Most men thought he looked tacky, but a certain class of woman found him irresistible and he did nothing to discourage their advances.

"Mr. Dobbs, how are you employed?" Ramon Quiroz, the Laurel County district attorney, asked his star witness. Ramon wore an ill-fitting brown suit. He was short, fat, and laid-back. He was also extremely tough to beat in court.

The question about employment proved to be a stumper for Lester Dobbs, who stared at Ramon the way he might if the prosecutor had asked him to explain quantum mechanics. Dobbs fidgeted in the witness chair and looked uncomfortable in the cheap blue suit that Quiroz had purchased for him.

"I ain't employed right now," Dobbs answered after a lengthy pause.

"That's true, Mr. Dobbs," Ramon agreed with admirable patience, "but before your arrest you did work, did you not?"

"Sure."

"Well, then, why don't you tell the jury what kind of work you performed."

"I worked construction for Mr. McCann," Dobbs answered, nodding toward Aaron Flynn's client. At the mention of his name, the defendant reluctantly shifted his gaze from Melissa Arnold's breasts and focused his attention on his chief accuser.

"What exactly were you constructing?"

"Sunnyvale Farm."

"Which is?" Ramon prompted.

"A housing development. We was building forty-three homes, or was supposed to before the money run out."

"How did you learn that Mr. McCann's project was in trouble?"

"He told me. That's why we did it. For the money, so's he could pay off his creditors and keep the project going."

"Objection," Aaron Flynn said, rising to his feet.

"Yes, Mr. Dobbs," Judge Schrieber lectured, "please listen carefully to the question and only answer what you are asked."

"Jurors," Schrieber continued, "please ignore everything Mr. Dobbs said, except his statement that Mr. McCann told him that the Sunnyvale project was in trouble."

"Mr. Dobbs, you are an ex-convict, are you not?" Ramon continued.

"Yes, sir. Several times."

"Did Mr. McCann know this?"

"Oh, yeah. That's why he thought I'd help him, because I'd been in prison. He said he needed someone with criminal experience."

Flynn objected on the grounds that the answer was not responsive and the judge lectured Dobbs again. Dobbs didn't appear to be bright enough to understand what he was doing wrong. If the jurors suspected the same thing, they might also conclude that Dobbs was too dumb to make up his testimony.

"Mr. Dobbs, why don't you tell this jury how you came to be involved in the kidnapping and murder of Patty Alvarez."

"Okay. Best I recollect, it was one evening in April," Dobbs said, turning toward the jurors. "I was sittin' at the bar in the Red Rooster Tavern, mindin' my own business and drinkin' a beer. Mr. McCann come in the tavern. Next thing I know, he's askin' me if I'd like to join him for a beer in a booth."

"Was it unusual for you and Mr. McCann to have a drink together?"

"Yes, sir, it was. In fact, this was the first time I'd ever talked to Mr. McCann, except on the job, and then it would be about problems on the site, stuff like that."

"What did you two talk about?" Ramon asked.

"Nothin' much, at first. Sports, the weather."

"Did the conversation turn to Sunnyvale at some point?"

Dobbs glanced over at McCann. He looked as if he was embarrassed that he was testifying for the state.

"Mr. McCann told me that Sunnyvale might not get built. There was money owed or some such. If he couldn't come up with it, the project was doomed. That's how he said it, 'doomed.'"

"What did you say to that?"

"Well, I was wonderin' if I'd lose my job, because it paid pretty good. Mr. McCann said everyone would lose his job if he couldn't pay off the loan. Then he asked me about the prison. Which one I'd been in, whether it was hard to be inside. It caught me by surprise, because he just jumped from one subject to another without no warning."

"Did you tell him about prison and what you did to be sent there?"

"Yes, sir. He seemed right interested. Especially when I told him that I've been in for aggravated assault and armed robbery."

"Now, just so the jury will know, those were two different convictions?"

"Yes, sir."

"And you've also been convicted of assault twice where you didn't go to prison."

"I got probation on that."

"Okay. Now, what happened after you told Mr. McCann all about prison?"

"Nothin' then. We just drunk some more beer, talked about some fight. Mike Tyson, I think. Then he looked at his watch and said he had to go. And he did."

"So, the defendant didn't mention anything about Mrs. Alvarez?"

"Not till the next time."

"And when was that?"

"About three days later. I was walkin' to my car after work when Mr. McCann stopped me. He asked me if I was interested in making some extra money. I said, 'Sure.' He said to meet him in the parking lot of the Red Rooster at ten. I thought I misheard him, so I asked him if he'd said the parking lot. He said this was a private matter and he didn't want no one to know we was talking."

"What happened in the parking lot of the Red Rooster?"

"Mr. McCann drove up and told me to get in this car he was driving. It wasn't his normal one, which is this bright red sports car. This one was black, a plain old Ford. Anyway, I got in and he drove me out into the desert where it was only the two of us and he asked me what I would do for fifty thousand dollars."

Several jurors turned to look at each other and there was murmuring in the back of the courtroom.

"What did you answer?"

"I thought he was kidding, so I joked back that I'd do most anything. Then, just in case it wasn't a joke, I told him I wouldn't kill no one. That's when he asked if I would commit a crime short of murder and I asked him what he meant."

Dobbs took a sip of water before turning back to the jury.

"Mr. McCann told me that his company was in big trouble, but he had a foolproof way of fixing up his problems. He asked me if I'd heard of Martin Alvarez. I said, 'Sure.' Everyone in Desert Grove knows who he is. Mr. McCann said that Mrs. Alvarez—Patty, he called her—was the light of Mr. Alvarez's life and that he would do anything to protect her from harm, including paying over a large sum of money that could be used to keep the Sunnyvale project afloat. I asked how much money we was talking about and Mr. McCann said that Martin Alvarez could part with one million dollars without batting an eye."

"What did you tell the defendant when he said this?" Ramon asked.

"I said, in that case, I was gonna want more than fifty thousand to help."

5

Desert Grove was baking and the ancient air conditioner barely stirred the air in the courtroom. The judge called the morning recess and most of the observers filed out to get a cool drink or wash their faces in the rest room, but

Martin Alvarez did not move. Soon he was alone in the front row staring hard, first at Dobbs, then at Paul McCann. Ramon Quiroz saw what was going on. He leaned across the low railing that separated the gallery from the judge and attorneys and whispered something to Alvarez. When Quiroz was through talking, Martin stood and left the courtroom.

When court resumed, Dobbs testified that Paul McCann knew that Patty Alvarez loved to ride in the desert and that she rode in the morning before the heat of the day. According to Dobbs, McCann planned to ambush her out of sight of the hacienda. Alvarez would be tied up, blindfolded, and taken in the back of a van to the basement of an abandoned house in the next county. The plan called for Dobbs to baby-sit Alvarez while McCann negotiated the ransom. Nothing went the way it was supposed to.

"Mr. McCann picked me up in his van real early. We drove out to this spot in the desert where there's this big outcropping of rock that Mrs. Alvarez always passed and we parked the van behind the rocks so Mrs. Alvarez wouldn't see it."

"What happened next?"

"We waited until Mr. McCann said he saw her coming. He had binoculars, but even I could see the dust. So we put on our ski masks and took out our guns. . . ."

"Who supplied the guns?"

"Mr. McCann."

"Go on."

"The plan was that Mr. McCann would jump out and wave his hands to stop the horse. Then I'd grab Mrs.

Alvarez and tie her up. Only, it didn't work that way. Mr. McCann was standing out there waving and she did slow down. Then something spooked her and she spurred the horse and tried to ride past us. Once she took off, that would be that. And that's when Mr. McCann done it."

"Did what, Mr. Dobbs?"

"Shot the horse. BAM! It was like in the movies. The horse was up on its hind legs, pawing at the air. It was almost like slow motion that horse rearing up, the blood pouring out. It paused up in the air for a moment, then took two steps back and toppled over, right onto the rocks and right on top of Mrs. Alvarez.

"I just stood there watching. I couldn't believe it. The shot was real loud, like a thunderclap. Then there was a dull thunk when Mrs. Alvarez's head hit the rocks and a thud when the horse came down on top of her. When I heard the thunk I knew we were in big trouble. Right away I was thinking that she was dead, and I was right."

"What did Mr. McCann do after he shot the horse?"

"He just stood there like he was paralyzed. I did, too, but I recovered after a moment. The first thing I did was ask him why he did it, but he was just staring. I don't think he planned shooting the horse. I think he just did it on the spur of the moment."

"What happened next?"

"I ran over to Mrs. Alvarez. She was a mess. Her head was mashed between the horse and the rock. Mr. McCann staggered over. He could barely keep his feet. He tried to ask me if she was dead, but he couldn't say the word."

"What word is that?"

"'Dead.' He just couldn't say it. So I said it for him. As

soon as I did he just sat down in the dust and started talking to himself."

"What did he say?"

"'Oh, God, oh, God.' He said that a few times and 'What are we gonna do now?' I told him we should get the fuck—uh, get outta there."

"Did he agree?"

"No. He put his hands over his ears and told me to shut up so he could think. I said, 'Fine,' but I was plannin' to take the van if he didn't move soon. Then, just as I was getting ready to go, he did something that surprised me."

"And what was that?"

"He took out his cell phone and made a call."

"Mr. Dobbs, until this point how many people did you think were involved in the kidnapping?"

"Two. Me and him."

"Did you discover that there was a third person in on the plot?"

"Yes, sir, but I don't know who it was, because I only heard Mr. McCann's side of the conversation and he never mentioned a name."

"Please describe the phone conversation to the jury."

"It was short. First, he said everything had gotten . . ." Dobbs paused and looked up at the judge. "Uh, can I use the F-word, Your Honor?"

"Accuracy is very important, Mr. Dobbs," Judge Schrieber replied. "Please make sure that you use the exact words that you claim the defendant used."

"Okay," Dobbs said, turning back to the jurors. "He said everything had gotten fucked up and he explained about having to shoot the horse when Mrs. Alvarez tried to escape. Then he listened for a while. Mr. McCann had his mask off by then and I could see him turning red like he was being chewed out. After a minute I heard him ask what he should do. He nodded his head a few times, then hung up. I asked him who he was talking to, but he said it was none of my business. I said it damn well was because I was an accessory to this whole thing, including Mrs. Alvarez being dead. That's when he told me the plan."

"Which was?" Ramon prodded.

"To pretend she wasn't dead. To bury the body and demand the ransom anyway. He told me that was the only way any of us would get any money."

"What did you say to that?"

Dobbs shrugged. "I said, 'Okay.' I was in it for the money and Martin Alvarez wouldn't know his wife was dead. What difference would it make?"

6

Court broke at five when Lester Dobbs finished his testimony. Aaron Flynn said a few words to his client and packed up his papers while the guards took Dobbs back to the jail. After law school, Flynn had received no offers from the firms and government offices in Phoenix and Tucson. Desperate for work, he had applied to the Laurel County District Attorney's Office on the day a deputy DA resigned. Two years later Flynn left to set up a solo practice in a shabby storefront office a few blocks from the courthouse. He scraped by, paying the bills by taking anything that came in the door, until Paul McCann came along.

McCann planned to turn land on the outskirts of Desert Grove into a housing development called Sunnyvale Farm and he put Flynn on retainer to deal with his legal affairs. Flynn thought that McCann would be a constant source of easy money, but he was soon spending all his time on McCann's problems. First there were labor troubles, then Flynn had difficulties obtaining permits from the county supervisors. He was perplexed until someone let slip the fact that Martin Alvarez was interested in the land upon which McCann was building. Within months McCann was on the verge of bankruptcy and he blamed Martin Alvarez for his problems. When the FBI cut a deal with Lester Dobbs for his testimony, no one was shocked when he named Paul McCann as the man who'd hired him to help kidnap Patty Alvarez.

As Flynn was getting ready to leave the courtroom, Paul's wife, Joan, an anorexic woman with pale skin and jet-black hair, approached him. Flynn suspected that her physical appearance and high level of anxiety were the direct result of living with his client. She had filed for divorce twice, backing out when Paul promised to be faithful and stop beating her. Joan worked as Gene Arnold's legal secretary and it was her salary and savings that were paying Flynn's retainer.

"Mr. Flynn," she asked nervously, "can I speak to you?"

"Of course, Joan."

"What did you think of Dobbs's testimony?"

"Tough to say," Flynn said, hedging. He had learned that honesty was not the best policy with Joan. She was as fragile as a Fabergé egg. Since her husband's arrest she had bitten her nails to the quick and developed a nervous tic in the corner of her left eye.

"You don't believe him, do you?"

Flynn put a comforting hand on her shoulder. "Paul swears he's innocent, Joan. I'm his lawyer."

The answer seemed to pacify her. If she realized that it completely evaded her question, she didn't call him on it.

"I'll be a witness, won't I?" she asked for the millionth time.

"Of course."

"He was fishing. I saw him leave before dawn. He had all of his fishing gear in the van."

"That will help Paul for sure," Flynn told her in a soothing voice. "And the lab found nothing in Paul's van that showed that Mrs. Alvarez was ever in it."

The ransom money had not been found either. And the tracks on the logging road were from a stolen car that had been abandoned several days later in another county.

"I'm afraid, Mr. Flynn. I don't know what I'll do if Paul is sent to prison." She looked away. "He's not easy to live with. You know he's hit me and he's cheated on me. You know that."

"I know, Joan."

"But he can be so loving."

The way she said it made Flynn feel that she was trying to convince herself of the truth of what she was saying as much as she was trying to convince him.

"The night he proposed, he drove me out to Bishop's Point. We were alone. There was a full moon and the stars filled up the sky. He said he wanted to stay there with me forever. I believe he meant that. We would have been okay if we could have just stayed there."

Joan's shoulders shook as she sobbed. Flynn wrapped her up in a hug.

"Now, now," he said before releasing her. He held out a handkerchief so she could dry her eyes. When Joan handed it back, she tried to smile, but her lips just twisted and she choked back another sob. Flynn touched her shoulder again.

"Hang in there, Joan. The case will be over in a day or so."

"I'll try," she said, then smiled bravely and walked away, leaving Aaron Flynn very much relieved.

By the time Flynn arrived at his office it was 5:30 and his secretary was gone. Flynn was taking his trial materials out of his briefcase when Melissa Arnold knocked lightly on the office door, startling him.

"Sorry to frighten you, Mr. Flynn," Melissa said in a mocking tone. She leaned her hip against the doorjamb. "I believe you wanted to discuss the preparation of a daily transcript of Lester Dobbs's testimony."

"Yes, I did, Mrs. Arnold," Flynn answered nervously. He found it impossible to maintain his composure when he was alone with Gene Arnold's wife. "Why don't you shut the door and come in."

"Preparing a daily transcript is hard," Melissa said as she crossed the room. "I'll have to work late and it's such lonely work."

"Maybe I can help you solve that problem," Flynn said.

Melissa pressed against him and silenced him with her lips. Flynn grabbed the hem of her skirt and hiked it up until he had his hands on her silk panties. Moments later they were on the couch ripping at each other's clothes.

7

In closing arguments, Aaron Flynn played up the deal Dobbs had cut with the district attorney. The man was basically walking away, Flynn told the jurors. He was even out of jail pending sentencing on the attempted kidnapping count, which was the only charge the state was going to bring against him. But even though the jury knew Dobbs had a motive to lie, he seemed to be telling the truth and Paul McCann had no alibi for the time of the kidnapping. Two hours after they retired to deliberate, the jury was back with a verdict of guilty on all charges, including the charge of murder.

McCann didn't take the verdict well. He broke down. He screamed and cried. He swore he was innocent and that Dobbs was lying. Flynn promised to fight his case all the way to the United States Supreme Court if necessary. The appeal he promised would begin as soon as Melissa Arnold, the court reporter, prepared the transcript of the case.

But that never happened. One week after Paul McCann's trial ended, Melissa Arnold disappeared.

Someone was knocking on Martin Alvarez's bedroom door. He sat up groggily and stared at the clock on his end table. It was 2:30 A.M.

"Señor Alvarez," a man called out. Alvarez recognized the voice of one of his guards.

"Come in."

A barrel-chested young man entered the bedroom.

"What is it?"

"Señor Arnold is here."

"What does he want?"

"He wouldn't tell me, but he's very upset."

"All right. Take him to my office, and see if he wants something to drink. I'll be right down."

The day after his arrest, Lester Dobbs had led the police to Patty Alvarez's grave in the desert. Martin was home when he got the news that Patty was really dead. He had identified the body, returned to his hacienda, and remained there, leaving only to attend Patty's funeral and Paul McCann's trial. Several friends had tried to pay condolence calls, but Martin had turned them away. This was different. Gene Arnold was more than Martin's lawyer. He had worked for Martin for peanuts when Martin was nobody. He had always been there for him when times were hard.

Alvarez dressed quickly. When he walked into his office he found his friend and lawyer pacing back and forth, his cheeks tear-streaked and his hair uncombed.

"She's gone," Gene said.

"Who's gone?"

Gene slumped on a chair and buried his head in his hands.

"Melissa," he moaned.

Gene Arnold was five eight, balding, and had the start of a paunch. He was not much to look at, in other words, which made his marriage to Melissa Arnold so surprising. He had met her during a deposition in Los Angeles, where she was working as a freelance court reporter. According to Gene, she had just left a terrible marriage. He had been pulverized by her looks and had proposed after one date. They married at a wedding chapel in Las Vegas and honeymooned at Caesars Palace.

Almost from the day he came back to Desert Grove with his bride, the gossips said Melissa had married Gene for his money. Martin and Patty Alvarez saw a lot of the couple and it had been Patty's opinion that Melissa was never in love with her husband—he was someone safe and comfortable who would worship her and never betray her.

Alvarez poured Arnold a tall Scotch and forced him to take a drink. When Gene was calm enough to speak coherently, he told Martin what had happened that day.

"Melissa left for work this morning. I went to the office. Around nine-thirty, Marge called from Mel's chambers to ask if Melissa was sick." Gene looked up, his face the very picture of despair. "She never made it to work, Martin."

Martin's first thought was that she had run out on Gene and the tedium of Desert Grove. He knew Melissa had grown tired of Gene and the town fairly quickly. Martin based his conclusion on the fact that she'd come on to him at his Fourth of July barbecue. Martin had rebuffed her gently and had never told anyone about the pass, but he watched her closely after that and noticed her flirting with more than one man.

"Marge said no one had seen Melissa at the courthouse. I called home, thinking she was sick and had gone back to the house. There was no answer, so I drove home in case she was sleeping or had fainted or . . ."

"And she wasn't there?"

Gene shook his head. It was still hard for him to talk.

"But all her clothes were there. So were the suitcases. There wasn't any note. She hasn't run off, Martin."

A feeling of dread began to grow in Martin's stomach.

"Did you call the sheriff?"

"No. What would I have said? I mean, she was only gone for a few hours. I was worried, but after I called the hospital and they said she wasn't there, I kept thinking that she would call and explain what happened. The sheriff wasn't going to do anything, anyway, until there was proof that something had happened to her."

"And now there is?" Martin asked fearfully.

"There . . . there was a call." Gene stopped and caught his breath. "The voice was disguised. It was so low that I couldn't understand it at first."

Gene started to cry again. Finally, he choked out what he had to say.

"They have her. It's the people who took Patty."

Martin felt sick.

"It's the same people," Gene sobbed. "The caller said so. They'll kill her if I call the police. What should I do? I love her. I've got to save her."

Gene looked at Alvarez for an answer, but Martin couldn't think straight.

"Did they let you talk to Melissa?"

"No. I asked, but they refused."

"What do they want?"

"Seventy-five thousand dollars or they're going to kill her."

"Can you get your hands on that much money?"

"Just. I've got a retirement account. The money means nothing to me. It's Melissa. If they kill her . . ."

"What are you supposed to do?"

"The kidnappers are going to contact me around five tonight at my house. They said they're watching me and they'll know if I go to the cops or have a tap put on my phone."

"What do you want me to do, Gene?"

Arnold raised his eyes to Alvarez's face. It was a block of stone.

"I can't risk going to the police or the FBI. Look at the mess they made in your case."

Martin nodded. Gene leaned forward, his hands clasped like a supplicant before a king.

"Can you bring them the money, Martin?" Arnold looked down. "I . . . I'm not brave. Look at me. What could I do to save her? But you're tough. If there was a chance, you could fight them . . ."

His voice trailed off. The plea was pathetic and desperate.

"That makes no sense at all, Gene. I'm no Rambo, and these guys won't fight fair. This isn't like one of those kung fu movies where the villain throws down his weapons and fights the hero hand to hand. They'll have guns and they'll shoot me in the back if it suits them. They shot it out with the FBI."

"I'm sorry. You're right, I don't know what I was thinking." Gene sounded thoroughly defeated. "I have to take the chance that Melissa is alive and that they'll return her to me if I pay them."

Alvarez looked at the clock on his desk. It was a little

after three. His mind was racing. He doubted that Melissa Arnold was still alive, but that didn't mean that he would let his friend deal with her killers. They were the people who murdered his Patty and this was a chance for revenge.

"Let me take you home," Alvarez said calmly, giving none of his feelings away. "I'll stay with you. Let's see what they say. Then we'll decide what to do."

8

By the time the call came, the money was waiting inside a gym bag and Martin had reached a decision. Gene had the receiver pressed to his ear before the second ring. Martin heard him say, "I understand" and "Yes," then, "Is my wife—" and knew by the way Gene's features crumbled that they had hung up on him without letting him talk to Melissa or assuring him that she was all right.

"Gene?" Martin asked softly.

Arnold stared at the phone.

"What did they say?"

"There's a side road off the highway." He sounded dazed. "It's near the bridge that crosses the McPherson River where they have the picnic grounds."

"I know it."

The McPherson River was twenty miles from Desert Grove in a deep canyon. The Park Service had developed a picturesque area near it. Rafters set out from a small park with a picnic area. Last summer, Martin and Patty had rafted that river with Gene and Melissa.

"Tonight, as soon as it gets dark, I'm supposed to drive

up the road for a mile and park the car near the trail to the river. They want me to walk down to the river and follow the trail until it curves around the cliff side. I'm supposed to leave the money there and drive home."

"What then?"

"They didn't say."

It was a strange plan. The trail from the road to the picnic area was the only way in or out. On the other hand, at night, the location was pretty isolated and the kidnapper would see anyone who tried to follow Gene.

"I'm going to take them the money," Martin said.

Gene looked startled. "Forget that. I was crazy to ask you before."

"Someone has to wait here in case Melissa comes home."

"I can't ask you to do this for me."

"You're a good friend, Gene. And I'm not asking for your permission."

Gene started to argue, but the determination he saw on Martin's face stopped him.

"Thank you," he whispered. "I'll never forget this."

It was cold in the desert that night, and Martin was wearing jeans and a windbreaker to fight the chill. The bag of money bumped against his legs as he descended toward the river. Tucked in his waistband was a licensed .45-caliber automatic. A hunting knife hung from his belt in a scabbard. Martin had a simple plan. He would kneecap the person who came for the money, then torture him until he told Martin where to find Melissa Arnold and named everyone involved in the kidnappings.

In sunlight, this was a beautiful spot—high red cliffs, carefully cultivated greenery at the jump-off spot, and the always soothing shush of the rapidly flowing water. At night, with the possibility of a killer lurking in the dark, the spot lost a lot of its glamour.

There was no light except the stars and a half-moon, so Martin moved slowly. It was about a quarter mile until the cliff jutted out where the river turned. The first rapids, a gentle class two, was a short distance past the bend. The trail narrowed where the river curved. A little ways on it dwindled to a footpath. Martin walked past the curve of the rock and looked around. There was scrub brush and not much else except for the high cliff wall. If someone was lurking behind one of the many outcroppings of rock, he wouldn't be able to see them. Martin left the money then walked back along the path and hid in the shadows.

Nothing happened for forty minutes. Then Martin heard a muffled footfall. Clouds suddenly moved across the moon and Martin could barely make out the person bent over the gym bag. He tried for a better look and dislodged a rock. In the stillness the tumbling stone sounded like a stack of bottles shattering in a supermarket aisle. The kidnapper turned and Martin went for his gun. While he was leveling the .45 he heard the crack of a gunshot and felt searing pain in his left shoulder. Martin staggered a few paces, then fell. His head struck the ground. Struggling to stay conscious, Martin fired a shot to discourage the kidnapper from coming over to finish him off.

Two more shots rang out and Martin crawled for cover.

Something splashed in the water. Martin peered around the rock. Two muzzle flashes lit up a small raft as it floated rapidly downriver. Martin came up shooting, but the raft was around the bend in the river and out of sight. His shoulder felt like it was on fire. He became nauseated and his legs gave way. Adding to his misery was the knowledge that his incompetence may have cost Melissa Arnold her life.

Martin stumbled up the trail, which seemed impossibly steep and long. After what seemed like hours, he reached his car. He had to fight to stay conscious during the drive to Gene Arnold's house and he let himself collapse on the car horn as soon as he came to a stop in the front yard. Gene was at his side in moments, blanching at the extent of Martin's bleeding as he pulled his friend from the car. With a grunt, he slung Martin's good arm across his shoulder and supported him as they crossed the yard. When they were inside, Gene called the hospital. Then he called the sheriff.

9

"Feel up to talking, Martin?" Detective Norm Chisholm of the Laurel County Sheriff's Office asked as soon as he walked into Martin's hospital room.

"Sit down. I've been expecting you. Any word yet on Melissa?"

Norm shook his head.

"How's Gene doing?"

"Not good. You two weren't acting very smart."

"Don't make me feel any worse than I do already. Gene wouldn't let me call the police. He was terrified that the kidnapper would kill Melissa." Martin's features clouded and his voice caught. "The way the FBI handled Patty's stakeout really spooked him."

Chisholm had no comeback for that, so he asked Martin to tell him what had happened by the river. When Alvarez was through, Chisholm brought Martin up to date.

"We sent a forensic crew to the take-out point down-river from where you were shot. That's where the kidnapper left the river, but we don't have a clue to who he is."

"Nothing?"

Norm shook his head. "Martin, what kind of couple are they?"

"Melissa and Gene?"

The detective nodded.

"Gene worships her."

"And Melissa? She seem happy?"

"Desert Grove is a change from the big city, and there is the age difference," he answered after a pause. "Why do you ask?"

"Gene never said anything to you about marital problems?"

"No, he didn't, Norm. Where is this going?"

He shrugged. "Probably nowhere. I'm just ruminating."

When Norm left, Martin called Gene Arnold, who seemed inconsolable. The pain pills the doctor had given Martin dulled his senses, but not enough to banish the guilt he felt for failing his friend.

10

When Norm Chisholm walked into Ramon Quiroz's office two days later he looked excited. The detective sat across from the DA and handed him an affidavit signed by Aaron Flynn.

"I want you to write up an affidavit for a search warrant for Gene Arnold's house, his cabin near the Meander River, his car, and Melissa Arnold's car. You can use Aaron's affidavit to establish probable cause."

Quiroz looked puzzled. "What's going on?"

"You know that court reporters type a kind of shorthand onto a strip of paper in a stenograph machine while court is in session."

Quiroz nodded.

"Well, there's a computer disk in the machine that acts as a backup. When a lawyer needs a transcript, the court reporter puts the disk in her computer and uses a software program that translates the stenographic notes into English. Flynn needs to get started on Paul McCann's appeal. He called up Judge Schrieber to find out who's going to prepare the transcript of McCann's trial now that Melissa Arnold is missing. A couple of other lawyers had the same question about their cases because Melissa was their court reporter. The judge told Flynn that he'd arranged for another court reporter to prepare the transcripts, but she can't do it because they can't find the disks or Melissa Arnold's notes. They've checked her office at the courthouse and they called Gene. He says they're not in his house. The judge thinks they could be in Melissa's car, but the car is still missing. The notes are essential, right?"

"Sure. When you appeal a conviction the appeals court looks through the record to see if the judge made a mistake during the trial that could have affected the verdict. Without the record, there can't be an appeal."

"Okay. I want to search Gene's house and that little cabin he keeps by the Meander River for Melissa's notes. That will make the search legal because they're government property."

"Why don't you just ask Gene to let you look around?"

"I don't want to alert him. Gene's become a suspect."

"You're not serious."

"There's nothing concrete yet. The neighbors say that Gene and Melissa have been arguing pretty heavily recently. She may have been thinking of leaving him."

"You think he killed her and faked everything?" Quiroz asked incredulously. "Martin was there when he talked to the kidnappers on the phone."

"He was there when a call came in, but he didn't hear the other side of the conversation. Gene could have arranged for someone to call him, then he could have gone upriver to Angel Ford and rafted downriver to the drop."

Quiroz shook his head. "What if Martin had gone back to Gene's immediately, instead of waiting? Gene wouldn't have been there. It would have given the whole plot away."

"No. He'd just tell Martin that the kidnappers called, told him where to find Melissa, he drove there, and his wife wasn't where they said she would be, or something like that."

"So do you think that Gene was involved in the Alvarez kidnapping?"

Chisholm thought for a moment before shaking his head.

"No, that was Paul McCann, all the way. But Dobbs got everyone thinking that there was a third conspirator out there, and maybe that gave Gene the idea for his fake kidnapping."

"I don't buy it. I know Gene. He couldn't kill someone, and he worshiped Melissa."

"Ramon, you've been in this business long enough to know that anyone can kill under the right circumstances. Anyway, I'm not saying that Gene's guilty, but he is a suspect. Maybe this is a wild-goose chase, but I wouldn't bet on it."

11

Two days later, at nine in the evening, Martin Alvarez's phone rang. It was Gene. He sounded on the verge of hysteria.

"I'm in jail. They're saying I killed Melissa."

"Try to calm down, Gene. Is anyone with you who can hear what you're saying?"

"Ramon, Norm Chisholm. I know these guys. I can't believe they're doing this."

"I'm coming down now to see you. Be strong and do not say anything. If they try to talk to you ask for the Miranda rights. Do you understand?"

"Yes. Thank you, Martin."

"Put Ramon on."

A moment later the DA was on the phone.

"What the fuck are you doing, Ramon?"

"This is hard for me, too, Martin, but we've got evidence."

"That Gene murdered his wife?"

"Yes."

"Bullshit. Gene's the gentlest person I know. You fucked up."

"We searched Gene's cabin, the Meander River place. The clothes Melissa was wearing on the day she disappeared were stuffed into a dresser drawer. They were covered with blood. We haven't done a DNA test yet, but the lab's done some preliminary tests. It's Melissa's blood type. We also found her car parked behind the cabin."

"Then someone planted the stuff. Gene's not stupid. If he killed her he'd never leave incriminating evidence around."

"I'm not going to get into this with you, Martin. I'm the elected DA in this county and I've got to do my job."

Martin held his tongue. Ramon was right. It would just get Quiroz's back up if he tried to throw his weight around.

"Can I visit Gene?"

"Yeah, but you'll become a witness if he talks to you about the case."

"I'll keep that in mind. What about you? Are you going to grill him?"

"No. Gene's so messed up right now that a judge would toss out anything he said. If he killed Melissa I'll nail him, but I want to do this right."

They were keeping Gene away from the other prisoners at the end of the cell block. The sheriff had put a suicide watch on him and a guard was sitting outside his cell. Arnold was lying on a metal cot, staring at the ceiling. The guard let Martin into the cell door and he sat on the edge of the cot.

"I didn't kill her."

Martin put his hand on his friend's shoulder. "I know that, Gene."

"She was everything to me." His eyes watered. "My life's . . . I mean, Jesus, Martin . . ."

Gene sobbed so hard that his body shook. He drew up his knees and rolled into a fetal position facing the concrete wall.

"She was going to leave me. She said she was bored, that I bored her. I told her I'd go anywhere, just to be with her."

"Ah, Gene."

Martin reached for Gene's shoulder and gave it a reassuring squeeze. Gradually, Gene's breathing steadied and he wiped his eyes, but he still wouldn't look at Martin.

"I don't care what they do to me."

"You've got to care. You didn't kill her. If you don't fight, the real killer will get away."

"It doesn't matter. They showed me her clothes. They were drenched with blood. She's dead. Finding who killed her won't bring her back."

"Listen to me, Gene. Nobody knows how you feel better than I do. Nobody. But you can't give up. You've got to fight."

Gene didn't answer.

"Do you have any idea what happened, why the clothes and her car were found at the cabin?"

Gene shook his head.

"The cabin is almost two hours away. If the kidnapper was some stranger he wouldn't know about the cabin."

That got Gene's attention.

"There . . . there was someone else. She had a lover."

"Do you know who?"

"She wouldn't say." Gene leaned his head against the wall and shut his eyes. "She could be cruel, Martin. There was a side to her that you didn't know."

Gene's head bowed.

"I'm not much in bed. She was so young, so vigorous. I couldn't please her. She taunted me. Made fun of me. And she said there was this man, someone who . . . who made her feel . . ."

"People say things they don't mean," Martin managed. "Stupid things." Gene opened his eyes and looked directly at Martin.

"I don't think she ever loved me. I think she was escaping from something and used me to get away. As soon as she had the time to really look at me, she realized the mistake she'd made."

"Don't run yourself down like this. You've been through so much you're not thinking straight. I've seen Melissa and you together. She did care," Martin lied. "She couldn't fake that."

Gene turned away. To Martin he seemed the very image of hopelessness.

Martin made it home from the jail at midnight. His wound ached, but his heart ached more, and his mind was racing. After twenty minutes of tossing and turning in bed, he gave up.

It was a hot night, but there was usually a cool breeze on the veranda. Martin filled a glass with Scotch and ice and sat down by the pool. The stars were bright and there were few clouds. If he had never known Patty, it might have been a perfect moment, but Patty was dead, Gene Arnold was locked up in the Laurel County jail, and someone was laughing at everyone. But who?

Lester Dobbs had testified that Paul McCann called someone on his cell phone after he murdered Patty. Whom did he call? Suddenly Martin sat up straight. Did McCann call anyone? The only reason everyone believed that a third man was involved in Patty's kidnapping was because Lester Dobbs claimed to have overheard Paul's phone conversation in the desert.

Alvarez took a sip of Scotch and let his mind wander. What if Dobbs had made up the story about the third man? Dobbs had been out of jail when Melissa was kidnapped. Did anyone know where he'd been at the crucial times? There was definitely another person with Dobbs at the Alvarez drop site, but maybe there were only two people—not three—involved in the plot to kidnap Patty Alvarez.

It was time to talk to Lester Dobbs.

Dobbs had been living in a trailer park on the outskirts of town; a privilege he'd earned when he agreed to turn state's evidence. His trailer was at the far end of the last row; beyond it were wide-open spaces. Martin neared the trailer door. Somewhere in the hills a coyote howled. The sound unnerved him. He collected himself before knocking on the metal door.

No one answered the knock. Martin strained to hear movement inside the trailer. A stiff wind rattled the metal siding.

"Dobbs! Open up!"

The coyote howled again and an eerie wailing answered his call. The coyotes were hunting. So was he.

Martin took out his .45 and opened the door. He paused for a moment, listening. Then he stepped inside praying that Dobbs was not waiting for him in the dark. Another step. Nothing. Martin touched a switch on the wall. Light filled the narrow confines of the trailer. Martin turned slowly and saw a sink filled with unwashed pots and dishes and a countertop littered with empty beer cans. Dobbs's clothes were scattered along the floor leading to his bed. Then he noticed a shape under the covers on the bed, and the hair stood up on the nape of his neck.

"Lester," he called, but he knew that Dobbs was not going to answer.

Martin pulled back the thin green blanket and the sheet, then stepped back and stared. A deep, jagged gash started on one side of Dobbs's throat and ended at the other. The sheets were coated with dried blood. If Dobbs knew anything about the identity of Melissa's kidnapper, he had taken the information to the grave.

"He's been dead for two days," Norm Chisholm told Martin. They were sitting in a police car. It was seven in the morning. Alvarez was cradling a cup of steaming-hot coffee. It tasted like battery acid but helped him keep his eyes open.

"Did anything in Dobbs's trailer connect him to Melissa?"

"Nothing so far, and the forensic guys have been over every inch of the place. But I didn't expect to find anything. We questioned Dobbs as soon as Gene reported the kidnapping. He had an alibi."

"Then why kill him?" Martin asked. "It doesn't make any sense."

"Dobbs must have known something that threatened the kidnapper. Maybe he lied when he testified that he didn't know the person McCann called after he killed Patty."

"Does this let Gene off the hook?" Martin asked hopefully.

"Afraid not. Dobbs was killed the night before we arrested Gene. Gene was alone all evening. He has no alibi."

12

A week after Dobbs's murder, Paul McCann's wife was waiting for Aaron Flynn by the door to Judge Schrieber's courtroom.

"Will you get him out?" Joan asked, anxiously twisting the strap of her purse. Her blue eyes were sunk in their sockets and there were dark shadows around them.

"I think so, Joan, but there are no guarantees in this business." Flynn patted her on the shoulder and smiled. "We'll have our answer soon."

Joan started to say something, but she stopped when

she saw Martin Alvarez bearing down on her husband's attorney.

"Ramon told me what you're trying to do, Flynn."

"I'm trying to do my job, Martin. This isn't personal."

"It's personal to me," Alvarez said in a chilling tone. "Your client is safer in jail, safer on death row, than he'll be if he walks out of this courthouse."

"Martin, this is not the way," Flynn said in a conciliatory tone.

"McCann killed my wife. If the law doesn't punish him I won't wait to find out if God will. Let him know that."

"You're asking for a new trial, Mr. Flynn?" Judge Schrieber said. He had read Flynn's motion and the memorandum of law in support of it and he looked very troubled.

"Yes, Your Honor. My memo sets out the relevant cases and statutes. Read together, they hold that you must order a new trial if an appeal can't be prosecuted because the reporter's notes have been lost or destroyed through no fault of the defendant, every reasonable effort has been made to find a substitute for the missing record, and the defendant has made a prima facie showing of error or unfairness in the trial.

"I've submitted a list of potential trial errors that I would have asserted as bases for reversal on appeal. There is no substitute for the missing record of Mr. McCann's trial. The police have made every reasonable effort to recover it and the record is missing through no fault of Mr. McCann."

"What do you say to Mr. Flynn's argument, Mr. Quiroz?" the judge asked.

Ramon rose slowly, as if trying to delay the inevitable.

"I agree that Mr. Flynn has raised several issues that could lead to reversal, though I don't think they actually would."

"But that's not the test, is it?" Judge Schrieber asked. "He doesn't have to prove he would win. You aren't asserting that?"

"No. I agree that Mr. McCann has met the test of making his prima facie case on the possibility of error in the trial. I don't agree on much else, though. For instance, the police have searched pretty thoroughly, but they're not through looking. I think the court should give them more time."

"Where are they going to look, Your Honor?" Flynn asked. "They searched both of Mr. Arnold's residences, Mrs. Arnold's car, her office, his office. This appeal has to be prosecuted quickly. We can't wait indefinitely in the hope that years from now the transcription tapes may show up."

"Mr. Quiroz," the judge asked, "do you have anything more than wishful thinking that leads you to believe that the lost record in this case will soon be recovered?"

Ramon shook his head. "No, Your Honor, I don't. I just feel that it's too soon to give up."

"Is there a substitute for the missing record?"

"No, Your Honor. None that I know of. It seems that the notes and backup disks for every case that Mrs. Arnold had on appeal were with her when she was abducted and there are no copies."

"If that's so, and you have no real hope of finding the originals, and the defendant had made a prima facie case for the possibility of reversal, what choice do I have except to grant this motion for a new trial?"

"We would argue that Mr. McCann is at fault here. How do we know that he wasn't involved in the kidnapping of Mrs. Arnold?"

"Your Honor," Flynn retorted, "this is an argument that grows out of sheer desperation. Mr. Quiroz prepared the warrant that led to the arrest of Gene Arnold for his wife's murder. There has never been a hint of a suggestion that Mr. McCann, who was in jail at all times relevant to the Arnold case, had anything to do with the second kidnapping."

"Mr. Quiroz?" the judge asked.

Ramon knew when he was whipped and he simply shook his head.

"Mr. Flynn, if I could find any legal reason to deny your motion I would do so," the judge said. "But there isn't any and I am sworn to follow the law, even when I don't want to." He paused. "I am going to order a new trial for Mr. McCann."

"Your Honor, I have a further motion," Flynn said quickly. "I move for an order dismissing the charges against Mr. McCann. If this case were retried today it would have to result in a judgment of acquittal as soon as the state rested. Mr. McCann has always maintained his complete innocence and we have always contended that Lester Dobbs accused Mr. McCann in order to escape his just punishment for Mrs. Alvarez's murder. Without the testimony of Lester Dobbs there is no evidence connecting Mr. McCann to the kidnapping of Patty Alvarez."

"Mr. Quiroz, is there an official copy of Mr. Dobbs's trial testimony?" Judge Schrieber asked.

"No, sir."

"Did Mr. Dobbs testify in the grand jury?"

"Yes, but there's no transcript."

"Even if there was," Flynn interjected, "it wouldn't be admissible against Mr. McCann because I had no opportunity to cross-examine Mr. Dobbs."

"I believe Mr. Flynn is correct," the judge said. "Mr. Quiroz, is there any legally permissible way to present the testimony of Lester Dobbs to a jury in a second trial?"

"Not that I can think of at this moment."

Judge Schrieber was lost in thought. He tapped his pen against the dais. When he spoke he looked very unhappy.

"Mr. Flynn, I am not going to dismiss the charges against Mr. McCann today. New evidence may be discovered. However, I am very reluctant to keep Mr. McCann in jail under the current circumstances.

"Mr. Quiroz, I am going to give you one week to convince me that there is a legal basis for keeping Mr. McCann in jail. If you can't, I'm going to be forced to set him free."

When Ramon Quiroz returned to the district attorney's office he found a furious Martin Alvarez waiting for him.

"What are you going to do about this?"

"There's nothing I can do, Martin. Unless we find new evidence, McCann is going to walk."

"That's insane."

Quiroz shook his head. "That's the law."

"There's got to be something you can do."

"Martin, I've been dreading this since I learned that Melissa's notes disappeared. I once went through something just like it with Gene Arnold and I knew what could happen. I was hoping that Flynn wasn't sharp enough to figure out what to do."

"What do you mean you went through something like this with Gene?"

"Remember when Bob Champion and Gene were partners?"

Martin nodded.

"Bob represented some young kid charged with auto theft. They picked the jury and the state put on some witnesses. There was a three-day weekend because of a national holiday. When the trial started again no one could find the kid. He just took off. Judge Milbrandt decided that the defendant's failure to appear was willful and ordered the lawyers to go on with the trial in his absence. The jury found the defendant guilty. The judge couldn't sentence him unless he was present, so he issued an arrest warrant.

"Three years ago they caught the kid in Canada. He was sent back for sentencing. Bob had retired by this time and Gene filed a notice of appeal, but the court reporter couldn't find her notes. They were in a box of old transcription tapes that she'd destroyed. Gene couldn't appeal because there wasn't any way to prepare the transcript without the notes, but he found that statute Flynn cited and the court had to order a new trial."

Martin left the DA's office. As he drove home he remembered that Joan McCann was Gene Arnold's legal secretary. If she knew about the auto theft case, she would also know that Judge Schrieber would have to order a new trial for Paul if Melissa's notes were lost. Did Joan love her husband enough to kill Melissa Arnold and Lester Dobbs? Was the ransom demand merely a smoke screen that had hidden a plot to free Paul McCann from prison? Was she capable of committing a double murder?

Martin tried to remember everything he knew about Joan McCann. She had exhibited signs of tremendous stress lately. Martin had assumed that she was worrying about her husband's fate, but what if her gnawed nails and weight loss had been physical manifestations of unbearable guilt.

13

A week passed. There were no new clues in the murder of Lester Dobbs, Melissa Arnold's body and the tapes were still missing, and Ramon Quiroz had not been able to come up with a legal theory that would keep Paul McCann in jail. Early Friday morning, Quiroz and Aaron Flynn slipped in the back door of the courthouse and stole down the corridor to Judge Schrieber's chambers. It was 7:00 A.M. and no one else was around. Ramon had phoned the judge the previous evening and convinced him that meeting in secrecy was necessary because of the threat that Martin Alvarez had made to Flynn.

"Good morning, Ramon, Aaron," Judge Schrieber said. He did not look happy as he signed the paper that sat in front of him. "I'm dismissing the case against Paul McCann and signing this release order. Everything has been done over at the jail to assure that McCann can walk out the door the minute you present this. I've arranged for you to go in and leave by the back door. I also instructed the jail personnel that anyone who leaks McCann's release is headed to prison for contempt. That should ensure your client's safety, at least for today."

Flynn drove his car behind the jail and knocked on the rear door. Sheriff Cobb was waiting with McCann, who was dressed in the clothes in which he had been arrested. The sheriff read the release order and told Paul he could go. Cobb looked as happy about this state of affairs as the judge.

As soon as they were in the car Flynn's client closed his eyes, put his head back, and said, "Hallelujah. I am so fucking grateful to be out of that hellhole that I might actually go to church."

"If I were you, the church would be in some city on the other side of the planet. I don't think Martin Alvarez is going to let this rest."

"Well, fuck him," Paul answered angrily. "Alvarez doesn't scare me."

"What are your plans?" Flynn asked.

"A hot shower, an edible meal, a good fuck, and a decent night's sleep."

"And after that?"

"I don't know. I'm thinking of moving. This trial showed me how many friends I have in Desert Grove. Besides, Sunnyvale is dead and your fees about wiped me out."

Flynn pulled the car as close as he could to Paul's front

door and prayed that Martin Alvarez wasn't out in the desert with a sniper scope. As soon as the car stopped Joan rushed out of the house. Her arms were around Paul's neck before he was standing. He let her kiss him, but Flynn didn't see much fire on his part. Then Joan walked around to Flynn's window and placed her hand over his.

"I'll never forget you for this, Mr. Flynn. God bless you."

14

The call from Joan McCann came at eleven o'clock. To Martin, she sounded like a woman on the brink of hysteria.

"I'm calling from my car. I'm following Paul. You've got to help me."

"How can you be following Paul? He's in jail."

"The judge dismissed his case, this morning. They sneaked him out of jail because they were afraid of you. Then . . . then he beat me up. He said things to me . . ."

She started to cry. Martin did not understand half of what she said, but he understood that Paul McCann was leaving town without his wife.

"He killed Patty. I can prove it."

Now Martin was completely focused.

"How do you know that?"

"Mr. Flynn came back an hour ago. He was very upset. He took Paul into the den, but I listened at the door. Someone called Aaron at home and said he had Melissa's notes and the disks. He wanted two hundred thousand dollars for them. Aaron told him it wasn't a scam. When Patty was murdered, she was wearing a topaz ring you'd given her for your anniversary, right?"

Martin's heart lurched. He remembered Patty's exclamation of joy when she saw the present and recalled the kiss she'd given him.

"Yes, she was wearing the ring. The police held back that information. How did you know?"

"Aaron told Paul that the caller described it."

"What did Paul say to Flynn?"

"He was angry. He claimed he didn't have two hundred thousand dollars. He said he thought the caller was a con artist. They argued for a while. Then Mr. Flynn left. As soon as he was gone, Paul started packing. I asked him what he was doing and he told me to shut up. He . . . he said I made him sick, that he was leaving me for good."

Joan burst into sobs again and Martin waited for her to calm down.

"What do you want from me?"

"I want you to stop him. Before he gets the money and escapes."

"What money?"

"The ransom money."

"How do you know he has it?"

"He's going to Laurel Canyon State Park, to the caves. He must have hidden it there. Why else would he go to the park in the middle of the night? If he has the ransom money, Mr. Alvarez, he killed Patty."

"Why are you calling me? Why aren't you calling the police?"

"I don't want him arrested. I want him dead."

Laurel Canyon State Park was a twisting, turning maze of dry riverbeds and towering cliffs that was known to rock climbers all over the world. At the base of some of these cliffs were caves. There was a parking area near the entrance and Martin found Joan McCann parked at the far end of the lot where she'd told him she'd be. McCann's car was at the head of a trail that led down to the caves.

"He has a fifteen-minute head start. You'd better hurry. He's on the Bishop's Point trail. It's where he proposed to me," Joan added bitterly.

Martin had been to the park many times and knew the trails by heart. He put his gun in the waistband of his pants and grabbed a flashlight before starting on a path that led up to Bishop's Point, a lookout spot with an awesome view, and wound down to the desert floor, where there were several caves.

It took twenty minutes to reach the base of the cliff along the narrow footpath. Martin switched on the flashlight for a few seconds and played it over the rock-strewn floor at the foot of the cliff face. Then he walked toward the mouth of the nearest cave. There were large boulders on both sides of the entrance. Martin edged around one rock formation and peered into the cave hoping to see the beam of Paul's flashlight, but there was only stygian darkness.

"You son of a bitch," McCann screamed, just before he cracked Martin's cheekbone with his pistol. Martin staggered backward and swung the flashlight. It caught McCann on a raised forearm but didn't stop him. McCann aimed a punch at Martin's wound. The pain was blinding. A kick to the knee knocked Martin's legs out from under him and sent him to the ground. He tried to get up, but McCann kicked him in the ribs, then stomped on his head. Just when Martin thought he would pass out the beating stopped.

McCann collected Martin's automatic from the ground, where he'd dropped it after the first, surprise blow. Martin was certain that there were broken bones in his face. His ribs stung, but he didn't think they were broken. He struggled into a sitting position.

"Did Joan tell you I was coming here?" McCann asked in a hate-filled voice.

Martin held his tongue. McCann glared at him.

"It doesn't matter. You're not here because of that bitch. You're here for the money. Well, you'll see the money, all right. You're going to dig for it. Then you and I are both going to disappear. Now get up."

He gestured with the pistol and Martin made it to his feet with only one minor stumble. McCann pointed the flashlight beam into the cave and Martin preceded him inside. It was cold, but Martin was in too much pain to notice. The cave was deep and the roof, which was about nine feet high at the entrance, quickly dropped, so that they were soon moving forward in a half crouch. After they had walked for fifteen minutes the roof rose dramatically and they found themselves in a high-ceilinged chamber. McCann told Alvarez to stop in front of a large pile of rocks that looked as if they had been undisturbed for centuries.

"Start digging. The bag is at the bottom of that mess. It took me almost two hours to put it there."

McCann propped the flashlight on a mound of rocks

on the other side of the cave so that it pointed at the pile that concealed the money. Martin started throwing rocks from the top of the pile off to one side. Every movement hurt, but digging in the rock pile was keeping him alive and giving him time to think.

After a while McCann eased himself into a sitting position against the far wall. His gun was aimed at Martin, who was certain it would soon grow heavy. As he dug he kept an eye out for a few heavy rocks. Every time he spotted one, he moved it to a spot where he could grab it quickly.

Martin's chance came after he had been working for half an hour. The barrel of the handgun wobbled then sagged downward. Then McCann leaned his head back and closed his eyes for a second. Martin was moving before he opened them. The first rock hit McCann in the forehead. He screamed and fired, but he wasn't aiming. Martin was on him before he could focus, smashing down with a second rock that sent McCann's head ricocheting off the wall, stunning him. A moment later Martin had the gun.

"Look around you, Paul," Alvarez said when he was certain that McCann was fully conscious of his situation. "This cave is where your body is going to rot."

McCann paled.

"You should be happy. I'm going to bury you with your blood money. You'll have an eternity to spend it in hell."

Anger suffused Martin's features as he aimed the gun.

"Goddamn you for killing Patty," he said, but he never pulled the trigger. Another gun fired from behind Martin. The explosion reverberated in the cave. Martin pitched forward, unconscious.

Part V

Deep Cover

THIRTY

"I don't know how much time passed before I regained consciousness," Alvarez said. "When I came to I wished I hadn't."

He paused for a moment, reliving the agony of those moments.

"How did you get out of the cave?" Kate asked.

"Joan McCann brought the police. She was attacked while she was waiting for me."

"Who . . . ?"

"She doesn't know. The person was wearing a mask. He put a gun to her head and forced her to tell where I'd gone, then she was knocked out. When she came to I hadn't returned, so she called the police. I was barely alive when the search party found me and Paul."

"McCann was still there?"

"He was dead, shot between the eyes. The ransom money was gone."

"Did Aaron Flynn have an alibi?"

"He was never a suspect. Six months later he quietly left town. I had no idea where he'd moved until today."

"Did anyone else connected with the case move away?"

"Joan. She left within three months. She visited me several times at the hospital while I was recuperating. The last time, she told me that she couldn't stay in Desert Grove any longer."

"Was there a theory about the identity of Paul McCann's killer?"

"No. I'm certain that McCann and Lester Dobbs killed Patty, and that the same person murdered McCann and Dobbs. In the end, the most widely accepted theory was that an outsider was behind the plot."

"Do you believe that?"

"Absolutely not," Alvarez said, his voice as hard as granite.

"What happened to Gene Arnold?"

"I hired the best criminal lawyer in Arizona to represent Gene. He convinced Ramon that there wasn't enough evidence to hold him. It was obvious to everyone that Melissa's clothing and the car had been planted at the cabin. The crime lab was all over the place and couldn't find any evidence that Melissa or Gene had been there recently. Melissa's body was never recovered, so there was no forensic evidence connecting Gene to the murder. All they had were the arguments and Ramon wasn't going to prosecute Gene on the basis of a few domestic spats."

"Were there any new developments after you were shot?"

"Not until now."

"Can you think of anything else that might help, Mr. Alvarez?"

After a moment Martin shook his head. "You realize, of

course, that Gene's death may have nothing to do with what happened here. It was a long time ago."

"That's true, but Aaron Flynn . . . The coincidence bothers me."

"Life is full of coincidences."

Kate stood and extended her hand. "Thanks for seeing me."

Alvarez took her hand and held it for a moment before releasing it. Kate handed him her card.

"If you think of anything else, please call me."

Martin nodded just as his assistant appeared on the patio.

"Anna will see you to your car. Good luck."

Martin Alvarez watched Kate Ross cross the terrace. Though she looked nothing like Patty, the investigator reminded him of her. They both had the same purposeful stride, and Patty had always shown a core of strength that he sensed in Kate Ross. Alvarez closed his good eye and rubbed his temples. There were times when he imagined that his wife was still with him, taking her morning ride, just out of sight and soon to return. Thoughts like that were calming, like a belief that he and Patty would be reunited in a life after death.

There were other times when memories of Patty stoked an impotent rage. It was that rage that was building as Martin entered the hacienda and went to his office. As soon as he closed his door he picked up the phone. A man answered in Spanish.

"You know who this is?" Alvarez asked.

"Yes."

"I have work for you. Come on the evening plane."

THIRTY-ONE

Saturday morning, Daniel bolted out of sleep thinking that he was still in his cell. When he realized that he was safe in Kate's guest room he fell back on the bed. Daniel was normally an early riser, but he had slept past nine. Just being in a place where the lights were not on twenty-four hours a day and screams and moans did not jerk him awake at all hours had been a luxury greater than silk sheets.

There was a note from Kate on the kitchen table. She had taken an early flight to Arizona and hadn't wanted to wake him. He wished she had. He remembered how happy he had been to see her waiting for him at the jail and he missed her already.

Daniel reread Kate's note. He liked holding something that she had touched and reading something that she had written just for him. Kate was very kind and very thoughtful. There hadn't been many people like that in Daniel's life. In truth, Kate was the single positive note in the sorry mess that had become his life. Despite their barely knowing each other, Kate had made sure that a top defense attorney represented him, she was paying some of his legal fees, and she was letting him stay with her—knowing that he was charged with murder. Her support conveyed her complete confidence in his innocence. He couldn't imagine getting through his ordeal without her.

After breakfast, Daniel wandered aimlessly around the house, flipped channels on the television, and quickly lost interest in a science-fiction novel he found in Kate's bookcase. Its plot wasn't nearly as surreal as his life. What had happened to him? A little more than a week ago he'd been living a dream he had never dared imagine as a child. Now someone had stolen that dream. Daniel wanted his life back.

One of the worst things about jail was being forced to stay inside. Daniel realized that he needed to get out in the world. He called Joe Molinari.

"How's the convict?" Molinari joked.

"I'm cooped up at Kate Ross's house and I'm going nuts."

"Ross, huh? That'll make juicy office gossip."

"There's nothing to gossip about. I'm hiding from reporters and Kate was kind enough to put me up."

"Of course."

"You're a pig, Molinari."

"I assume you didn't call just to insult me."

"True. Do you want to go for a run? I've got to get some exercise."

"Sounds good."

"Can you drive me over to my apartment so I can get my car and my running gear?"

"No problem. See you soon."

A fire-engine-red Porsche pulled up in front of Kate's house. Joe honked the horn and waved.

"Jesus, Molinari, I'm trying to be inconspicuous."

"Don't worry," Joe said as he peeled out, "you're too ugly to attract attention. Everyone will be looking at me."

Daniel relaxed and enjoyed the ride. It was cool, but the sun brought everyone out and the streets of northwest Portland were crowded with strolling couples.

"Go around the block once," Daniel instructed when they were a few streets from his apartment building. "I want to make certain that there aren't any reporters waiting for me."

"This celebrity thing is going to your head. Who do you think you are, O.J.?"

"Hey, I'm feeling a lot of empathy for O.J. at the moment."

As the Porsche cruised by Daniel's apartment house, a large man in jeans, a black windbreaker, and a baseball cap came out of the front door and crossed the street to a black pickup truck. He looked familiar, but Daniel was certain he had never seen him in the building. When they came around the block the next time, the pickup was gone.

Molinari parked in the street and Daniel ran up the stairs. Kate had been right about the chaos inside. The cops had obviously never heard that neatness counts. Daniel didn't feel like dealing with the mess right away. He grabbed his workout gear and changed in the bathroom, then he stuffed some extra clothes in a duffel bag and ran down to the small lot at the side of the building where his car was parked.

With Molinari following behind, Daniel drove past the zoo and the Forestry Center and parked up the road from the Vietnam Memorial. The two men stretched before taking off through the woods along one of the trails that wound through Washington Park. It took a while for Daniel to get his rhythm, and it didn't help that the first half mile was uphill.

"Feel like telling me what's going on?" Molinari asked.

"You shouldn't get involved."

"From what I can see, you don't have too many people on your side. I'd like to be one of them."

Daniel knew that he probably shouldn't talk about his case with Molinari, but Joe was one of the few people at the firm who'd stood by him. And he was smart. Maybe Joe would see something that he had missed. It would also be a relief to be able to talk about everything he'd kept bottled inside.

Daniel started with the night that Susan conned him into reviewing the discovery and ended with his arrest. The only part of the story he omitted was the call from Arthur Briggs and his presence at the cottage. The prosecutor couldn't prove he'd been at the scene of Briggs's murder and Daniel didn't want to make Joe Molinari a state's witness.

"Any brilliant insights you'd care to share?" Daniel asked when he was through.

"Not really, but it's sure a funny coincidence that Flynn got lucky again so soon after finding the Kaidanov letter."

"What do you mean?"

"Jaffe demolished Fairweather under oath. After Oregon Mutual sees a transcript of her testimony they'll be begging Reed, Briggs to settle and Flynn will collect a nice fat attorney's fee."

As they ran up a small rise Daniel suddenly remembered that Flynn had sent one of his associates to sit in on his hearing. An odd thought occurred to him. Did Flynn know what was going to happen when Fairweather took the stand? Was Flynn the guardian angel who sent Amanda the videotape of Fairweather's speech?

"You know, I just got a crazy idea," Molinari said as they started downhill. "Do you think it's possible that Aaron Flynn has a mole at Reed, Briggs?"

"Like in the spy novels?"

"Seriously, think about it. How did Kaidanov's letter get into the box of discovery? How did a tape from Arthur Briggs's office find its way to Amanda Jaffe?"

The trail narrowed and the men ran single file in silence until it widened giving Daniel time to think. He liked Flynn. He remembered how natural he'd been with Patrick Cummings. Daniel knew that Flynn was flamboyant and aggressive. He didn't want to think that he was dishonest.

"Someone at Geller could have included Kaidanov's letter by mistake when they compiled the discovery," Daniel said.

"You told me that everyone at Geller swears that they've never seen that letter or the Kaidanov report," Molinari countered.

"They would if they're lying."

"But how would someone at Geller know about Fairweather's case?" Joe insisted. "It has nothing to do with Geller Pharmaceuticals. If someone at Reed, Briggs sent Amanda that tape to help Flynn they could also have slipped the Kaidanov letter into the discovery."

"Okay, suppose you're right. Who's the mole?"

"Oregon Mutual was Briggs's client, so, technically, the suit against Fairweather was Briggs's case, but Brock Newbauer and Susan Webster were doing most of the work on it. They'd know about the videotape."

"Brock and Susan are also on the Insufort team," Daniel said.

"Something happened after you left that fits into my theory," Joe told Daniel. "Briggs called a meeting on the day he was killed to discuss what to do in the Insufort litigation. Brock Newbauer was complaining that he wanted Geller to settle, but Briggs wouldn't listen to him."

"Is Brock running the Geller defense now?"

"Technically, but I'm guessing that Susan is calling the shots."

"Why do you say that?"

"Brock only made partner because his family owns Newbauer Construction, one of our biggest clients. He's a joke around the firm. Haven't you noticed how long he takes for lunch, and have you ever smelled his breath when he gets back? He could never get a handle on a case as complex as the Insufort litigation. The science would be beyond him. Briggs represented the Newbauer account, which brings in mucho dinero. He had to baby-sit Brock to keep the client happy."

"And you said that Brock wanted Geller to settle?"

Molinari nodded.

"If Flynn does have a mole at Reed, Briggs that's exactly what he would want."

THIRTY-TWO

The next morning, the sun was hiding behind a lead sky and there was a threat of rain in the chill air. Daniel was sore from his run and he limped out of bed. After breakfast, he watched the first half of a Seattle Seahawks' game on TV, but Kate's house was beginning to feel claustrophobic. He remembered the mess in his apartment and drove over at halftime.

The apartment didn't look any better than it had the day before. Daniel turned on the football game and watched while he straightened up. Everything was in decent shape by the time the game ended. Daniel was wondering when his life would be put back together when the phone rang. His hand hovered over the receiver as he debated whether to take the call. He had no desire to talk to a reporter, but it could be a friend and it would be nice to talk to someone who cared enough to call.

"Hello?"

"Daniel Ames?" a man asked. He had an accent—Slavic, Russian perhaps.

"Who is this?"

"We have to meet."

The man sounded desperate.

"About what?" Daniel asked cautiously.

"I witnessed Arthur Briggs's murder." The answer was rushed. "I know you didn't kill him. That's why you're the only one I can trust."

The hair stood up on the back of Daniel's neck. "Dr. Kaidanov?"

"Will you meet with me?"

"Will you go to the police and tell them I'm innocent?" Daniel asked excitedly.

"We must talk first."

"Fine, where are you? I'll come right away."

"No, not in daylight. You might be followed. Tonight at ten come alone to Rest of Angels Cemetery. I'll meet you near Simon Prescott's mausoleum."

"You're joking?"

"I lost my sense of humor when those bastards tried to kill me at the lab."

"But a cemetery, after dark?"

"Rest of Angels is where my mother is buried. Are you going to be there?"

"Yeah, don't get excited."

"I've earned the right to be excited. I've been running for my life for almost a month. You should be able to relate to that."

As soon as Kaidanov told Daniel how to find the mausoleum, he hung up and Daniel dialed Kate's house, hoping that she was back from Arizona, but all he got was her answering machine.

THIRTY-THREE

Daniel left for Rest of Angels at 9:30 without having heard from Kate. The main gate closed at sundown. Kaidanov had instructed him to park in a housing development that was separated from the cemetery by a shallow ravine and a quarter acre of forest. Daniel put up the hood from his windbreaker. Heavy rain had turned the walls of the ravine to mire. He slid down one side then scrambled up the other. By the time he was out of the depression, he was shivering and covered with mud.

Rest of Angels sprawled across a hundred and twenty-five hilly and wooded acres overlooking the Columbia River and was surrounded by another hundred and seventy-five acres of forest. On summer days the cemetery was a serene and picturesque shelter for the dead. When Daniel broke out of the forest, the rain-slashed graveyard looked like a set from *Dracula*.

A cemetery after dark would never have been his first choice of a place to meet, especially with a murderer running loose. The mausoleums and monuments provided excellent cover for a killer. Daniel ran between the graves to the Prescott mausoleum, then ducked behind the crypt.

The rain and the biting wind were making him miserable and he pulled the strings of his hood tighter to protect his face, all the while looking around for Kaidanov. His senses were strained to the limit, but the downpour made it hard to hear and his hood limited his peripheral vision.

"Ames."

Daniel spun around, fist cocked. He held his punch when he recognized Kaidanov. The scientist looked as miserable as Daniel felt. Water ran down his face and beaded a mustache and beard that Daniel had not noticed in the picture on the liquor cabinet in Kaidanov's living room.

"You scared the shit out of me," Daniel said as he sagged against the tomb.

"We don't have much time," the Russian answered. He was shivering and his voice trembled from the cold. "I want you to tell Geller Pharmaceuticals that I'll testify that my study is a hoax."

"The results aren't real?" Daniel asked, stunned by Kaidanov's revelation.

"Of course not."

"And Insufort is safe?"

"I don't have time for this," Kaidanov said impatiently. "You tell Geller's people that I want money and protection. I'm not meeting anyone until I've been paid and all of the safety precautions have been arranged to my satisfaction."

"Why me?"

"Because I don't know who to trust at Reed, Briggs or Geller. I want one million dollars. That's cheap considering how much I'll save them. I also want a safe house and bodyguards." Kaidanov looked around nervously. "They tried to kill me at the lab. Then they tried again when they murdered Briggs."

"Who tried to kill you?"

"I don't know. I never met anyone. I received my instructions by phone or in the mail or at a drop. They paid me to transform that building into a lab and to phony up the study. They told me the results they wanted."

"Why did you do it?"

Kaidanov shrugged. "Gambling debts. They promised me enough to pay them and more. I was stupid. I believed them."

"Do you know who killed Arthur Briggs?"

"I'm sure it was the same person who tried to kill me at the lab, but I didn't see his face. Everything happened too fast. Arthur warned me and I got away. I was lucky at the lab, too." Kaidanov laughed. "That fucking monkey. It saved my life."

"The monkey that was shot?"

"I was seconds away from being set on fire when the little beast came out of nowhere. It was amazing. Its coat was solid flame and it still had the strength to attack." The Russian shook his head in awe. "The last thing I saw was its teeth sinking into the killer's shoulder."

Kaidanov shuddered. Blood, skin, and brains spattered Daniel's face. He stepped back instinctively, making a strangled sound as he stared in shock at the remains of Kaidanov's face. The scientist lurched forward and clutched Daniel's jacket. His back absorbed the next bullet. The explosion acted like a slap. Daniel shoved the body away and jumped behind the mausoleum, barely avoiding a bullet that nicked the edge of the crypt and sprayed him with rock chips.

Daniel sprinted between the graves toward another mausoleum. Someone was running parallel to him, several rows over. The killer pulled up and assumed a shooting stance. Daniel dove behind a stone angel just as the angel's head exploded.

Daniel scrambled forward, crablike, but he held out little hope of escape. It wouldn't take long for the killer to figure out that he was unarmed and helpless. He took a quick look around. The mausoleum was two rows away. The killer would expect him to head for it because it provided the best shelter, so he started circling back toward Kaidanov's body, hoping that the heavy clouds and rain would cloak his movements.

Daniel risked a look over his shoulder and saw a figure racing toward the mausoleum. As soon as it disappeared he leaped up and raced away. A gun fired and Daniel felt the wind track of a bullet speeding by his cheek. He shifted gears and ran all out, dodging behind the tallest monuments and widest headstones. Another bullet ripped the fabric of his hood and creased the side of his head, sending him sprawling headfirst into a granite slab. Fighting for consciousness, Daniel gritted his teeth and struggled to one knee, then tumbled back down. Footsteps pounded the ground, drawing closer. A shot. Daniel braced for the impact, but none came. Two more shots, but from opposite directions, then another and another. Daniel looked around. A figure was firing toward his assailant, who turned and fled.

"Stay down," Kate Ross yelled. Daniel crawled behind

a large headstone. His head was throbbing. When he touched the skin above his left ear, blood dampened his palm and pain flared in his temple.

Kate crouched beside him, a gun in her hand.

"Get up. We've got to go, *now*!"

Daniel braced himself on the headstone and levered himself to his feet, before doubling over from nausea. Kate gripped his arm.

"Suck it up and move."

Daniel stumbled forward like a drunk with Kate following, gun in hand. Gradually, his head cleared enough for him to get his bearings.

"Where's your car?"

"Over there," Daniel said, pointing toward the ravine where he'd come in. Kate worried that the shooter was waiting in the woods, but she angled toward the trees. Daniel had all he could do to keep his feet moving. At some point Kate took his arm, steadying him. Kate breathed a sigh of relief when they entered the woods without incident.

When they found Daniel's car, Kate took his keys and helped him into the passenger's seat, then went around to the driver's side. The dome light went on. Kate got a good look at Daniel's face and gasped. Daniel stared in the rearview mirror. His blood drenched the left side of his head and Kaidanov's blood and brains speckled his face and the front of his windbreaker.

"Oh, Jesus," he said as a wave of nausea rolled through his stomach. He pushed open the door and threw up on the macadam. Kate put a hand on his back.

"How badly are you hurt?" she asked.

Daniel ran the back of his hand across his mouth and squeezed his eyes tight.

"It's not all my blood," he managed. "Kaidanov . . ."

Another wave of nausea hit him and he gritted his teeth.

"The scientist you came to meet?" Kate asked.

Daniel nodded. "His body is back there by the mausoleum."

Kate made a decision. She punched in a number on her cell phone and Daniel looked at her.

"I'm getting you an ambulance."

"No," Daniel gasped. "They'll send me back to jail."

Kate gave their location to 911, then dialed another number.

"You're hurt and there's been a murder," she answered as she waited for the party on the other end to pick up.

Daniel was too weak to talk and almost too dizzy to think, but he shook his head. Kate grabbed his shoulder and squeezed.

"Do you trust me?" she asked.

Daniel used most of his energy to muster a nod.

"Then stick with me." A voice on the other end of the phone distracted her.

"Hello," she said. "It's Kate Ross, Amanda. I'm with Daniel Ames. We need you."

THIRTY-FOUR

When Billie Brewster and Zeke Forbus drove up, the medics were treating Daniel's head wound in the back of an ambulance. An officer was stationed at the rear of the ambulance, guarding Daniel. The detectives conferred with him for a few minutes. Then the officer pointed to Kate's car, where Kate Ross and Amanda Jaffe had taken shelter from the rain. Billie ran over and knocked on Kate's window. Kate got out of the car just as Forbus joined his partner.

"Why couldn't your boyfriend commit murder on a sunny afternoon?" he grumbled.

"Daniel didn't kill anyone," Kate snapped, too exhausted to be polite.

Forbus barked out a sour laugh and threw a thumb over his shoulder toward the uniform. "Harris told me the bullshit story you gave him about a mysterious stranger and your heroic rescue. Sounds a little like *Lethal Weapon Nine*."

"Listen, you fat—"

"Hey!" Billie shouted, stepping between them. "We're all tired and we're all wet. Let's try to act civilized, okay? I do not want to play referee to you two."

Forbus smirked as Amanda Jaffe joined the trio. Kate glared at Forbus.

"Tell us what happened!" Billie said.

"I already gave a statement," Kate answered belligerently, still annoyed.

"Then repeat it to me," Billie asked calmly. "Please."

Kate looked at Amanda and the lawyer nodded.

"I was out of town on business. When I got home there was a message from Daniel on my answering machine. He said that Sergey Kaidanov had called him."

"The missing scientist?" Billie interjected.

Kate nodded. "Kaidanov wanted Daniel to meet him at Rest of Angels. He was going to testify that his study was a hoax, but he wanted to be paid. He wanted Daniel to negotiate with Geller Pharmaceuticals."

"Why Ames?" Forbus asked.

"Kaidanov was at the cottage when Arthur Briggs was killed. He knew Daniel didn't kill Briggs, so he trusted him."

"This is what Ames told you?" Forbus asked skeptically.

Kate nodded.

"I don't suppose he has a witness to back him up?"

"Let her tell the story," Billie told her partner.

"By the time I got here Kaidanov was dead. I saw Daniel go down. The killer was trying to finish him off. I started shooting and scared him away."

"Where's your gun?" Forbus asked.

"I turned it over to the first cop who showed up. It's already bagged."

"What were you using?" Billie asked.

"A nine-millimeter Glock. You should find a lot of spent shells out there. I was spraying shots."

"Sounds familiar," Forbus muttered.

Billie's head snapped around and she glared at Forbus. He shrugged and held up his hands, but Kate caught his cruel smile.

"Where's the body?" Billie asked Kate.

"In the cemetery. There should be someone out there already. They called for forensics."

Billie was about to ask another question when a car pulled up. Mike Greene opened an umbrella and ran over.

"I should have stayed in L.A.," he swore. "Hi, Amanda, ladies and gentlemen. What have I missed?"

Billie quickly repeated what Kate had told her.

"Where's Ames?" Greene asked when she was finished.

"In the back of the ambulance," Amanda answered.

Greene thought for a moment. Then he looked at Daniel's lawyer.

"Let's get out of this rain and talk. There's a Denny's down the road."

"We've got to get over to the cemetery to scope out the crime scene," Billie said. Greene nodded and Amanda followed him to his car.

Kate turned to Billie. "What are you going to do about Daniel?"

"He's a suspect, Kate."

"Damn it, Billie, I told you what I saw. Daniel was supposed to die, too. He's been shot. Take a look at his wound. He'd be dead if I got here a few minutes later."

"This is the second crime scene Ames has been caught at."

"You didn't catch him. I called 911 with his consent. We could have been long gone if he gave the word. You'd never have connected him to the killing if he didn't wait here."

"You've got a point."

"The person who killed Briggs and Kaidanov is a cold-blooded psychopath. Daniel's nothing like that."

"Is this your heart or your head talking?" Billie asked, watching her friend carefully.

"How many times do I have to say it? I saw someone shoot Daniel."

"Who?"

"It was dark. Everything happened very fast."

Billie was quiet for a moment. When she spoke she looked uneasy.

"I'm gonna be blunt, Kate. Right now I've got a murder victim and a guy who's charged with another, connected murder. What Ames has is a witness who came on the scene after the victim was killed, and that witness is a friend of the suspect—maybe a very good friend."

"You think I'm lying?" Kate asked, aghast at the accusation.

Billie broke eye contact for a moment. When she reestablished it she looked embarrassed.

"What happens to Ames isn't my call. Mike Greene and Amanda Jaffe will work out the details. Right now all I want to do is get my work done and go home to a hot drink and a very hot bath. You should get out of the rain."

THIRTY-FIVE

When Mike Greene and Amanda Jaffe returned, the ambulance was gone and Daniel was under guard in the back of a patrol car. In view of Kate's account of the shoot-out and Daniel's wound, Greene decided that there was too much uncertainty to arrest Daniel.

The shock of being seconds from death, the discomfort from his wound, and the discovery that Kaidanov's study was a hoax gave Daniel a lot to think about during the ride to Kate's house. As soon as they were in the door Kate led him into the bathroom. His clothes were still covered with gore.

"Give me those," Kate said while she filled up the bathtub. "I'll put them in the wash to get this . . . stuff off."

Daniel stripped and settled into the scalding water. The painkillers he'd been given by the EMTs had kicked in. He closed his eyes and drifted off, but a recurring vision of Kaidanov's head exploding kept him from falling asleep, as did the sudden understanding that the only person who could tell the police that he did not murder Arthur Briggs was dead.

The water cooled off and Daniel hoisted himself out of

the tub. Every movement hurt. After he dressed in clothes that Kate had left for him, he limped into the living room. She was sitting on the couch clutching a glass of Scotch. The bottle stood in front of her on the coffee table. Kate's eyes were closed and her head was back. She looked exhausted. Daniel felt guilty that he had only been thinking about himself.

"Are you okay?" he asked anxiously. "Can I do anything?"

Kate opened her eyes and shook her head.

"What's wrong?"

"I was in a shoot-out once before. I never thought I'd have to go through that again."

Daniel sat next to Kate on the couch. "I saw how you looked at the lab when Forbus called you Annie Oakley. Was that because of the shooting?"

Kate nodded.

"What happened?"

Kate closed her eyes and pressed the glass to her forehead.

"There wasn't enough action in solving computer crimes, so I asked for a transfer to narcotics," Kate said in an exhausted monotone. "About six months after I went undercover I busted Clarence Marcel, an enforcer for Abdullah Hassim, a major dealer.

"While Clarence was out on bail, he and Abdullah had a falling-out over three missing kilos of cocaine. Clarence decided to rat out Abdullah in exchange for witness protection. I'm the one he called to set up the deal. The DA had an orgasm when I told him. He'd been trying to catch Abdullah for years. Only problem was Clarence insisted on turning himself over at the Lloyd Center mall at high noon. I told the DA that Clarence's plan was insane—too many people could get hurt if Abdullah tried to take out Clarence—but the DA was so desperate to turn him that he went along with it."

Kate took a stiff drink. "I remember every second of that afternoon," she said, a faraway look in her eyes. "It was Christmas. Carols were being piped through the loudspeakers, kids were skating at the ice rink, and the mall was packed. We were supposed to meet Clarence in front of a camera store. There were shoppers all over the place: a pregnant woman with her child, a Hispanic family, a cute, blond kid about twelve in a baggy Spider-Man sweatshirt.

"Clarence appeared out of nowhere and our guys moved to surround him. Watching from the doorway of a record store across the way were two black teenagers in Oakland Raiders gear. I was window-shopping, next door. As soon as they spotted Clarence they pulled out automatic weapons."

Kate shook her head slowly.

"I shot the first one in the chest. He fell sideways into the guy on his right, who had his finger on the trigger of an Uzi. I shot the second guy. He stumbled forward, spraying bullets into the crowd. A mother and daughter went down, one of our men was hit. There was complete panic and everybody started diving for cover.

"The crowd had separated Clarence from our guys and he took off for the nearest exit. I went after him. Running hard on his heels was the little white kid in the Spider-Man sweatshirt. Just as they reached the exit the kid said something and Clarence stopped and turned. I had almost caught up with him when this hole appeared in Clarence's forehead."

Kate touched a spot above her right eye.

"Who shot him?"

"It was the fucking kid. He was working with the brothers in the Oakland Raiders togs. Later on we found out that the hit wasn't his first." Kate shook her head as if she still couldn't believe it. "He was twelve years old and he did it for two Baggies."

She paused, drained her glass, then refilled it.

"I thought someone behind me had killed Clarence. It never dawned on me that it was the kid until he shot me, too. I was so shocked that I froze. Then he shot me again and I started squeezing the trigger. When the other cops got there every pane of glass in the exit door had been blown out, the kid was lying in a pool of blood with his chest torn apart, and I was standing over him jerking that trigger even though there wasn't a bullet left in my gun."

"How could you still be standing?" Daniel asked, awed by Kate's story.

"On TV, people fly through the air when they're shot or they fall down and die. That's not the way it happens in the real world. I've heard of shoot-outs where robbers took shot after shot and kept coming. Even a person who's shot in the heart could have as much as a minute to act before he bleeds out and goes unconscious. I didn't even know I'd been hit until I saw the blood. That's when I collapsed."

"Jesus, that's amazing."

"The DA didn't think so," Kate concluded bitterly. "Neither did the press. They called the shoot-out 'The Holiday Massacre.'" She looked at Daniel. "They needed a scapegoat, so they chose me. I'd lost Clarence and I killed a little kid. It didn't matter to the press that the kid was a hired assassin. I was expendable. I could have fought it, but I'd had enough, so I resigned."

"It sounds to me like you have nothing to feel bad about."

Kate smiled without humor. "I don't feel bad. I never did. After the shooting I had to visit a shrink. It was department policy. He told me it was common to experience feelings of guilt even when a shooting was righteous, but I never felt guilty and that really bothered me."

"What about tonight?"

Kate looked directly at Daniel. "Truth?"

"Of course."

"I was pumped. My motor was going every second I was trading shots."

"That's adrenaline."

Kate shook her head. "I know what adrenaline feels like. This was something different. This was a high like no other. So, what does that say about me?"

"It says that you're too hard on yourself. Are you forgetting that you saved my life? You're my hero, Kate."

Kate's laugh was sharp and biting.

"I mean it," he insisted. "I'd be dead if it wasn't for you. What you did was very brave."

Kate touched his cheek. "You're sweet."

Daniel reached up and took Kate's hand. It was light as a feather. He turned her palm and kissed it. She hesitated for only a second. Then she pulled Daniel to her and kissed him. Daniel winced. Kate sat back.

"Are you okay?" she asked, alarmed.

"Never felt better," Daniel answered, grimacing.

Kate laughed.

"I hate to say this," Daniel said, managing to smile, "but I'm in no condition to play Don Juan tonight."

Kate squeezed his hand. "Do I get a rain check?"

"Most definitely." He grinned. "I've got to thank you properly for riding to my rescue."

She laughed. "I did arrive in the nick of time, didn't I?"

"Just like the cavalry"—Daniel smiled—"but please feel free to rescue me sooner in the future."

THIRTY-SIX

The slender, dark-skinned man was waiting patiently for Claude Bernier when the photographer reached the landing of his third-floor walk-up. Bernier hesitated even though his visitor was dressed in a conservative suit and carrying a briefcase. He had been robbed at gunpoint recently and the man looked sinister enough to make him uneasy,

"Mr. Bernier?" the man asked in a heavy Spanish accent.

"Yes?" Bernier answered warily.

"My name is Juan Fulano and I am here to do business with you."

Photographers—even those with Claude's talent—had to scramble to make a living, and the mention of business erased the last of his doubts. He unlocked his door and invited Fulano inside. The apartment was small but clean. The walls were decorated with Bernier's photographs and the works of friends. Claude put down the bag of groceries he was carrying on the table in his narrow kitchen.

"I don't have much in the fridge," he apologized, "but I could make us some coffee."

"Not necessary."

Bernier led Fulano into the living room and offered him the most comfortable chair. Fulano sat down and carefully crossed his left leg over his right.

"How can I help you?" Bernier asked.

"I am interested in buying a copy of a photograph that was originally purchased from the Pitzer-Kraft Gallery in late February by a lawyer named Gene Arnold."

"Are you with the police?"

"No, Mr. Bernier. Why do you ask?"

"The police in Portland, Oregon, called me about that photograph. Do you know that Arnold was murdered?"

Bernier's visitor nodded. "Why did the Oregon authorities contact you?"

"They want a copy of the photograph, too."

"Have you sent it to them?"

"No. I just found the negative. It was misplaced. I'm mailing a print to Portland tomorrow."

Fulano smiled. "I wonder if I could induce you to sell me a copy of the photograph as well."

"Sure. I can make another copy."

"How much do you require?"

Bernier did a quick calculation based on the quality of Fulano's clothes.

"Fifteen hundred dollars," he said.

"A reasonable price, but the photograph would be worth five thousand to me if you would do me a small favor."

Bernier managed to conceal his surprise and excitement. He had never sold a photograph for that much money.

"What would you want me to do?"

"Do the authorities in Oregon know that you've located the negative of the photograph?"

"No. I just found it this morning."

"The five thousand is yours if you wait to send the photograph until I tell you to do so."

"I don't know," Bernier answered, suddenly worried. "It's a murder investigation. The detective I spoke with thought the people in the picture might be involved in Mr. Arnold's death."

"I, too, am interested in discovering the identity of Mr. Arnold's killer. I have no desire to obstruct a police investigation."

"Then why do you want me to wait to send the photograph to the police?"

Bernier's visitor leaned back and steepled his fingers. "Is five thousand dollars a fair price for your photograph?"

"Yes."

"Is it more than fair?"

Bernier hesitated, certain that the man knew he had inflated the price.

"It's very generous."

"Then I would hope that you would permit me to simply say that your assistance is important to me."

Bernier considered the proposition for a moment more before accepting.

"Do you think you could have the photograph for me by this evening?" Fulano asked. "I have an early flight."

"That shouldn't be a problem. Come by at eight."

Bernier's visitor opened his briefcase and handed him a stack of currency.

"A down payment," he said. "I hope you don't mind cash."

THIRTY-SEVEN

The aroma of coffee lured Daniel out of a fitful sleep the next morning. When he limped into the kitchen Kate was finishing her breakfast. She looked up from the paper and smiled.

"How are you feeling?" she asked.

"I'm okay," Daniel answered unconvincingly. He poured himself a cup of coffee.

"I forgot to ask, last night. Did anything happen in Arizona?"

She nodded as Daniel put two slices of bread in the toaster.

"I'm pretty certain I know why Gene Arnold came to Portland."

Daniel carried his coffee to the table and Kate told him about the kidnappings in Desert Grove and her discovery that Aaron Flynn had been Paul McCann's attorney.

"So you think Gene Arnold recognized Flynn in the photograph?"

"I can't think of any other reason for him to come here."

"But why—" Daniel stopped in mid-sentence. "The guy!"

"What?"

"Saturday, Joe Molinari took me to my apartment to get my running gear. When we pulled up I saw a man leave my apartment house and get into a black pickup. I was certain I'd seen him someplace before. I just remembered where. The day I dropped off the discovery Flynn and this guy came into the reception area together. I got the impression he worked for Flynn."

"Describe him to me."

"He looked like a weight lifter, a big neck, thick shoulders. I'd guess he was in his forties."

"Burt Randall. He's Flynn's investigator."

"Why would he be at my place?"

Kate was quiet for a moment. "Did you tell anyone other than me that you were going to meet Kaidanov at the cemetery?"

"No."

"Then how did the killer know?"

"Maybe someone followed Kaidanov."

"That doesn't work," Kate said. "If the people who wanted him dead knew where he was, they would have killed Kaidanov before he could tell you that the study was a hoax."

"Maybe I was the one who was tailed."

"But they'd have to know you were meeting Kaidanov. Kaidanov called you at your apartment, right?"

Daniel nodded.

"Randall knows all about electronic surveillance. You may have a tap on your phone."

"Is there any way you can tell?"

"I know someone who can sweep your apartment."

"Shit. The only person who could clear me is dead and my apartment might be bugged. This is getting worse and worse."

THIRTY-EIGHT

Paul Durban, a chubby, bespectacled man in a white shirt, gray slacks, and a gray sweater vest, finished his sweep of Daniel's apartment as Kate and Daniel watched from the couch. Durban concentrated his equipment on an area of molding for a few moments, then he turned to Kate.

"One bug in the phone, one in the bedroom, and one in here."

"Thanks, Paul. You know where to send the bill."

"Anytime," he said as he gathered up his equipment and left.

Durban had placed each listening device in its own evidence bag and left them on the coffee table. Daniel picked up one of the plastic bags and examined the bug.

"I've been doing a lot of thinking," he said. "Until Kaidanov told me that his study was a hoax, I was sure that Geller was trying to cover up Kaidanov's results. Now that I've learned about Aaron Flynn's connection to Gene Arnold, I've been looking at everything that's happened in a different light."

Daniel put the bug down.

"When I dropped off the discovery I had a talk with

Flynn. He told me that he'd hired more than twenty people to deal with the Insufort case and had leased another floor in his building to house them. That had to cost him. Now add in the expense of hiring experts at three hundred to six hundred dollars an hour and the other assorted expenses of litigation and you're looking at hundreds of thousands of dollars in costs.

"Flynn made a lot of money from his other cases, but I bet he's plowed a lot of that dough back into the Insufort case. That's a good investment if he wins. In some of the Insufort cases, the plaintiffs are permanently injured babies. You're talking about a lifetime of damages. There's lost earning capacity, medical costs, lifetime care. The life expectancy of a male is around seventy-two years and a female's life expectancy is a little under eighty years. What kind of care does a severely handicapped child need? There's nursing care, doctors' visits, psychiatric counseling for the parents. We're talking a hundred thousand dollars a year, easy. Now multiply that by seventy or eighty years and multiply that by the number of plaintiffs. Potentially that's millions in attorney fees. When the first few plaintiffs showed up, Flynn must have thought that his ship had come in. I bet he started spending money like crazy, figuring he'd make a fortune when the cases were over."

"But the studies failed to show a causal connection between Insufort and the birth defects," Kate said.

"Exactly. And Flynn figured out that it was only a coincidence that the plaintiffs were taking Insufort and their children had birth defects. That's when he decided that he had to manufacture evidence."

"I see a problem," Kate said. "Flynn would have to put on admissible evidence to prove Insufort causes birth defects. If the study is phony it would be torn apart by Geller's experts at trial."

"The operative words here are 'at trial,'" Daniel said. "That's where evidence is put to the test and a fraud can be exposed. But what happened when Kaidanov's lab was destroyed? The media jumped to the conclusion that Geller was covering up problems with Insufort. That's what we believed, and it's what a jury might believe. Now someone has murdered Kaidanov and Geller Pharmaceuticals has the obvious motive. With Kaidanov dead and the lab destroyed, Geller can't refute his study results. They can claim they're phony, but they can't prove it. There's going to be tremendous pressure on Geller to settle rather than run the risk of a catastrophic jury verdict."

"You're right," Kate said. "If the case settles, no one gets to show whether or not Insufort is safe."

"And Aaron Flynn wins a huge attorney fee instead of losing millions of dollars in costs."

Kate hesitated. "If Flynn is behind Kaidanov's hoax, why did he try to hide the results of the study by erasing it from the hard drive on Kaidanov's computer? Wouldn't Flynn want us to find the study?"

The question stumped Daniel for a moment. Then he brightened.

"When I broke into Kaidanov's house it looked like a hurricane had swept through it, but there was one thing in that house that was untouched and sitting exactly where it was supposed to be."

"The computer!"

"Whoever trashed Kaidanov's house left his computer alone so I couldn't help but notice it in the wreckage. He couldn't have done more to draw my attention to it if he painted it red and stuck sequins on it."

"You're right. They wanted us to think that there had been an unsuccessful attempt by Geller's people to erase the file, but a pro would have left no trace on the hard drive. It was a snap for me to recover the study."

"There's something else, Kate. Think about this. Flynn finding Kaidanov's letter in the documents Geller produced was like buying a winning lottery ticket. But that's not the only time that Flynn's gotten lucky. The eyewitness in my murder case just happens to be April Fairweather, the defendant in another one of his cases. Then a guardian angel sends my lawyer a videotape that enables her to destroy Fairweather so badly that the insurance company Flynn is suing will have to settle. Bingo, Flynn collects another big attorney fee."

"That is quite a string of good luck," Kate mused.

"What if Flynn is making his own luck? I talked with Joe Molinari about my case when we ran. He wondered if Flynn's got a mole at Reed, Briggs who stole the tape and put the Kaidanov letter into the discovery."

"Did he say who he thought it was?"

"Brock Newbauer or Susan Webster. Both of them are involved with the Insufort and the Fairweather cases."

Kate was quiet for a moment. When she spoke Daniel could tell that she was upset.

"You might be onto something. About a year ago Brock Newbauer settled a lawsuit because Aaron Flynn found a witness no one outside our office was supposed to know about. The way I remember it, aside from the lawyers, only our client was supposed to know that this guy existed. A lot of people in the firm were upset when they received Flynn's witness list. There were rumors that someone at Reed, Briggs tipped off Flynn, but they never came to anything. The next time you talk to Joe Molinari ask him about the Romanoff case. He was working on it with Newbauer. It was shortly after you started at the firm."

Kate thought for a moment before making a decision.

"I think our best chance of clearing you is to help the police find the person who killed Briggs and Kaidanov. I'm going to show Billie the bugs. We can tell her about Burt Randall. She'll question him and find out who told him to install them. I'll tell Billie about Flynn's connection to Gene Arnold. We'll nail him."

THIRTY-NINE

When Kate walked into the Taco Bell, Billie Brewster was working on a burrito in a back booth. Kate bought a cup of black coffee and slid in across from her.

"What, no password? I thought this was a top-secret meeting."

Kate smiled. "I'm here to talk about Kaidanov's murder."

"And I thought you wanted some fashion tips." Billie took a bite of her burrito. "I assume there's going to be a little quid pro quo here."

Kate nodded.

"A neighbor who lives near that ravine heard the shots and looked out her window. She saw someone run out of the woods a little before you and Daniel came out, but it was too dark for her to give any kind of ID. She also saw a car drive off without lights, but can't tell us the make or color. That's all we've got."

"I think you should take a hard look at Aaron Flynn and Burt Randall, Flynn's investigator."

"This on the up-and-up?"

Kate nodded.

"Aaron Flynn has lots of important friends," Billie said.

Kate leaned across the table. Her voice and her stare were intense.

"Kaidanov phoned Daniel's apartment to set up the meeting at the graveyard. Daniel didn't tell anyone except me that he was meeting Kaidanov there at ten, but the killer knew. The day before the call, Daniel saw Burt Randall leaving his building. I had Dan's apartment swept for bugs and my technician found these."

Kate placed the evidence bags containing the bugs on the table. Billie whistled softly.

"Randall must have planted them and whoever listened to Daniel's calls knew that Kaidanov would be at Rest of Angels at ten o'clock."

The detective picked up evidence bags and studied the listening devices.

"Okay, you've got me thinking about Randall," she said. "Why Flynn?"

Kate told Billie everything she had learned in Arizona about the Alvarez and Arnold kidnappings.

"I'm certain that Gene Arnold was killed because Flynn was afraid that he would expose his connection to the Arizona kidnappings."

"Was Flynn ever a suspect in the Alvarez or Arnold murders?"

"Not that I know. But I called your friend at the Benson Hotel. He went over Arnold's phone records. Gene Arnold called Aaron Flynn's office from his room."

"Why would a hotshot lawyer like Aaron Flynn be killing people and setting monkeys on fire?" Brewster asked.

Kate told the homicide detective how much money Flynn would make if he won the Insufort litigation and how much it would cost him if he lost it.

"You think Flynn or Randall killed Arthur Briggs?" Billie asked.

"I'm certain of it. Kaidanov was going to tell Briggs that the study was a hoax. The study was all Flynn had going for him. He had to kill Kaidanov and anyone he talked to."

Billie took a bite of her burrito and mulled over all she'd just learned.

"I think I'll pay a visit to Mr. Flynn," she said.

FORTY

Zeke Forbus was at his desk in the Justice Center writing a report when his intercom buzzed.

"I've got a caller on line two for a detective who's working on the Ames investigation," the receptionist said.

"Though he works from sun to sun, a detective's work is never done." Forbus sighed. The receptionist laughed. "I'll take it, Millie."

"Detectives," Forbus said as soon as he punched line two.

"Ask Arthur Briggs's secretary what Daniel Ames said when he called her the afternoon her boss was murdered," a muffled voice said. Then the line went dead.

Zeke Forbus flashed his badge and told the receptionist at Reed, Briggs that he wanted to talk to Renee Gilchrist. Then he took a seat and leafed through a magazine while he waited for Renee to appear. As soon as she walked into the reception area, Forbus remembered her. She was tall and sleek and easily distracted him from the article he had been reading.

"Ms. Gilchrist?" Forbus said.

When she nodded Forbus showed Renee his identification. Renee looked nervous.

"I'm one of the detectives investigating the murder of Arthur Briggs. We spoke right after your boss was killed."

"Oh, yes. I remember."

"Is there someplace quiet where we can talk now?"

"There's a room down the hall that's not being used."

"That'll do."

"What's this about?"

Forbus smiled. "Why don't we get settled first."

As soon as they were inside, Forbus shut the door and motioned Renee into a seat. The room was small and the air close. Forbus moved slowly to the table and took his seat, staring at Renee the whole time and not saying a word. The detective enjoyed using his size to advantage in a situation like this and he felt a surge of pleasure when Renee lowered her eyes. He had intentionally scooted his chair close to her so their knees were almost touching.

"After we talked the first time I wrote a report."

Forbus pulled three folded sheets of paper out of his inside jacket pocket and pushed them across the table. Renee looked at the report nervously but did not reach for it.

"Read it," Forbus ordered.

Renee hesitated, then started turning the pages. When she finished she looked at the detective expectantly.

"Anything missing?" he asked.

"Missing?"

"Yeah. Is there anything that you should have told me that's not in there?"

Renee looked confused. "What do you mean?"

"I got a call from someone who thinks you're concealing information in this investigation."

Renee's shoulders hunched a little and she looked down at the table.

"Ms. Gilchrist, how did you and Daniel Ames get along?"

"Okay. Fine."

"Care to elaborate."

"He . . . We worked together."

"Do you like him?"

The question seemed to startle Renee. "Like him?" she repeated. "Well, I mean, he's a nice guy, sure."

"That's not what I'm talking about, Ms. Gilchrist. You two ever date?"

"No! He did a lot of work with Mr. Briggs. I just saw him in the office."

"So you'd have no reason to cover for him, to conceal evidence that would prove he killed your boss?"

"Certainly not," she answered, but there was a tremor in her voice.

Forbus smiled. He leaned back and studied Renee. She shifted on her chair.

"Then I suppose you have a good reason for not telling me about the phone call you got from Ames on the day your boss was killed?"

Renee hesitated.

"Did he call you, Renee?" Forbus demanded, putting emphasis on the secretary's first name. "Do you understand that it's a felony to obstruct a police investigation?"

Renee's eyes dropped and she fidgeted in her seat.

"I'm gonna ask you once more: Did you get a call from Daniel Ames on the day Arthur Briggs was killed?"

"Yes," Renee answered, her voice barely above a whisper.

"Good, Renee. You just took the first step toward staying out of jail. Step two is to tell me what Ames said."

FORTY-ONE

When Billie Brewster entered Aaron Flynn's suite of offices, she was as impressed by the lobby as Daniel had been, but Brewster had no trouble separating her admiration for the things someone owned from her opinion of the person who owned them. Flynn's office was as impressive as the lobby. It was paneled in mahogany and decorated with fine art and tributes to Flynn's courtroom triumphs. When Flynn's secretary brought the detective to meet him, he rounded his polished oak desk and crossed the Persian rug that covered his hardwood floors.

"Sit down, Detective Brewster," he said, flashing a warm smile and giving Billie's hand a firm shake. "Can I get you anything to drink?"

"I'm okay, thanks," Billie answered as she settled onto a comfortable couch that sat against one wall. Flynn sat opposite her, completely at ease.

"How can I help you?" he asked.

"Have you heard about the shooting at Rest of Angels Cemetery last night?"

The lawyer's smile disappeared. "It was in the morning

paper." Flynn shook his head sadly. "Dr. Kaidanov's death was a tragic loss."

"You knew him?"

"No, but I was hoping that he would be the key witness for several clients of mine who have given birth to babies with defects we believe were caused by Insufort, a Geller Pharmaceutical product. Dr. Kaidanov authored a study that showed that the product was harmful. He disappeared before I could question him about his work."

"Did you try to find Dr. Kaidanov?"

"I've had my investigators trying to locate him since I learned about the study."

"Is Burt Randall one of the people you were using?"

"Yes. Why?"

"Did you instruct Mr. Randall to put a tap on Daniel Ames's phone?"

"A tap! Of course not."

"Mr. Flynn, I've received information that your investigator did exactly that, which we both know is quite illegal."

"Of course I know that. That's why I would never do such a thing." Flynn paused. "Ames. Isn't he the young man charged with killing Arthur Briggs?"

Billie nodded.

"I'm completely lost, Detective. What makes you think that Burt would do something like that? If you're going to make serious accusations against one of my employees, I have a right to know the basis for them."

"I'm sorry, but this comes from a confidential source. You understand confidentiality, being a lawyer and all," Brewster said, feigning a friendly smile.

"Well, I don't know what to say. This is very unsettling."

"Is Mr. Randall here? I'd like to speak to him."

"I don't believe he came in today."

"Can you give me his home address and phone number?"

"I'd have to ask Mr. Randall for his permission, first. Why don't I arrange to have you meet him here, tomorrow?"

"I appreciate the offer, but I need to see him today."

"Then I can't help you."

"Or won't," Brewster answered, her smile gone. "Mr. Flynn, does the name Gene Arnold mean anything to you?"

The question seemed to take Flynn by surprise. "I knew a lawyer named Gene Arnold years ago when I was practicing in Arizona."

"That's the Gene Arnold I'm interested in. He was stabbed, then set on fire at the primate lab where the Kaidanov study was conducted."

Billie watched Flynn's reaction carefully.

Flynn seemed confused. "Gene was the dead man at that lab?"

She nodded.

"My God. What was he doing there?"

"I thought you might be able to tell me."

"I have no idea. I haven't seen Gene in years."

"What was your relationship to Mr. Arnold when you did know him?"

Flynn shrugged. "'Relationship' would be too strong a word. We were acquaintances. Both of us practiced law in

Desert Grove, which is a fairly small town. There weren't many attorneys in Desert Grove, so we socialized at Bar Association meetings, things of that sort. We were adversaries on occasion, legally speaking, though this was some years ago. I don't remember any specific cases offhand."

"Do you know of any connection between Mr. Arnold and the Insufort litigation?"

"None."

"So he didn't mention the lab or the Insufort case when he called you?"

"Why would he call me?"

"I don't know, but the phone records from the Benson Hotel show a call from Mr. Arnold's room to your office that lasted fifteen minutes."

"I never spoke to him. I told you, I haven't seen him or spoken to him since I left Desert Grove."

"If you didn't talk to him when he called, who did?"

Flynn spread his hands and shrugged his shoulders. "I have no idea, Detective."

Billie told Flynn the date and time of the call.

"Were you in the office when he phoned?" she asked.

"I can't say for certain."

"Fifteen minutes is a long time, Mr. Flynn. Mr. Arnold must have been talking to somebody."

"Maybe I was on another line and he held for a while, then hung up. I frequently have phone conferences that last an hour or more. I'm involved in cases all over the country. I'm even representing some of the families from that air crash in India."

"Would your staff be able to help? Maybe they remember the call."

"I'll ask, but I'm assuming this would have been several weeks ago, right?"

"Your billing records would show what you were doing when Mr. Arnold called, wouldn't they?"

"They might."

"Will you ask your secretary to make a copy of them for me?"

"I'm afraid I can't do that. It would violate client confidentiality." Flynn smiled. "There's that word again."

Brewster studied Flynn. He seemed to be getting a second wind.

"Can you think of any reason why Gene Arnold would be in Portland?"

"No."

"You represented Paul McCann, didn't you, the man accused of killing Patty Alvarez?"

"Yes."

"And you know about the murder of Mr. Arnold's wife."

"I wasn't involved in that case," Flynn answered, shifting uneasily in his chair.

"Could Mr. Arnold's visit have had anything to do with the death of his wife and Martin Alvarez's wife?" Billie asked.

Flynn looked very uncomfortable. "I can't think of how it could."

Billie waited a moment, watching Flynn closely. "Well," she said as she stood up, "I guess that does it. Thank you for your time."

Flynn stood, too. "If there's anything I can do . . ."

Billie handed Flynn her card. "The time sheets for the

day Mr. Arnold called. Why don't you think about letting me see them."

As soon as the door closed behind Billie Brewster, Aaron Flynn told his secretary to hold his calls. Then he dialed a number he knew almost as well as his own. A moment later the call went through.

"We got a serious problem," Flynn said, speaking urgently into the phone. "A very serious problem."

FORTY-TWO

One wall of Geller Pharmaceuticals' conference room was glass and provided a view of the atrium with its indoor waterfall, but no one in the room was looking at the view. Their attention was focused on J. B. Reed, who had just entered with Brock Newbauer and Susan Webster in tow. At six five and almost three hundred pounds, Reed, Briggs's most powerful partner was used to being the center of attention.

Isaac Geller crossed the conference room and grasped Reed's hand.

"Thank you for coming, John," Geller said. "How are you holding up?"

"It's been hard, Isaac," Reed answered, shaking his head sadly. "Art and I were more than law partners."

"I know."

"We go back to high school. We founded the firm."

"We're all still in shock," Geller said.

Reed's features hardened into a look of rocklike determination.

"I'm stepping in, Isaac. That's why I'm here, to let you

know that I'm making these lawsuits my number-one priority."

"And none too soon, either," interjected Byron McFall, Geller's president, as the lawyers took their seats at the conference table. "Kaidanov's murder couldn't have happened at a worse time."

McFall's callousness made Geller flinch, but no one noticed. Their eyes were on Reed.

"How is this going to affect our position?" McFall asked.

"I've been briefed about the case by Brock and Susan," Reed replied, "but I don't have enough of a handle on the facts yet to give you an intelligent answer. Susan?"

All eyes turned toward Susan Webster, the elegant associate who had taken the seat next to Reed.

"Sergey Kaidanov's murder is a public relations nightmare, Mr. McFall. I pulled up several stories on the Kaidanov killing on the Internet. It's front-page news all over the country. The press is hinting that Geller Pharmaceuticals is behind the destruction of the lab and Kaidanov's death because the company wants to cover up his study. There's pressure on the district attorney to start an investigation. Not surprisingly, Aaron Flynn is talking to every reporter he can find. If he brings this case to trial we'll never find twelve jurors who haven't heard the rumors."

Isaac Geller closed his eyes and shook his head. He looked exhausted.

"What do you suggest we do?"

Susan looked at Reed. "Maybe I should wait for Mr. Reed to get up to speed on the case before offering any advice."

"That's okay," Reed prompted. "I want to hear where you think we are in the case."

"I'd start discussing a settlement, Mr. Geller," Susan said reluctantly. "It could be a bloodbath if we go to trial."

"Goddamn it!" Byron McFall said bitterly. "We had nothing to do with that lab or the study or Kaidanov's murder."

"That may be irrelevant if everyone believes that we did," Susan said evenly. "We should approach Mr. Flynn with a reasonable offer. There are good arguments for admissibility and exclusion of the evidence of the murders, the study, and the destruction of the lab. Right now neither side knows what Judge Norris will let in at trial. This is the best time to feel out Flynn. If Norris rules in his favor he'll want to try every case, and once he wins one of them we won't be able to hold back the flood."

Geller's in-house counsel made a comment just as Susan's cell phone rang. Newbauer, who was seated to Susan's left, watched her answer it and noted her surprise. She walked to the far end of the conference room, away from the others, and continued her conversation in a voice too low to hear. She seemed concerned when she returned to the conference table.

"Anything wrong?" Newbauer asked.

"No," Webster answered unconvincingly.

Kate Ross split her attention between the *New York Times* crossword puzzle and the exit to Aaron Flynn's garage. An hour after she'd seen Billie Brewster leave Flynn's building, Flynn's car appeared. Kate put down the paper and followed him across town to the Sunset Highway entrance. It was almost 6:30 and the traffic had thinned out. Kate stayed several car lengths back as Flynn headed toward the coast. After half an hour, the lawyer left the highway and took a route that wound through farm country. Ten minutes later he pulled into the dirt parking lot of the Midway Café, a run-down roadhouse with a neon sign that advertised beer and fried chicken. It was the type of place where truckers and farmers stopped for coffee and pie, and high-priced lawyers rarely entered.

Kate drove by the restaurant then made a U-turn and parked at the far end of the lot just as Flynn was walking inside. Moments later another car pulled into a parking space near the door and Susan Webster got out.

"Bingo," Kate said to herself. She thought about following Susan inside, but the restaurant was too small. Kate leaned over her seat. When she surfaced, she was holding an expensive camera with a telephoto lens.

Thirty minutes later the door to the restaurant opened and Susan Webster and Aaron Flynn walked out. Kate snapped off several shots.

Juan Fulano had been surprised to see another car following Aaron Flynn from his office building to the roadside café. He had been careful to stay far enough back of both cars so he would not be seen. When Kate parked in the lot Fulano drove down the road, made a U-turn, and pulled to the side of the road, where he waited until Aaron Flynn and Susan Webster came out of the restaurant. His only worry was that Flynn's tail would follow him after he left the diner, but she did not.

As soon as Flynn drove away Fulano turned on his

headlights and followed. Flynn stayed on the highway until he was back within the Portland city limits. When he turned off the highway, Fulano followed at a discreet distance. Once he was certain that Flynn was going home, Fulano fell farther back to give Flynn time to park. Then he found a spot on Flynn's block where he stayed, watching Flynn's house. When the lights went out near midnight, Fulano drove back to his hotel and phoned in his report to Martin Alvarez.

FORTY-THREE

Billie ran a check on Burt Randall after visiting Aaron Flynn's law office. Besides getting his address, she had discovered that Randall was an ex-marine with combat experience and former LAPD. Deciding that discretion was the better part of valor, the detective had a patrol car follow her to Randall's house. Brewster drove along Northwest Twenty-third until she reached Thurman, then turned left into the hills. Randall's modern A-frame was set back from an unpaved street on the outskirts of Forest Park. A black pickup truck stood in the driveway.

"Let's you and me go to the front door," Billie told Ronnie Blanchard, a uniformed officer who had played linebacker at Portland State. "Radison can cover the rear of the house."

"Sounds like a plan," Tom Radison, Blanchard's partner, said. He headed toward the back of the house.

"You know this guy's background," Billie said. "Let's not take chances."

The house was dark. Billie rang the bell. There was no answer. She tried again while Blanchard tried the door. It was unlocked. The officer looked at Billie and she nodded. He edged the door inward.

"Mr. Randall," Billie called out. Silence. "I'm Billie Brewster, a police detective. Are you home, sir?"

The living room had a vaulted ceiling. The dying rays of the sun cast a pale light through ceiling-high picture windows. Billie pointed to a dark hallway. Blanchard edged down it while Billie cautiously climbed the stairs to a sleeping loft that overlooked the entryway and the living room. The moment Billie's head cleared the landing she knew something was wrong. She gripped her weapon a little tighter before climbing the rest of the stairs in a crouch. The blinds were closed and all Billie could tell was that there was someone sprawled across the bed.

"Mr. Randall?" she said loudly.

There was no answer.

"I do not fucking like this," Billie mumbled to herself as she stepped onto the landing. As soon as her vision adjusted Billie made out Burt Randall in a T-shirt and boxer shorts. There were two bloodstained holes in the T-shirt and a third in the center of Randall's forehead.

FORTY-FOUR

Daniel was fixing dinner in Kate's kitchen when he heard her car pull up. She was holding a roll of film when she walked in the door.

"What's that?"

"Photos of a secret meeting between Aaron Flynn and Susan Webster. Tomorrow morning, I'm going to have a talk with that little bitch. If she'll admit she's been working with Flynn to fix Insufort, we may be able to nail him."

"That's terrific," Daniel said.

The phone rang and Kate answered it. She listened intently for a moment, then swore.

"What's wrong?" Daniel asked.

"It's Billie," Kate told him. "Randall is dead, murdered."

Kate listened while Brewster described the crime scene.

"No sign of a struggle?" Kate asked.

"None," Billie told her.

"When was Randall killed?"

"Medical examiner's rough guess puts the death

around the time Kaidanov got it, give or take an hour either way."

"It sounds like someone is tying up loose ends," Kate said. "Did you talk to Flynn?"

"Yeah, but I didn't get a thing. He was very nervous when I asked him about the call from the Benson. He denied talking to Arnold, even though the call lasted fifteen minutes. And he refused to let me see his time sheets so I could find out who was with him when the call came in. I'm sure he's hiding something."

"With Randall dead, we won't be able to prove that Flynn ordered him to bug Daniel's apartment."

"With Randall dead, we can't prove a thing against Flynn." Billie sighed. "I phoned Claude Bernier. He's still having trouble finding the negative. If we ever get a print of the photograph, and Flynn's in it, I might be able to get a search warrant for Flynn's time sheets."

"Go get some sleep," Kate said. "You sound all in."

"Good advice."

Kate hung up. "That was Billie Brewster. Burt Randall's been murdered."

"Then we're fucked. The cops are not going to go after someone like Aaron Flynn without proof."

"Maybe I can crack Susan with the photos when I—"

Kate froze. Then she smiled.

"What?" Daniel asked.

She started toward the door to her basement workshop.

"Come on. We're going to take a trip in cyberspace."

Daniel followed Kate downstairs. She flipped on the light and headed to one of her computers.

"One of the reasons Reed, Briggs hired me was to advise them on computer security. If you want to know how to protect files, you have to know how to invade them. I'm going to hack into Flynn's computer."

Kate checked her watch. "Flynn's employees should be home by now, so we're good to go."

"What are you looking for?" Daniel asked as Kate started pounding her keyboard.

"If he operates like most lawyers, Flynn posts his time sheets to his law office server," she answered while focusing her attention on her monitor. "They stay there until his secretary uploads them to her workstation when she does his billing. I should be able to access the time sheet for the fifteen minutes when Gene Arnold called Flynn's office. If someone was with Flynn when Arnold's call came in, we'll soon know."

"How are you going to get in?"

"That's simple. I'll access the files at Reed, Briggs and get Flynn's E-mail address. That'll give me his Internet Protocol address. Once I log onto Flynn's server, I'll use the software that found Kaidanov's password to get the password for Flynn's law office server. When I'm in, I can go to any file in the server and download any information in the file to my computer."

"It can't be that easy. What if Flynn has security?"

"He might have installed a firewall to block unauthorized intruders, but I doubt it's one I can't circumvent. The best defensive software has weaknesses. Even Microsoft has been hacked. I doubt Flynn put a lot of money into his security system. Most law firms don't."

"Can this be traced back to you?"

Kate laughed. "I'm going to give Flynn's server a frontal lobotomy when I'm through. I'll erase the transaction. It'll look like someone randomly logged on by mistake and was kicked off."

"You're sure about this?"

"Relax. This is what I do. In three to four hours we'll know the name of the person Flynn was with when Gene Arnold called."

FORTY-FIVE

Alice Cummings lived in a cheap garden apartment behind a strip mall and a car wash a few blocks from Portland's worst commercial avenue. Daniel remembered how tired she had looked wheeling Patrick's stroller into Aaron Flynn's lobby on the day he delivered the boxes containing the discovery documents. She looked worse today.

When Cummings visited Flynn she'd been wearing makeup and a dress. When she opened the door, she was in soiled jeans and a stained sweatshirt and there was no mascara or pancake makeup to hide the lines that the pressure of raising a handicapped baby had etched in her face.

"Hi," Daniel said, flashing a pleasant smile. "You probably don't remember me, but Aaron Flynn introduced us about a month ago."

Alice examined Daniel's face. Her eyes lingered on the bandage that covered his head wound, but only for a moment. He hoped that she did not recognize him from one of the television news programs that had filmed him at the courthouse.

"We met in the lobby of Mr. Flynn's office. I was just leaving as you came in for your appointment."

Alice brightened. "Oh, yes. Now I remember. Did Mr. Flynn send you?"

"Can I come in?" Daniel answered, finessing the question.

Alice stepped aside and let Daniel into a small front room.

"How's Patrick?" he asked.

"He had a bad night, but he's sleeping now."

Daniel heard the resignation and exhaustion in Cummings's voice. Kate had looked up Alice in the records at the courthouse. Daniel knew that her husband had filed for divorce soon after Patrick's birth, which meant that she was raising her son alone.

"When he has a bad night yours must be rough, too," he said.

"My nights are never as bad as my baby's. Sometimes I wonder how he goes on, but he's never known anything else."

Alice rubbed her hands on her jeans and surveyed her front room. There was laundry on the sofa. She took a toy off an armchair and motioned Daniel toward it.

"Please, sit down. Can I get you some coffee?"

"I'm fine," Daniel said, waiting for Alice to push some of the laundry aside and take a seat before he sat down.

"Has Mr. Flynn heard anything?" she asked anxiously. "We're really counting on him."

"I'm not here about your case." Alice looked confused and Daniel felt horrible about deceiving her. "It's something

Mr. Flynn wanted me to ask you about. Do you remember visiting his office in early March?"

She nodded. "That was my first time. I . . . I read about the Moffitts. I wanted to see if he could help me, too."

"So you remember the consultation?"

"Of course."

"Because a matter came up in another case I need your help with. It has to do with a phone call that Mr. Flynn insists that he received while you were with him. Another lawyer is claiming that the call never took place. Mr. Flynn's time sheets indicate that he was meeting with you when the call came in. Do you remember a call interrupting your meeting? Or the receptionist talking to Mr. Flynn over the intercom while you were with him?"

Alice thought about it for a moment. "Yes, I do. There was a call. Mr. Flynn apologized when his receptionist interrupted the meeting. And . . . Of course! Now I remember. Mr. Flynn was upset when his secretary buzzed him. He told her that he didn't want our meeting interrupted. She was speaking on an intercom and I heard her. She said the man was calling about a murder and was very insistent. That's one of the reasons I remember the call. I don't hear people discussing a murder very often."

"That's the call I need to know about," Daniel said, trying to sound businesslike. "Do you happen to remember the caller's name? That would be very helpful."

"His last name was Arnold," she said with a laugh. "My father's first name is Arnold, so I remember it perfectly."

Daniel laughed, too, even more enthusiastically than Mrs. Cummings.

"Wow," he said, "that was easy. Thanks."

"I'm glad I could help. Mr. Flynn has been so good to Patrick and me. I don't know what we'd do without him. He's going to get us the money for Patrick's operations. I don't have health insurance and my husband walked out when Patrick was born." She looked down. "He couldn't take it. He couldn't even look at Patrick," she said softly. "If Mr. Flynn wasn't fighting this case for us . . ."

Daniel felt sick inside, both for her plight and for deceiving her. He couldn't imagine how she would feel when Flynn was arrested and she learned that her suit against Insufort was baseless. Daniel said good-bye, feeling like the worst kind of traitor. Partway down the block he looked back. Alice Cummings smiled and waved hopefully from her front door. Daniel couldn't bring himself to wave back.

FORTY-SIX

Susan Webster looked up when Kate Ross walked into her office and closed the door behind her.

"Yes?" Susan said.

Kate sat down without being asked and laid the envelope she was carrying on Webster's desk.

"It's Kate, right?" Webster asked after a moment of silence, annoyed when Kate continued to sit and stare.

"That's right."

"Why are you here?" Susan demanded.

"Show-and-tell," Kate said, opening the envelope and handing Susan a picture of her and Aaron Flynn standing outside the Midway Café.

Susan flushed, then glared at Kate. "How dare you follow me."

"If you don't like it, why don't we both go up to J. B. Reed's office? You can complain that I'm harassing you and I'll tell J.B. about your clandestine meeting with Aaron Flynn."

Susan gave herself time to calm down by looking at the photograph again.

"Why are you showing me this?" she asked.

"I want you to know that I'm onto your arrangement with Flynn."

"Aaron and I don't have an arrangement."

Kate smiled. "Beer and fried chicken never struck me as your cuisine of choice. I always pictured you as more the Pinot Noir and coq au vin type."

"Cute," Susan answered sarcastically, "but I didn't pick the restaurant. Aaron wanted to meet where no one would see us. He chose the Midway Café. As you said, I don't usually do business over fried chicken and beer. Neither does anyone else at Reed, Briggs, so we knew we'd be alone when we discussed settling the Geller case."

"Why would Flynn discuss a settlement with you? Brock Newbauer is the lead attorney."

Susan laughed. "Brock is clueless in a case of this complexity. Flynn knows I'm running the show. And he didn't want Brock around when he tried to bribe me." Kate's eyebrows went up. "Aaron offered me a job at his firm at significantly more than I'm making if I convince Geller to settle."

"Which I assume you're trying to do."

"Of course, but not because I plan to leave Reed, Briggs. The Insufort case is a sure loser in court. We have to settle to save the company."

"Was Arthur Briggs murdered so you could control the Insufort litigation?"

"What!"

"You can stop the act, Susan. I know you're helping Flynn fix the Insufort and Fairweather cases."

"What are you talking about?"

"Before Kaidanov died, he told Daniel that his study is

a hoax. Flynn's plan is going to fail and you're going down with him."

"You better think twice before you threaten me, Ross."

"I don't make threats," Kate said. "Either you go to the police and confess or I'll make sure that J.B. and the DA learn about your deal with Flynn."

Susan shot to her feet. "Listen, you bitch. If you say one word of this to anyone, I'll sue you for slander and see that you're fired. Joe Molinari can't keep a secret. Everyone knows that Ames is staying with you. Why don't you tell J.B. your ridiculous theory and see if he believes you? But don't forget to tell him you're fucking the man who killed his best friend."

Kate colored, but she held her temper.

"I'll give you until the end of the day to decide what to do. After that, you're on your own."

Kate walked out and Susan slammed her hand on the desk. Was Ross bluffing, or would she really go to J. B. Reed? Then she suddenly realized that Kate had said that Daniel Ames could testify that Sergey Kaidanov's study was a hoax. She sat down heavily. Before he died did Kaidanov give Ames hard evidence to back up his claim?

Susan tried to calm down so she could think more clearly. After a moment she dialed Aaron Flynn's office.

FORTY-SEVEN

There was an urgent message from Amanda Jaffe for Daniel on the answering machine when Daniel returned to the house. He called her office immediately

"We have a problem," Amanda told him as soon as they were connected. "Mike Greene wants to reopen your bail hearing."

"How can he do that? The judge already ruled I could stay out."

"Mike has a witness who can corroborate April Fairweather's testimony."

"Who?" Daniel asked, alarmed.

"Did you call Renee Gilchrist after you heard Arthur Briggs's message on your answering machine?"

Daniel's face fell. "Oh, shit."

"I take it that's a yes?" Amanda said sharply. Daniel could tell that she was upset and disappointed in him. "It would have been nice if you'd let me know that there was a land mine right in front of us."

"I knew they'd interviewed Renee once. I didn't figure they would talk to her again."

"Well, they did. Someone dropped a dime on you."

"What's that mean?"

"An anonymous caller told Zeke Forbus to ask Gilchrist about a call you made to her on the day Briggs was shot. She told Forbus that you said Briggs wanted to meet that evening at the cottage where he was killed to talk about the Insufort case."

Daniel felt sick. "Greene let me go at the cemetery. He saw my head wound. I thought he was convinced that I'm innocent."

"No. He just had some reservations about last night's shooting, and Forbus is still certain that you killed Arthur Briggs. He's the one who's pushing Mike. Now tell me what happened with Renee Gilchrist."

"I couldn't figure out why Briggs wanted to see me," Daniel said, "so I called to talk to him. Only he'd left. So I asked Renee if she knew about a new development in the Insufort case that involved me. When she asked why I wanted to know, I told her about Briggs's call."

"You know what you said to her is admissible as an exception to the hearsay rule because you're the defendant," Amanda said. "The judge can consider your statements as proof that you intended to meet with Briggs."

"Do you think that's enough to change Judge Opton's decision on bail?"

"Come on, Daniel, be smart about this. Bail could end up being the least of our problems."

When Kate walked into her house, Daniel was sitting on the couch in the dark. One look told her that something was wrong.

"What happened?" she asked.

Daniel told her about Amanda Jaffe's call.

"I don't think Renee's testimony will be enough to convince the judge to deny bail," Kate said. "They still can't prove that you killed Briggs. The best they can do is place you at the crime scene."

"Renee can also corroborate Fairweather's testimony about my argument with Briggs after he fired me."

"How did things go with Cummings?" Kate asked to change the subject.

"I can prove that Flynn got a call from Gene Arnold," Daniel answered without looking at her. "Alice Cummings was in Flynn's office when Arnold called. She even remembers Arnold's name."

"That's great!"

"Yeah."

Daniel should have been thrilled, but he sounded depressed.

"What's going on, Dan?" Kate asked with concern.

"When we bring down Flynn, we'll also be destroying his suit against Geller."

"So? The suit shouldn't have been brought in the first place."

"But Flynn convinced Alice Cummings that it should. She lives in this tiny apartment. She has nothing. Her son, Patrick, desperately needs medical attention, and he's not going to get it because of us."

Kate sat on the couch next to Daniel.

"Remember, I told you that my sister went through this with her baby? She's a good person and no one knows why her baby was born the way it was. And remember what you told me about life being unfair, about bad things happening to people for no reason? It's true. We have to accept that, even when it's hard, even when we need something to rail against. Insufort is not responsible for Patrick's birth defect, and the courts aren't always the right place to go for help."

"I still feel like I robbed that poor woman. I used her to get at Flynn. The end result is that I'll be killing her dreams and Patrick's future."

"You have to bring down Flynn. He's a murderer."

"That doesn't make me feel any better."

Kate put her arms around Daniel. "Don't get down on yourself, Daniel. You're a good man. I can see how hard this is for you, but we're so close. Don't fold when we're almost there."

Daniel sighed. "I'm okay. I just wish—"

Kate put a fingertip to his lips. "Don't," she said. Then she kissed him—once quickly, her lips lingering the second time. They looked at each other for a moment, then Daniel let himself go, losing himself in the contradictory softness of her breast and hard muscles of her back. After a moment they broke their kiss. Daniel closed his eyes and rested his cheek against her hair. It smelled sweet and felt so soft. Kate was a haven from all the bad things that had happened to him.

Daniel felt Kate move and he opened his eyes. She stood up and took his hand. "Come on," she said softly, pulling him slowly to his feet and toward the bedroom.

FORTY-EIGHT

The call from Susan Webster had confirmed Aaron Flynn's worst fears. Before he died, Kaidanov had told Daniel Ames that his study was a fraud. But Flynn didn't know if Ames could prove the study was a hoax. Without proof, all Geller would have was the hearsay testimony of a man charged with murder and Flynn was certain he could still force a settlement.

"Alice Cummings is on line two," Aaron Flynn's receptionist announced.

Flynn debated not taking the call for a moment, but little Patrick was worth a bundle if everything worked out.

"Good afternoon, Alice," Flynn said in his heartiest voice. "How's my boy?"

"He had a rough night."

"I'm so sorry. What can I do for you?"

"I hope I'm not interrupting, but it's been bothering me since your associate left. He never said if you needed me to sign anything about the phone call. I can come down anytime."

"The phone call?"

"From Mr. Arnold." Flynn's eyes shut reflexively and a

sick feeling spread through his gut. "Your associate said a lawyer is claiming that you never talked with him, but I remember it very clearly. Did you want me to sign an affidavit?"

"What was this associate's name, Alice?"

"You know, I can't remember. I'm not certain he even told me. But you introduced us. It was several weeks ago. I wheeled Patrick into the lobby in his stroller and you brought him over to meet us."

Flynn felt a flash of fear.

"Ah, yes," he said. "Well, I appreciate your call, but I won't need you to sign anything. The matter has been resolved. Thank you for calling, though. Give Patrick a kiss for me," Flynn said as he hung up.

"Everything is falling apart," Aaron Flynn said as soon as he was through the front door. A look of panic was etched on his face. "Ames found the client who was with me when Gene called."

"How did he do that?"

"How the fuck should I know? He just did and she remembers Gene's call. She just phoned me. She wanted to know if I needed her to sign an affidavit that could be used as evidence. Jesus Christ!"

"You've got to calm down so we can think this out."

"There's nothing to think about. If that homicide detective, Brewster, finds out I lied about Gene's call, we're dead."

"Who is the client?"

"Alice Cummings, the mother of one of the Insufort brats."

"Where does she live?"

"I don't know offhand."

"But it's in your file?"

"I can get it."

"We have to kill her."

"What?"

"We have to kill her and Ames and Ross."

"You're insane."

Flynn felt a hand snake through his hair. Then warm lips brushed his and a hand stroked his crotch. It took all of his willpower, but he broke away and headed for the couch. Flynn heard a cruel laugh behind him.

"You didn't mind when I took care of Briggs, Kaidanov, and Randall. Why are you so squeamish now?"

"Alice is . . . She's just this woman."

"No, Aaron, she's not just some woman. The bitch is a witness who can put both of us on death row, not to mention rob us of millions we have worked very hard to earn." A hand strayed to his zipper. "I'll kill them to protect you—to protect us—so we can be together."

A finger brushed the tip of his penis, emphasizing the point.

"You can't do this again," Flynn protested weakly.

"We can do anything."

Flynn was having trouble thinking. There were warm lips on his, fingers stroking his nipples, and a hand as soft as silk inside his fly.

"If it bothers you, I'll take care of Cummings while you take care of Ames and Ross."

Flynn's eyes went wide. "I can't. I've never killed anyone before."

"It's easy, baby," he heard as his body moved against its will to the rhythm set by the fingertips, tongue, and lips that were everywhere at once. "I'll tell you how to do it. Besides, we don't have a choice. The cops don't know about Cummings yet. If they did, she wouldn't have called you. That means that Ross and Ames haven't told them yet. We've got a window of opportunity here, but we've got to move, and I can't be in two places at once."

Flynn wanted to protest, but he was having trouble thinking. One part of his brain knew that someone who killed so easily could kill him, too, but the part of Flynn's brain that craved sex whispered that he was safe because only he could collect the millions from the Insufort settlement. And his partner had sworn they would be together after he'd banked his attorney's fee, living on a beach in an exotic country with servants and hot sex whenever he wanted it. That's what he'd been told and he wanted to believe—had to believe to rationalize the things that had been done and would be done for the millions they craved.

Juan Fulano smiled as he pulled down the binoculars. He'd gotten a very good look at the person Flynn was meeting before the front door closed. Martin would be pleased. Fulano took out his phone and made a long-distance call to Desert Grove, Arizona.

FORTY-NINE

Kate's doorbell rang at two in the morning. After the third ring, she staggered out of bed in a T-shirt and sweatpants. Daniel pulled on a sweatshirt and followed her to the front door. Kate looked through the peephole and was surprised to see Aaron Flynn looking wild-eyed and agitated.

"It's two in the morning, Flynn. What's going on?" she asked.

"I'm desperate. We have to talk. I need help. I'm afraid."

Daniel and Kate looked at each other.

"Let him in," Daniel said. "This could be our break."

Kate opened the front door. Flynn had barely stepped inside when he turned and struck her viciously in the head with a gun butt, sending her into the wall. Daniel started forward as Kate slid to the floor, but Flynn extended a .22 pistol in his direction.

"Get inside," he ordered as he bolted the door.

Daniel hesitated.

"Do it," Flynn screamed, pointing the gun at Kate. His hand was shaking badly.

Kate was dazed. Blood trickled from a gash on her cheek. Daniel helped Kate to her feet and stepped backward into the living room.

"Why couldn't you stay out of this?" Flynn shouted. "Why did you have to go to Alice Cummings?"

Flynn was sweating and his eyes were wild. Daniel knew that he had to keep him talking.

"You framed me for murder," he said. "Now you're angry because I'm trying to clear my name?"

"You stupid bastard. You're going to die, your girlfriend is going to die, and Cummings is going to die, too, and it's your fault."

Daniel was stunned. "You don't have to kill Alice."

"You put her in this position."

Kate sat on the arm of the couch and put a hand to her head. Daniel took a step forward.

"Stop! I *will* kill you," Flynn said as if to reassure himself that he could do it.

Out of the corner of his eye, Daniel saw Kate pull herself together. She was taking in the situation, focusing on Flynn.

"I know you've got someone at Reed, Briggs who's helping you," Daniel said to Flynn. "Tell the cops who it is. We can help you cut a deal."

Kate stood up.

"Goddamn it, stop," Flynn shouted as he moved the gun between Daniel's body and Kate's. He'd been told to kill them quickly and get out, but he was having trouble pulling the trigger.

Daniel lunged. Flynn fired into his torso. Daniel grunted with pain as he hit Flynn with every ounce of his strength. Flynn staggered into the door and fired again, shocked that Daniel hadn't fallen. The second shot stunned Daniel, but he still had enough strength to drive his thumb into Flynn's eye. Flynn screamed. Daniel's knees gave way. Flynn lashed out, using the gun as a club, and knocked Daniel to the floor. As he fell Kate made a spearhead with her rigid fingers and struck Flynn in the larynx. His hands flew to his throat and the gun dropped to the floor.

Flynn had trouble seeing and breathing, but he lashed out with a wild punch that caught Kate in the temple, dazing her. Flynn grabbed Kate by the throat. She tried to break the hold, but he kneed her in the stomach and she sagged. A blow to Flynn's crotch went wide and glanced off his thigh. Kate couldn't breathe. Her sight dimmed and she lashed out ineffectively in a panic. Flynn smashed her head into the wall and her body grew limp. Then there was an explosion. Blood bathed the side of Flynn's head and the grip on her throat relaxed.

Kate staggered away from Flynn and gasped for air. Flynn fell to the ground. Daniel was on one knee holding Flynn's gun. Then he toppled over on his back and clutched his stomach, now saturated with blood.

Kate dropped beside him. "Oh, God! Daniel!"

A wave of nausea swept through him. Daniel's vision blurred, but he forced himself to speak.

"Nine-one-one," he croaked. "Save Alice Cummings."

"Don't talk," Kate said as she pulled up his shirt so she could see the bullet wounds. Daniel tried to give Kate Alice Cummings's address but he felt like he was lost in a patch of fog. He knew that Kate was talking to him because he could see her lips move, but he couldn't hear her words. Those lips were the last thing he saw before he slipped away.

FIFTY

Aaron Flynn's partner pulled on a ski mask and cut across a yard that backed on the ground-floor garden apartment where Alice Cummings lived. A door at the back of the house opened onto the postage-stamp-size patch of lawn, which was enclosed by a low wood fence. The screen door was unlocked and the lock would not be much of a challenge. The plan was to jimmy the lock and cut the bitch's throat. To kill or not to kill the kid, that was the question. If he was as fucked up as Flynn said, the brat was probably better off dead.

The door only took a few minutes to open. Flynn's partner pulled a hunting knife from a sheath and took a step into the apartment.

Alice Cummings sat up in bed. Her clock read 2:13. The house was quiet, but she was certain that a noise had awakened her. Maybe Patrick was having a dream and made the noise in his sleep, because he was quiet now.

Alice lay down and closed her eyes. It was always a blessing when Patrick slept. She'd put him down at ten and crashed immediately. Five hours was good.

Alice's eyes opened wide again. She was certain that she'd just heard something. She slipped out of bed and walked to the bedroom door, which she always kept open so she could hear Patrick, and peered into the front room. Nothing seemed out of place.

The only part of the apartment she couldn't see was the kitchen, which was at the back. She edged along the wall. As soon as she turned the corner Alice saw that the back door was open.

The moment Flynn's partner took a step into Alice Cummings's apartment, a sixth sense warned her of danger. She was half turned when a damp ether-soaked cloth pressed across her mouth and nose and a muscular arm circled her chest, pinning her arms to her side. She tried to kick free as she was hoisted off her feet. She knew she only had moments before she passed out. In desperation she raised her heel and jammed it down on her attacker's instep. He swore, but his grip did not weaken. As she was dragged back across the lawn she saw the stars swirling above her, twisting in faster circles.

Alice froze at the entrance to the kitchen. Was someone in her house? Was Patrick safe? She switched on a light as she rushed to his room. His door was open. She stopped at the railing to his crib. He was curled on his side, breathing fitfully but sound asleep.

Relieved, Alice checked the rest of the small apartment. When she returned to the kitchen a cold wind swept through the door. She shivered as she pushed it shut. Then she turned the lights off so she could see outside, pressing her nose to the kitchen window to see every inch of the yard and beyond. She saw nothing strange. But someone had definitely tried to get in. Why had they left? Who had they been?

FIFTY-ONE

Kate tried to keep her face neutral when the police guard showed her into Daniel's hospital room. There were bruises on her face and the gash on her cheek had required stitches. But Daniel's injuries had been far more severe.

"You look awful," she said.

"Gee thanks," he said, his voice subdued by painkillers. "You look pretty ugly yourself."

Kate smiled, relieved that he could joke. "That picked my spirits up." She sat down next to Daniel's bed. "Now I'm going to pick up yours. Amanda and I had a long talk with Mike Greene. I think we convinced him that Flynn framed you. Amanda is pretty certain your case will be dismissed by the time you're discharged. Also, Alice Cummings is okay. When the police got to her house she told them that someone tried to break in. Her back door was wide open. But nothing happened."

Suddenly Daniel grimaced. Kate took his hand. "Are you okay?"

"Yeah. My meds must be wearing off. But I'll be fine. The bullets went through my small bowel. I only had to have minor surgery. I should be out of here in a few days."

"Charging Flynn's gun was very brave. You saved my life."

Daniel smiled. "Turnabout is fair play. Besides, I wasn't worried. I remembered what you said."

Kate looked confused. "About what?"

"You know, about how being shot in real life is different from TV. Flynn's gun was a twenty-two. I knew it would-n't pack the wallop of a larger-caliber gun, and I knew you knew all that judo stuff." Daniel shrugged. "I figured I'd get in a few good punches to soften him up and you'd fin-ish him off and call the medics."

Kate looked horrified. "You idiot. That only works if you're shot in the body. You'd be dead if Flynn had shot you in the head."

Daniel's eyes widened in mock horror. "You never told me that," he said. Then he laughed.

Kate shook her head. "You really are hopeless. I'm going to have to stick around to baby-sit you."

Billie Brewster knocked on the door.

"Thought I'd drop by and see how you're doing," she said.

"What happened with Webster?" Kate asked. Then she turned back to Daniel. "Billie questioned her today."

"Either she's innocent or she's got ice water for blood," Billie said.

"Did you hit her with the photographs?"

"She's sticking with the story she told you. She denies having anything to do with fixing cases for Flynn and she's got an answer for everything."

Billie suddenly remembered the envelope she was carrying. "By the way, I got this in the mail. It's Bernier's photograph. Flynn is in it, but Webster isn't. I thought you might be able to tell me who the woman is."

Kate took out the photograph. Daniel leaned over to see it.

"Oh, shit," Kate said, and she suddenly knew why Gene Arnold had almost fainted when he saw Claude Bernier's photograph.

FIFTY-TWO

Anna Cordova escorted Kate Ross and Billie Brewster across the terrace to the poolside table where Martin Alvarez was waiting. Alvarez stood as Kate introduced the detective.

"Claude Bernier finally sent us a copy of the photograph that Gene Arnold bought in New York. Flynn is in it, and we've identified the woman he's with."

"Really. Who is she?"

"Renee Gilchrist, a secretary at Reed, Briggs," Kate said. "Flynn represented the plaintiffs in a number of lawsuits that my firm was defending. We think that Gilchrist was working with Flynn to fix those cases."

"What does she say about that?" Alvarez asked.

"We haven't been able to ask her," Billie answered. "She disappeared the same day that Flynn was killed."

"That would certainly indicate guilt, wouldn't it?" Alvarez said.

"It's definitely suspicious."

"Do you think this woman was involved in Gene's murder?"

"Yes, we do," Billie said. "That's why we're here. Kate

has a theory about why Mr. Arnold was killed and she thinks you can help us find out if it's correct."

Alvarez spread his hands. "Anything I can do . . ."

Kate took Bernier's photograph out of the envelope she was holding and set it on the table. Alvarez showed no emotion as he studied the photograph.

"Is that Melissa Arnold, Gene's wife?" Kate asked. "The woman who was supposed to have been kidnapped and murdered seven years ago?"

Alvarez nodded slowly. His eyes never left the photograph.

"Here's what Billie and I think happened," Kate said. "When the FBI botched the arrest at the drop site, McCann got away with the ransom money, but Lester Dobbs was arrested. Dobbs cut a deal and named McCann, the only other person in the plot that he could identify. McCann was arrested quickly, but not before he hid the ransom money.

"I'm guessing that McCann refused to tell Melissa where the money was unless she got him out of jail. There was also the threat that he would cut a deal to save himself. That's when Melissa conceived the brilliant idea of faking her kidnapping.

"Looking back, Melissa had to have been involved. When she faked her own kidnapping, she only asked for seventy-five thousand dollars, instead of the million dollars she asked from you. Seventy-five grand was an amount that Gene Arnold could cover from his retirement account. Melissa would have known Arnold's financial situation."

"Of course," Billie interjected, "Melissa's kidnapping

was only a smoke screen to cover up the real reason for her plan: the destruction of her court reporter notes, which would force the judge to order a new trial. After she murdered Lester Dobbs, the court had to let McCann out of jail and she was able to kill the only witness who could identify her and get away with the money. No one thought Flynn was involved, so he was home free. Even McCann might not have known. And no one was looking for Melissa, because everyone thought that she had suffered the same fate as your wife.

"Then Mr. Arnold saw Melissa and Flynn in Bernier's photograph and flew to Portland. He phoned Flynn from his hotel the day he landed, Flynn or Melissa killed him and burned the body in the lab."

Alvarez shook his head. "I can't believe it, but it must be true."

Kate studied him carefully. She was certain that her news had not come as a surprise.

"It's too bad we can't find Melissa," Brewster said. "Whoever burned down the lab was bitten by a rhesus monkey. The medical examiner has a swab with material she found on the monkey's teeth. If we had Melissa we could run a DNA test that would prove she was at the lab. We also have an impression of the monkey's teeth that we could match to any bite marks she has on her shoulder."

"Do you have any leads?" Alvarez asked.

"Actually, we do," Billie answered. "It's another reason we came to see you. Claude Bernier called me, yesterday. His conscience was bothering him. It seems that a Hispanic gentleman visited him the day after Kate told you about Mr. Bernier's photograph. He called himself Juan Fulano. I'm told, by a Hispanic friend, that Juan Fulano is the Spanish equivalent of 'John Smith.' Is he right, Mr. Alvarez?"

"Yes."

"Fulano wanted to purchase a copy of Bernier's photograph, but he paid Mr. Bernier to do something else. Can you guess what that was?"

"I have no idea," Alvarez answered coolly.

"Mr. Fulano asked Bernier to hold off sending us the photograph until he gave the okay. Paid extra for the favor. Then, the day after Melissa Arnold disappeared, Fulano gave the okay to send the photo to Portland. Interesting, no?"

"I'm afraid I don't follow you."

"Don't you, Mr. Alvarez?" Billie asked. "You know, I made some inquiries about you to police acquaintances in Mexico and Arizona. They say you're straight now—have been for a while. But they say you ran with a very rough crowd early on. The type of people who would think nothing of abduction or murder."

Alvarez did not act offended by the accusation. "Your information is correct. I was very wild in my youth. But those days are behind me."

Billie stared hard at Alvarez. He returned the stare without blinking.

"If I asked you to predict the future would you hazard a guess for me?" the homicide detective asked.

"I have no psychic powers, Detective."

"I give you my promise that your answer will stay with the three of us."

Alvarez considered Billie's request for a moment. "Ask your question."

"My department has limited funds. I'd rather spend them on crime fighting than on a wild-goose chase. What would you guess my chances are of finding Melissa Arnold alive?"

As Alvarez thought about the question he looked at the two women. They stared back impassively. Alvarez made a decision.

"Melissa is a very clever woman, as you have discovered. My guess would be that someone so clever would be able to disappear without a trace. Whether she is alive or dead is not for me to say, but I would guess that she will never be found."

Then Alvarez shrugged and his features softened. "But the police have all sorts of modern devices I know nothing about. Really, crime detection is not my area of expertise."

Billie stood and Kate rose with her. "Thank you for your time, Mr. Alvarez," the detective said. "Kate has told me how deeply you loved your wife. I'm sorry if we uncovered old wounds."

Kate picked up the photograph and replaced it in the envelope. Alvarez did not glance at it.

As soon as the women were out of sight, he entered his office and closed the door. Then he took a copy of Claude Bernier's photograph from a wall safe concealed behind a small painting. He studied it one last time, then set it on fire. As Melissa Arnold's image burned, Alvarez turned toward the photograph of Patty Alvarez that stood in a prominent place on his desk. A tear appeared at the edge of Alvarez's good eye. He made no effort to wipe it away. He dropped the burning photograph in a wastepaper basket and watched it turn to ash.

"It's over, Patty," he whispered. "It's over."

FIFTY-THREE

"Come in, Joe," J. B. Reed said as his secretary showed Joe Molinari into his corner office. Reed was puzzled by Molinari's visit since he was not working on any of Reed's cases. To be honest, he only remembered Molinari's name because his secretary had told it to him when she buzzed him to say that one of the associates wanted to talk to him.

"What can I do for you?" Reed asked as Molinari sat down. He noticed that Molinari did not seem nervous or deferential the way most of the new associates were in his presence.

"Something is going on that you need to know about."

"Oh?"

"Just before he died, Mr. Briggs fired Daniel Ames." Reed's features clouded when Molinari mentioned his friend's murder and accused murderer. "That was wrong."

"I don't see how any of this is your business, Mr. Molinari," Reed snapped.

Molinari met Reed's fierce gaze and returned one of his own.

"It's my business," Joe said forcefully, "because Dan is a friend of mine and someone has to tell you what he's done for this firm and Geller Pharmaceuticals."

Daniel was engrossed in a thriller when J. B. Reed and Isaac Geller walked into his hospital room. Daniel paused in mid-sentence and stared, as surprised by their appearance as he would have been if Mark McGwire and President Bush had strolled into his room.

"How are you feeling?" J. B. Reed asked.

"Okay," Daniel answered tersely.

"I've come to apologize for agreeing to have you fired," Reed said.

Daniel waited for Reed to go on. The senior partner saw how tense Daniel looked and he smiled.

"I don't blame you for being very angry with our firm, but we didn't have the whole picture until Joe Molinari explained everything to me."

"Joe?"

Reed nodded. "You have some very loyal friends at Reed, Briggs. I've also spoken to Kate Ross. Molinari came to my office two days ago and read me the riot act. Said the firm owed you an apology. When he finished explaining what you'd risked for our client, I called Isaac immediately."

"I don't believe I'm exaggerating when I say that your actions may have saved my company, Mr. Ames," Geller told him. "If Flynn's scheme had worked we would have had to take Insufort off the market and I can't begin to imagine how much the company would have lost paying off legal judgments."

"I know there is no way to repay you for what you've gone through," Reed said. "The disgrace of being fired, the time you spent in jail, not to mention being shot . . . It's terrible, and I sincerely regret any part Reed, Briggs had in your ordeal, but Mr. Geller and I want to try to make it up to you. I want you back at the firm and we're prepared to give you a hefty raise."

"And Geller Pharmaceuticals wants to reward you with a substantial bonus," Isaac Geller added.

Daniel was stunned and did not answer right away.

Reed smiled broadly, fully expecting Daniel to leap at his peace offering. After all, what young lawyer in his right mind would reject a chance to work at Reed, Briggs?

"I know this must come as a shock, so there's no reason to rush your decision," Reed said. "Concentrate on getting well and call me at your convenience."

"I am overwhelmed by your generosity," Daniel said, thanking both men, "but I don't need any time to think. Actually, I've had plenty of time to think while I was in jail and while I've been recuperating. I appreciate the offer to come back to Reed, Briggs, but I don't really fit in at the firm. I respect the work you do, but I would be more comfortable working at a smaller firm, one that represents the type of person I grew up with, people who don't have anyone else to look out for them."

"Surely you must see how much good a company like Geller can do," Reed said, amazed at Daniel's rejection of his generous offer.

"I do, and I know how sleazy and dishonest a lawyer like Flynn can be, but you'll always be able to find top-notch lawyers to represent your clients, Mr. Reed. You pay for the best and you get the best." Daniel smiled. "I don't know where I fit in, but I'd like to try and level the playing field a little."

"Well, if that's what you want, you must do what you think is best. But the offer is open if you change your mind."

"Thank you. I appreciate that."

Reed started to leave.

"You know, there is one thing you two can do for me, if you're still feeling generous."

"What's that?" Isaac Geller asked.

FIFTY-FOUR

Daniel woke up slowly to the sound of the surf. When he opened his eyes he could see sunlight through the thin curtains that covered the picture window in the bedroom of the beach house. He stretched and smiled. The first thing Amanda had said when Judge Opton dismissed all the charges against him was, "I bet you've never had a job interview like this before." Then she offered Daniel the use of her beach house so he could get away from Portland and the press. His interview with the rest of the partners at Jaffe, Katz, Lehane and Brindisi was set for next Wednesday.

Daniel hoped that he would get the job with Amanda's firm, but he had no regrets about turning down J. B. Reed. Amanda Jaffe had let him see firsthand that there was another, better, way to use his law degree. Still, Daniel had not walked away from his meeting with J. B. Reed and Isaac Geller empty-handed. Alice Cummings would not have to worry about Patrick's medical expenses anymore. Daniel had sold Isaac Geller on the public relations bene-fits that Geller Pharmaceuticals would reap by agreeing to help Alice's son. Daniel didn't want any credit for the good deed. Knowing that Patrick would have a chance at a normal life was payment enough.

Daniel rolled onto his side and noticed that Kate was not in bed. In the past few days he had learned that she was an early riser. Daniel smiled at the thought of her.

Amanda's house stood on a bluff overlooking the Pacific, which was calm today. Last night, Kate and Daniel had sipped hot buttered rum and let the heat from the bedroom fireplace warm them while they watched a brutal storm assault the beach. This morning, the sand was littered with driftwood.

Daniel washed up and found Kate on the phone in the kitchen. She smiled when he walked in. He poured a glass of orange juice and sat down at the kitchen table while Kate finished her call.

"That was Billie," she said as soon as she hung up. "She found out some more information about Gilchrist. Her name was originally Melissa Haynes. Her father was a colonel in the army. He was away a lot and she grew up wild. Billie says she had a string of juvenile arrests, some involving violence, but her father used his influence to get her out of most of her scrapes.

"When she turned eighteen Melissa left home and moved to California. She married an actor wannabe, but the marriage lasted less than a year. She went to secretarial school, then learned how to be a court reporter. Gene Arnold met her during a deposition in L.A."

"Is Billie certain that Renee was Flynn's partner?"

"She'll probably never be able to prove it, but everything makes sense if Renee was the mole at Reed, Briggs. She was in a perfect position to slip the Kaidanov letter into the discovery and send Amanda the videotape. If Kaidanov called Briggs at his office to arrange the meeting at the cottage, Renee would have answered the phone and could have eavesdropped on their conversation. But there's something else that convinces me that Renee is guilty.

"We were never able to figure out why Arthur Briggs wanted April Fairweather to meet him at the cottage on the night he was killed."

"Right. It made no sense, since her case and the Insufort case were totally unrelated."

"I'm certain that Briggs never wanted Fairweather at the cottage. Renee was in the waiting area when Fairweather saw you blow up at Briggs. I bet she heard Briggs leave the message on your answering machine asking you to meet him at the cottage. I think Renee told Fairweather to go to the cottage so she would see you leaving after Briggs was murdered. With you as the main suspect, no one would look at anyone else. But better still, Renee knew that your lawyer would use the videotape to thoroughly discredit Fairweather when she was under oath, assuring another hefty attorney fee for Flynn that she would share."

"Renee probably made the anonymous call that tipped off Zeke Forbus about my call to her."

"That's my guess. But I don't think we'll ever know for certain."

Daniel stood up and took Kate in his arms. "I don't want to talk about the case anymore. We're out here to forget about it."

"If you don't want to talk about the case, what do you want to do?" Kate asked mischievously.

"I'd like to kiss you, but I'm afraid you'll use your self-defense moves on me."

"I might if there was a bed nearby."

"I guess ugly women need judo to get a handsome guy like me in the sack."

The next thing Daniel knew, Kate was behind him and had him in a hammerlock. The idea of resisting never entered his mind.

The Last Innocent Man

For Joseph and Eleonore Margolin,
great parents and good friends,
and Doreen, Daniel, and Amy,
the home team.

ACKNOWLEDGMENTS

With special thanks to Don Nash for his support, Bill Phillips, Laura Evans, and Mike Mattil for their help, and Jed Mattes for finding this book a home.

And additional thanks to Irwyn Applebaum, Elisa Petrini, and everyone at Bantam for everything you have done for me.

And finally I want to express my gratitude to Jim Tower for taking the time to share his knowledge of Mercedes-Benz cars with me, and to Dan Bronson for his excellent screenplay and his advice on a knotty plotting problem.

PART I

TRIALS

1

David Nash could see the storm clouds closing in on Portland from his office on the thirty-second floor of the First National Bank Tower. The rain would be a welcome relief from the June heat. The first large drops started falling on the river. David watched for a while, then turned his back to the window. Across the room Thomas Gault shifted his position on the couch.

The newspapers called David 'The Ice Man' because of his unruffled appearance in court, but Gault deserved the title. It was almost eight o'clock. The jury had been deliberating for two days. But Gault dozed, oblivious to the fact that twelve people were deciding whether he should be convicted of murder.

The telephone rang and startled David. Gault opened his eyes. The phone rang again and David answered it. His heart was beating rapidly as he raised the receiver. His hand felt sweaty against the plastic.

'Mr. Nash,' Judge McIntyre's bailiff said, 'we have a verdict.'

David took a breath to calm himself. His mouth

was dry. It was always the same, no matter how many times he heard those words. They were so final, and despite his record of victories, they always left him with a feeling of despair.

'I'll be right over,' David said, replacing the receiver. Gault was sitting up and stretching.

'Moment of truth, old buddy?' he asked as he yawned. He seemed to be experiencing none of the tension that David felt.

'Moment of truth,' David repeated.

'Let's go get 'em, then. And don't forget how you're feeling. I want to interview you as soon as we hear the verdict. I talked to my editor this afternoon, and he's hot to get the book into print as fast as he can. Capitalize on the publicity.'

David shook his head in amazement.

'How can you even think about that book now, Tom?'

Gault laughed.

'With what you're charging me, I have to think about it. Besides, I want to make you famous.'

'Doesn't anything ever get to you?' David asked.

Gault studied David for a second, his grin momentarily gone, his eyes cold.

'Not a thing, old buddy. Not a thing.

'Besides,' he said, the grin back in place, 'I've been through a hell of a lot worse than this in Africa. Remember, those twelve peers of mine can't kill me. Worse comes to worst, I get a few years off to write at state expense. And the worst

THE LAST INNOCENT MAN

ain't gonna come, old buddy, because I have faith in you.'

Gault's smile was infectious, and despite his misgivings, David found he was smiling.

'Okay, Tom, then let's go get 'em.'

Outside, the rain and wind were twisting the large American flag that hung from the building across the street, winding it around itself and whipping it to and fro. One of America's symbols taking a beating, David mused. If he was the lawyer everyone said he was, the blind woman with the scales would also go down for the count when they arrived at the courthouse.

IF DAVID HAD not been famous already, the Gault case would have made him so. Reporters from Paris and Moscow had flown into Portland to cover the trial of the handsome defendant who looked like a movie star and wrote like Joseph Conrad.

At nineteen, Gault, a member of a violent L.A. gang, had been given a choice between jail or the Army. Gault loved the military and was a natural for Special Forces training.

At twenty-six, Gault turned mercenary, putting his skills to work in East and West Africa.

All during his years abroad, Gault had been indulging another passion, writing. Plotted and fleshed out during his African sojourn, and completed during six months of furious activity in a cheap apartment in Manhattan, *Plains of Anguish* made Gault rich and established him as a writer of note. The novels that followed increased his literary reputation. But they were not the only reason Gault's name was newsworthy.

Shortly after the movie version of his second novel was released, Gault married his leading lady. The gossip columns were suddenly full of stories about Gault's latest affair or drunken brawl. When Gault drove his Rolls-Royce through the bedroom wall of his wife's lover's beach house, the missus called it quits. Gault, fed up with Hollywood, headed for the quiet of the Pacific Northwest.

A year later Gault emerged from seclusion, carrying the manuscript for *A Ransom for the Dying*, which won the Pulitzer Prize. While working on the book, he had met Julie Webster, whom he was presently accused of beating to death.

Julie Webster Gault, the daughter of a former secretary of commerce, was beautiful, spoiled, and rich. To her parents' horror, she married Thomas Gault after a brief courtship that consisted of several violent couplings in various odd places and positions. The marriage was doomed from the beginning.

Julie Webster was incapable of loving anyone but herself, and Thomas Gault was similarly afflicted. By the time the novelty of working their way through the *Kama Sutra* wore off, the couple realized that they could not stand each other. Gault's drinking, which was excessive in the best of times, got worse. Julie started wearing high-neck sweaters and sunglasses to cover her bruises. Then, one evening, someone beat Julie Gault to death in her bedroom on the second floor of their lakeside mansion.

The police arrested Gault. He swore that he was innocent. He told them he had been sleeping off a drunk when screams from his wife's bedroom awakened him. He said he found Julie lying in a pool of blood and had knelt to take a pulse. A sudden movement behind him had made him turn, and he had seen an athletically built man of average height with curly blond hair standing above him. The intruder struck him on the head, Gault told the police, and he was unconscious for a few moments. When the police arrived, there was blood on Gault's hands and bathrobe and a bruise on the left side of his face.

Whether Thomas Gault or a mysterious stranger had taken Julie Webster Gault's life was the subject of a two-month trial. Famous writers and movie stars took the stand, either recounting the Gaults' marital battles or coming to the writer's defense. As the case neared its end, David was worried. Then Gault took the stand.

During the time that David represented him, Gault had not shown a single sign that his wife's death disturbed him. To the contrary, he seemed happy to be rid of her. But Gault was a great actor, and his performance as a witness had been superb. He emerged from two days of direct and cross-examination as a sympathetic figure. He had even broken into tears once while testifying. The jury had been sent from the room and never saw how quickly Gault recovered his composure.

Gault was like that. He had an innate ability to tune in on, and manipulate, the feelings of other people. David found him a fascinating yet frightening man. An original in whom he sensed a quality of evil. Everything he knew about Gault made him believe that the writer's detachment was genuine. Nothing appeared to touch him. Still, he wondered how Gault would react if the jury found him guilty.

FLASHBULBS EXPLODED, AND a thin, attractive woman from NBC just missed David's lower lip with a hand-held mike. David made a brief comment to the press as he elbowed his way through the crowd toward the courtroom. Gault followed, laughing and chatting with the reporters.

A local photographer asked Gault to pose for a picture, and Gault paused, sweeping his stylishly long brown hair backward to reveal his handsome profile. At a little under six feet, with a figure kept trim by constant exercise, Gault produced a good photograph.

Cameras clicked and the courtroom doors swept open. A stir of almost sexual excitement filled the courtroom when Gault entered. David watched the faces of the women. They wanted Gault. Wanted the thrill of lying next to him and wondering if his gift would be love or death.

Gault headed down the center aisle toward the low gate that separated the spectators from the bar of the court. A man dressed in jeans and a plaid shirt said something to Gault, which David missed. Gault laughed and raised his hand in a clenched fist salute.

David followed Gault to the counsel table. Norman Capers, the district attorney, was already in place. He looked tired. The bailiff was talking to a courtroom guard. David nodded to him as he sat down. The bailiff went into chambers to tell the judge that the parties were ready. A moment later he left to get the jury.

David felt dizzy. He turned toward Gault, curious to see if his client was showing any signs of tension. He was surprised to see the writer's eyes riveted on the door that led to the jury room. There was complete silence in the spectator section.

The door to the side corridor opened and David watched the jurors walk in. They moved silently, in single file, into the jury box. There were no smiles, and they scrupulously avoided looking at Gault or the lawyers.

David felt slightly nauseated. These were the worst moments. He scanned the box for the foreman. The folded white paper was in the left hand of juror number six, a middle-aged schoolteacher. He tried to remember back. How had she reacted to the testimony? Was it a good or bad sign that she had been chosen foreman?

The noise in the courtroom stopped. The bailiff pressed a button on the side of the bench that signaled the judge's chambers. Judge McIntyre entered from a door behind the dais.

'Be seated,' the judge said. His voice trembled slightly. He, like Capers and Nash, had been worn down by the grueling trial.

'Has the jury reached a verdict?' the judge asked.

'We have,' the foreman replied, handing the verdict form to the bailiff.

Gault leaned forward and followed the paper from the jury box to the judge's hand. Someone coughed in the back of the courtroom, and a chair moved, scraping along the floor.

Judge McIntyre opened the white paper slowly and read it carefully. Then, without looking at Gault, he read,

'Omitting the caption, the verdict reads as follows: "We the jury, being first duly impaneled and sworn, do find the defendant, Thomas Ira Gault, not guilty as charged in the indictment." . . .'

There was silence for a moment; then someone in the courtroom began to cry. David expelled a deep sigh and leaned back in his chair. Gault had not moved, as if he had not heard. There was pandemonium in the rear of the court as reporters pushed forward to reach the counsel table.

In the confusion the jurors were forgotten. David watched them file out. Not one of them looked at the man they had just acquitted. Not one of them shared the joy the spectators were expressing. David knew why. In order to acquit, the jury did not have to believe Thomas Gault was innocent. The law required an acquittal if the jurors harbored a single reasonable doubt about a defendant's guilt. David was a master at creating reasonable doubt, and once again he had prevailed. But David knew what the verdict would have been under a less stringent standard. From the start Gault had proclaimed his innocence. Never once had he deviated from his original story. But David never believed that Gault was innocent. Not for a moment.

David stood up and moved away from the counsel table. Norman Capers had left the courtroom quickly. David wanted to shake his hand. He had tried a good case. Gault was being embraced by well-wishers as flashbulbs exploded around him. The solemnity of the courtroom had given way to a carnival atmosphere. The reporters were swarming around Gault now, but David knew he would be next.

David tried to feel something positive from his victory, but he was empty inside. There was no joy, no exaltation, at winning a case every other criminal lawyer in the country would have given his right arm to try.

He remembered how he had felt after his first murder case. It was funny. There had been no big fee involved. Hell, the case had been a court

11

appointment. There had been no publicity. With the exception of a few old men who spent their retirement watching trials, no one bothered to come.

The defendant was a petty thief who had made the big time by shooting a shopkeeper during a liquor-store holdup. There had been nothing of worth in David's client and no question of his being anything but guilty, but that had not mattered to David, who had been overwhelmed by his trust. A man's life depended on the exercise of David's skills, and he had pushed himself to the point of exhaustion, knowing, all along, that he would fail. He had tried every legal motion, explored every avenue, but it had not been enough.

The guilty verdict had been returned quickly. Afterward David had talked with his client for an hour in the interview room of the county jail. The man did not seem to care. But David cared. That evening, alone in his office, David cried tears of frustration, then went home and got quietly drunk.

Those had been good days. There were no tears anymore. No emotional investments. All that was left was the winning and the money; recently, he was beginning to wonder if even that was important. David had reached goals that other lawyers only dreamed of achieving. He was a senior partner in a prestigious law firm, he was nationally known, and he was wealthy. All this had been accomplished at a whirlwind pace that left little time for reflection. Now that he had reached the top, he had time to catch his breath and look around. He wasn't sure he liked what he saw.

'How many does this make?' a reporter from the *Washington Post* asked.

'I'm sorry?' David said.

'How many murder cases in a row?'

David shifted away from his black thoughts and became 'The Ice Man.' If any of the reporters noticed his initial distraction, no one mentioned it.

'I'll be truthful with you,' he said with a confidential smile. 'I've lost track. Six seems right, though.'

'Why do you think the jury acquitted Gault?' a reporter with a foreign accent asked.

'Because he is innocent,' David answered without hesitation. 'If Tom hadn't been a celebrity, they wouldn't have prosecuted him. But I'm glad they did. Gave you fellows work and kept you off the street.'

'And made you a fat fee,' someone shouted.

The reporters laughed and David joined them, but he didn't feel like laughing. He was bone tired and he wanted to go home.

There was a stir to David's right, and he turned his head. Gault was moving toward him, his hand outstretched. The mass of reporters and well-wishers parted slowly, and David had time to study his client's face. For a brief second Gault winked; then their hands touched.

'I owe this man my life,' Gault roared. 'This

man is the king. And I am going to get him so drunk tonight he won't be able to defend anyone for a year. Now, any of you suckers who want to join us, form a line. I have enough booze back at my place to get even a reporter drunk. So let's get going.'

Gault grabbed David with one arm and draped the other over the shoulders of the thin, attractive woman from NBC. David knew it was useless to try to bow out. The crowd swept him along. On the courthouse steps David caught a glimpse of Norman Capers getting into a car parked a block away. David envied him his solitude and his clear conscience.

2

It was an old wooden door.

The type you expected to find in a high-school classroom. Long ago someone had painted the windowpane in the upper half a light green to give the occupants of the room more privacy. The lock still worked, but the mechanism was slightly out of line. The door opened with a metallic click, and David looked up from his file. A teen-age girl dressed in a dirty white T-shirt and ill-fitting jeans hesitated in the doorway. Monica Powers, the deputy district attorney, stood protectively behind her.

'This is Mr. Nash, Jessie,' Monica said. David stood. Detective Stahlheimer continued to work on the tape recorder at the far end of the wooden table. It was hot and humid outside, but it was cool in the room. The wire mesh in the room's only window threw crisscross shadow patterns across the detective's broad back.

'Mr. Nash represents Tony Seals,' Monica continued. The girl looked puzzled.

'T.S.,' Monica said, and Jessie nodded. David watched her carefully. She was nervous, but not afraid. He imagined that she would never be afraid again, after what she had been through.

The girl interested him. Nothing about her suggested that she was a survivor. Her body was loose and sloppy. She wasn't ugly. 'Plain' was a better word. Unkempt strands of brown hair straggled down past her shoulders. The shoulders were rounded and the arms heavy. David would have picked her to fail, to fold under pressure. She hadn't. There was steel there, someplace. A fact worth noting when he began to prepare his cross-examination.

'Mr. Nash wants you to tell him what happened on the mountain. He'll probably ask you some questions, too.'

'Do I have to?' the girl asked. She looked tired. 'I've said it so many times.'

'But not to me, Jessie,' David said in a firm, quiet tone.

'And why should I tell you . . . help you, after what they done to me?' she challenged. There was no whine in her voice. No adolescent stubbornness. Monica had told him she was sixteen. It was an old sixteen. A runaway for the past year and a half. Then, this. Life had leapfrogged her over adolescence.

'So I can find out what happened.'

'So you can get him off.'

'If there's a way to do it. That's my job, Jessie, and I'd be lying if I said otherwise. But lawyers usually don't get guilty people off, and I want to find out what happened so I can decide whether to tell T.S. to go to trial or plead guilty or what. Only I won't be able to tell him one way or the other if I don't hear your version of what happened.'

Jessie looked down at her sneakers, thinking. It was working, David thought. His power over people. The ability to persuade. The trick he had used so many times was now as natural a part of him as his arm.

At thirty-five, David still looked open and honest, like a little boy at an American Legion oratorical contest. Jurors trusted him. When he looked them in the eye and told them that his client was innocent, they believed him. When he told a witness, like Jessie Garza, that he was interested only in finding out the truth, they spoke to him. More than once David had seen the shock on the face of a witness as something innocently revealed during an interview was used to destroy the prosecutor's case.

Jessie shrugged and walked over to a chair near Detective Stahlheimer, turning her back to David.

'I don't care,' she said. She didn't say anything else, David noted. She knew the routine.

'I think it's ready,' Stahlheimer said. Monica sat down across from David and beside the girl. She was immaculately dressed, in a double-breasted charcoal-pinstripe cutaway jacket, a matching skirt, and a cream-colored, ruffle-front blouse. Monica looked more beautiful now than she had when they were married. Their eyes met for a moment; then David looked away. He always felt a bit uncomfortable

17

when he had a case with Monica. Their divorce had been relatively amicable, but being in her presence stirred up feelings of guilt best left buried.

'This is Detective Leon Stahlheimer,' the detective said into the mike. 'It's Thursday, June sixteenth. The time is ten-oh-seven A.M. I am present in a conference room at the Juvenile Detention Center for the purpose of an interview with the victim in an attempt murder. Present are Jessie May Garza, Deputy District Attorney Monica Powers, and David Nash, the attorney for Anthony Seals.'

Stahlheimer stopped the tape and played it back. David took a pad out of his attaché case and wrote the date, the time, and 'Jessie May Garza' at the top. Monica leaned over and said something to the girl which he did not catch. Jessie crossed her fat forearms on the table and rested her head on them. She looked bored.

'Okay,' Stahlheimer said.

'Jessie,' David started, 'I represent Tony Seals, one of three boys who you claim tried to kill you several weeks ago. The purpose of this interview is for me to find out what happened and, more specifically, what part Tony . . . You know him as T.S., don't you?'

She nodded.

'You'll have to talk, Jessie, so it goes on the tape,' Monica said.

'Yes. T.S. It meant "Tough Shit," he said. I never even knowed it meant Tony.'

'Okay. I'll say "T.S.," then.'

'It don't make no difference to me.'

'Now, Jessie, I don't know what impression you have of lawyers from TV or the movies, but I'm no Perry Mason and I'm not trying to trick you here. The purpose of this talk is to find out what happened, and if I ask a question you don't understand or if you say something you want to change, ask me to explain the question or just say you want to change what you said. Okay?'

The girl said nothing.

'Why don't you just start at the beginning.'

Jessie sat up, then slouched back in the chair.

'Like, when?' she asked.

'Well, when did you first meet T.S., Sticks, and Zachariah?'

'I don't know. It was at Granny's. Whenever I started living there. Because Zack was there already, you know, and then T.S. and Sticks moved in about a week after I got there.'

'Who is Granny?'

'I don't know her last name. I heard someone call her Terry once.'

'What does Granny have going on over at her place?'

'Well, it's where a bunch of people used to crash. There was always guys who worked the carnivals when they came through. Then she used to let people fix up speed, and she used to do acid and everything, and then everything changed because Zack and Sticks

OD'd. All of them came damn close to OD'ing on pure heroin and, let's see, and so like, so like her old man's in the Navy or used to be, and she changed old mans. This guy Norman is now her new old man.'

'Is he young?'

'Oh, he's about twenty-three.'

'But she's quite a bit older, isn't she?'

Jessie laughed sarcastically.

'Like a hundred.'

'She liked having young boys like T.S. and Sticks around?'

'Yeah. She dug it.'

'Did she go with Zack for a while?'

'No. She brought Zack into the house to bring him off the needle from speed 'cause he was gettin' to the point where he needed speed all the time.'

'Were you guys speeding quite a bit the night it happened?'

'I hadn't took speed for almost two weeks 'cause the last time I did, I overacted on it.'

'What about Sticks and Zack?'

'No. Like I said, they quit speed and chemicals altogether 'cause they almost OD'd.'

'And T.S.?'

'Man, like he was constantly fucked up. Yeah, he was doin' speed and acid. But I don't know what he was into that night specifically, except for pot, 'cause we was all smoking that.'

'Well, did he seem awake and aware that night or what? How did he look?'

'I guess he was stoned. We all were, a little.'

'When you say "stoned," what do you mean? Can you describe how T.S. looked?'

'Well, he was talking slow and his pupils were big and he was dreamy. I don't really remember that much. I remember in the car, going up to the park, I was in the backseat with T.S. and he was tripping out, you know, like gazing off in his own little world. My problem remembering is I took some downers before we left and I slept through most of the ride.'

'Why did you go out there?'

'Around two that afternoon Zack tells me how there are pounds buried out by the park in a place he knows and how they're gonna get it that night. So I asked if I could go.'

'Were Sticks and T.S. around when he said this?'

'Oh, yeah. Sticks was teasin' and sayin' how they shouldn't take me, but Zack said I could come.'

'And T.S.?'

'He didn't say nothin' I can remember.'

'Okay, what happened when you got to the park?'

'Well, it took a while. I remember Sticks was driving, but Zack had to take over because Sticks was tired and got lost. Then, when we got to the place where Zack said it was, we didn't find it right away.

'We parked the car and Sticks crawled into the backseat to sleep. Then me and Zack and T.S.

went into the woods a ways until we came to the railroad tracks. There was one shovel, which Zack carried, and T.S. had a flashlight. I remember about four trains goin' by, because Zack would say to turn off the flashlight when they came, so no one would see us.

'Anyway, we walked up and down the tracks and every so often Zack would say he thought this was it. Then he'd change his mind. Finally he said this was it at a spot about twenty feet from the tracks, and we started digging.'

'Did you dig, too?'

The girl looked directly at David and smiled, as if amused by some private joke.

'Yeah, I dug. I dug almost the whole goddamn hole. Zack did almost nothin' and T.S. dug a little, but mostly he held the flashlight. And when I'd get tired, Zack would say to keep diggin' or I wouldn't get any of the weed.'

'Did you get sore?'

'Sure, but I wanted the pot.'

'Do you think there really was marijuana out there?'

'I really kind of doubt it in my mind now, because . . . well, at first, I thought . . . yeah, really, I thought there was some out there, because Zack kept sayin' dig, dig, dig, like he was determined to get it. But, now, well, when I got shot, I was in the hole and I've been thinking about it a lot. Now I think they was having me dig my own grave.'

22

David felt a chill. Just a moment, then it was gone. He saw the acne-marked, hollow-cheeked face of Tony Seals during their interview at the county jail. The eyes dull, the dirty, uncombed hair thick with grease. He was suddenly sick with himself.

'How did it happen?' David asked. 'The shooting, I mean.'

'Like I said, the tracks was behind us and I had been digging for a long time and I was tired. T.S. was standing above me and behind me to my right with the flashlight. I couldn't see Zack, but I think he was to my left, because when the train came, he was the one that said to put out the light, and I'm pretty sure the voice came from there.

'Every time a train would come the light would go out. This time the light went out and Zack said, "Keep digging." I said okay, then I heard the shot out of my left ear.'

'What happened then?'

'I was in the hole and I froze. I didn't feel no pain right then, but I was scared. I called for T.S. and Zack, but they didn't say nothing. It was dark and cold, and when the light didn't go back on, I called again. I was feeling weak and I slumped down in the hole and I was leaning against the side of the hole on my stomach with my head and arms just over the rim.

'I called again and this time I seen their shadow. They was about forty-five feet away near some trees and I yelled, "I've been shot," and they walked back.

Zack said, "Let's see," and he squatted on the edge of the hole and said he didn't see nothin', just a clot of dirt on my shirt. Then T.S. and Zack looked under the shirt with the flashlight, and they said they still didn't see nothin'.

'I told 'em again I was shot and I was getting more tired. They said they'd go for help and walked off. I said, "No," I was comin' with them, but they just walked off and I crawled out of the hole by myself.'

The look of boredom had disappeared from Jessie's eyes, and David could see that she was reliving the incident. She had a faraway look, and there was a rigidity in her body that had not been there before. Monica gave Jessie a glass of water, then looked across at David. He could read her unspoken criticism of him for representing Tony Seals.

'The car wasn't far from where we was digging, but it was hard getting back. I was feeling weak and I couldn't breathe. By the time I got there, all three of 'em was by the back of the car talkin'. I asked 'em to help me, but they acted scared and stood away, like they didn't want to be near me. The back door was open where Sticks had got out, so I laid down in the backseat. The pain started gettin' real bad then and I was cryin' and blood started coming out of my mouth and nose and I got so dizzy I shut my eyes and just laid there. I could taste the blood and that was scaring me worse than the pain. Someone started the car and I thought we were going to the hospital, 'cause that's what I asked them and they said they would.'

'Do you remember the car stopping?'

'When they dumped me out?' Jessie asked bitterly. 'Yeah, I remember that. I was lying with my head on the driver's side, but facing the back of the car and the car had been bouncing a lot like we was on a dirt road and then they stopped and the passenger door opened. Sticks or Zack, I don't know who, said to get out. That there was a kind of a plant that would stop the bleeding. I knew what they were up to, so I said I couldn't move, I was in pain. Then T.S. and Sticks grabbed my legs and pulled and Zack was on the other side pushing me out. I tried to go into the front seat and I was hanging on underneath the seat and they was pulling me out by the feet. I was really scared then, 'cause it was so dark and I didn't want to be alone. Then Zack said again how I should let go because there was a plant that stopped bleeding and I said, 'Bullshit, there's no plant that stops bleeding. Take me to the hospital.' And that's when Zack hit my fingers with the gun and I let go and they dragged me onto the ground a ways from the car.

'I lay there. I think I was cryin' 'cause they were gonna leave me alone in the dark and the pain was gettin' worse. I heard the car door slam and I yelled to them to take me with them. I even said I wouldn't take none of the pot. Then I heard two shots and I just shut up. I laid there not moving until the car drove off. I didn't move then, either.

I thought maybe one of them was waiting for me to move.

'About two minutes later they turned around and fired the rest of the shots in the gun off at me.'

It was very quiet in the room. David was having trouble taking this in, which was unusual for him. He was an old pro at this sort of thing. How many mutilated bodies had he seen in photographs or in person? How many human tragedies had he been involved in? What was this girl to him?

'How close did the shots come to you?' David asked.

'One bullet spit up dirt right near my head. So did another.'

'Did you hear any of them say anything when they left?'

'Yeah, someone said, "I think we got her," but I don't know who.'

'Do you know who shot at you from the car?'

She shook her head and put it down on her crossed arms again. She looked very tired.

'How did you get down to the bottom of the mountain? It's several miles from where the shots were fired.'

'I crawled.'

'Crawled?'

'I got scared lying there. I stayed curled up for a while, but the pain wouldn't stop and there was no sound up there. Just the wind and animals in the woods. I didn't want to stay put, so I crawled. And it took hours and it hurt so much.'

There were tears in her eyes and David felt dead inside.

'But I wasn't gonna let them do this to me. So I crawled and sometimes I walked a ways and I got to the bottom and just fell in that ditch, and anytime a car come by or a truck I'd pull myself up. That was the worst. Even worst than the shooting and being alone. No one would stop for me or help me.'

The tape recorder spun on. The rays of the sun created splotches of light on the tabletop. Monica placed her arm around Jessie's heaving shoulders and spoke soothingly. David stared at the wall. It took every ounce of control he had learned in the courtroom to keep his features from showing any emotion. Sometimes he wondered if that wasn't one trick he could do now without trying.

MONICA AND DAVID agreed to meet by the reception desk, and Monica took Jessie back to the girls' detention area. It was a little past noon and the reception room was empty. David sat down on a couch in the corner. The interview had shaken him, and he wanted some time to calm down.

A teenage boy walked up to the reception desk and David thought about the man-boy, Tony Seals, whom he was being paid so much money to represent. Eighteen years old, his brains burned out by controlled substances, not caring about anything or anyone, not even himself.

And the boy's parents. David would never have come into the office the day after the Gault verdict if Anton and Emily Seals had not been old and valued clients of his firm, and close personal friends of Gregory Banks, one of the senior partners and David's closest friend.

During the meeting Anton Seals had sat straight-backed and expressionless, wearing his conservative pinstriped suit like a uniform. His only show of emotion had been the constant stroking of his wife's hand. Emily Seals had also kept her composure, but David could see that her eyes were red-rimmed from crying. The Sealses represented old money. They were elegant people. Neither of them fully understood what their son had done to Jessie Garza, himself, or their lives.

'Why did you shoot Jessie Garza?' David had asked Tony Seals yesterday at the county jail. Even now David did not know why he had asked the question. You didn't have to know why a person violated the law to get him off.

'She was a pain in the ass.'

'You shot her because . . .'

'Well, you know, she knew how to get drugs, so we used her like that for a while, but she was a pain in the ass. Then she tore up some marijuana plants that Sticks had growing. So we were talking about what a pain in the ass she was and how no one

28

liked her because she's got such a big mouth and Zack says he'll bump her off.'

'Just like that?' David had asked. 'Just because of the plants?'

'I guess so. Zack was always talking like that. About how he was a hit man. He said he'd killed guys before, but Sticks and me didn't believe him even though he was always flashing this gun around. We didn't think he'd use it.'

'Why didn't you try to get Zack to take her to the hospital after she was shot?'

'I did say we should back at the hole, but Zack said, "Don't worry about her, she's just gonna die," so I forgot about it. Besides, I was real tired and I didn't want trouble with the cops.'

David saw Monica walking toward him and he stood up.

'Is she okay?' David asked when they were outside.

'It depends on what you mean by "okay." Physically, she's doing fine. Psychologically . . .' Monica shook her head. 'She's one tough cookie, Dave, but I don't know. And her ordeal on the mountain isn't the worst part. We're holding her until the trials are over; then we want to send her back to her parents in Montana. Only they're not sure they want her.'

'Shit,' David said.

'Yeah,' Monica answered bitterly, 'but that's life, right? Why the interest?'

David shrugged.

'She got to you, right? You better watch that, Dave. It's bad for the old "Ice Man" image.'

'Give me a break, Monica,' David said without anger. 'I'm not in the mood.'

Monica sensed his exhaustion and backed off.

'Say, I haven't congratulated you yet on the Gault verdict.'

The way she said it, David wasn't certain it was a compliment, so he said nothing.

'Norm says you tried a good case.'

'We both did.'

'Who's going to play you in the movie?' Monica asked with a mischievous grin. David laughed.

'You angling for a part?' he asked.

'Oh, I don't know. Maybe if Tom Cruise gets the lead.' She struck a pose. 'Whadda ya think? Do I still have what it takes?'

'Yes, Monica, you still do.'

And they were suddenly too close to personal problems for comfort.

'Look,' David said to change the subject, 'is there any possibility we can deal on this one?'

'Not a chance, Dave,' Monica answered.

'Not even if I threw in Tom Cruise?' David asked with a smile.

'Not even for Tom Cruise.'

'That's what I thought, but I had to try.'

'You always do.'

They stood together for a moment, until they both realized they had run out of conversation.

'Take care of yourself,' Monica said. David knew she meant it. She was the one who had been hurt most by their divorce, and that fact always made him feel bad.

'You, too,' he told her. They walked out to their cars, and David watched Monica drive off; then he shut his eyes and sat in the hot car for a moment while the air-conditioning came on. He didn't need a case like this so soon after Gault. He needed a vacation. But, then, he always did. He couldn't remember the last time he had not been under pressure. The difference was he had never thought about it before.

3

Darlene Hersch was out of breath by the time she reached the squad room. The clock over the water fountain told her the bad news. She had sprinted from the car and she was still late. There was nothing she could do about it now. Only she hated to make a bad impression. All the other officers in the special vice unit had been on the police force for several years. She was new, and it looked bad to be the only late arrival.

The squad room was small. The dull-green paint on the walls was peeling, and the linoleum-tile flooring buckled in places. Rows of clipboards hung from two of the walls. A bulletin board occupied the third. All the space in between was covered by cartoons about police work, bulletins about office procedure, and a large poster that gave instructions about what to do in the event of a fire.

A sink and a countertop ran along the outer wall. The countertop was littered with paper cups, and two pots of coffee steamed next to the room's only window. The center of the room had been taken over by two long Formica-topped tables. Sandra Tallant and Louise Guest, the other policewomen on the squad, sat at the end of the table near the door. Darlene slid onto a metal bridge chair and hoped Sergeant Ryder would not notice that she was late.

'Have another rough night, Darlene?' Ortiz asked in a loud voice. Darlene flushed. Neale grinned and Coffin snickered. Sergeant Ryder looked up from the desk at the front of the room, and Darlene turned her head and glared at Ortiz. Ortiz winked. The bastard.

Ortiz perched on the countertop near the coffee-pots. He was handsome, and he knew it. With his dark complexion, shaggy mustache, and thick black hair, curled and cared for like D'Artagnan's, he played the lady's man. Darlene thought he was an asshole.

Sergeant Ryder stood up and checked his notes on the clipboard he always carried. A big, insecure man, he was always rechecking his facts, as if he feared that they would change if he did not keep constant track of them.

'Are we all here?' he asked rhetorically. He had known the precise number of people in the room every minute since he had arrived.

'Okay, for those of you who have not been keeping up with the captain's weekly bulletin on developments in the law, last week the public defender filed a motion claiming that the equal-protection rights of Vonetta Renae King were being violated. . . .'

'They got us there,' Ortiz called out. 'Vonetta's been violated more than any whore I know.'

Coffin giggled and Ryder stared at him. Coffin covered his mouth and coughed.

'Is it all right if I continue, Bert?' Ryder asked in a tired voice. He knew there was no way to keep Ortiz from acting the clown. He also knew that Ortiz was one of his best vice cops. It all balanced out.

'As I was saying, the public defender is claiming that the prostitution laws are being unfairly enforced, because only the . . . er . . . females are being arrested. Since the statute makes anyone guilty who offers or agrees to have sex for a fee, the PD is saying that that includes the trick too.

'Chief Galton agrees. You ladies will work with a male cover. You are to stay within eye contact at all times.'

'Sergeant?' Darlene asked.

'Yes.'

'I've been thinking about this. We'll be dressing up like prostitutes, right?'

'Yes.'

'Well, what about entrapment? I mean, isn't that planting the idea in the john's head?'

'The legal adviser said it's not, but it's best to let him bring up the subject of sex and the price.'

'How far are we going to have to go to make a bust?' Louise asked.

'Yours is made pretty well already,' Ortiz said. Coffin laughed, then looked embarrassed and stopped.

'Come on, Bert, for chrissakes. This is important,' Ryder said.

And it was important, Darlene thought. And god-damn Ortiz and Coffin and Neale. Why wouldn't they take the women seriously instead of treating them like secretaries in uniform?

'That's a good question. The way the law reads, you don't have to . . . er . . . uh, have sexual relations with the trick to make a case. The law is broken if the male offers or agrees to have sexual intercourse, which you ladies know what that is, or deviate sexual intercourse, which is, uh, as the statute says, contact between the, er, genitals of one person and the, er, mouth or, er, anus of another.'

Ryder blushed. Actually blushed! Darlene wanted to laugh, but it was too sad a state of affairs. Why wouldn't he say 'blow job' or 'asshole' or any of the other words he used when women weren't around?

'So if you get such an offer for money, you can make the arrest.'

'How are we going to work this?' Ortiz asked.

'I don't want any arrests made alone on the street. We don't want anyone freaking out on us. Bring the trick to your male cover. There's less likelihood of trouble with a man there.'

'What if the trick wants you to get in his car?'

'Absolutely not. We don't get into cars. I don't want you ladies isolated from your cover. If a trick asks you to get in his car, tell him there are cops

35

around, and they'll make a pinch if they see you get in the car. Suggest a meet where your male cover is waiting. If the trick insists, brush him off.

'Okay, any more questions? No? Good. Now, I want good collars. There are certain judges, and you know who I'm talking about, who are going to jump at a chance to throw out these cases. You just wait until we bag a doctor or some big-shot attorney. So don't give them the chance.

'All right, I want Tallant and Coffin to work the area around Ninth and Burnside. Louise, you and Neale take the area by the Hilton. And Darlene and Bert, you take the park blocks.'

DARLENE STRAIGHTENED HER tight black miniskirt and dipped her knees so she could adjust her blond Afro wig in the sideview mirror of the unmarked police car. The California-surfer-girl effect produced by her straight blond hair, large blue eyes, and deep tan had been destroyed by false eyelashes, tons of pancake makeup, and gobs of red lipstick. Grotesque, she thought, as she put the finishing touches on the wig.

'Not bad, Darlene,' Ortiz chuckled. 'You may be in the wrong line of work.'

'Stuff it, Bert,' she snapped, still angry at him for the incident in the squad room.

'You know, Darlene, your trouble is you never took the time to get to know me. Now, if we had a drink after the shift, you'd get to see the real me.'

36

'Look,' she said, straightening and looking him in the eye, 'I don't have time for any of your macho shit tonight. Hand me my coat, please.'

There was heavy emphasis on the 'please.' Ortiz laughed and pulled a cheap rabbit coat out of the trunk. Darlene was wearing a fire-engine-red sweater that left her little room to breathe. She kept the coat open so the sweater showed. Black panty hose and high black boots completed her official whore uniform. She checked her purse to make sure she had not forgotten her service revolver.

Ortiz had picked a darkened parking lot for his surveillance post. An office building occupied the other half of the block on the same side of the street. There was a jewelry store, a shoe-repair shop, a beauty salon, and an all-night café across the way. The only illumination came from a series of evenly spaced streetlights.

'What's the plan?' Ortiz asked, suddenly all business.

Darlene looked up and down the street. It was a one-way street going south.

'I'll walk down the block to the corner, across from the café. That way I can get the traffic on both streets. Will you be able to see me from here?'

'Yeah. Just stay under the streetlight on the corner. This building blocks a little of my view.'

'If I get a proposition that's good enough for an arrest, I'll pat my wig. Then I'll have the trick come to the lot.'

'How are you going to do that?'

Darlene hadn't thought about the story she would use to lure the trick to Ortiz. Ortiz leaned against the side of the car watching her.

'I'll tell him I have a car in the lot and the keys to my room are in it. How's that?'

Ortiz stood up and stretched.

'Good. There's enough shadow here to keep me hidden until you're almost to the car.'

'Okay,' Darlene said. She turned her back to Ortiz and started across the parking lot. There were butterflies in her stomach, and she had a sudden urge to go to the bathroom. She always did when she was nervous, and she was suddenly nervous and a little scared.

'Darlene,' Ortiz called after her, 'don't take any chances.'

DARLENE HAD BEEN standing near the corner for fifteen minutes when the beige Mercedes drove by the first time. She got a fast look at the driver as he went by. Blond, good-looking. He had smiled at her. Darlene had smiled back, hoping he would stop, but he hadn't. Darlene had no idea why she had brought the rabbit coat along. It was way too hot for it. If she didn't get a nibble soon, she was determined to take it back to the lot. She glanced back toward Ortiz but couldn't spot him in the shadows.

The Mercedes drove by again and pulled to the curb across the street. The man signaled to her and she walked toward him, remembering to swing her hips as she went. She had to concentrate to keep from stumbling in her high-heel boots.

'Nice night,' the man said. He was a little nervous, but trying to be cool, Darlene thought.

'Nice enough,' she said. 'What are you doin' drivin' around in this big old car all by your lonesome?'

The man smiled. Probably married, Darlene thought. Where was the little woman while Papa was out cavorting? Bridge club? Maybe home watching TV while hubby is at a 'business' meeting. She could imagine how that pretty face was going to look when Papa had to explain to Mama that he had been arrested for prostitution.

'I'm just driving around, looking for a little fun. How about yourself?'

'I'm just hangin' around, sugar. Lookin' for a little fun myself.'

'I know a place where we can have a lot of fun. You want to come along?'

Darlene leaned over and rested her elbows on the window of the car. The top buttons of her sweater were open, and the blond man couldn't keep his eyes off her cleavage. This close, she could smell the liquor on his breath. He had been doing some heavy drinking, but he appeared to be able to hold it.

'I'd love to have some fun, sugar. What kind of fun did you have in mind?'

'Fun. You know,' he said evasively.

The trick was getting more agitated. Maybe he was new at the game. Darlene was beginning to get impatient. She wanted him to say the magic words so she could make her first arrest.

'Are you thinkin' of the kind of fun I'm thinkin' about?' she asked with a smile that she hoped looked lascivious.

The trick looked up and down the street.

'Look,' he said, 'why don't you get in and we can talk about it?'

'You have any money, sugar?' Darlene asked, trying to speed things up. The blond looked startled.

'Why?'

'The type of fun I'm thinking about could get expensive.'

The trick seemed very agitated. His eyes were darting back and forth rapidly.

'Look,' he said, 'I don't want to stand around here. There are cops all over. If you want to get in, get in.'

Darlene patted the wig with her right hand.

'Why are you worried about cops? I don't see any cops.'

'I can't wait anymore. Do you want to do business or not?'

Darlene felt her stomach churning. So close. She didn't want this one to get away. If she could just make him wait a minute. She was almost there.

ORTIZ SAT UP when the Mercedes slowed down.

He slouched back down in the front seat of the unmarked car when it sped up and drove on. This whole assignment was a waste of time, he thought. Busting some poor slob who wanted a little pussy and had to pay for it. That wasn't why he'd joined the force. Why did they have to take him out of narcotics just as he was beginning to get some heavy action? And working with Darlene Hersch . . . Jesus H. Christ, if that wasn't the luck of the draw. Miss Tight Ass herself. Then again, maybe she wasn't such a tight ass. Sometimes it was the ones who gave you the hardest time that wanted it the most and just wouldn't admit it to themselves. He wondered what she'd be like in bed. Good old Darlene. He chuckled to himself. Probably want to be on top. She sure acted like it most of the time.

There was that Mercedes again. And it was stopping. Ortiz sat up. Darlene was wiggling over and talking to the driver. He couldn't see much of the guy from this distance.

She was leaning over now and resting on the ledge of the driver's window. Must be a live one. Yup, she was patting her wig. Now all she had to do was get him to drive into the lot.

Ortiz was wearing a light jacket. His revolver was in a holster on his belt. He checked it. Someone who drove a Mercedes was probably going to be no trouble, but no use taking chances. Darlene was still leaning on the window. Nice ass. Even from this distance. Ortiz wondered what was taking so long.

41

Christ, he was tired. He had a thing going with a cocktail waitress at the Golden Horse, and they had been at it all night. He yawned and shook his head. He should cut down. Too many women could kill you. Just like cigarettes. Still, he ... What the—

Darlene was walking around to the passenger door and getting in. The car was driving off. Ortiz jammed his key into the ignition. The engine turned over and he started out of the lot. Shit! He remembered. The street was one-way, the wrong way. That dumb cunt. If he went around the block, he'd lose them for sure. It was late and the street was deserted. He made up his mind and wheeled right. His tires squealed when he made the turn. That stupid bitch. When he made his report she would be ... Of all the dumb things to do. He picked up the radio mike. He might need assistance on this one if the Mercedes got too big a lead. He was about to make the call when he changed his mind. If he reported what was happening, it would be real trouble for Darlene. He didn't want that. Besides, everything would be okay if he could keep the car in view.

He made the turn onto Morrison, and there it was. Two lights away, but there wasn't much traffic. He relaxed and slowed down. He didn't want the driver to spot him. Why did Darlene have to prove how hard she was? She wouldn't be half-bad if she could get the chip off her shoulder. He'd bawl her out for sure once they made the bust. No, he'd have

Sandra or Louise talk to her. She'd never listen to a man.

'WHAT'S YOUR NAME, sugar?' Darlene asked as they turned onto the freeway. The man turned his head and smiled. He had nice teeth. Straight and gleaming white, like a movie actor. A good-looking guy. She couldn't figure out why someone that good-looking would have to pay for it.

'What's your name?' the blond countered cautiously.

'Darlene.'

'A nice name. You shouldn't wear so much makeup, Darlene. A pretty girl like you doesn't need it.'

'Well, thanks,' she said, patting her hair as she looked in the rearview mirror. Ortiz was still there. Good. She had counted on Ortiz's following her. She had been nervous until she spotted him when they turned off Morrison. He would be fuming by now, she thought with satisfaction. Well, fuck him. This was going to be an A-one bust.

'You look like you have nice breasts, Darlene,' the trick said without taking his eyes off the road. There was a hard edge to his voice when he said it, and Darlene felt uneasy for a moment.

'Thank you,' she said. 'Do you have some special plans for them?'

The trick laughed but didn't say anything. Ortiz was several car lengths back. A moving van changed lanes, and its width blocked the police car from view.

'Wife doesn't treat you right, huh?' Darlene asked. The trick still didn't answer, but he did turn and look at her. He was smiling, but there was no laughter in his eyes. They made her nervous and she felt a fleeting sense of desperation.

'Well, Darlene will treat you right. Now, just what do you want Darlene to do for you?' she said, making her voice low and sexy.

THE TRUCK WAS still blocking Ortiz's view when the Mercedes turned onto the exit ramp. Ortiz swore and almost missed the turn. He still hadn't got close enough to get the license plate, and he couldn't afford to lose them. Traffic was heavy when he got to the end of the ramp, and the Mercedes's lead was increasing. He finally pulled into the traffic and the Mercedes disappeared. He slammed his fist on the dashboard but continued to scan the neon-lit restaurants and motel parking lots on both sides of the street. Nothing. Nothing. Come on. Where are you?

Then he saw it. The Mercedes was just stopping in front of the office of the Raleigh Motel. Ortiz tried to read the license as he passed the motel, but the angle was bad and he was going too fast. Through the rearview mirror he saw Darlene getting out of the car. He pulled quickly into the McDonald's next door to the motel.

*

44

'I DON'T WANT to discuss business here, Darlene, but I can assure you that you will be paid well.'

They were off the freeway, and she couldn't be sure that Ortiz had seen them exit. Damn that truck. There was something about this guy that was starting to bother her. He would not commit himself, and she was beginning to think that she had acted too hastily.

The trick turned the car into the parking lot of the Raleigh Motel. Darlene pressed the side of her purse and was comforted by the feel of the gun's outline. Ortiz wouldn't be frightened in a situation like this if he was busting a female prostitute. She looked out the back window. Where was he? She couldn't see the police car anywhere.

'I want you to register for the room,' the trick was saying. 'I'll pull around and park.'

'I don't . . .'

'There's nothing to it,' he said, smiling and handing her a roll of bills.

Darlene took the money and slid out of the front seat. The trick drove toward the rear parking lot, away from the motel office. An old man in a plaid shirt was squinting at a used paperback through a pair of thick-lensed, wire-rim glasses. He looked up when Darlene entered.

'I'd like a room,' she said.

The old man slid a registration card across the desk without comment. She took a pen from a plastic holder on the desk and filled in the squares for name and address using her own name and the address of the North Precinct. It would be good evidence when the case came to court.

'Thirty-five bucks in advance,' the clerk said. He was looking at her breasts without the slightest attempt at concealment.

'How come you didn't ask me how long I'm staying?' Darlene said as she laid down the money. The old man cocked an eyebrow at her, shook his head slowly, and took the money without answering.

'Second floor on the street side,' he said, handing her the key. The old man was reading again by the time the office door swung closed.

The office was separate from the motel rooms. Darlene crossed the parking lot and walked up the stairs past an ice machine. Her heels clanged on each metal stair and stopped when she reached the concrete landing that ran the length of the second floor on the outside of the building. Her trick was nowhere in sight. She paused outside the door of the motel room and looked down the length of the landing. She thought she saw someone standing in the shadows at the other end, but she wasn't sure. She was starting to feel nervous again. This guy could be a freak. She decided to keep her hand on her gun. She could do it by simply putting her hand in her purse. She'd have to keep some distance between them.

She opened the door and flipped on the light. The combined odor of cleaning fluids and stale air

46

assailed her. Where was the air-conditioning unit? Motel rooms always depressed her. They were so sterile and so impersonal. She often thought that hell must be a series of motel rooms where people sat, alone and unconnected.

There was a queen-size bed covered by a faded yellow bedspread. Two pillows were tucked under the spread and two cheap, natural-wood-colored end tables with matching lamps flanked the bed. A dresser with a large mirror faced the bed. A color TV perched on one corner of the dresser; a phone, with instructions for dialing out-of-town and local calls, sat on the other. Two sagging Scandinavian chairs were the only other furniture. Darlene sat in the one facing the door and put her hand in her purse. The door opened.

'Hi, Darlene,' the trick said. He was of average height, maybe a little under six feet. His slacks were light brown. The flowered shirt looked expensive. So did his polished shoes. She noticed that he locked the door when he closed it, and she tightened her grip on the revolver.

'Why did you do that?' Darlene asked nervously. The trick grinned.

'I thought we could use a little privacy,' he said. He had been moving toward her, but he stopped when he reached the bed.

'Why don't you take your clothes off?' he asked quietly. 'I want to see those breasts we were talking about.'

47

Darlene decided everything had gone too far. She had made a mistake and she wanted to get out. Maybe the guy was a freak. Maybe he just wanted her to get nude, then he'd beat off. There'd be no violation of law. Just some sick bastard whose wife didn't satisfy him. She'd be a laughing-stock. She felt ill. Why hadn't she followed instructions?

'Look,' she said, 'this isn't a peep show. If you want to have sex, say so, or I'm leaving.'

'Don't go, Darlene,' he said, 'I'll make it worth your while.'

His voice was husky now. She could almost feel his sexual desire. He was moving again. Almost to her. Darlene made her decision. She was going to end this right now. She would say he propositioned her. She had to. She'd make up a story. The trick would cop a plea anyway. He'd be too embarrassed to go into court for a full-blown trial.

'Forget the money, mister,' she said, standing. 'You'll need it for a lawyer.'

The trick froze.

'What?' he said.

'You heard me. I'm a cop and you're under arrest.'

FROM THE CORNER of the McDonald's lot Ortiz watched Darlene climb the stairs. She walked to the door near the far end of the landing and looked around before entering one of the rooms. A few seconds later a blond man walked out of the

48

shadows at the other end of the landing and walked quickly to the door. It was too far to get a good look, but the man was slim and athletic looking. He could see the flowered shirt and tan slacks pretty clearly.

When the door to the motel room closed, Ortiz started to worry. He should be up there, but he didn't want to ruin her bust. He tried to decide what to do. Ryder had paired them because of his experience. If anything happened to Darlene, it would be his fault. Ortiz made up his mind. He sprinted across to the motel.

Ortiz heard the scream as he reached the stairs to the second floor. He froze and there was a crash and a second scream. The lights were on and he could see the man's blurred silhouette through the flimsy motel curtains. It was all happening very fast. He realized that he was not moving.

The lights went out and he took the stairs two at a time. Someone was moaning in the room. Someone was breathing hard. He crashed the heel of his shoe into the door just above the lock. There was a splintering sound, but the door held. He swung his foot again and the door crashed inward. The globe lamp that hung outside the door turned the room a pale yellow. Darlene was sprawled like a rag doll against the side of a chair in the far corner of the room. Her head hung limply to one side, and blood trickled from the corner of her mouth. There was a jagged red slash across her neck, and the floor around her was covered with blood.

Something exploded across Ortiz's eyes and he dropped his gun. He was propelled into the room and he felt a burst of pain in his neck and upper back. His head crashed into the metal edge of the bed as he twisted and fell. He slumped against the bed. There was a man standing in the doorway, in the light of the globe lamp. Standing for a moment, then bolting like a startled deer. Ortiz felt consciousness slipping away. He tried to concentrate on the face. The blond, curly hair. He would never forget that face. Never.

4

'David, come over here. There's someone who wants to meet you.'

David looked around and saw Gregory Banks standing near the fireplace with several other people. Gregory was a political ally of Senator Martin Bauer, and he had organized this cocktail party at his spacious riverfront home to help raise funds for the senator's reelection.

Gregory was a large man. An ex-boxer and ex-Marine, he had started his adult life as a longshoreman and union organizer, then gone to night law school. Gregory worked as a lawyer for the unions, and the unions had made him a wealthy man.

The summer before his last year in law school, David had driven cross-country and fallen in love with Portland. One week after graduation, David said goodbye to his family and flew west from New York to take the Oregon bar examination. He had never regretted the move. East Coast law schools tended to push their graduates into corporate practice and left them with a feeling that there was something grubby and demeaning about opening a solo practice and actually going into a courtroom. In

Portland the feeling was different. There still existed a spirit of individualism that encouraged a person to try to make it on his own. Within a week of passing the bar, David hung out his shingle on the fourth floor of the American Bank Building.

David was good and soon developed a reputation as the man to see if you were charged with a serious crime. He also volunteered to take ACLU cases, pro bono. While working on a prison-rights appeal, David met Gregory Banks, another volunteer. Despite the difference in their ages, they hit it off immediately. One evening, Banks invited David home for dinner and broached the possibility of David's joining his firm. David took a week to decide. He disliked the idea of giving up a measure of his independence, but he liked the idea of being associated with Gregory Banks. He accepted, and by the time the firm moved its offices to the First National Bank Tower, he was a name partner.

'David, this is Leo Betts, a professor at the law school,' Gregory said, introducing a tall, hawk-nosed man with greasy, shoulder-length hair. Professor Betts was standing next to a mousy woman in her early thirties.

'And Doris, his wife,' Gregory added. David shook hands with the professor.

'Leo read your brief in the Ashmore case.'

'An excellent job. I'm having my first-year criminal-law class read it as an example of first-class appellate argument.'

'I'd look on it as a punishment assignment,' David said. 'It was over a hundred pages.'

Everyone in the group laughed, and Gregory indicated another couple, a short, balding man and his tall, elegantly dressed wife.

'John and Priscilla Moultrie. John's with Banker's Trust and Priscilla teaches at Fairmount Elementary School.'

Gregory had an annoying habit of introducing a person by telling his line of work. David nodded at the couple, but his attention was on an attractive young woman who had wandered over and was standing on the fringes of the group.

'What is the Ashmore case, Gregory?' Mrs. Moultrie asked. The young woman was watching him and their eyes met momentarily.

'Isn't Ashmore that fellow who raped and murdered those schoolchildren?' her husband asked.

'Yes,' Professor Betts answered with a smile. 'David was able to get the conviction reversed by the state supreme court two weeks ago. A monumental job. He convinced the court to overrule a line of cases going back to eighteen ninety-three.'

The young woman smiled tentatively, and David nodded. He would make a point, he decided, to talk to her as soon as he could break away from the conversation. The Ashmore case was not one of his favorite subjects.

'Does that mean he'll go free?' Mrs. Moultrie asked.

'No,' David sighed. 'It just means that I have to try the whole mess over again. It took a month the last time.'

'You defended that man?' Mrs. Moultrie asked in a tone that combined amazement and disgust.

'David is a criminal lawyer,' Gregory said, as if that were an adequate explanation.

'Maybe I'll never understand, Mr. Nash' – she seemed to have used his last name intentionally – 'but I knew one of those children, and I don't see how you could have represented someone who did what that man did.'

'Someone had to represent Ashmore, Priscilla,' Gregory said.

'I heard he tortured those children before he killed them,' Mrs. Moultrie said.

David almost instinctively said, 'That was never proved,' but he realized in time that, for Mrs. Moultrie, that was not the issue.

'A lawyer can't refuse to represent someone because of the nature of his crime,' Professor Betts said.

'Would you have represented Adolf Hitler, Professor?' Mrs. Moultrie asked without humor.

There was a moment of uncomfortable silence. Then Professor Betts answered, 'Yes. Our judicial system is based on the premise that an individual charged with a crime is innocent until proven guilty.'

'But what if you know your client is guilty,

Mr. Nash? Know for a fact that he held three schoolchildren captive for several days, raped them, then murdered them?'

'Oh, now, Priscilla. That's unfair,' her husband said. His face was red, and it was clear that he disapproved of the course the conversation had taken.

David felt uncomfortable. Professor Betts had been defending him, but why did he need a defense for doing something that he was ethically obliged to do? Why should this woman he had never met before feel such obvious hostility toward him?

'I'm afraid I can't discuss the facts of the case, Mrs. Moultrie. I'd be violating my client's confidence if I discussed his guilt or innocence with you.'

'Hypothetically, then. I really want to know.'

'You represent a guilty man as hard as you do an innocent man, Mrs. Moultrie, because the system is more important than any individual case. If you start making exceptions with the guilty, sooner or later you'll make exceptions with the innocent.'

'So you represent people that you know are guilty?'

'Most of my clients are guilty.'

'And you . . . get them off . . . win their trials?'

'Sometimes.'

'Doesn't it ever bother you?'

DAVID WATCHED THE scattered lights on the houseboats moored across the river. The sun was down and a cool breeze drifted inland, gently rearranging the lock of thick brown hair that fell across his forehead. It was pleasant standing on the terrace. The shadows and stillness soothed him.

Somewhere upriver the shrill blast of a tanker's horn punctuated the darkness. The sound died and the river was at peace again. David wished that he could restore his inner peace as easily. The discussion about the Ashmore case had upset him. It had stirred something inside that had been lurking for too long. Something ugly that was starting to crawl into the light.

This morning at the juvenile home, interviewing that young girl. What happened? When she was describing her ordeal, he had felt shame and pity for her. He had become emotionally involved. That should never have happened. He was a professional. One of the best. He was not supposed to feel pity for the victim or revulsion for his client.

Something was definitely wrong. He was getting depressed too much lately, and the feeling was lasting too long. There had been times in recent weeks when his mood would plunge rapidly from a high, floating sensation into deep melancholy for no apparent reason. And that feeling. To live with it too long was to experience a kind of death. It was as if his spirit evaporated, leaving his body a hollow shell. He would feel empty and disoriented. Movement was impossible. Sometimes he would sit immobile, on the verge of tears, and his mind would scream, 'Why?' He was in excellent health. At thirty-five, he was at the top of his profession, making more money than he ever had. Everything should have been going so well, but it wasn't.

There had been a time when losing any case had been a deep, personal defeat, and winning, a magnificent triumph. David had lost those extreme feelings of involvement somewhere along the way. One day he had won a very difficult case, and it just did not matter. Another time a client received a long prison term, and he felt nothing. His world had shifted from dark black and bright gold to shades of gray.

If his professional life was empty, his personal life was even more so. He had heard more than once that he was envied by other men for the steady parade of beautiful women he escorted. Few people knew that the routine had grown old a long time ago.

His one attempt at marriage had been a disaster that lasted officially for two years, but which ended emotionally after eight months. Monica resented the long hours he worked, and in truth, he was rarely home. There had been so many big cases. He was just starting to reach the top then. Everyone wanted David Nash, and there didn't seem to be enough time for his own wife.

There had been violent arguments and too many stony silences. Monica had accused him of infidelity. He denied her accusations, but they were true. He was trying cases in other states now, and if some Texas filly wanted to warm his bed . . . well, he was a star, wasn't he? In the end the constant bickering exhausted them both, and whatever had motivated them to marry was not strong enough to keep their marriage together.

Monica had gone to law school after the divorce. David thought she had done it to compete with him. It was certainly not coincidence that led her into criminal prosecution. The tension was there whenever they tried a case against each other. David sensed that their legal battles were, for Monica, only an excuse for carrying on a personal battle of which he had never been a part. That, of course, was the problem with their marriage. If David had cared about Monica, it would never have broken up. But he had ignored her, and he felt guilty that she still felt a need to prove something to him.

David had seen little of Monica between the divorce and her graduation from law school. After she joined the district attorney's office, their friendship had renewed. They were much better friends than spouses. Sometimes David wondered if he hadn't made a mistake with Monica, but he knew that if he had, it was too late to rectify it. Their problem was that they had met at the wrong time.

David took a sip from his glass. The gin tasted too sweet. He carried the drink to a corner of the terrace that was not illuminated by the lights from the house and sat down on a lawn chair. He closed his eyes and tilted his head back, letting the chair's metal rim press into the back of his neck.

Monica was an attractive woman, and she was a different, stronger person than she had been when they'd met. David was different, too. He had toyed once with the idea of trying to reestablish their relationship, but had given up on the idea. He wondered what she would say if he tried.

The terrace door opened and a splash of sound interrupted David's thoughts. He opened his eyes. A woman was standing with her back to him, staring across the river as he had moments before. She was tall and slender, and her long, silken hair looked like pale gold.

She turned and walked along the terrace with a dancer's grace. The woman did not see him until she was almost at his chair. He was hidden by the shadows. She stopped, startled. In that frozen moment David saw her set in time, like a statue. Blue eyes wide with surprise. A high, smooth forehead and high cheekbones. It was the woman he had seen earlier on the fringes of the group that had been discussing the Ashmore case.

The moment ended and the woman's hand flew to her mouth. She gasped. David stood up, placing his drink on the terrace.

'I'm sorry if I frightened you,' he said.

'It's not your fault,' the woman answered, waving her hand nervously. 'I was thinking and I . . .' She let the sentence trail off.

'Okay,' David said, 'you've convinced me. We're both at fault. How about calling it a draw?'

The woman looked confused; then she laughed, grateful that the awkward moment was over.

'My name is David Nash.'

'I know,' the woman said after a moment's hesitation.

'You do?'

'I . . . I was listening when you were talking to that woman about the murder case.'

'You mean that Ashmore business?'

'She upset you, didn't she?'

Now it was David's turn to hesitate.

'It wasn't pleasant for me to try that case, and it won't be pleasant to retry it. I don't like to think about it if I don't have to.'

'I'm sorry,' the woman said self-consciously. David immediately regretted his tone of voice.

'You don't have to be. I didn't mean to be so solemn.'

They stood without talking for a moment. The woman looked uneasy, and David had the feeling that she might fly off like a frightened bird.

'Are you a friend of Gregory's?' he asked to keep the conversation going.

'Gregory?'

'Gregory Banks. This is his house. I thought you were with that group that was talking about the case. Most of them are Gregory's friends.'

'No. I really don't know anyone here. I don't even know why I came.'

She looked down, and David sensed that she

was trapped and vulnerable, fighting something inside her.

'You haven't told me your name yet,' David said. The woman looked up, startled. He held her gaze for a moment and saw fear and uncertainty in her eyes.

'I'm afraid I have to go,' she answered anxiously, avoiding his question.

'But that's not fair,' David said, trying to keep his tone light. 'You know my name. You can't run off without telling me yours.'

She paused, and their eyes met again. He knew that she was debating whether to answer him and that her answer would determine the course of the evening.

'Valerie,' she said finally. 'Valerie Dodge.' And David could tell by the firmness in her voice that Valerie had resolved her doubts in his favor, at least for the moment.

David had a lot of experience with women, and there was something about this one that he found intriguing. Common sense told him to go slowly, but he noticed a change in her mood. When she told him her name, she had committed herself, and his instincts told him to take a chance.

'You're not enjoying yourself here, are you?' he asked gently.

'No,' she answered.

'I wasn't either. I guess that woman upset me more than I'd like to admit. Look, I'd like to make a suggestion. I know a nice place in town where we can grab a late supper. Are you interested?'

'No,' she said, momentarily dashing his hopes. 'I'd rather you just take me to your house.'

DAVID'S CANTILEVERED HOUSE strained against the thick wooden beams that secured it to the hillside. In the daytime you could stand on one of several cedar decks and look across Portland toward the snow-capped mountains of the Cascade Range. In the evening you could stand in the same place and see the Christmas-light grid of the city spreading out from the base of the hill.

The house was modern, constructed of dark woods that blended into the greenery of the West Hills. It had three stories, but only one story showed above the level of the road, the other two being hidden by the hillside. The house had been custom-built to David's specifications, and the east wall was made almost entirely of glass.

David helped Valerie out of the sports car and led her down a flight of steps to the front door. The door opened onto an elevated landing. The landing looked down on a spacious, uncluttered living room, dominated by a huge sculptural fireplace that resembled a knight's helmet with the visor thrown back. The fireplace was pure white and the carpeting a subdued red. There were no chairs or sofas in the room, but a seating platform piled high with pillows of various colors was incorporated into the sweep of the rounded, rough-plastered walls. The only other furnishings in the room were a low, circular light wood table and several large pillows.

A spiral staircase on the left side of the room led upward to the bedroom and down to the kitchen area. A balcony that ran half the length of the third floor overlooked the living room.

'This is magnificent,' Valerie said, taking off her shoes and walking barefoot across the carpet to look at a large abstract painting that hung to the left of the fireplace.

'I'm glad you like it. Do you want the grand tour?'

She nodded, and he led her downstairs into the kitchen and dining room, then back to the second level. The den was located on the south side of the house, and it looked out onto the hillside. It was small and cluttered with briefs, legal periodicals, books, sheets of paper, and pens and paper clips. A bookcase was built into one wall, and a filing cabinet stood in one corner. The walls were decorated with framed clippings from some of David's best-known cases. Valerie skimmed the texts of a few of them.

'Did you win all these cases?'

'Those and a few more,' he answered, pleased that she had noticed them.

'Are you famous?'

David laughed.

'Only in circles that you're not likely to travel in.'

'Oh, for instance?'

'Murderers, dope fiends, pimps, and rapists.'

'How do you know I'm not a rapist?' she asked. She had attempted to ask the question coolly and casually, but a tremor in her voice betrayed her nervousness. She heard the tremor and looked away, embarrassed, when he looked at her.

'I still haven't shown you the top floor,' David said evenly. He led her up the spiral staircase to his bedroom. The lights were off and the bedroom curtains had not been drawn shut. They could see the moon floating above the pine shadows.

Valerie walked across the room and pressed her forehead against the cool glass of the picture window, watching the lights of the city. David stood beside her and gently touched the smooth skin of her shoulder. She turned to face him and he took her in his arms. His lips pressed softly against hers. She hesitated for a moment, and her body tensed under his touch. Then she flung her arms around him, pulling him into her, returning his kiss with great passion.

David stepped back, surprised at the ferocity of her reaction. Valerie looked into his eyes and unfastened the straps of her summer dress. It floated down the long lines of her body in slow motion. She stood in the moonlight, her face in shadows.

David took off his clothes, his eyes never leaving her. Her body was magnificent. An athletic figure with breasts that were small and perfectly formed. He watched the gentle rhythm of her breathing and the rise and fall of her rib cage under her smooth, tanned skin.

They touched and she melted into him. They stroked each other, and he forgot where he was and who he was. There was desperation and abandon in her lovemaking, and she moved under him with violence and passion until her body suddenly arched and her eyes closed tight. He could feel her fingers digging into his back and he heard her gasp, then moan.

They held each other for a while; then David rolled slowly to his back. She pressed her head to his chest and sighed. He wound his fingers through her long blond hair. His fingers strayed to her cheek. It was damp with tears.

'Don't cry,' he whispered.

'I'm always sad after I make love. Really make love. I feel . . . I don't know . . . as if I'd lost something.'

He sat up and gently pushed her back. Moonlight illuminated her hair and made it look like strands of gold against the pale blue of the pillow cover.

'You're very beautiful,' David said. She turned her head away from him.

'Have I said something wrong?' he asked.

'No . . . I . . . it's just that . . .'

He placed a finger over her lips, then kissed them. The longing he felt for her welled up in him. She drew him down.

'I HAVE TO go,' she said. 'It's very late.'

He looked at the digital clock on his nightstand. It was after midnight.

'Why don't you spend the night? I promise to cook you a terrific breakfast in the morning.'

Valerie looked suddenly worried.

'I can't stay, David. It's . . . I just can't.'

'Why?' David asked, concerned by her sudden change of mood.

'Please, David. It has nothing to do with you. I can't stay. That's all. Can you take me back to Mr. Banks's house? I left my car there.'

David nodded. She stood up and walked to the bathroom, picking up her clothes on the way. He watched her from the bed. She pressed the light switch, and floor-to-ceiling mirrors reflected her in a halo of light. Each part of her body was like a piece of fine sculpture. The long, thin arms, the well-formed legs, the flat, muscular stomach. He wanted to touch her again.

She moved out of his line of vision, and he heard the shower door open. David lay back on the bed and looked at the ceiling. They had been good together sexually. He felt as if he were giving a part of himself when he was inside her, instead of simply taking. He had not felt that way in a long time.

The shower started and David turned his head toward the bathroom door. He didn't want Valerie to leave and he wondered why she had to. The obvious answer was that she was married. That would explain her nervousness at the party. Would it make any difference to him if he found out she was married? No, he decided.

The water stopped and David started to dress. He wondered what it would be like to love somebody. What he and Monica had was not love, but he had never felt as strongly about any other woman. He thought about Gregory Banks and his marriage, which had lasted so long. What was the secret? Was it all chemical? Was he missing something that other men had?

Valerie finished combing her hair and turned off the bathroom light. David put on a pair of slacks. He looked at her while he buttoned his sport shirt. Valerie walked around the room, glancing out the window, fingering objects, not looking at him. He wanted to see her again. There was something about her. He wanted to know if what he felt for her was a product of the magic of the evening or something more.

They rode down from the hills in silence. The view was very beautiful, and neither wanted to break the spell it created. Most of Gregory's guests had left, but there was still noise coming from the big house. Valerie's car was at the foot of the long, winding driveway. David stopped behind it. He turned off the ignition and they sat in the dark.

'I'd like to see you again,' David said.

She looked suddenly nervous, as if she regretted the evening.

67

'Is something wrong?' he asked.

'David,' she said slowly, 'I don't want you to misunderstand. I enjoyed . . . had a wonderful time . . . being with you. But I'm a little confused just now.'

She stopped. He wanted to hold her. To press her. To make her commit herself. But he knew that would be a mistake.

'All right,' he said. 'I'm glad we spent the evening together, too. If you feel the same way, you know how to get in touch with me.'

Valerie looked down at her lap, then turned quickly and kissed him, opened the door, and walked to her car. David watched her drive off. He was tired and a little down, but he didn't start back immediately.

5

Sunlight streamed through the glass wall of David's bedroom, and he stretched. The warm morning sun made him feel lazy and relaxed. He opened his eyes. A bird was singing and he could see green pines profiled against a clear blue sky. He should have been elated. Instead, he felt a sense of loss. Nothing overwhelming, but real enough to put him off his stride.

In the bathroom he splashed cold water on his face, brushed his teeth, and shaved. He returned to the bedroom and began to perform calisthenics in front of a full-length mirror. He enjoyed watching the play of his muscles as they stretched and contracted. When he broke a sweat, he did some stretching exercises to loosen up his legs. Then he slipped into a pair of shorts and a T-shirt and laced up his running shoes.

David's house was on a three-and-a-half-mile road that circled around the hill back to his front door. His morning run took him past sections of wooded area and other modern homes. There were a few other joggers out and he nodded at them as he went by. This run had become a daily routine for the past five years. His body had become a victim of the sedentary nature of the legal profession. Turning thirty had made him self-conscious about the softening process he was going through. So it was back to the weights and miles of jogging and an attempt to return to the muscle tone of his youth.

It was nine o'clock. He had slept later than usual, but that was okay. He had no court appearances and, at the moment, nothing very pressing to work on other than the Seals case.

Halfway around, David spotted a pretty girl running in front of him. She made him think of Valerie Dodge. Valerie had had a strange effect on him. Perhaps the mysterious way she had ended the evening was responsible for his desire. Perhaps it was the mixture of passion and reticence that had permeated their lovemaking. When they were in bed, she held him so tight; then, just when he thought she was giving herself completely, he would suddenly feel a tension in her that implied a spiritual withdrawal from the act. It had been confusing, yet entrancing, suggesting a mystery beneath the surface of the slender body he was holding.

David sprinted the final quarter mile to his house. He showered and dressed for work. He had decided that he could not wait for Valerie Dodge to call him. He was going to find her.

'BAUER CAMPAIGN HEADQUARTERS.'
　'Joe Barrington, please.'
　'Speaking.'

'Joe, this is Dave Nash.'

'Some party last night, Dave. Tell Greg thanks a million.'

'I'm glad it worked out all right.'

'The senator was really pleased.'

'Good. Look, Joe, the reason I called was for some information. You helped Greg draw up the invitation list for the party, right?'

'Sure. What can I do for you?'

'I met a woman at the party. Her name is Valerie Dodge. Tall, mid-twenties, blond hair. I promised I'd give her the answer to a legal question and I lost her phone number. I called information, but she's not listed.'

'No problem. Give me a minute and I'll get the list.'

'Dave,' Joe Barrington said a minute later, 'doesn't look like I can help you. There's no one named Dodge on the list. Did she come with someone?'

'No. She was alone.'

'That's funny. I'm certain everyone we invited was on the list. Of course, Greg might have invited someone on his own. Or the senator. Do you want me to check?'

'Would you?'

'No problem. It might take a few days, though. We're all backed up here.'

'That's okay. There's no rush. She'll probably call me in a day or so if she doesn't hear from me.'

'Tell Greg thanks. Don't forget. The senator's

going to drop him a line personally, but it might take him some time to get around to it.'

'I'll tell him. Thanks again.'

David hung up and learned back in his chair. No name in the phone book or on the list. Maybe Valerie Dodge wasn't her right name. If she was married, she might have given him a phony. He had to see her again. The more mysterious she became, the greater became David's desire. He closed his eyes and started thinking of ways to track her down. By lunchtime he still hadn't thought of any.

ORTIZ HEARD RON Crosby enter his hospital room. He turned his head toward the door. It took a lot of effort to do even that. His twin black eyes and bandaged nose made him look like a boxer who had lost a fight. His head throbbed and his broken nose hurt even more.

'Ready to get back to work, Bert?' Crosby asked. Ortiz knew Crosby was just trying to cheer him up, but he couldn't smile.

'Is she . . .?' Ortiz asked in a tired voice.

'Dead.'

Ortiz wasn't surprised. No one had told him, but he knew.

'Can you talk about it, Bert?' Crosby asked. He pulled up a gray metal chair and sat down beside the bed. This wasn't the first time he had been in a hospital room interviewing a witness in a homicide. He had been on the force for fifteen years, and a homicide detective for eight of those. Still, it was different when the witness was a fellow cop and a friend.

'I'll try,' Ortiz answered, 'but I'm having trouble getting it all straight.'

'I know. You have a concussion. The doctor said that it's going to make it hard for you to remember for a while.'

Ortiz looked frightened and Crosby held up his hand.

'For a while, Bert. He said it goes away in time and you'll remember everything. I probably shouldn't even be here this soon, but I was gonna drop in to see how you were, and I figured it wouldn't hurt to pump you a little.'

'Thanks for coming, Ron,' Ortiz said. He shut his eyes and leaned back. Crosby shifted on his seat. He was short for a policeman, five eight, but he had a big upper body and broad shoulders that pushed past the edges of the chair back. He had joined the force in his late twenties after an extended hitch in the Army. Last February he turned forty-two, and gray was starting to outnumber black among his thinning hairs.

'I can't remember anything about the murder. I vaguely remember a motel, but that's it. I can remember the car, though,' he said, brightening. 'It was a Mercedes. Beige, I think.'

The effort had taken something out of him, and he let his head loll like a winded runner.

'Did you get a license number or . . .?'

73

'No, I don't think so. It's all so hazy.'

Crosby stood up.

'I'm gonna go and let you get some rest. I don't want to push you.'

'It's okay, Ron. I . . .' Ortiz stopped. Something was troubling him.

'What does Ryder think?' he asked after a while. 'I mean, does he think I . . .?'

'He doesn't think anything. No one does, Bert. We don't even know what happened.'

Ortiz put his hands to his head and ran them across the short stubble that covered his cheeks. He felt drained.

'What if it was my fault? I mean, they put me with Darlene because she was new, and what if . . .?'

He didn't finish.

'You've got enough to worry about without taking a strong dose of self-pity. You're a good cop and everybody knows that. You worry about getting better and getting your memory back.'

'Yeah. Okay. I just . . .'

'I know. See you, huh?'

'See you. Thanks again for coming.'

The door closed and Ortiz stared at it. The drugs they had given him were making him sleepy, but they didn't get rid of all the pain. They just made it bearable. He closed his eyes and saw Darlene. She had been an annoyance. Really juvenile. Had he screwed up because he had got mad at her? He wished that he could remember what had happened. He wanted to help get the killer, but, most of all, he wanted to know if it was his fault that a young policewoman was dead.

6

The first half of July was cool and comfortable. There was a subdued sun, light breezes, a mad array of flowers, and underdressed girls in eye-catching getups. Then, overnight, the breeze disappeared, the sun went mad, and a thick, unmoving mass of hot air descended on Portland, wilting the flowers and making the girls look tired and worn. To David the oppressive heat was merely a meteorological expression of his mood. The torpid air had a dehydrating effect that wore away the energy of the city, and, in a similar way, David could feel his mental and spiritual energy draining away, like wax slowly dripping down the sides of a candle.

All his attempts to locate Valerie Dodge had failed, and she had not called him. Perhaps David desired her because he could not find her, but her absence gnawed at him, confronting him with the void that was his personal life.

Work provided no escape. It only deepened his depression. The Gault case had brought him many new clients, all guilty and all hoping that he could perform a miracle that would wash away their guilt. His work on their behalf disheartened him. More and more he felt that he was doing something he should not.

The originality that had characterized David's early legal career was giving way to a highly polished routine that let him move through his cases without thinking about them. His success as a lawyer was due to his brilliance and his dedication. Others might not notice, but David knew he was no longer giving his best effort. So far that had made no difference in the results he had achieved. But someday it would. On that day he would know, even if no one else did, that he was no different from the ambulance chasers and incompetents who practiced at the gutter levels of criminal law.

The trial of Tony Seals was scheduled for late July, and David was working on his final preparations when the receptionist told him that Thomas Gault was in the reception room. David had seen little of the writer since the trial, except for a half-day interview for background on the book. David had not felt much like talking about Gault's case, but he was sharing in the proceeds of the book and was obligated by contract to cooperate. The interview had taken place the day after the trial, and a week after that Gault had taken a vacation in the Caribbean, then gone into seclusion to finish the book.

David did a double take when his office door opened. Gault laughed. He loved to shock people, and his appearance provided a low-grade jolt. Below the neck Gault looked the same. It was his head that had changed. His long brown hair had been shorn off, leaving a gleaming skull, and his upper lip sported a Fu Manchu mustache.

'Jesus!' David said, to Gault's delight. 'Have you taken up professional wrestling?'

'I'm changing my image,' Gault answered with a grin.

'Sit down,' David said, shaking his head. 'What brings you to town?'

'The book. My editor wants me to beef up the final chapters, so he suggested that I get a little more of your thinking about the trial.'

'What do you want to know?'

'I don't know. It was his idea. What you ate the morning of the main event. Who does your clothes. Think of something. After all, I'm doing the work, but you're getting part of the profits. Take an interest.'

'Tom, I have no idea what would interest your readers. Give me a hint.'

'You ever play any sports in high school or college?'

David shrugged.

'I ran a little track in college and wrestled some.'

'Okay. Why don't you tell me how trying a case compares to the feeling you get just before a sporting event. How's that?'

David thought for a few minutes before answering.

'I don't think they're that similar,' David said. 'Winning or losing at sports depends on your performance during the sporting event, but a lawyer can't win a case at trial. Or, anyway, not usually.'

'What do you mean?'

'Well, the facts of each case are determined by the time the case gets to you. All the facts might not be revealed, but they're there. So a lawyer wins his case before trial by finding out, through investigation, what the facts are. A lawyer can't change the facts, but once he knows what the facts are, he can deal with them. Try to get the jury to look at them in a certain way. And there is usually more than one way to look at the facts.

'A few years back I represented a man who tried to hold up a minimart. He walked in with a shotgun and told the manager to give him the money or he would kill him. The manager was a feisty little guy, and he whipped out a handgun and shot my client through the neck. When the police arrived, my man was lying in a pool of blood holding the gun, and there were five eyewitnesses who swore that he tried to rob the place. The DA charged my client with armed robbery. Those were the facts I started with. Want to guess the verdict?'

Gault smiled.

"It has to be not guilty, but how did you do it?"

'There were other facts we didn't know about when we started. When they took the defendant to the hospital for surgery, they took a blood sample.

One of the routine checks the hospital makes before performing surgery is to find out how much alcohol a person has in his system. My man was loaded. He had consumed so much alcohol that I was able to get two prominent psychiatrists to testify that a person in his condition would not be able to form the intent to commit the crime, and the district attorney must prove intent as one of the elements of the crime of armed robbery.

'The next step was to find out why my client drank like that. It turned out that his wife had died and he had gone to pieces. When I got him, he was already an alcoholic.

'Finally, we had to figure out why he had been at the minimart in the first place. My investigator asked around, and it turned out that our boy had been blotto that day. Two of his buddies had planned the robbery and sent him inside. He was so drunk, he didn't know what he was doing. In fact, he doesn't remember what happened to this day.

'When we presented all the facts to the jury, they acquitted. It wasn't what we did at trial, but the investigation before trial, that mattered. Getting the facts, then presenting them in a favorable light at trial.'

'And is that what you did in the case of State versus Thomas Ira Gault? Manipulate the facts?' Gault asked with an impish grin.

David looked straight at Gault without smiling. The question had caught him off guard.

'Yes,' he answered.

'You know, David,' Gault said, 'there is something I've always wanted to ask you. All the time you were defending me, and doing such a bang-up job, what did you think? Guilty or innocent? Tell me.'

'Guilty,' David said without a moment's hesitation. Gault threw back his head and laughed loudly.

'Terrific. And you still worked your ass off. David, old buddy, you are a pro. Now, do you want to know something?' Gault asked in a conspiratorial tone.

'What?'

'Is that attorney-client thing – the privilege – is that still in effect?'

David nodded, very tense.

'Anything I tell you is secret, right? No police, nobody else finds out, right?'

David nodded again. Gault leaned back in his seat and grinned.

'Well, I did it, old buddy. Beat the shit out of her. Ah, she deserved it. She was a real bitch. I mean the original bitch. Anyway, I was tanked. Really polluted. But randy. Very hot to trot. And do you know what? She turned me down. The bitch would not spread. I couldn't let her get away with that, could I, Dave? I mean, I was really ready for some exotic stuff. Not your missionary position. No, sir. I was going to dick her good. But she said no dice, so I decked her. It felt great.'

Gault paused for effect. David didn't move.

81

'Have you ever hit a woman? No? It feels terrific. They're soft. They can't take the pain.'

Gault closed his eyes for a moment, and a beatific expression possessed his features.

'Julie was very soft, Dave. Soft in all the right places. And she adored pain. Loved it. So I gave her the ultimate in pain. I gave her death.'

Gault paused and looked directly at David.

'What do you think of that, Dave?'

David didn't know what to say. He felt sick. Gault's face had hardened into a sadistic mask as he talked, and the handsome features looked twisted and grotesque. Then the face split open and Gault began to shake with laughter.

'Oh, you should see your face. God!' he roared between breaths. David was confused by the sudden change.

'It's not true. I made it all up,' the writer gasped. 'What terrific dialogue. You should see your face.'

'I don't . . .' David started.

'It's a joke, son. Get it? A joke. I didn't kill Julie. She was a bitch, all right, and I'm not broken up about her death. But, shit, she was a human being and I'd hate to see anyone go the way she did.'

Gault stopped and David tried to speak. He didn't know whether he wanted to hit Gault or get a drink.

'You son of a bitch,' he said finally.

'Really had you going, didn't I?'

'Jesus.'

'Serves you right for thinking I did it in the first place.'

But David didn't know what to think. There had been something about the expression on Gault's face when he was making his confession . . .

'Aren't you going to say anything, old buddy?' Gault asked, his grin spread across his face.

'I don't know what to say,' David answered, his tone betraying some of the anger that had replaced his initial shock and confusion.

'Aw, come on, Dave. You're not mad, are you?'

'Dammit, Tom,' David said, his face flushed, 'that's not something to kid about.'

'Now, that's where you're wrong, boy-o,' Gault answered. 'The first thing you learn when you are soldiering is that Death is a joke. The ultimate prank, old buddy.'

Gault leaned across the desk. He was talking toward David, but David sensed that Gault was speaking to himself.

'Death is everywhere, and never forget that. The more civilized the surroundings, the harder it is to spot the little devil, but he's there, hiding in the laundromat, peeping out from your microwave oven. He's got more camouflage here in Portland, but he's always present.

'Now, there's two ways of dealing with Death, old buddy: you can fear him or you can laugh at him. But I'll tell you the truth: it don't make no difference how you treat him, because he treats us all the same. So when you're in the jungle, where you see Death every day standing buck naked right out in the open, you get to know the little devil real well and you learn that he is a prankster and not a serious dude at all. And you learn that it's better to die laughing than to live each moment in fear.'

Gault stopped abruptly and sat back in his chair. 'I hope I remember that,' he said. 'Be great in my next book, don't you think? Real profound.'

'Very, Tom,' David said, still unsure of what to make of Gault's confession and disconcerted because of his uncertainty. 'Look, do you mind if we work on the book some other time?'

'Hey, I didn't upset you, did I?'

'No, Tom,' David lied, 'I just didn't expect you and I've got some things to do. Why don't we get together sometime next week?'

'Sounds good,' Gault said, standing. 'I'll give you a call.'

Gault started to leave, then stopped with his hand on the doorknob.

'One thing, Dave. If that had been the truth, if I really had killed Julie, would you have kept it a secret?'

'I never reveal a client's confidence.'

'You're all right, old buddy. And you should take care of yourself. You don't look so hot. Get more sleep.'

Gault winked and he was gone.

7

It took David a long time to calm down after Gault left. Was it all a joke? Gault had a sadistic streak in him. He had enjoyed seeing David wriggle on his hook. But when he was discussing the murder, he seemed so sincere, he seemed to be reliving an experience, not creating one. David didn't know what to think, and the worst thing was that the attorney-client privilege prevented him from discussing with anyone what Gault had said.

The intercom buzzed and David was grateful for the diversion. It was Monica calling from the district attorney's office.

'Can you come over, Dave?' she asked.

'Sure. What's up?'

'I want to talk to you about Tony Seals.'

'What about him?'

'I'll tell you when you get here,' she said with a trace of bitterness. 'And bring your shopping cart. We're giving the store away today.'

A NARROW CORRIDOR led back to the depersonalized cubbyholes that passed for offices at the district attorney's office. Monica had seniority and rated a corner cubbyhole somewhat larger than the rest. Her sole attempt at humanizing her work space was a framed Chagall lithograph that added a splash of color to the white and black of her diplomas.

Monica was working on a file when David entered, and she waved him toward a chair. There were two in front of her desk, and he took a stack of files off one and placed them on the floor, then glanced at the newspaper that was draped over the top file on the other chair. Monica looked up.

'I need Seals's testimony and I'll give him immunity to get it,' she said without ceremony.

David said nothing for a second. He was watching Monica's face. When he was certain she was serious, he asked, 'Why do you need his testimony?'

'Because he is the only one other than Zachariah Small who can testify that Sticks pulled the trigger up on the mountain. Without him Sticks will get off.

'We had an informant who heard the three of them talking after they shot Jessie. Sticks and Zack were bragging about shooting her, and it was pretty clear that it was Sticks who shot from the car.'

'Why don't you use your informant?'

'He's gone. He split shortly after we interviewed him. He's a transient who was staying at the Gomes house when the boys were arrested. I guess he got scared when he realized that we wanted him to testify. I've got the police looking for him, but even if we found him, I'm not sure how much good he'd be to us. He has a police record and he's a drunk.'

David was churning inside. He leaned forward slightly.

'We get complete immunity?'

'Yes.'

David stood up. 'I'll talk to my client.'

THE GUARD LED Tony Seals into the interview room at the county jail. The room was long and narrow, and a row of rickety wooden folding chairs was scattered along its length. There was one Formica-topped table at the far end. David sat in front of it, watching his client walk toward him.

'Buzz me when you're through,' the guard said, pointing to a small black button set in a silver metal box under some steam pipes near the barred door. Then he slammed the door shut and David heard the key turn in the lock.

On visiting day this room was usually jammed full of anxious wives and girlfriends, talking in quiet tones to men they might not be making love to for a long time. But this was early on a weekday, and David and his client were alone.

T.S. smelled worse than the last time they had met. There was a body odor that prisoners at the county jail had that was unique and vile. It was the type of smell you could believe would never be scrubbed away.

David searched his client's eyes as the gangly teen-ager shuffled toward him with a loose, puppetlike gait that made him look as if he had straw where bones should be. The eyes were vacant and as lifeless as his perpetual half smile.

'Hi, Mr. Nash,' T.S. said. He had a soft voice that rarely fluctuated with any emotion.

'Sit down, T.S.'

T.S. did as he was told. He always did. David wondered if he had ever initiated an action in his life. Monica was right. It had to have been Sticks and Zachariah. He was dealing with a boy who lacked free will. Another person's creature who got from point A to point B by suggestion only.

'How've you been?'

'Okay, I guess.'

'I want to ask you a few questions, T.S., and I want truthful answers. This is important, so you have to be straight with me.'

'Sure, Mr. Nash.'

'Who shot Jessie when you were down at the hole? The first shot.'

'That was Zack.'

'You didn't shoot her?'

David detected a flicker of fear.

'Honest, Mr. Nash. I didn't never shoot her.'

'And up on the mountain? Who shot at her there?'

The boy's right hand raised slowly and began to pick at a whitehead on his cheek. The tip of Seals's

88

tongue licked his lower lip, then darted back into his mouth.

'Well?'

'Uh . . . well, there was Zack. He done it first, right after we left her. Then we drove off some and Sticks said we should make sure. So we turned around and Sticks asked Zack if he could take a shot and Zack give him the gun.'

David watched T.S. closely. Remembering anything seemed to exhaust him. He wondered what it would be like to go through life with a brain that worked so slowly.

'T.S., did you ever shoot the gun?'

The hand dropped from the pimple and T.S. looked afraid.

'No, honest. They don't say I done it, do they?'

'I want to know.'

'No, no. Zack said he'd let me try, but I was too bummed out. I said no and Sticks just took another shot.'

'What do you mean, bummed out?'

'I was tired,' T.S. said, sagging back in his chair, as if he had forgotten that he had been frightened only seconds before. He went back to worrying the pimple.

'T.S., just between us, if you hadn't been tired, would you have shot her?'

T.S. considered the question and David wondered why he had asked it. What difference did it make? He had won. T.S. would be a free man after he testified at the trials of his former friends, and David would have earned his fee. Why did he need to know the truth about this idiot boy who would soon be at large again?

'Yeah, I guess,' he said. The pimple burst and white pus squeezed through his fingers. David felt cold and alone. The empty room was suddenly too close, and he wanted to get out.

'The district attorney has offered us a deal, T.S. She feels that she needs your testimony to convict Sticks and Zack. If you are willing to testify against them, she will grant you complete immunity. Do you know what that means?'

T.S. shook his head. His fingers were at work on another pimple.

'It means you go free. That they drop the charges against you for shooting Jessie.'

The fingers still worked, the stare was still vacant.

'I can go home?' he finally asked.

'After you've testified.'

'I have to testify in court?'

David nodded.

'Gee, I don't know,' he said. Seals was trying to piece it together. David leaned back and let him think. He was floating and he needed some air. Dizzy. If he had some water.

'I guess it would be okay,' T.S. said finally. There was no excitement, no elation. David wondered if Seals even cared. For T.S. the world was a torment where everything was too complicated. He was a man made for prison where the rules and regulations set him free from the arduous task of having to make decisions.

'You'll have to get on the witness stand in court and say exactly what happened, and you'll have to take a lie-detector test first, so the district attorney can be sure you're being truthful. Will you do that?'

'If you say so,' the boy said. He had stopped picking his face apart and thought for a second. 'I can really go home?'

'Yes, T.S.'

T.S. smiled, but only for a brief moment. Then he looked at David.

'You know, the guys in here said I was lucky to have you as my lawyer. They said you'd beat the rap for me.'

David stood to go. It was very warm in the narrow room and he needed air badly. He looked down at the idiot boy at the table and saw him back on the streets, the way he'd be in six months or a year. Back on drugs. Doing . . . what? Would he pull the trigger next time? Would there be a next time? David knew there would be, because he could see with his own eyes what Tony Seals was. His hands began to itch as if they were very dirty.

'I THOUGHT YOU'D gone home,' Gregory Banks said.

David was sitting in his office in the dark. His

jacket was folded over the back of a chair on the other side of his desk, and his tie was undone. He had turned his desk chair so that it faced the river, where a tugboat flowed with the current like a firefly tracing the path of a piece of carelessly thrown black ribbon.

'Just thinking,' David said. He sounded down.

'Want to talk, or should I leave?'

David swiveled around and faced his friend.

'Do you ever wonder what the hell we're doing, Greg?'

Banks sat down.

'This does sound serious,' he said, half joking.

'I just made a deal with the DA. Tony Seals is going to get complete immunity.'

'That's great!' Gregory said, puzzled by David's mood. He was close to the Sealses, and he knew what this would mean to them.

'Is it? What do I do six months from now when Tony kills someone and his parents want to hire me because I did such a good job today?'

'The DA made the offer, Dave. You were just representing your client.'

'*Jah, mein Herr*, I vas chust following orders,' David said bitterly.

'Why don't you tell me what brought all this on.'

'I don't know, Greg,' David said. Gregory waited patiently for him to continue. 'I guess I've just been taking a good look at the way I earn my living, and

I'm not sure I like what I see. There are people out there hurting other people. The cops arrest them, the prosecutors prosecute them, and I shovel the garbage right back into the street. You know, that's an apt metaphor. Maybe they should start calling us sanitary engineers.'

'I think you're getting a little melodramatic, don't you? What about that kid you helped out? The college kid who got busted with the marijuana. He was guilty of a felony, right? Should he have been convicted? If you hadn't beaten that case, he wouldn't be in medical school. And you beat that case using the same legal arguments you used to get that heroin dealer off last year. You can't have two systems of justice.'

'Maybe not, Greg. Your arguments, as always, are very logical. That's what makes you such a good lawyer. But I just made a deal today that is going to permit a very sick young man, who made a young girl dig her own grave and left her to die, to walk out of jail scot-free.

'You know, when I got into this business, I saw myself as a knight in shining armor defending the innocent, the unjustly accused. How many innocent people have I represented, Greg? After a while you realize there aren't any innocent men, only a lot of guilty ones who can pay pretty good for a smart lawyer. So at first you rationalize what you're doing, but eventually you're just in it for the money.'

'Look, Dave, I know what you're going through.

I've been through it, too. Anyone who practices criminal law and has a conscience has to deal with the conflict between that idealized crap they teach you in law school and the way the real world is, but the picture you're painting isn't accurate either.

'You are a good lawyer and you do good, honest work. There are innocent people who get arrested. There are people, like that college kid, who are guilty but shouldn't be convicted. In order to help them, you have to help people like Tony Seals. It's the system that's important. It's the only thing that keeps this country from being Nazi Germany. You think about that.'

'I do, Greg. Look, I know what you believe and I respect you for it. My problem is, I don't know what I believe in anymore. I know what I used to believe in, and I'm beginning to think I sold that out when the money started getting too good.'

Gregory started to say something, then changed his mind. He remembered the agonies he had gone through over this same question. He never had to find an answer, because he'd stopped taking criminal cases, except those that interested him, when he'd started doing more and more work for the union. Greg had made his fortune by winning big verdicts in personal-injury cases and dealing tough at negotiating sessions for union contracts. Getting out of criminal law was no problem for him.

David was different. He had no interest in any other area of the law. He had tried to branch out, but he had always come back to his criminal practice. And why not? He made a good living at it and he loved what he did. Only now he was beginning to question his worth because of his work.

'You want to go get a drink?' Gregory asked. It was quiet in the evening offices. A few associates staying late to work on problems assigned by the partners made an occasional disturbance in the dark rhythms. David stood up and put on his suit jacket.

'I think I'll just go home.'

'I could tell Helen to set another place for dinner.'

'No, I'd rather be by myself.'

'Okay. Just promise me you won't let this drag you down.'

'I'll try,' David said, making an effort to smile.

After David left, Gregory walked back to his office. He looked at his watch. It was late. He was working too damn late recently. He'd have to cut that out. He sighed. He'd been telling himself that since he started practice, what was it, over twenty years ago. That was a long time, twenty years.

He sat at his desk and started to proofread the brief he had been writing. Poor David. There were advantages to being in your fifties. Growing up was hell and you never really stopped. You thought you did when you got out of your teens. Then you found out that the crises were just starting.

David was a good boy, though. A sound thinker.

What he needed was a case he could believe in. There had been too many hard cases lately. He needed to feel his worth again. A good case would come along. It was the law of averages.

PART II

THE LAST INNOCENT MAN

1

Judge Rosenthal looked across the courtroom toward the clock that hung above the empty jury box. The last witness had just been excused, and there was plenty of time before lunch.

'You might as well argue now, gentlemen,' he said to the two attorneys seated at opposite tables in front of the bench. Walter Greaves struggled to his feet. He had been fighting a battle with arthritis, and, the judge reflected sadly, he seemed to be losing. That was too bad. He'd known Wally for thirty years, and he had a genuine affection for him.

The judge let his eyes wander over to opposing counsel. Larry Stafford provided a perfect contrast to Greaves. He looked so healthy that he made the judge self-conscious about his own physical condition. There had been an upsurge of work during the past few weeks, and he had been passing up his noontime squash games. He was suddenly aware of the pressure of his waistband against his belly. The pressure made him feel guilty and uncomfortable, and he tried to take his mind off it by listening to Greaves's argument.

When Greaves sat down, the judge nodded

at Stafford. The young lawyer had been before Rosenthal on a few occasions representing Price, Winward, Lexington and Rice, Portland's largest law firm. Rosenthal considered him to be conscientious and thorough, if not exceptionally bright.

Stafford was dressed in a lightweight plaid suit that was conservative enough for the courtroom, yet sufficiently summery to fit in with the unseasonably mild September weather. Stafford was just under six feet in height, but his slim, athletic build made him look taller. When he spoke, the pure white of his teeth contrasted with his deep tan. The boy was good-looking enough to be an actor, Rosenthal thought.

'As the Court is aware, and I set this out in full in my trial memorandum, the Uniform Partnership Act permits a limited partner to have some degree of control over the conduct of the business with which he is involved. Mr. Tish has done nothing more than the limited partners did in the Grainger case or the Rathke case. I don't want to go into this too much more, because I'd just be repeating the brief, but I don't see where the plaintiffs have established liability. If the Court has any questions . . .'

'No, Mr. Stafford. I'll tell both of you gentlemen that this question is too close for me to make a decision now. I've read your briefs, and I want some time to do some independent research before resolving this. I'll try to have a written opinion in a week or so. If you have any supplemental authorities, you can submit them in letter form. Anything further?'

The attorneys shook their heads.

'Then we'll adjourn. Have a nice lunch, gentlemen.'

The judge rose and disappeared through a door behind his seat. Larry Stafford started collecting his notes and putting them into his file in an orderly manner. The notes, written in a neat, precise hand, were set out on index cards. Andrew Tish, Stafford's client, asked for an opinion on how the case had gone. Stafford tucked a law book under his arm and hefted his attaché case as he shook his head and started for the courtroom door.

'No way of telling with Rosenthal, Andy. The guy's bright, and he'll give a lot of thought to the case. That's about all I can say.'

Walter Greaves was waiting in the hall outside the courtroom.

'Larry.'

Stafford stopped and asked Tish to wait for him.

'I talked with my people, and they're willing to come down on the settlement offer.'

'I'll tell Tish, but I'm going to advise him to hang tough.'

'I'm just conveying my client's offer.'

Stafford smirked and walked down the hall that led to the elevators. The courthouse had four corridors that ran along the sides of an empty central shaft. Greaves picked up his briefcase and walked toward the rear of the building. He did not like dealing with Stafford. He was too cocky. Very . . . superficial – that was the word. Nothing under the surface. Come on like Mr. Nice Guy one minute, then you find out you've been double-crossed. And in this case it had not been necessary to do some of the borderline ethical things the boy had done. Hell, Stafford had him dead to rights. His clients were just trying anything they could to prop up a dying business. Greaves shook his head and moved aside to get out of the way of a young man dressed in jeans and a work shirt. This young man had a dark complexion, a shaggy black mustache, and thick black hair and he was staring down the corridor toward Judge Rosenthal's courtroom.

'AND THEN WHAT happened, Officer Ortiz?'

'My job was to wait outside the residence in case any of the suspects attempted to escape. The other officers went inside to execute the search warrant, and Officer Lesnowski and I waited near the front of the building.'

'Did you actually take part in the search?'

'No, I did not.'

'What happened then?'

'Shortly after, Officers Teske and Hennings exited the residence with the two prisoners and a bag containing evidence. Officer Teske gave me the evidence bag, and he and Hennings drove to the station house with the prisoners.'

'Did you talk with either of the prisoners or look in the bag?'

'No, sir.'

'I have no further questions, Your Honor.'

Judge McDonald nodded toward the public defender, who was conferring with his client, a teenage black man accused of possession of cocaine. Ortiz relaxed. He had been cross-examined by this asshole before, and he expected the interrogation to be long and stupid, even though he had no information of interest to anyone.

But the prospect of cross-examination didn't bother him. He was happy just being back at work. First there had been the stay in the hospital, then the vacation he had not really wanted to take. The department had insisted, though. It wanted him to rest and get his memory back, because his memory was the only thing the department had left in the Darlene Hersch case.

He had dropped in on Crosby before going to court, and nothing had changed. No fingerprints, no other witnesses, no leads. Crosby had moved around the edges, not wanting to ask the question directly. Probably under the orders of some department shrink. So Ortiz had answered the unspoken question. Nothing had changed. He still had trouble sorting out what had happened. His memory was getting better every day, but it blurred and faded, and even when his idea of things seemed clear, he could not be sure if what he was seeing was what had really happened.

The public defender was still gabbing, and Ortiz shifted in his chair in the witness box. Thinking about his memory and that night had spoiled the feeling of peace he had experienced when he had started giving testimony. It was Darlene that troubled him. He was afraid of the pictures he would see when his memory came back. Afraid that he had been responsible for her death. Everyone assured him that it wasn't so, but how did they know? How could they be so sure of what had happened that night?

The public defender looked up from his notes. Ortiz waited for the questions, grateful for a chance to escape from his own thoughts.

'Officer Ortiz, what happened to Officer Murdock and Officer Elvin after Teske and Hennings left the scene?'

'They remained in the residence.'

'Thank you, I have no further questions.'

'You're excused,' the judge said. Ortiz was surprised he had gotten off so easily. Maybe the schmuck was learning.

Jack Hennings, Ortiz's partner, looked up from his newspaper when the courtroom door opened.

'You're on,' Ortiz said.

Hennings handed the paper to Mike Elvin and went through the door. Ortiz turned toward Elvin to ask for the sports section when he noticed two men talking at the other end of the corridor. His hand started to shake and his chest felt suddenly constricted. The two men concluded their conversation, and the older man walked toward him. Ortiz did not see him. His eyes were riveted on the younger man – the blond. He had started down the hall that led to the elevators, but Ortiz was seeing him in a different place. He was remembering a man with curly blond hair walking quickly along the landing that ran outside the rooms at the Raleigh Motel, and he was seeing a face spotlighted for a moment in the doorway of the motel room where Darlene Hersch had died.

The older man passed him, and the blond disappeared around the corner.

'Tell Jack to wait for me,' he said to Elvin. Elvin looked up, but Ortiz was already halfway down the corridor.

There was no one in the hall when Ortiz reached the corner. He looked up at the floor indicator. Both elevator cars had reached the ground floor. Ortiz walked back toward Judge Rosenthal's courtroom. The law student who served as the judge's clerk was reading a textbook in the empty courtroom and munching on a sandwich.

'Excuse me,' Ortiz said. The boy looked up.

'There was a lawyer in here just now, with blond hair. Can you tell me who he is?'

'Why do you ask?' the boy asked suspiciously.

Ortiz realized that he was dressed for undercover work and looked as grubby as the degenerates he had to mix with. He walked across the room and flashed his badge.

'Now, can you tell me his name?'

The boy studied his badge, then hesitated. Ortiz knew he was thinking about the constitutional rights his professors had told him he had.

'I don't know if – ' the boy began.

'You'd better,' Ortiz said softly, and there must have been something in his tone, because the boy spoke.

'Stafford. Larry Stafford.'

'And where does he work?'

'The Price, Winward firm. It's in the Standard Plaza Building.'

Ortiz put his badge away and headed for the door. Halfway there, he stopped and turned.

'This is official police business, you hear, and I don't want this mentioned to anyone. If it gets back to me that you opened your mouth, you're in serious trouble.'

There was a pay phone near the elevators. The phone book had two listenings for Lawrence Dean Stafford. Ortiz wrote them both down; then he called homicide. Ron Crosby answered.

'This is Bert Ortiz, Ron. I want you to check something for me. I need the make of car for Lawrence Dean Stafford, 22310 Newgate Terrace.'

'Why do you want to know?'

'Just do it for me by this afternoon, okay? I'll be back to you.'

'Does this have something to do with the Hersch case?'

'Everything.'

THE LUNCH HOUR crawled by and Ortiz made his second call to Crosby shortly after one.

'I've got your information,' the detective said quietly. The tension on the other end of the line was the tip-off. Crosby had struck pay dirt. 'There are two cars registered to Lawrence Dean Stafford. The first is a Porsche and the second is a Mercedes-Benz.'

Ortiz said nothing. He was cradling the phone and staring at the wall of the phone booth, without seeing it or feeling the plastic thing in his hand. He was back on Morrison Street and the Mercedes was right in front of him.

'Is this your man, Bert?'

'I think so, but I have to see his face.'

'You saw the killer's face?'

'Before I blacked out. I know the man's face.'

'Where are you? I'll be right over.'

'No. Let me handle this. You get a DA and have a judge on standby to issue a search warrant. I want to be sure.'

'What are you going to do?'

'Follow him. If it's the car, I'll know. Then we can search for the clothes. But I want it all legal. I don't want this one to slip away.'

*

'PRICE, WINWARD, LEXINGTON and Rice,' the receptionist said in a pleasing singsong.

'I'd like to speak to Larry Stafford.'

'Who shall I say is calling?'

'Stan Reynolds. I was referred to Mr. Stafford by an old friend.'

'Please hold and I'll see if Mr. Stafford is in.'

There was a click and the line went dead. Ortiz held the receiver to his ear and waited. Thirty seconds later there was another click.

'This is Larry Stafford, Mr. Reynolds. Can I help you?'

'I hope so. I'm in a kind of a bind and I was told you're the man to see. I run a small construction company. Spec housing. I'm doin' pretty good now financially, but I'm beginnin' to have some hassles with my partner, and I need some advice fast.'

'Well . . .' Stafford said, and Ortiz could hear paper rattling, 'I've got a spot open tomorrow at . . . Let's see. How about three o'clock?'

Ortiz was taking in the voice and trying to size up the man. The voice had strong, confident qualities, but there was a slick gloss to the tones, as if the timbre and pitch were learned, not natural.

'Gee, I was hopin' I could see you today.'

'I'm afraid I have a pretty full schedule for the rest of the afternoon.'

'I see,' Ortiz said. He paused, as if thinking, then asked, 'How late will you be at your office?'

'My last appointment should be over at seven.'

Ortiz paused again.

'Well, I guess I can wait until tomorrow.'

'Good. I'll see you then.'

They hung up and Ortiz stepped out of the booth. He was across the street from the Standard Plaza. The light changed and he crossed the street. It took him ten minutes to find the beige Mercedes in the underground garage. It was near the fire door toward the rear of the second parking level. He checked the license number against the number Crosby had given him; then he left the building. All he had to do now was wait for seven o'clock.

ABNER ROSENTHAL WAS a small, dapper man with a large legal reputation. He had made a fortune as a corporate lawyer, then taken an enormous cut in salary to become a circuit-court judge. It was common knowledge that he had passed up several opportunities to be appointed to the state supreme court because he enjoyed being a trial judge. Rosenthal especially liked criminal cases, and he had developed an expertise in the area of search-and-seizure law. The police usually sought him out when they needed a search warrant in a particularly sensitive case.

The doorbell rang just as the judge was finishing dinner. His teenage son started to stand, but Rosenthal waved him down. Monica Powers had called him earlier to alert him that there was a breakthrough in the Darlene Hersch case.

'Sorry to bother you, Judge,' Monica said when the door opened. 'Do you know Ron Crosby and Bert Ortiz?'

'I've met Detective Crosby before,' the judge said as he led them into his den. 'I don't believe I know Officer Ortiz.'

As soon as they were seated, Monica handed the judge the search warrant and the affidavit Ortiz had sworn to in support of it. The affidavit set out all the information that Ortiz felt supported his belief that Lawrence Dean Stafford had murdered Darlene Hersch and that evidence of that crime could be found in Stafford's house. The judge looked grim when he finished reading it. He looked at Ortiz long enough to make the policeman feel uncomfortable.

'Are you aware that Larry Stafford was in my courtroom this very day, Officer Ortiz?'

'Yes, sir.'

Rosenthal reread a section of the affidavit.

'I've read this, but I want you to tell me. Are you positive that Larry Stafford is the man you saw at the motel?'

Ortiz's mouth felt dry. Was he positive? Could he have made a mistake? No. He had waited outside Stafford's office at seven. He had seen Stafford leave the office. He had seen the face of Darlene's killer.

'Larry Stafford killed Darlene Hersch,' Ortiz answered, but there was a slight quiver in his voice.

'And you, Miss Powers?'

'I don't like this any more than you do, Judge, but I've worked with Officer Ortiz before, and I trust his judgment.'

The judge took a pen out of his pocket.

'I'm going to sign this warrant, but you'd better keep a tight lid on this if you don't make an arrest. This case is going to be sensational. If you're wrong,' he said, looking directly at Ortiz, 'the publicity alone will be enough to destroy Larry Stafford's career at a firm like Price, Winward. Do you understand me?'

'Yes, sir,' Ortiz said.

No one spoke when Rosenthal signed the warrant. Monica picked up the documents and they left, Monica for home and Ortiz, Crosby, and a second carload of men for Larry Stafford's house.

NEWGATE TERRACE WAS a long, winding, tree-lined country road fifteen minutes from down-town Portland. At uneven intervals driveways led the way to expensive homes, few of which were visible from the street. Stafford's home was at the end of a stretch of straight road. A row of tall hedges screened the house from view, and the policemen were not able to see it until they had driven a short distance up the driveway. The house was a two-story Tudor design painted a traditional brown and white. The grounds had the well-manicured look of professional care, and there were several large shade trees. The driveway circled in front of the house, and Ortiz imagined the

Mercedes parked in the garage that adjoined it on the left.

The young woman who answered the door was puzzled by the appearance of two carloads of uniformed policemen at her doorstep.

'Mrs. Stafford?' Ron Crosby asked.

'Yes,' the woman answered with a tentative smile.

'Is your husband home?'

'Yes.'

'Could you please ask him to come to the door?'

'What's this all about?'

'We have a matter to go over with your husband. I'd appreciate it if you would get him.'

The woman hesitated for a second, as if hoping for more of an explanation. She got none.

'If you'll wait here, I'll get him,' she said, and walked toward the end of the hall, disappearing around the back of a staircase that led upstairs from the foyer. Ortiz watched her go and his stomach tightened. In a few moments the man who killed Darlene Hersch would come down that hall.

Ortiz was in uniform, and he had placed himself at the rear of the small group of policemen. He wanted a long second look at Stafford before the lawyer got an opportunity to recognize him. Crosby and two policemen had stepped into the foyer to await Mrs. Stafford's return. A moment later Larry Stafford, dressed in Bermuda shorts and a red-and-black-striped rugby shirt, walked down the carpeted corridor. His wife trailed behind, more visibly worried now.

'What can I do for you?' he asked with a wide smile. Ortiz concentrated on the face. There was so much light in the hallway, and there had been so little in the motel room. Still, he was sure. It was him.

Crosby handed Stafford the search warrant. Ortiz watched him carefully as he read it. If Stafford was nervous or upset, he did not show it.

'I'm afraid I don't understand . . . What did you say your name was?'

'Crosby. Detective Ron Crosby, Mr. Stafford.'

'Well, Detective Crosby, I don't understand what this is all about.'

'That is a search warrant, Mr. Stafford. It is an authorization by a judge to search your house for the items listed in the warrant.'

'I can see it's a search warrant,' Stafford said with a trace of impatience. 'What I want to know is why you feel it is necessary to invade my privacy in the middle of the night and rummage through my personal effects.'

'I'd prefer not to go into that right now, Mr. Stafford,' Crosby said quietly. 'If you'll just permit us to do what we came for, we won't take much of your time.'

Stafford scanned the warrant again.

'Judge Rosenthal signed this warrant?' he asked incredulously.

'Yes, sir.'

Stafford said nothing for a moment. There seemed to be a private war waging inside him. Then he relaxed.

'Search if you want to. I'm sorry if I gave you a hard time. It's just that I've never had anything like this happen before. I'll even make it easy for you. I own several sport shirts of this type,' he said, indicating the list of clothing set out in the warrant, 'and at least three pair of tan slacks. Why don't you come up to my room and I'll show you. Then, if you're not satisfied, you can search the house.'

Stafford was not reacting the way Ortiz had expected him to. The man was too self-possessed. Maybe he was wrong. After all, he had gotten only a fast look at the murderer's face, and he was dazed and in pain at the time. And there was the lighting. No, there had been enough light. The globe outside the motel room was very bright. Still, it had been so fast.

Stafford started to climb the stairs to the second floor with his wife close behind. Ortiz stayed to the rear as several officers followed Crosby. Two men stationed themselves in the foyer.

Stafford's bedroom was toward the rear of the house. It was bright and airy and had a decid-edly masculine feel about it. A sliding glass door led to a small balcony, and Ortiz glanced out into the darkness. A twin bed sat against the north wall. It was unmade, and the edge of one of the blankets touched the hardwood floor. A large walk-in closet occupied the east wall, and an expensive-looking chest of drawers stood to their right as the party entered the room. Stafford pulled out one of the middle drawers and stood back.

'My sport shirts are in here. My slacks are in the closet.'

Crosby signaled to Ortiz and the policeman stepped over to the closet. He opened the louvered doors and started to examine several pairs of slacks that hung on a long row of wooden hangers. He pushed several aside before stopping at a pair of tan slacks. He wasn't positive, but they were close. It was the shirt he could be sure about. The flowered pattern was distinctive.

He finished sorting through the hangers, then walked back down the line and selected the tan pants. He looked at Stafford. The man had not changed his expression of detached interest, and he had given no indication that he recognized Ortiz.

'Let me see the shirts,' he said to Crosby. The detective stepped back, and Ortiz carefully lifted one shirt after another out of the drawer, placing them in a neat pile on top of the chest of drawers. Midway down, he stopped. It was sitting there. A shirt of brown and forest-green with a leaf-and-flower design. The shirt that the man who killed Darlene Hersch had been wearing. Ortiz called Crosby aside, and the two men conferred in the corridor. Mrs. Stafford stood on one side of the room, nervously shifting her attention between her husband and the door to the hallway. Crosby and Ortiz reentered the room. They looked grim. There were two other policemen with them. That made a total of six officers, and the large bedroom was beginning to shrink in size.

'Mr. Stafford, I am going to have to place you under arrest.'

Mrs. Stafford blanched, and her husband's composure began to slip.

'What do you mean? Now, see here. I . . .'

'Before you say anything, Mr. Stafford, I have to advise you concerning your constitutional rights.'

'My rights! Are you insane? Now, I've cooperated with you and let you into my home. What nonsense is this? What am I being arrested for?'

Crosby looked at Stafford, and Ortiz watched for a reaction.

'I am arresting you for the murder of Darlene Hersch.'

'Who?' Stafford asked, his brows knitting in puzzlement. Mrs. Stafford's hand flew to her mouth, and Ortiz heard her say, 'My God.' Crosby began reciting Stafford's Miranda rights.

'You have a right to remain silent. If you choose to—'

'Wait a second. Wait a second. Who is Darlene Hersch? Is this a joke?'

'Mr. Stafford, this is no joke. Now, I know you're an attorney, but I am going to explain your rights to you anyway, and I want you to listen carefully.'

Mrs. Stafford edged over to her husband with a slow, sideways, crablike movement. Stafford was beginning to look scared. Crosby finished reciting Stafford's rights and took a pair of handcuffs from his rear pocket.

'Why don't you change into a pair of long pants and a long-sleeved shirt?' Crosby said. 'And I'm going to have to cuff you. I'm sorry about that, but it's a procedure I have to follow.'

'Now, you listen to me. I happen to be an attorney—'

'I know, Mr. Stafford.'

'Then you know that as of right now you are going to be on the end of one hell of a lawsuit.'

'Getting excited is not going to help your situation, Mr. Stafford. I'd suggest that you keep calm and have your wife contact an attorney.

'Mrs. Stafford,' Crosby said, turning his attention to the lawyer's wife, 'you had better contact an attorney to represent your husband. He will be at the county jail within the hour.'

The woman acted as if she had not heard Crosby. Stafford started toward her, stopped, and looked at Crosby.

'May I talk to my wife in private for a moment?'

'I can send most of my men out, but someone will have to stay in the room.'

Stafford started to say something, then stopped. He seemed to be back in control.

'That would be fine.'

Stafford waited to go to his wife until all but one policeman had left. She looked confused and frightened.

'Larry, what's going on?'

Stafford took her by the shoulders and led her to the far corner of the room.

'This is obviously some mistake. Now, call Charlie Holt. Tell him what happened and where I am. Charlie will know what to do.'

'He said murder, Larry.'

'I know what he said,' Stafford said firmly. 'Now, do as I say. Believe me, it will be all right.'

Stafford changed his clothes and his wife watched in silence. When Stafford was finished, Crosby put on the handcuffs and escorted the prisoner downstairs. Ortiz watched Stafford closely. He said nothing as they led him to the car. He walked with assurance, his back straight and his shoulders squared. Mrs. Stafford stood alone in the open doorway. Ortiz watched her shrink in the distance as they drove away.

2

'There's a Mr. Holt to see you, Mr. Nash,' the receptionist said. "He says it's urgent."

David looked at his watch. It was eight-thirty. He had been at the office since seven working on a brief that was due in two days, and he was only half-done. He was tempted to tell Charlie to come back, but Charlie would not be at his office this early unless there was an emergency. He sighed.

'Tell him I'll be right out.'

He finished editing a paragraph and carefully moved his work to one side. He placed an empty legal pad on his blotter, straightened his tie, and put on his suit jacket.

Charlie Holt was pacing in front of the bar that separated clients from the well-endowed redhead who served as the receptionist at Banks, Kelton, Skaarstad and Nash. Only Charlie was not looking at the girl. His eyes were straining toward the swinging doors that opened onto the lawyers' offices. Charlie was a tall, balding securities lawyer who had never lost the military bearing he had acquired in the Marines. His movements were always sharp and jerky, as if he were on parade. It was an exhausting experience spending time with Charlie: you always felt like a passenger in a sports car driving on a winding mountain road at top speed.

David pushed through the swinging doors and Charlie rushed toward him.

'Thanks, Dave,' Holt said quickly, pumping David's hand. 'Big trouble. Sorry to interrupt so early.'

'That's okay. What's up?' David asked as he led Holt back down the corridor to his office.

'Larry Stafford, one of our associates. Do you know him?'

'I think I met him at the bar-association dinner last month.'

Charlie sat down without being asked. He looked at the floor and shook his head like a man who had given up hope.

'Really shocking.'

'What is?'

Holt's head jerked up. 'You didn't read it in the papers?'

'I've been here since seven.'

'Oh. Well, it's front page. Bad for the firm.' He paused for a moment and thought. 'Worse for Larry. He's been arrested. Wife called me last night. In tears. Doesn't know what to do. Can I help? I went out to the jail, but I'm no criminal lawyer. Hell, I'd never even seen the jail before this morning. Your name naturally came to mind, if you'll take it.'

'Take what, Charlie? What's he charged with?'

'Murder.'

'Murder?'

Holt nodded vigorously.

'They say he killed that policewoman. The one who was pretending to be a prostitute.'

David whistled and sat down slowly.

'He's very upset. Made me promise to get you out there as soon as I could.'

Holt stopped talking and waited for David to say something. David started to doodle on the legal pad. A lawyer. And that murder. That was a hot potato. Lots of press and TV coverage. A good investigation, too. The police were not going to go off half-cocked and look bad later. They would make damn sure they had a good case before they moved. And it would be better than damn good before they arrested an associate from the biggest and most influential law firm in the city. Hell, half the politicians in town had received sizable contributions from Seymour Price.

'Who's footing the bill, Charlie? This will cost plenty.'

'Jennifer. Mrs. Stafford. They have savings. She has family. I asked her and she said they could manage.'

'What do they have on him, Charlie?'

Holt shrugged. 'I don't know. I told you, I'm no criminal lawyer. I wouldn't even know who to ask.'

'What do the papers say?'

'Oh, right. Something about an eyewitness.

Another policeman. Jennifer says they searched the house and took some of Larry's shirts and pants.'

'That's right,' David said, remembering one of the newspaper stories he'd read. 'Bert Ortiz was working with her and got knocked unconscious. But I didn't know he'd seen the killer.'

'You know this Ortiz?'

'Sure. He's a vice cop. He's been a witness in several cases I've tried.'

'Will you go out and see Stafford?'

David looked at the half-finished brief. Did he want to get involved in a case this heavy right now?

'Jennifer swears he didn't do it. Says they were home together the night the girl was killed.'

'She does? Do you believe her? After all, she is his wife.'

'You don't know Jenny. She's a peach. No, if she says so . . .'

David smiled, then laughed softly. Holt looked at him quizzically.

'I'm sorry, Charlie. It's just that you don't run across too many innocent men in this business. They're about as rare as American eagles.'

David felt a surge of excitement at the thought. An honest-to-goodness innocent man. It was worth a look. He'd finish the brief tonight.

'AM I GLAD to see you,' Larry Stafford said. The guard closed the door of the private interview room, and David stood up to shake hands. Stafford was dressed in an ill-fitting jumpsuit.

'Sit down, Larry,' David said, indicating a plastic chair.

'How soon can you get me out of this place?' Stafford asked. He was trying to keep calm, but there was an under-current of panic flowing behind his pale-blue eyes and country-club tan.

'We'll be in front of a judge later this morning, but this is a murder case, and there's no requirement that the judge set bail.'

'I . . . I thought they always . . . there was always bail.'

'Not on a murder charge. If the DA opposes bail, we can ask for a bail hearing. But there's no guarantee that the judge will set an amount after the hearing, if the DA can convince the court that you may be guilty. And even if the judge does set an amount for bail, it could be high and you might not be able to make it.'

'I see,' Stafford said quietly. He was trying to sit straight and talk in the assured tone he used when conferring with attorneys representing other people. Only he was the client, and the news that he might have to remain in jail caused a slight erosion in his demeanor. A slumping of the shoulders and a downcasting of the eyes indicated to David that the message was starting to get through.

'On the other hand,' David said, 'you are an attorney with a good job. You're married. I doubt

123

the district attorney's office will oppose bail, and if they do, I'm pretty sure most of the judges in the courthouse would grant it.'

Stafford brightened as he clutched at the straw David had held out to him. David did not like to build up a client's hopes, but in this case he was certain that his evaluation of the bail situation was accurate.

'How have you been treated?' David asked.

Stafford shrugged.

'Pretty well, considering. They put me by myself in a small cell in the, uh, "isolation." '

'Solitary.'

'Yes.' Stafford took a deep breath and looked away for a second. 'All these terms. I never . . . I don't handle criminal cases.' He laughed, but it was forced laughter, and he moved uncomfortably on the narrow seat. 'I never wanted to get involved in it. Now I wish I'd taken a few more courses in law school.'

'Have the police tried to interview you yet?'

'Oh, yeah. Right away. They've been very polite. Very considerate. Detective Crosby. Ron is his first name, I think. Treated me very well.'

'Did you say anything to him, Larry?'

'No, except that I didn't do anything. He . . . he read me my rights.' Stafford laughed nervously again. 'Just like television. I'm still having a hard time taking this seriously. I half believe it's some fraternity prank. I don't even know anything about the case.'

'What did you say to the police?' David asked quietly. He was watching Stafford closely. People who were not used to the police or prison situations often talked voluminously to police detectives who were trained to be polite and considerate. Once the prisoner was cut off from his friends and family, he would open up to any concerned person in hopes of getting support. The voluntary statements of helpless men were often the most damaging pieces of evidence used to convict them.

'I didn't say anything. What could I say? I don't know anything about this.'

'Okay. Now, I want to say a few things to you and I want you to listen very carefully. I am going to explain the attorney-client relationship to you. I know you are a lawyer by profession, but right now you are a prisoner charged with murder, and the lawyer in you is not going to be functioning very well, because people are never very objective when they are dealing with their own problems.'

Larry nodded. He was leaning forward, concentrating on every word.

'First, anything you tell me is confidential. That means that not only won't I tell anyone what you say to me, but I cannot, by law, reveal the contents of our conversations.

'Next, you should tell me the truth when we discuss this case. Not because I will be offended if you lie to me, but because if you tell me something that is not true, I may go off half-cocked in reliance

125

upon what you've said and do something that will hurt your case.'

David stopped and let the point sink in. Stafford looked very uncomfortable.

'Dave . . . look, I want to get one thing clear. I'm not going to lie to you, because I didn't do anything. I have nothing to lie about. This whole thing is one ridiculous mistake, and I can promise you that I am going to sue those bastards for every cent in the city treasury when I'm finished with this business. But there is one thing I want to get straight between you and me. I . . . I have to be sure that the lawyer who represents me believes me. I mean, if you think I'm lying . . . well, I don't lie, and when I say I'm innocent, I am innocent.'

David looked straight at Stafford, and Stafford returned his stare without wavering.

'Larry, what I'm telling you I tell every one of the people I represent, and I tell them for a reason. Let me make one thing clear to you. You don't want a lawyer who believes you. You want a lawyer who will clear you of the charges against you. This isn't Disneyland. This is the Multnomah County Jail, and there are a large number of well-trained people in this county who, at this very moment, are conspiring to take away your liberty for the rest of your life. I am the only person who stands between you and prison, and I will do everything in my power, whether I believe you or not, to keep you out of prison.

'If you want someone to hold your hand and say

that they believe you and tell you what a good guy you are, there's a baby-sitting service I know of that can take care of that. If you want to get off, that's another matter, and I'll be glad to take your case.'

Stafford looked down at the floor. When he looked up, he was flushed.

'I'm sorry,' he said, 'it's just that . . .'

'It's just that you're scared and cut off from your family and friends, and you're confused and you want to know that someone is on your side. Well, I'm on your side, Larry, and so is your wife and Charlie Holt and a lot of other people.'

'I guess you're right. It's just so . . . so frustrating. I was sitting in my cell and thinking. I don't even know how this happened.'

'It has happened, though. And that's what we have to deal with. Can you tell me where you were on the evening of June sixteenth and the early-morning hours of June seventeenth?'

'Is that when the murder occurred?'

David nodded.

'What day of the week was that? A weekday or weekend?'

'June sixteenth was a Thursday.'

'Okay. Without my appointment book and talking with a few people, I couldn't say for sure, but I probably worked at the office and went home.'

'How late do you usually work?'

'I put in pretty long hours. I'm still an associate at Price, Winward. Hoping to make partner pretty soon, but you know what that's like. And I had a fairly complicated securities case I was working on about that time. I was probably at the office until seven at least. It could have been later. I really can't say until I see my book.'

'Who would have that?'

'Jennifer. My wife.'

David made a note on a yellow lined legal pad.

'Let's talk about you for a bit. How old are you?'

'Thirty-five.'

'Education?'

'I went to law school at Lewis and Clark,' Stafford said. David nodded. Lewis and Clark was a private law school located in Portland.

'I was back east for my undergraduate work.'

'Are you from the East Coast?'

'That's hard to answer. My father was in the military. We traveled a lot. Then my folks got divorced, and I lived with Mom on Long Island, New York, until I went into the Army.'

'You were in the service?'

Stafford nodded.

'Was that before or after college?'

'After college and before law school.'

'Did you go to work for Price, Winward right after law school?'

'Yes. I've been there ever since,' Stafford said. David noticed something peculiar in the way Stafford answered, but he moved on.

'Larry, have you ever been convicted of a crime?'

'I had some trouble in high school. Minor in possession of beer. But that was cleared up.'

'I'm only interested in criminal situations after the age of eighteen where you were either found guilty by a jury or by a judge or pleaded guilty.'

'Oh, no. I never had anything like that.'

There was a knock on the door and the guard stuck his head in.

'He's got to go to court soon, Mr. Nash.'

'How much time have I got, Al?'

'I can give you five minutes.'

'Okay. Just knock when you're ready.'

The door closed, and David started collecting his material and placing it in his attaché case.

'We'll finish this later. I'll meet you at the courthouse.'

'I'm sorry about that business before. About . . .'

David stopped him.

'Larry, you're under more pressure now than I've ever been, and I think you're holding up very well, considering. I'm going to try to find out what the DA has on you, then I'll meet with you again and we'll start plotting strategy. Try to relax as much as you can. This is out of your hands now, and there isn't much you can do. So try not to brood about the case. I know that that's impossible advice to follow, but you pay me to do your worrying, and you'll be wasting your money if you do that part of my work for me.'

Stafford smiled. It was a broad, brave smile. He grasped David's hand in a firm grip.

'I want to thank you for taking this case. I feel much more confident now with you on it. You've got quite a reputation, if you don't know that already. And one more thing. I know you said it didn't matter, and I believe you, but I want you to know that I am innocent. I really am.'

THE PHONE RANG just as Monica was leaving her office. She hesitated for a moment, then answered it.

'Monica, this is Ron Crosby.'

'Oh, hi, Ron. I was just on my way up to arraign Stafford, and I'm going to be late. Can I call you back?'

'No. Hold on. This is about Stafford. Does he get out on bail today?'

'I talked it over with the boss, and we're not opposing bail if David asks for it.'

'I see. Look, I may be onto something and . . . I don't think he should be out.'

'Why not?'

'Do you remember when we were talking? We figured Stafford was getting a little on the side without risking the dangers and entanglements of an affair. So he picks up a prostitute and panics when he finds out she's a policewoman.'

'That's what I think,' Monica said. 'His wife is the one with the money. If there was a divorce, it would hurt him more than her.'

'Right. That's what everyone was thinking. We saw Darlene as a policewoman. But she was posing as a prostitute. Maybe she was killed because Stafford thought she was a prostitute.'

'I don't get you.'

'I did some checking on Stafford. He's never been convicted of a crime or even arrested for one, but I did come up with something. This isn't the first time Larry Stafford's had problems with a whore.'

THE GUARD OPENED the steel door of the holding tank and told Larry it was time to go to court. He was polite and more deferential than he had been with the other prisoners. It made Larry feel uncomfortable. Another guard opened the door that connected the holding area to the courtroom. Larry hesitated at the threshold. He wanted to crawl inside himself and disappear. David had arranged for him to have the dignity of his own clothes, so that he did not have to parade in the uniform of a prisoner before all these people he knew, but the clothes did not prevent him from feeling shame and that nauseated feeling in the pit of his stomach that had grown worse since his arrest.

There was an embarrassed quiet when Stafford was led into the courtroom. Other lawyers looked away. The judge, a man he had appeared before only last week, occupied himself with a loose stack of papers. The bailiff, a young night student with whom he had sometimes chatted during court recess, would not look at him.

David hurried to Stafford's side and began telling him what would happen. Larry wanted to see Jennifer, but he could not bring himself to look at the packed courtroom. He felt he could hold himself together if he stared forward. He wanted to numb all feeling, freeze his heart, and melt away.

They were through the bar of the court now and standing in front of Judge Sturgis. An attractive woman was reading the charge against him, but he could not associate the words she was saying with himself. It was some other Larry Stafford she was talking about. And all the time, he concentrated on a spot just above the judge's head and tried to stand erect.

'Your Honor, I am David Nash, and I will be representing Mr. Stafford in this matter.'

'Very good, Mr. Nash.'

'Your Honor, I would like to raise the matter of bail. Mr. Stafford was arrested last night. As the Court knows, he is a member of the bar, he is married, and he is practicing with a well-respected firm . . .'

'Yes, Mr. Nash,' the judge interrupted. He turned toward Monica Powers.

'Is there any opposition to the setting of bail at this time, Ms. Powers?'

'Yes, Your Honor. The State would be opposed to the setting of bail at this time.'

David started to say something, then thought better of it. Instead, he addressed the Court. 'We would like to have a bail hearing scheduled as quickly as possible then, Your Honor.'

Monica turned toward him.

'I should tell counsel that we are taking this case directly to the grand jury this afternoon, and we expect to arraign Mr. Stafford in circuit court in one to two days.'

'We'll set a hearing date anyway, Ms. Powers,' Judge Sturgis said. 'You can reset the hearing in circuit court if an indictment is handed down, Mr. Nash.'

'Do I have to stay in jail?' Stafford whispered.

'Yes,' David said. He looked at Monica, but she seemed uncomfortable and looked away from him, he thought, intentionally.

'But I thought—'

'I know. I don't know what's going on, but I'll find out as soon as this is over.'

The clerk set a hearing date and David marked it on his folder. The next case was called and Monica started to leave. David touched her elbow.

'Can I talk to you for a second?'

She looked undecided, then nodded.

'I'll wait for you in the hall,' she said, then hurried out.

'Larry, I'll be in touch soon. I want to find out why there was opposition to your bail.'

'You've got to get me out of here,' Stafford said.

The guard was gesturing Stafford back toward the holding area, and a new prisoner was being led into the courtroom. 'You don't know what it's like in that place.'

'We'll have a hearing on the bail in a few days and get this cleared up. I—'

'I don't know if I can take it in that stinking hole for two more days. I want out now, dammit. That's why I hired you.'

David stopped and looked directly at Stafford. His voice was quiet, but firm.

'Larry, you have to start adjusting to the fact that, guilty or innocent, you are accused of a crime. You may not be able to get out of jail. The DA may convince the judge that bail is inappropriate. You have to get hold of yourself or you are going to be a mess by the time we get to trial.'

Stafford was breathing heavily, and David could see the rapid beating of a pulse near his temple. Suddenly, he sagged and his breathing quieted.

'You're right. I'm sorry. I should know enough about the courts to know that nothing is going to happen right away. There's no reason it should be any different because I'm the one in trouble.'

'Good. I'm glad you understand that. I'll see you soon, Larry.'

MONICA WAS STANDING in the hall near the elevators.

'What was that all about?' David asked.

134

'Our office is opposed to your client's release on bail.'

'You made that quite obvious in there,' he said, pointing over his shoulder. 'I want to know why. Stafford's no junkie who's going to split the minute the jail door opens. He's married, with a job—'

'I know all that. It makes no difference.'

'Why? What have you got on him?'

'You'll get all your discovery in the normal course when he's arraigned in circuit court,' Monica said abruptly. Something was upsetting her.

'I know all about discovery procedures, Monica. I'm asking you now, as a colleague who's—'

'Look, David, I'm putting you on notice. This one is different. No breaks and nothing that isn't procedure according to the books.'

'Whoa. Slow down. I've always been square with you, haven't I?'

'Yes. And this has nothing to do with you or me. This one is different, and I mean it. There is more to this case than you know.'

'Like what?'

The elevator door opened and Monica stepped inside.

'I can't discuss it and I won't. I'm sorry.'

David watched the door close and turned back toward the courtroom. Monica had never acted this way before, and it troubled him. When they had a case together, they discussed it. They tried to be as honest with each other as the rules of the game allowed. David's initial impression of Larry Stafford had been favorable, but Monica had said that there was more to the case than he knew. Did that mean that she had conclusive evidence of Stafford's guilt? Had Stafford lied when he'd said he was innocent?

The courtroom door opened and someone called his name. He looked up and saw Charlie Holt approaching. He had not noticed him in the packed courtroom.

'What was this about no bail?' Charlie asked.

David did not answer. He was staring at the beautiful woman who was following Charlie.

'Oh, sorry,' Charlie said. 'Dave, this is Jennifer Stafford.'

Only it wasn't. It was Valerie Dodge.

'I'M SORRY, DAVID. I didn't want to lie to you, but . . .' Her voice trailed off and she looked at her hands, clasped tightly in her lap. David sat across from her. They had both managed to carry on a normal conversation on the way to his office. Charlie was too distracted to notice the tension between them. David asked Charlie to stay in the waiting room, and they both walked to his office in silence. When David closed the door, Jennifer had taken a chair without looking at him.

'I don't know if I should stay on this case,' he said.

She looked up, startled.

'Oh, you must. Please, David. Larry needs you.'

'I'm not sure that I'm the best person to represent your husband.'

'Why? Because we slept together? Please, David. I don't know why I . . . We'd quarreled and . . .' She shook her head. 'I never did anything like that before. You have to believe me.'

'I do believe you. That doesn't matter. A lawyer is supposed to be objective, uninvolved. How am I going to do that?'

She looked down at her hands again, and David leaned back in his chair, trying to maintain control. The shock of meeting her in the courthouse was wearing off, and a deep depression was setting in.

'When Charlie suggested your name . . . at first I was going to say no, but I couldn't. Larry has to have the best lawyer. I can't let him . . .'

She stopped. David turned his chair slightly so she would not be in his line of vision.

'Do you love him?'

She looked up but didn't say anything.

'I asked you if you love your husband.'

He didn't really want to know. He had asked the question to hurt her. He felt confused and betrayed.

'Please don't,' she said. Her voice was almost a whisper, and he was afraid that she would cry.

'Do you love your husband?' David repeated forcefully.

'Does it matter? Do you ask that of every wife

who comes to you for help? Isn't it enough that I'm asking you for help?'

He still could not face her. She was right and he saw that. He was being a fool. A child. And she was asking for help. But to give her that help, he would have to build a barrier between them that might never come down. He swiveled the chair back toward her. She was sitting erect and watching him.

'I could give you the names of several other attorneys. All very competent.'

'No, I want you. I believe in you. I know you can clear Larry.'

'Who is Valerie Dodge?' he asked. She blushed and smiled.

'Dodge is my maiden name. The other one . . . Valerie . . . There's a TV show I watch. I didn't know what to say and that was the first name I thought of.'

David laughed. She hesitated a second to make sure that his laughter was real; then she laughed. A nervous laugh. Grateful that the tension had been broken.

'I tried very hard to find you. Called Senator Bauer's campaign committee, scoured the phone books.'

'I thought about you, too. There were times I wanted to . . . But I couldn't. Larry and I . . . we've had problems. He works very hard and . . . What happened that night. It just happened. But you can't let that interfere with Larry's case. Whatever

I feel for him, if it's love or . . . he is my husband and . . .'

She stopped and they looked at each other. Now it was his turn to avert his eyes. He felt very tired.

'I want to think, Jennifer. I'm mixed up now and I want some time to clear my head.'

'All right.'

'I'll call you in the morning and let you know what I decide.'

He stood up and she followed. He held open the door and she started to leave. They were close. Within inches of each other. His hand poised on the doorknob, the scent of her all around him. He wanted to hold her. She sensed it and pretended not to notice. The moment passed and he opened the door. When she was gone, he sat at his desk without moving for a long time.

3

David had not slept well. There had been clear skies and a bright slice of moon, and he had watched the stars from the darkness of his living room when he found he could not sleep. What was there to it? A woman he had slept with one time. Why should she matter, when none of the others he had taken to bed had mattered? He knew he would not find the answer with logic, the lawyer's tool.

What should he do? The answer was obvious. Get out. Obvious on paper, that is. But not in his heart, where the decision was being made. And it was not all that obvious, anyway, because one factor muddied everything over. What if Larry Stafford was innocent? Charlie Holt had told him that Jennifer said she had been with her husband the night Darlene Hersch was murdered, and Jennifer had told him when they were walking to his office from the courthouse that Larry was innocent. Stafford had said it too, and David believed him. On the other hand, was the man who had cuckolded the defendant the best man to represent him?

David had to give that a lot of thought. Now that he had found Jennifer, he did not want to let her go. He wanted to know if there was anything more possible between them. He had sensed that possibility when they had parted at his office.

Did he want the case because of Jennifer? Did he care about Larry Stafford at all? If it was just Jennifer, he knew he would have to give it up. But it wasn't just Jennifer, David told himself. If Larry Stafford was innocent, David could not stand by and see him convicted. There was more to this case than just a chance to see Jennifer again. Hadn't he felt the excitement when Charlie Holt had told him that Stafford might be innocent? David thought about Ashmore and Gault and Anthony Seals. When their cases had concluded, he had felt a sense of guilt, not pride. This was a case he could be proud of. He was the best criminal lawyer in the state and one of the best in the country. It was about time he started using his abilities the way they were meant to be used.

THERE WAS A note from Monica in his message box the next morning. An indictment had been returned, and a date for the arraignment had been set in circuit court. David made a note to himself to set a time for a bail hearing. The first thing he did when he reached his office was call Jennifer Stafford. She answered after the first ring.

'I'll represent Larry if you want me to.'

'Yes,' she answered after a brief pause. 'Thank you. I was afraid you wouldn't . . . Larry is very high on you. We talked about it yesterday evening.'

141

'You didn't tell him I was thinking about not taking the case?'

'Oh, no. He doesn't know anything about us.'

There was silence on the line.

'You haven't . . .?' she started.

'Of course not.'

There was another pause. Not an auspicious beginning. They could not relax with each other.

'Larry said that you have his appointment book at home,' he said.

'I think so. I'll look.'

'I'll need it as soon as possible. And the fee,' he added, feeling uneasy about asking her for money.

'Of course; Charlie told me. I'll go to the bank.'

Again, dead air. Neither of them knew how to fill the space.

'I'll let you know when the bail hearing is set,' David said, unwilling to let the conversation end.

'Yes.'

'And don't forget the book. It's important.'

He was repeating himself.

'If . . . if I find the book, should I bring it down this morning?'

Did that mean she wanted to see him? He felt very unsure of himself.

'We can set an appointment.'

'I could leave it with your secretary. If you're busy.' She hesitated. 'I don't want to bother you. I know you have other cases.'

'No. That's all right. If you find it, come down.

142

I'm pretty open this afternoon, and I have to talk to you anyway for background.'

'Okay. If I find it.'

They rang off. He leaned back, breathed deeply, and composed himself. This was no good. There was too much adrenaline involved. He wasn't thinking straight. Like some high-school kid with a crush. Stupid. When he felt he had himself in hand, he dialed Terry Conklin, his investigator.

'How you doing, Terry?'

'Up to my ass. And you?'

'Same thing. That's why I called you. I have a real interesting one. It'll probably take a lot of your time.'

'Gee, I don't know, Dave. I hate to turn you down, but I just picked up Industrial Indemnity as a client, and I've had to hire another guy just to handle their caseload.'

David was disappointed. Terry had been an intelligence officer in the Air Force and a policeman after that. When he got tired of working for someone else, he quit the force and started his own agency. David had been one of his first clients, and they were good friends. As Terry's reputation grew, he acquired several insurance companies as clients. The money end of his business was in investigating personal-injury claims, and he had little time now for criminal investigation, his first love. But he and David had an understanding if the case was big enough, and he had never let David down yet.

'It's the policewoman who was murdered at the Raleigh Motel,' David said. He was laying out the bait.

'Oh. Yeah? Some of my police friends were talking about that. They got someone, huh?'

'You don't read the papers?'

'I was in New Orleans last week.'

'My, my, aren't we getting to be the cross-country traveler. Business or pleasure?'

'A little of both. You representing the accused?'

David smiled. He was interested.

'Yeah. They arrested a lawyer from the Price, Winward firm.'

'No shit!'

David relaxed. He had him.

'Can you recommend someone to work on the case? I'd like someone good.'

'Hold on, will you? Just one minute.'

Terry put him on hold and David laughed out loud. When Terry got back on the line, they made an appointment to meet after work and drive to the Raleigh Motel.

JENNIFER SHOWED UP at three. She was dressed in a conservative gray skirt and a white blouse that covered her to the neck. Her hair was swept back in a bun. With glasses she would look like a librarian in one of those forties movies, whose hidden beauty was revealed when she let her hair down.

'I brought the book,' she said, holding out a

pocket-sized notebook with a black leather cover. David reached across the desk and took it, careful not to let their hands touch. He flipped through the pages until he came to June 16. Stafford had had an appointment at nine forty-five with someone named Lockett and another appointment at four-thirty with Barry Dietrich. David recognized Dietrich's name. He was a partner at Price, Winward who specialized in securities work. That would tie in with what Larry had told him at the jail. There were no other entries for the sixteenth, and David made a note to contact Dietrich.

'Is that any help?' Jennifer asked.

'It could be. Larry met with one of the partners on the day of the murder. I'll find out how late they worked.'

Jennifer nodded. She looked ill at ease, sitting erect with her hands folded in her lap, making an extra effort to look businesslike. David appreciated her discomfort. He felt rigid, and the conversation had an artificial quality to it.

'I want to talk to you about your relationship to Larry. Some of the questions I'm going to ask will be very personal, but I wouldn't ask them if the answers weren't important to Larry's defense.'

She nodded again, and he noticed that her hands clasped tighter, turning the knuckles of her left hand momentarily white.

'How long have you known Larry?'

'Just over a year.'

'How did you meet?'

'I was teaching school with Miriam Holt, Charlie's wife. She introduced us. Larry and Charlie play a lot of handball together.'

'How long after that were you married?'

'A few months. Four.'

It came out as an apology, and David looked down at his notes, sensing her embarrassment. Whether the jury found Larry innocent or guilty, this would be an ordeal for her. And it would never really stop. If Larry was convicted, she would be the wife of the young lawyer who had killed a policewoman he thought was a prostitute. Why had he needed a prostitute? They would look at her and wonder. What was wrong with her that she had driven him to that?

And if he was acquitted? Well, you never were, really. The jury might say you were not guilty, but the doubts always remained.

'Where do you teach?'

'Palisades Elementary School.'

'How long have you been teaching?'

She smiled and relaxed a little.

'It seems like forever.'

'Do you enjoy it?'

'Yes. I've always liked kids. I don't know. It can be hard at times, but I really feel it's worthwhile. Larry wanted me to stop teaching after we were married, but I told him I wanted to keep on.'

'Why did he want you to stop?'

Jennifer blushed and looked down at her hands. 'You have to understand Larry. He's very tied up in this manhood trip. It's just the way he is.'

'Has Larry ever cheated on you?'

There was a sharp intake of breath, and Jennifer looked directly at David.

'No,' she said firmly. 'And I think I would have known.'

'Has he ever struck you?'

'No,' she said after a moment's hesitation.

'Has he or hasn't he?'

'Well, we've quarreled, but he's never . . . No.'

'Do you consider Larry to be normal sexually?'

'What do you mean, "normal"?' she asked hesitantly.

David felt uneasy and unsure of himself. He had asked this type of question often enough in the past, but it had always been strictly for professional reasons. He was asking now as a professional, but there was something more. He wanted to know what the relationship between Larry Stafford and his wife was really like. He wanted to know how he stacked up sexually to the man he was representing. He wanted to know if Jennifer responded to her husband with the passion she had exhibited during their lovemaking.

'Are his sexual preferences unusual? Does he have any peculiarities?'

'I don't see why, what that would . . . Can't we talk about something else? This is very hard for me.'

'I know it's hard for you, but this case is heavily

147

concerned with sex, and I want you prepared for the questions the district attorney is going to ask you in open court.'

'I'll have to . . .? I couldn't . . .'

Jennifer took a deep breath, and David let her compose herself.

'Our sexual relationship is . . . just normal.'

Her voice caught, and David again watched her hands, tense and entwined, clasp each other rigidly.

'I don't know what you want me to say,' she said so softly that he had to strain to hear her.

'David, that evening you and I . . . It is true that Larry and I were having problems, but they had to do with his work, not our sexual relationship. He was working very hard. He didn't make partner last year and it deflated him. At first he just gave up. It was right after we got married, and he was talking about leaving the firm and trying something else: government work or going out on his own. Then he changed his mind and decided that he would be accepted if he just worked harder. Even harder than before. He was leaving early and coming home late. He was drinking, too. I hardly saw him at all, even on the weekends. And when I did see him, it seemed we were always quarreling.

'The evening I met you . . . I just blew up at him. Called him at the office. He came home all upset. I'd interfered with his work. Couldn't I understand? I told him I did understand. That I thought he considered his work more important than me. I walked out. Then I met you and . . . and it just happened. I wanted to hurt him, I guess. But it isn't . . . wasn't sex. We were . . . all right.'

She stopped, out of words, her energy spent. David didn't know what to say. He wanted to take her in his arms and comfort her, but he knew he couldn't.

'Besides,' she said, 'I don't see what any of this has to do with Larry's case. I told Charlie, Larry couldn't have killed that girl. He was home with me on that evening.'

'You're certain?'

'Yes. I would know. I mean, if he was out with another woman . . . He was with me.'

'You would swear to that in court?'

'Yes. I don't want Larry to go to prison. He couldn't take it, David. He couldn't take the pressure.'

'He seems to be holding up pretty well.'

'You don't know him like I do. He puts up a good front, but he's a little boy underneath. He's very good at seeming to be in one piece, but I know him well enough to see the cracks beneath the surface.'

David put down his notepad. The short interview had taken its emotional toll on both of them.

'I guess that's enough for now. I'm going to visit the motel after work and try to talk to the desk clerk. I'll let you know if I turn up anything.'

She stood, and he walked her to the door.

'I want to thank you for taking the case. I know it

was a hard decision for you. And I know that Larry will be safe with you.'

He didn't know what to say. She solved the problem by leaving quickly. He watched her walk away, hoping that she would turn and give him some sign, but she didn't and he returned to his desk, more confused than ever about their relationship.

There was a glass and a bottle of good bourbon in David's bottom drawer. He took his bourbon neat. It was some time since he had felt the need for a midday drink, but he had the feeling that there would be many more before he was through with the Stafford case.

TERRY CONKLIN WAS medium height, a bit chubby, and had a wide and continuous smile. He looked like the least dangerous person in any gathering, and people trusted and talked to him. That's what made him so valuable as an investigator.

Terry turned his Dodge station wagon into the parking lot at the Raleigh Motel. The wagon was strewn with debris left by Conklin's five children. It was a far cry from the flashy sports cars James Bond drove, and Terry liked to joke that it was part of his cover.

Terry had spent some time that afternoon in the morgue at the *Oregonian* reading everything he could find about the Hersch case. He had photocopied the clippings for David, who was finishing the last one as they pulled up in front of the motel office.

'Any help?' Conklin asked as he shut off the engine.

'They don't give me much more than I already know. Say, before I forget, the bail hearing's tomorrow and they'll probably put Ortiz on. Can you make it?'

'No problem,' Terry said as they headed toward the motel office.

Merton Grimes was an old man, stooped and slow to move. The cold weather was still holding off, but Grimes had on a heavy plaid shirt, buttoned to the neck, and a pair of soiled gray slacks. He was standing over a pot of coffee when David entered, and David had to cough to get his attention. Grimes looked put out and took his time shuffling across the room. David could see a section of the back room through a half-open door. There was a small couch covered by an antimacassar. A lamp rested on a low end table casting a dim light on the green-and-white fabric. David could hear the muffled sound of a TV whose volume had been turned low, but he could not see the screen.

'Mr. Grimes?' David asked. The old man looked immediately suspicious. 'My name is David Nash. This is Terry Conklin. I'd like to talk to you about the murder that occurred here a few months ago.'

'You reporters?' Grimes asked in a tone suggesting that he would not be upset if they were.

'No. I'm a lawyer. I represent the man who's been charged with the crime.'

'Oh,' Grimes said, disappointed.

'I'd like to see the room if I could and talk about anything you might know.'

'I already told what I know to the police. Damn place was like a circus for a week,' he said, nodding at the memory. 'Reporters and cops. Didn't do business no harm, though.'

He laughed and it came out more of a snort. The old man wiped his nose with the back of his hand and turned to a pegboard on the wall behind the desk counter. It took him a moment, but he found the key he was looking for. He started to reach for it, then stopped and turned back. He had a crafty look on his face, and David knew exactly what was coming next.

'You know, I ain't sure I should be doin' this. You representing a criminal and all. I don't know if the cops would like it. I could get in trouble.'

'I can assure you this is perfectly legal . . .'

'All the same . . .'

'And, of course, we would pay you for your time.'

'Oh, say, that's mighty nice of you,' Grimes said with a smirk. David wondered how much dough he'd pulled in from the press for exclusive tours. He laid a twenty-dollar bill on the countertop. Grimes looked at it for a moment, probably figuring if there was any way to get more; then his fingers made the fastest move David would see all evening, and the bill was gobbled up and stuffed into his trouser pocket.

'We can talk while we walk,' Grimes said, taking the key off the peg and shuffling toward the door. Conklin held it open, and he and David followed Grimes across the parking lot toward the motel rooms.

'She sure was a nice-lookin' gal,' Grimes said as they started up the metal stairs to the second landing. 'Didn't look like no hooker to me. I got suspicious right off.'

'You get plenty of hookers here?' Terry asked with a straight face.

'What's that supposed to mean?'

Terry shrugged.

'You said she didn't look like one. I just supposed . . .'

The old man weighed his answer for a second, then snickered.

'Yeah, we get our share. I don't take no cut, you understand. But there's a few that likes our accommodations. Cops don't care, so why should I?'

'Did you ever see the fella who was with the dead girl before that night?'

'Like I told the cops, he was out in the car and I didn't pay no attention to him. She come in and I was readin'. Then she took up most of my attention, if you know what I mean. Nice tits, as much of 'em as I could see. I just didn't have no interest in the john.'

'So you didn't get a good look at him at all?'

153

'I didn't say that. I seen him, but he didn't make no impression. And it was only a little look, when he come tearin' out of here after he killed her.'

'What do you remember seeing?'

'Nothin' much. A man in a car. I already been through this with the cops.'

'I know,' David said, 'and I appreciate your taking the time to talk to us now.'

They were on the landing and Grimes was leading the way toward a room at the end. Terry looked around, filing the layout away in his mind for future use. Grimes stopped and inserted his key in the door of the next-to-last room. The door opened. A large globe light to the right of the door hung above David's head and cast a pale-yellow glow over the door. Grimes put his key in the lock and pushed the door open.

'There she is. Course it's cleaned up now. It was some mess then, I can tell you.'

Grimes stepped aside, and David entered the unlit room. He turned and saw the neon signs on the boulevard. A reminder of the life outside. Here, in the sterile, plastic room, there was no sign of life or death. Just a twentieth-century motel limbo devoid of feeling. The shadowy figures of Grimes and Conklin wavered in the doorway like spirits of the dead. Grimes reached around the wall and found the light switch.

'There isn't much we can learn here,' Terry said

when he had toured the bedroom and bathroom. 'The DA will have pictures of the scene.'

David nodded.

'The papers say it was some young lawyer,' Grimes said.

'That's right.'

'That fits with what I seen. Fancy car he was drivin' and the long hair.'

'You saw his hair?' David asked.

'I said so, didn't I?'

'I must have misunderstood you. I thought you said he didn't make an impression on you.'

'He didn't. But I seen the hair. Brown hair.'

'You're certain about that?' David said, casting a quick look at Conklin.

'I'm gettin' along, but I ain't senile. Say, you think they'll put it in the papers when I testify?'

'No doubt, Mr. Grimes,' Terry said. Grimes smiled and nodded his head.

'I was in the papers once before. They had a robbery here and they listed me as the victim. I got the clipping in my desk.'

'I think I've seen all I want to. How about you?' David asked Conklin. The investigator just nodded. He and David walked onto the landing, and Grimes switched off the light and locked the door.

'Thanks for the tour,' David said when they reached the office.

'Anytime.'

'See you in court,' Conklin said.

The old man chuckled and shook his head. 'That's right,' he said. 'That's right.'

He was shuffling toward the back room as they drove away.

4

The main entrance to the county courthouse was on Fourth Avenue. David entered through the back door on Fifth. The rear corridor was jammed with police officers waiting to testify in the three traffic courts located there. Lawyers in three-piece suits huddled with straggly-haired dopers and stylishly dressed young women about defenses to their traffic citations. Court clerks shuffled people back and forth between the courtrooms and the large room where the fines were paid. An old lawyer listened patiently to the complaints of a young member of the bar, and an even younger district attorney tried to understand the testimony of a police officer as he prepared to try his seventh straight speeding case.

David pushed through the crowd and into the narrow alcove that housed the jail elevator. The courthouse jail was used to hold prisoners who had court appearances and for booking new arrestees.

The elevator stopped at seven, and David stepped up to a thick glass window and called through an intercom to a guard who was seated at a control panel.

'I'd like to see Larry Stafford. Do you have an empty booth?'

'Try two, Mr. Nash,' the guard said over his shoulder. David signed his name in the logbook. The guard pressed a button and a floor-to-ceiling steel gate swung open. David walked into the narrow holding area and waited for the gate to close. As soon as it clicked shut, the guard pressed another button. There was an electronic hum, and the solid-steel door at the other end of the holding area swung open. David walked to a door that opened into the conference area. Several identical booths were set up side by side. Each booth was divided by wire mesh that started halfway up from the floor. There was a chair on each side of the mesh and a ledge underneath it.

David took some papers out of his attaché case and read them while he waited for the guard to bring Larry Stafford. Stafford arrived a few minutes later, smiling and looking thinner than he had at the arraignment.

'It's good to see you, Dave,' he said through the mesh. There was no tremor in his voice, as there had been the last time they were together.

'How are you getting along?' David asked.

Stafford shrugged.

'I guess you can get used to anything. In a way, it's not all that bad. No clients yelling at me. No partners making demands. Plenty of sleep. If the food was a little better, I'd recommend the place.'

David smiled. Stafford seemed to have developed a sense of humor, and that was essential if he was going to get through his ordeal.

'You do look a little thinner than when I saw you last.'

'Yeah, well they cut down on all those fancy sauces here. It definitely helps the waistline.'

David took the appointment book out of his attaché case and held it against the wire mesh.

'We have some time before the bail hearing, so I want to go over some stuff. Does this help you remember any more about the night of the murder?'

Stafford read over the entry for June 16.

'Right. I was going to talk to you about that. I talked to Jenny and she mentioned the book. Call Dietrich. He'll tell you. We had a conference that night. Remember I told you about that securities case? Well, we were together until six, six-thirty. You can check the time sheets we keep at the firm for billing clients.'

'Okay,' David said, making a notation on his pad, 'but that doesn't help us too much. Hersch started her shift around ten-thirty, and she was killed about midnight.'

'Oh,' Stafford said, momentarily dejected. Then he brightened.

'It would still be good circumstantial evidence that I'm innocent. I mean, it doesn't make sense, does it, for me to have a normal business day, confer on a securities case, then slice up a policewoman. I mean the two are pretty inconsistent, aren't they?'

'Not necessarily. There are plenty of businessmen who use the services of prostitutes. Why should you be any different?'

'Okay,' Stafford answered eagerly, 'I've been thinking about that angle. But it won't work. Jenny will testify that we're happily married. You've seen Jenny, haven't you? What jury would believe that a guy married to someone as good-looking as that would waste his time with a whore? Right? It doesn't fit in.'

Stafford sat back and smiled, satisfied that he had won his case. David looked up from his notes and waited a moment before speaking. He noticed that his palms were damp, and for the moment he felt certain that he was more unsure of himself than was his client.

'A man married to a good-looking woman might seek the services of a prostitute if he and his wife were having difficulties with their marriage.'

Stafford continued to smile. He nodded his head to acknowledge the point.

'If. But there's no "if" about Jenny and me.'

'No difficulties at all? No arguments, no sexual difficulties or money problems? You'd better be straight with me on this, Larry, because putting you and Jenny on the stand will open the door for the district attorney, and if there's dirt, you can bet she'll find it.'

David thought about his evening with Jenny as he waited for Stafford to answer. A mental image of her, naked and in his bed, appeared, and he fought to erase it.

'We have spats. Who doesn't?' Stafford paused. 'Look, I'm going to level with you. Jenny and I have had our problems. What marriage doesn't? And you know what they say about the first year being the toughest.'

David thought back to his first year of marriage. It had not been pleasant for either of them. Vicious words, said for the sole purpose of hurting. Slammed doors and backs turned in anger.

'Hell, it was both our faults. I'm not an easy guy to live with sometimes. I didn't make partner last year and it really hurt me. Two other guys who were hired the same year I was made the grade, and I was pretty depressed for a long time. I don't suppose that was easy for Jenny to take.'

'How are you two sexually?'

Stafford reddened slightly. The question seemed to make him uneasy.

'I don't know. I'd say we do okay. I'm maybe more demanding than some guys. You might say I dig sex a little more than Jenny. She's more conventional in her, uh, tastes. Nothing I'd call a, uh, problem though.'

Stafford hesitated. He looked upset.

'Will . . . will they be asking about that at the trial? Our sex life, I mean?'

'It could come up. Why?'

'I don't know. It's just embarrassing, I guess. I don't mind talking to you. You're my lawyer and I trust you. It would be different in front of all those people.'

David glanced at his watch. The bail hearing was set for two and it was ten of.

'It's almost time to go to court,' he said, 'so I'm going to stop now. But I want to ask you one more question. You remember how surprised I was that the district attorney's office opposed bail at the arraignment? Well, I talked with Monica Powers after court, and she acted very peculiar. She hinted that they had some kind of surprise evidence I didn't know about. Do you have any idea what that might be, Larry?'

'Surprise evidence,' Stafford repeated. 'I can't think of . . .' He stopped for a moment, and David got the distinct impression that something was troubling his client.

'Look, I didn't do it, so what could they have? It doesn't make any sense.'

'You do some thinking on this, okay, Larry? I don't like surprises, and it looks like Monica is planning one. Remember what I told you about being straight with me. If you've done something that can hurt us, I want to know right now.'

'Dave, I have been one hundred percent square with you. There's nothing.'

'You're sure?'

'Absolutely. Say, how do my chances look today?' Stafford asked anxiously.

'I don't know. It depends on what kind of showing the State makes. One point for our side is that Jerry Miles is the presiding criminal judge this month.'

Stafford brightened. 'He's pretty liberal, isn't he?'

'He's good and he's fair. Keep your fingers crossed. I hope you'll be out of here by this evening.'

They shook hands and David buzzed the guard. Stafford was still waiting in front of the door when the guard let David out. On the elevator ride up to the courtroom, David tried to analyze his feelings about his client. He felt uncomfortable around Stafford. The man appeared to be open and honest, but David could not help feeling that Larry was using the same technique on him that David used on a jury. Or did he just want to feel that way? He had to face one very unpleasant fact: he wanted Jenny, and Larry Stafford was his rival for Jenny's affections.

David tried to stand back from his problem and be objective. Was Stafford lying to him? Was he really guilty? Were his uneasy feelings about Stafford generated by his emotional involvement with Jenny? He had given Larry a chance to lie today, and Stafford had not taken it. Although reticent at first to discuss his private life, Larry had eventually been candid about his marital problems,

163

and he had told David about his failure to make partner. And then there was Jenny. She swore she was with Larry on the night of the murder. She would not lie to him.

By the time the elevator doors opened, David was starting to feel better about his case. Jenny would make a good witness, and there was Grimes's testimony about the hair. The jury might not be totally convinced of the accuracy of the motel clerk's observations, but his testimony, combined with other evidence, could create the reasonable doubt needed for an acquittal. Now all David had to do was find those other pieces of evidence. He hoped some of them would be provided by the testimony at the bail hearing.

PRESIDING CRIMINAL COURT was at the far end of the corridor from the bank of elevators David had used. He was halfway to the courtroom when he saw Thomas Gault grinning at him from a bench near the courtroom doorway.

'You're just the man I wanted to see,' Gault said. David stopped and looked at his watch. Court would start in a moment, and he really did not want to talk to Gault anyway. Ever since Gault had shaken him with his false confession, David had gone out of his way to avoid the writer.

'I'm sorry, Tom, but I'm due in court.'

'The Stafford bail hearing, right?'

'Right.'

'That's what I want to talk about. I'm covering the case for *Newsweek*.'

'The magazine?' David asked incredulously.

'The same. They gave a lot of coverage to my trial, so I convinced them that it would be a neat gimmick to have someone who was just acquitted of murder cover a murder case. Hell, I'm their murderer-in-residence now. Besides, I did those articles on Cambodia and the article on the mercenaries for them.

'So what do you say? Is Stafford guilty? Come on. I need a scoop to beat out the local yokels.'

David couldn't help laughing. Gault was a leprechaun when he wanted to be, and his humor could be infectious.

'No scoops and no comment. How would you have liked it if I'd blabbed to reporters about your case?'

'But, Dave, I had nothing to hide. Can you say the same for Stafford? If I don't get facts from you, I'll have to make something up. I've got deadlines.'

'No comment,' David repeated. Gault shrugged.

'Suit yourself. I'm only trying to make you famous.'

'And I appreciate the effort, but I really do have to go.'

'At least say something memorable, old buddy. I've gotta have some snappy copy.'

David shook his head and laughed again. He opened the door and entered the courtroom. Gault followed him and took a seat in the back of the room where he would not be noticed.

'THIS IS THE time set for the bail hearing in State versus Lawrence Dean Stafford, case number C94-07-850. The State is represented by Monica Powers,' Monica said, 'and the defendant is present with his attorney, David Nash.'

'Are you prepared to proceed, Mr. Nash?' Judge Autley asked.

'Ready, Your Honor,' David answered stiffly. Clement Autley was the worst judge they could have gotten. Almost seventy, Autley was so erratic that many attorneys filed affidavits of prejudice against him rather than risk his unpredictable rulings at trial and subject themselves and their clients to his very predictable temper tantrums. Autley was not supposed to be on the bench today. Jerome Miles was. But Miles had the flu, and Autley had been shipped upstairs for the week.

'You may proceed, Mr. Nash.'

'Your Honor, I believe the burden is on the district attorney.'

'You're asking for bail, aren't you? Your motion, your burden,' Autley snapped.

'If I might, Your Honor,' David said, careful to maintain his composure and to address the judge formally. He had once seen Autley, in a fit of anger, hold a young lawyer in contempt for not using the proper court etiquette. 'Article one, section

166

fourteen of the state constitution states that, and I quote, "Offenses, except murder and treason, shall be bailable by sufficient sureties. Murder or treason shall not be bailable when the proof is evident or the presumption strong."

'In *State* ex rel. *August v. Chambers*, our supreme court held that if the State seeks to deny bail to a person charged with murder, it has the burden of proving that there is proof of, or a presumption of, the defendant's guilt which is evident or strong. In light of the Chambers case, it appears that the State has the burden, not Mr. Stafford.'

Judge Autley glared at David for a moment, then turned rapidly toward Monica Powers.

'What do you say to that?'

'I'm afraid he's right, Your Honor,' Monica said nervously. It was widely known that the one thing Autley hated more than young defense lawyers was any kind of woman lawyer.

'Then why are you wasting the Court's time? I have a busy schedule. You see all these people waiting here, don't you? Why did you let him go on and on if you agreed with what he said?'

'I'm sorry . . .' Monica started, but Autley waved a hand toward her.

'What's your evidence?'

Monica tendered to the judge a copy of the indictment charging murder. His bailiff, an elderly woman who had been with him for years, handed the document to him.

'I believe the indictment in this case should be sufficient. It establishes that the grand jury, after hearing testimony, decided that there was sufficient proof to indict for murder.'

Judge Autley scanned the document for a moment; then he handed it back to the bailiff.

'Bail denied,' he said without looking up. 'Next case.'

David was on his feet, waving a law book toward the judge.

'Your Honor.'

'I've ruled, Mr. Nash. Next case.'

'Your Honor, last month in the Archer case the Oregon Supreme Court ruled on this specific question and held that an indictment is not sufficient evidence to support a denial of bail in a murder case. I have the case here, if the Court would read it.'

'What case?' Autley asked, annoyed that the matter was not over.

'Archer, if you'd take a look.'

'Give it to me. But if this case isn't on point . . .' He let his voice trail off, leaving the threat dangling over David's head.

David handed the law book to the bailiff. Stafford leaned forward to say something, but David touched his leg and he sat back. Autley read the page twice, then turned his anger on Monica Powers.

'Don't they teach you the law anymore? Didn't you know about this case?'

'Your Honor, I—'

'You'd better have more than this, young lady,' Autley said, waving the indictment toward Monica, 'and you'd better produce it fast.'

'We do have further evidence, Your Honor. Officer Ortiz is prepared to testify.'

'Then call him.'

Monica gestured toward the first row of spectator seats, and Bert Ortiz rose from his seat next to Detective Crosby. He pushed through the gate that separated the spectators from the bar of the court and stopped in front of the bailiff.

'Do you swear to tell the truth, the whole truth, and nothing but the truth, so help you God?' the bailiff asked.

'I do,' Ortiz replied.

'Then state your name and spell your last name.'

Ortiz sat down in the witness box and spelled his last name for the court reporter. His throat felt dry as he did so, and there was none of the air of self-assurance about him that he usually had when he testified. He felt uncomfortable reliving the events of the murder.

'Officer Ortiz,' Monica asked, 'how are you employed?'

'I'm a police officer with the Portland Police Bureau.'

'How long have you been so employed?'

'It will be seven years this coming February.'

'Were you so employed on the evening of June sixteenth of this year?'

169

'I was.'

'And what was your assignment at that time?'

'I was working in a special vice unit. We were using policewomen disguised as prostitutes to arrest males who were soliciting prostitution.'

'Could you be more specific for the Court?'

Judge Autley leaned toward Monica and waved an impatient hand.

'I know what he means. Don't insult the Court's intelligence. Now, get on with this.'

'Very well, Your Honor. Officer Ortiz, who was your partner that evening?'

'Darlene Hersch, a policewoman.'

'When did you begin work?'

'The shift started at ten-thirty, but we weren't out on the street until about eleven-thirty. We had a meeting first.'

'Officer, please tell the Court what happened from the time you began work on the street until the time Darlene Hersch was murdered.'

Ortiz leaned forward slightly. There was tension in his shoulders and a tight feeling in his stomach. He looked down at the railing of the witness box and quickly ran his tongue across his dry lips.

'I was in our car in a parking lot on the corner of Park and Morrison, and Officer Hersch was on the far corner. Shortly after I started my surveillance, a beige Mercedes-Benz stopped and Darlene – Officer Hersch – got in. It drove off and I followed.'

'Were you able to read the license number of the car at that, or any other, time?'

'No.'

'Go on.'

'Officer Hersch was not supposed to enter a vehicle if asked. She was supposed to decoy the subject back to the lot, where we would make the arrest. She had strict orders not to do that.'

Ortiz stopped. He realized that he was trying to justify his actions by putting Darlene in a bad light. He looked up. Monica was waiting for him to continue. There was little sound in the courtroom. For the first time in a long time, he noticed the faces watching him.

'Officer Hersch got into the Mercedes and I followed the car to the Raleigh Motel. I saw Officer Hersch enter the motel office, and I saw the car drive around back. I parked in the lot of a fast-food place next door and took up a surveillance post.'

'To this point had you been able to see who was driving the Mercedes?'

'Not really. I had a look at him when Officer Hersch got into the car, but he was too far away. It was the same when he was letting her off at the motel office.'

'Go on.'

'Well, Officer Hersch was new. She didn't have much street experience. I started to worry about her being alone with the, uh, the subject.'

Ortiz paused again. He wanted to look for Crosby

but was afraid. Would the older man condemn him for letting things go as far as they had? He had been wrong. He should never have let Darlene go into that room alone. Even if it meant losing the collar, he should have stopped it as soon as he reached the motel. Should have parked in the motel lot and gone straight up to the room.

Ortiz looked over to the defense table. They had dressed Stafford in a suit. Very Ivy League. He looked more the lawyer than Nash. Their eyes met, and Stafford's face, for a brief instant, reflected contempt. There was no fear in his eyes, only ice. Humorless, emotionless, unlike Ortiz's own, which wavered with confusion and self-doubt. Ortiz looked away, defeated. And in that moment he felt the sick feeling in his stomach turning to hate for the man who had taken Darlene Hersch's life. He wanted that man. Wanted him more than he had ever wanted any other man he had hunted.

'I saw the subject walk along the second-floor landing and enter the room Officer Hersch had entered.'

'What did the man look like?'

'He was tall. About six feet. Athletic build. I would say he was in his late twenties or early thirties. I didn't see his face, but he had curly blond hair, and he was wearing tan slacks and a flowered shirt.'

'What happened after the man entered the motel room?'

'I . . . I crossed over to the motel lot and started up

the stairs. When I was halfway up, I heard a scream. I broke down the door, and then I was struck several times. I remember crashing into the bed. I must have hit the metal leg, because I passed out.'

'Before you lost consciousness, did you get a look at your assailant?'

'I did.'

'Do you see that man in this courtroom?'

Ortiz pointed toward Stafford. This time his hatred made him strong and he did not waver. David watched his client. If the identification upset him, he did not show it.

'The man I saw in the motel room is sitting beside counsel at that table,' Ortiz said.

'Officer Ortiz, if you know, what type of car does Mr. Stafford drive?'

'Mr. Stafford drives a beige 1991 Mercedes-Benz, model 300 SEL.'

'Is this the same car that you saw at the corner of Park and Morrison and later at the Raleigh Motel?'

'Yes.'

'At a later point in time, did you have an opportunity to search the defendant's home?'

'On September fifth we obtained a search warrant for Mr. Stafford's home. Detective Crosby, myself, and several other policemen arrested Mr. Stafford and conducted a search for clothing.'

'What did you find?'

'A shirt identical to that worn by the person I

saw at the Raleigh Motel, and tan slacks that were very similar to those worn by the killer.'

'I have no further questions,' Monica said.

'Officer Ortiz,' David asked, 'you were a full city block away from the Mercedes when you first saw it, were you not?'

'Yes.'

'As I understand your testimony, Officer Hersch was supposed to lead a person back to you if she was propositioned and you would then arrest him in the lot?'

'Yes.'

'And you were watching Officer Hersch from your car?'

'Yes.'

'Was the engine on?'

'In the police car?'

'Yes.'

'No.'

'And you were surprised when Officer Hersch got into the Mercedes?'

'Yes.'

'Park is one-way going south, is it not?'

'Yes.'

'Where was Officer Hersch when she got into the Mercedes?'

'At the corner of Park and Morrison.'

'Did the Mercedes turn up Park?'

'No. It proceeded down Morrison.'

'In order to follow it, wouldn't you have to go

up Park to Taylor, then back down Tenth?'

'No, sir, I went down Park the wrong way.'

'Then turned on Morrison?'

'Yes, sir.'

'How far away from the Mercedes were you when you spotted it again?'

'Two blocks, about.'

'And did you maintain that distance?'

'Yes.'

'You were too far back to read the license plate?'

'Yes.'

'Where was the Mercedes when you reached the motel?'

'I believe it had just stopped in front of the motel office.'

'Why didn't you get the license number then?'

'At that point I didn't realize it would be important. Besides, I was going too fast.'

'When did you next see the Mercedes that night?'

'I didn't. It was gone by the time I parked.'

'Let me see if I have this straight. You first saw the car from a distance of one city block, then you followed it from a distance of approximately two city blocks, and, finally, you saw it briefly as you passed by the motel lot?'

'Yes.'

'Now, you testified that the car you saw was a beige 1991 Mercedes-Benz, model 300 SEL, did you not?'

'Yes.'

'How do you know that?'

Ortiz looked perplexed.

'How do I know . . .?'

'The model and year and color?'

'That's the car Mr. Stafford drives.'

'Yes. But did you know the year and model and color on the night of the murder?'

'I . . . The color was beige. I could see that.'

'And the year and model?'

Ortiz paused.

'No. I only knew it was a beige Mercedes on that night.'

'So it could have been an '89 or an '85 Mercedes?'

'I later saw Mr. Stafford's car and it was the same one.'

'Do you know what a 1989 Mercedes looks like?'

'No.'

'Or an '85?'

'No.'

'The only time you saw the killer's face was just before you passed out, is that correct?'

'Yes.'

'Where were you and where was he, when you saw his face?'

'I was lying on my back on the floor looking up, and Mr. Stafford . . .'

'Your Honor, I move to strike that response,' David said. 'He's saying it was Mr. Stafford. That's a conclusion a jury or judge will have to draw.'

176

'Oh, let him go on, Mr. Nash. I've been around.'

Judge Autley turned to Officer Ortiz and smiled. David didn't like that. It was rare that anyone was graced with an Autley smile, and if the judge was bestowing one on Ortiz, that didn't bode well.

'Just say "suspect," Officer, and Mr. Nash won't get all bent out of shape.'

'Thank you, Your Honor,' Ortiz said. 'I was lying on my back on the floor, my head was against the bed, and the suspect was standing in the doorway.'

'Could you step down to the easel and draw a picture for us?'

Ortiz turned to the judge and the judge nodded. There was an easel with drawing paper and felt-tipped colored pens propped against the wall. Ortiz pulled the easel closer to the witness stand and picked up a black pen.

'This would be the doorway,' he said, tracing a rectangle on the paper. 'I was here, against the bed.' He drew a stick-figure bed and a stick-figure man. The man's head rested against a leg of the bed with its eyes facing the door.

'The door was open. It opened inward and it was half-open, about where I'd kicked it. I guess it must have swung back a ways. He was standing at the door frame, leaning into the room.'

'How far in?'

'Not much. I think his body was at a slight angle, and his right leg and arm were outside the door,

177

but the left leg and his left arm were inside the room a bit.'

'And where was his head?'

'Leaning down toward me. Looking at me.'

'You are certain?'

Ortiz looked directly at David. Then he looked at Larry Stafford.

'I will never forget that face.'

David made some notes, then directed Ortiz back to the stand.

'Were you seriously injured?'

'I was in Good Samaritan Hospital for a day or so.'

'What hospital?'

'Good Samaritan.'

'How long did you view the killer's face?'

'I don't know.'

'A long time?'

'No.'

'How long did the man stand there?'

'A few seconds. Then he bolted.'

'So you saw him for a few seconds?'

'Yes.'

'Less than a minute?'

'Maybe five, ten seconds. But I saw him.'

David consulted his notes. He looked at the judge.

'Nothing further, Your Honor.'

Judge Autley looked at Monica Powers.

'Any further witnesses?'

'No, Your Honor. The State feels that it has met the standards set out in the case law. Officer Ortiz is a trained police officer. He has identified the man he saw at the Raleigh Motel as being the defendant. His testimony is corroborated by the fact that the defendant drives a car similar to the car seen at the motel and has similar clothes.'

'Mr. Nash?'

'Your Honor, I don't feel that a five-second identification by a man who had just been struck sufficiently hard to require hospitalization is the type of proof that creates a presumption of guilt that is evident or strong as is required by the Chambers case.

'Furthermore, Officer Ortiz can only say that the car was a Mercedes. He embellished that description with information he learned later.'

'Have you made your record, Mr. Nash?'

'I do have several character witnesses here to testify in the defendant's behalf.'

'You won't need them. Officer Ortiz is not your ordinary witness, Mr. Nash. He is a trained and experienced policeman. I think his testimony is sufficient and I am going to deny bail.'

David saw Stafford sag for a moment beside him. Monica was collecting her papers and Ortiz was starting to leave the witness stand.

'I can take this up to the supreme court on mandamus, Larry. If we—'

'It's okay,' Stafford said in a defeated voice. 'I knew we were dead when I saw Judge Autley. You did a great job, Dave.'

'Do you want me to come back and see you?'

'No. It's all right. Just get the trial date set as soon as you can. I don't know if . . . Just set the trial date soon.'

Stafford walked over to the guard, who led him back to the holding area. David saw Terry Conklin fold a secretarial notebook and head for the door of the courtroom. Jennifer was waiting just outside the courtroom.

'He's not getting out. The judge denied bail,' David said bitterly. He was disappointed. He had wanted to win, because he wanted Jennifer to see him win and because he thought that Stafford should be out. But he had lost, and it was starting to get to him: the shock of the court's rapid-fire decision was just wearing off, and the fact that bail had been denied was just seeping through.

'He didn't seem to even listen,' Jennifer said incredulously. 'He didn't even let you put on our witnesses.'

'I know. I'll petition the supreme court for a writ of mandamus, but I doubt they'll grant one. They rarely reverse a discretionary decision of a judge unless there's a gross abuse.'

'Well, isn't this . . .?' Jennifer started.

David shook his head. 'No. He just gave a lot of credence to Ortiz's testimony. Another judge might

180

not have. That son of a bitch. Maybe I should have . . .'

David stopped himself.

'Look, Jenny, I'm going to meet with my investigator. I know we lost this time, but I developed several important points during my examination of Ortiz. Points that could win us the trial. And that's the important thing.'

'Won't it be the same at trial? They'll take his word because he's a policeman. They won't believe . . .'

David put his hand on her shoulder before he realized what he was doing. Jennifer looked startled, and he recalled the first time they had touched; saw her standing with her forehead pressed against the cold glass of his windowpane. He released his hand slowly. She looked away.

'At trial we'll have a jury and it will be different,' he said, but his thoughts were elsewhere. 'Juries are very fair. They do make the State prove its case, and I think the State is going to have a harder time than it thinks, if I'm right about a few things. Now, let me get to work, okay?'

'Yes. Of course. I . . . Thank you, David.'

'Don't thank me. So far all I've done is lose.'

'You'll win in the end. I know.'

They both stood in the hall, unwilling to break away. When David finally turned and walked over to Terry Conklin, he felt very depressed.

IT TOOK ONLY a few minutes with Conklin to restore his spirits. They walked from the courthouse to the Shingle Tavern, discussing the case as they went. Conklin had spotted the same thing David had, and the fact that his investigator had been thinking along the same line sent his adrenaline pumping. If they were right, David would have an excellent shot at an acquittal.

'When can you get on it?' David asked excitedly.

'I'll do it this evening, if I can find the man I need.'

David sipped his beer, then bit into his ham sandwich.

'I want Ortiz's medical records. Do you know anyone at Good Sam?'

Conklin thought for a moment. 'It might cost a few bucks, but I think I can swing it.'

'Don't worry about the money. There are a few other things. See if I'm right on the Mercedes and check the shirt.'

'I'll do that this week.'

'Good. You know, Terry, I'm starting to feel very good about this case. Very good.'

RON CROSBY WORKED the long, sauce-covered noodles around his chopsticks until he had them where he wanted them. Then, with a swift, stabbing movement, he jabbed the rolled noodles into his mouth.

'This place makes the best Chinese food in town,' he said. A piece of chewed noodle slipped out of the side of his mouth, and he nudged it back with his chopstick.

'How does it look, Ron?' Ortiz asked. He was toying with his food and had eaten little of it.

'Nash is smooth. That's why he does so well. He scored a few points, but Stafford's still in jail, isn't he?'

'Only because Autley was on the bench. He wouldn't let the pope out on bail. I'm not fooling myself. I made a lousy witness, and Nash didn't take the gloves off like he will at trial.'

Crosby put down his chopsticks. 'What's bothering you, Bert?'

'Nothing. It's just . . . Well, I feel responsible for . . . If I'd acted sooner, Darlene might still be alive. And now . . . I want that bastard, Ron, and I'm afraid I'll screw up again and Nash will get him off.'

'You didn't screw up the first time. Nobody thinks you did. Hersch was green and she was trying to prove how tough she was. She's dead because she broke the rules. And Nash isn't going to get Stafford off, anyway.'

Something in Crosby's tone made Ortiz look up.

'What's that supposed to mean?' he asked.

'Eat your noodles and I'll tell you,' Crosby answered, pulling a folded police report from his inside pocket. 'Do you know a pimp named Cyrus Johnson?'

'T.V.? There isn't a vice cop in town who doesn't know that asshole.'

'Check out this report,' Crosby said, handing it to Ortiz, 'then have a talk with T.V. It might prove interesting.'

CYRUS (T.V.) JOHNSON was probably the easiest person to find in the city of Portland. Every evening he parked his pink Cadillac outside the Jomo Kenyatta Pool Establishment so junkies would know where to make their connections, and his whores would know where to bring their take. T.V. was not the biggest pimp or pusher in Portland, but he was the most notorious. He had once had the temerity to be interviewed as part of a locally produced television special entitled *Drugs in Our Schools*, and thus the sobriquet.

Ortiz parked his car in front of the Cadillac and tried to make out T.V. through the haze of smoke that obscured the activity going on behind the storefront window. He could not see Johnson, but that didn't matter: he knew exactly where he was. T.V. always held court from an expensively upholstered armchair he had had the owner install in the rear of the pool hall. The armchair, surrounded as it was by the room's shabby furnishings, was a symbol of T.V.'s affluence, and it was understood that heavy penalties attached if anyone else used it.

Ortiz snaked his way around the players and their extended cues, aware that the noise level dropped as soon as he neared a table. A few players turned to watch him, but none moved out of his way. It was a game that Ortiz was used to playing. You trained yourself to suppress the anger that the defiance kindled inside you. A white face in a place like the Kenyatta usually meant cop, and the men who played their pool here had no use for him.

T.V., as usual, was dressed in one of his flamboyant outfits. He hadn't always dressed like the stereotype pimp before his television appearance, and it was only by coincidence that he had been wearing an ankle-length fur coat and garish gold jewelry when the television cameras had happened along. But the word was that T.V.'s television performance had been the high point of his life, and since that day he had dressed to fit the part in case the cameras should call again.

T.V.'s nostrils flared as Ortiz approached, and he sniffed the air.

'We havin' bar-be-cue tonight, Kermit?' he asked the large man standing to his left, in an exaggerated Negro accent.' 'Cause I believe I smell pig.'

The large man fixed Ortiz with a cold, challenging stare. Ortiz recognized Kermit Monroe, a bodyguard who had played pro ball for Detroit before injuring a knee.

'You seem to be in good spirits, T.V.,' Ortiz said calmly.

'Why, sho' nuff, massah. We colored folks is always happy.'

'Do you think you can cut your routine long enough for us to have a little talk?'

185

The grin faded and T.V. eyed him suspiciously. Ortiz was no stranger. He had busted T.V. twice, but neither rap had stuck. The last time Ortiz had split T.V.'s lip. T.V. was vain about his looks and had not shown up at the pool hall for a week. He had also taken out his anger on one of his girls and sent her to the hospital. T.V. held Ortiz responsible for the girl's lost earnings, as well as his humiliation.

'Whatcho want to talk about?'

'In private,' Ortiz said, gesturing toward Monroe.

'Uh-uh. I got nothin' to say to you I can't say in front of my friends.'

'Why don't you piss off, Ortiz?' Monroe said. His voice was deep and smooth. Ortiz didn't show it, but he was afraid. He knew Monroe would not hesitate to kill a policeman. He might even enjoy it.

'I want some information about a white man who had some dealings with you and one of your girls a few years back,' Ortiz said, ignoring Monroe and pulling a mug shot of Larry Stafford out of his pocket. He noticed Monroe's hand move inside his leather jacket when his own hand moved.

'Girls? What girls he talkin' about, Kermit?' T.V. asked Monroe over his shoulder.

'I heard Ortiz don't like girls. I hear he likes little boys,' the bodyguard said with a sneer.

T.V. took the photo and studied it. If he recognized Stafford, it did not show.

'This is your boyfriend, Ortiz?' T.V. asked.

'You like to do it with boys, Ortiz?' Monroe

asked, echoing his boss. There was no emotion in his voice.

'Do you know him?' Ortiz asked T.V.

T.V. smiled. 'I ain't never seen this white boy, massah.'

'I think you have.'

Ortiz noticed that the noise in the pool room had stopped. He suddenly regretted his decision to come alone.

'You sayin' I'm lying, Ortiz?' T.V. asked. Monroe moved a step closer to Ortiz. T.V. took another look at the mug shot.

'You know, Kermit, this looks like that white boy who offed the lady pig. I read about that in the papers. The word is that Ortiz here fucked up. The word is she's dead because of you.'

He directed his last shot at Ortiz, and it scored. Ortiz could feel his stomach tighten with a mixture of rage and anguish. He wanted to strike out, but his own uncertainty about his role in Darlene's death sapped him of his will. T.V. read the uncertainty in Ortiz's eyes, and a triumphant smirk turned up the corners of his lips. Ortiz stared at him long enough to collect himself. Then he took the picture back.

'It's been nice talking to you, T.V. We'll talk again.'

He turned his back on Monroe and Johnson and walked back through the maze of black figures. There was laughter behind him, but the ebony faces in front of him were blank and threatening.

His hand was shaking as he turned the key in the ignition. He felt dizzy and slightly nauseated. He had made a fool of himself. He knew it. Suddenly he was filled with rage. That black bastard was going to talk to him. That son of a bitch would tell him what he wanted to know. And he knew just how to make him tell.

5

David looked down at the stack of papers scattered across his desk. He had brought home a legal memorandum in the Stafford case to proofread, but he was too tired to go on. He closed his eyes and massaged his eyelids. The pressure felt good.

He stood up and stretched. It was ten-thirty. He looked out his den window. A pale-yellow half-moon was peeking around the side of the hill.

It was two weeks after the bail hearing, and the case was starting to shape up nicely. Conklin had secured a copy of Ortiz's medical file, and it had proved interesting reading. His idea about the Mercedes had panned out, too. Most important, Terry Conklin had finally got around to taking the shots he wanted at the motel. The pictures had not been developed yet, but Terry was confident that they would show what they both thought they would.

David had learned a lot about Larry Stafford, too. He and Terry had talked to people who knew Larry. A picture had emerged of a person who was always under a little more pressure than he could handle. Larry was a striver, never secure with what he had, always reaching for the pot of gold at the end of the rainbow.

Larry's father had divorced his mother when Larry was in his teens. Larry stayed with his mother, who was never able to cope with the destruction of a life she had built around one man.

Larry's father was a military man and a stern disciplinarian. Larry idolized him. Although there was no truth to it, Larry half believed that his father had left because Larry had not lived up to his expectations. He had spent the rest of his life trying to prove himself.

Larry had not just joined the Army, he had joined the Marines. In college and law school he had studied constantly, pushing himself to the point of exhaustion. Socially it had been the same story. He read all the books on self-improvement, drove the latest sports cars, often piling up debts to get them, and dressed according to the latest trends. Anyone who did not know Larry well would assume that he had achieved the success he sought, but Larry had achieved only a state of perpetual fear that drove him toward goals he could never reach.

David had come to feel sorry for Stafford. Jenny was right when she said he was like a little boy. He had no idea of what was really important in life, and he had spent his life running after the symbols of success. Now, just as he had grasped those symbols, they were going to be stripped away.

Stafford had married wealth and beauty, but his

marriage would not last. Jenny was protective of her husband, but David knew that it was out of a sense of duty, not love. He felt sure that when the trial was over, no matter what the outcome, Larry Stafford would lose his wife.

Larry would never make partner at Price, Winward, either. David had talked to Charlie Holt about that. Before his arrest there had been no clear consensus among the partners. Stafford did not have a first-class legal mind, but he did well in matters that required perseverance. Stafford's arrest had unbalanced the scales. The firm could not afford the publicity. If acquitted, Larry could look forward to a year more as an associate to give the appearance that the firm was fair, but it would be made clear to him that there would never be an offer of a partnership.

The doorbell rang and David went to answer it. Jennifer Stafford was waiting when he opened the door.

'Can I come in?' she asked, a bit unsure of herself.

'Of course,' he said, stepping aside.

Jenny was dressed in jeans, a black turtleneck, and a poncho. Her long hair was tied back in a ponytail. She looked very beautiful.

'I was going to call,' she said hesitantly, 'but I was afraid you would tell me not to come.'

'Don't be silly,' he said a little too quickly. 'I've been locked up with my law books all evening, and I can use some human companionship.'

David watched her wander across the living room. There was a fire in the fireplace, and Jenny stood in front of it, her back to him.

'Can I get you a drink?' David asked.

'Please.'

The liquor was in another room and he wanted a chance to settle down. Jenny had not been to his house since the night they had made love. Now she had come to him, and he was very unsure of himself. There had not been a moment since he had seen her again at the courthouse that he had not wanted her, but there was an unspoken understanding between them that made any personal discussions taboo.

Jenny was sitting in front of the fire, leaning against a large pillow, when he returned with her drink. He sat beside her, listening to the logs crackle and watching the flames twist and curl.

'How have you been?' he asked.

'Busy. School's back in session. I've had lesson plans to prepare, and they've given me a class of exceptional children. They really keep you on your toes.'

'Have you had any problems because of the case?'

'No. Actually, everyone has been very kind. John Olson, our principal, told me I could stay out for the whole trial.'

'That's great.'

'My folks have been unexpectedly supportive, too.'

'Why, didn't you expect them to be?'

'Mom's never approved of Larry. You know how mothers are.' Jenny shrugged. 'Anyway, Mom even volunteered to go to the jail with me on visiting day.' Jenny laughed suddenly.

'What's so funny?'

'Mom at the jail. You wouldn't understand unless you knew her.'

Jenny laughed again. The laugh was warm and open, without a trace of the self-consciousness that had characterized their relationship from the start. David wanted to hold her very much at that moment. She must have sensed this, because she stopped and her smile faded.

'David, I want you to be honest with me. Are you going to win? Will Larry be acquitted?'

'I think so. The State's whole case rests on Ortiz, and I think I'm going to be able to take him apart.'

David expected Jenny to ask him how he planned to get to Ortiz, but she didn't. Instead, she stood up and walked toward the window. He rolled onto his side and watched her.

'If Larry was convicted . . .' she started. 'If you didn't do your best to . . .'

She didn't finish. He stood up and walked over to her. When he spoke, his voice was firm.

'But I wouldn't do that and you wouldn't want me to. That's not the solution to our problem, Jenny.'

'David, I—'

193

He stopped her by placing the tips of his fingers against her lips.

'We're both under a lot of pressure, Jenny. I should never have taken this case, but I did. I've tried to kid myself, but a lot of the reason was so I could see you again. That's a very bad reason, but there it is and there's nothing I can do about it.'

'Oh, David,' she said, and it sounded like the sigh of a lost soul. David put his arms around her and they stood there, her head on his shoulder, not holding tight, but holding soft and caring.

'You don't know how much I've wanted you,' she said, 'but I couldn't hurt Larry. After that evening . . . I felt so confused and guilty. And I didn't know what the evening meant for you. You were so self-assured, as if you had done . . . been to bed with other women so often. I was afraid that it had just been sex for you and that I would make a fool of myself.'

'It was never just sex,' David whispered.

'Then Larry was arrested and Charlie told me to hire you. It made it worse for me, but Larry needed you.'

'And I need you, Jenny, very much.'

She looked up at him. She was frightened. They both were. Then their lips met, and they sank down on the soft carpet and made love in front of the fire.

Afterward she slept curled up in his arms. When David was certain he would not wake her, he eased her down and covered her with a blanket. Flame shadows played across her face, and she looked as peaceful as a sleeping child.

David put another log on the fire; then he sat across from Jenny so he could see her. She had come so close to saying something he did not want to think about. He could lose the trial, and their problems would be solved. But he would not. He would win an acquittal for Larry Stafford by trying the best case he had ever tried.

What kind of life could he and Jenny have together if he intentionally lost Larry Stafford's case? Even if no one else ever knew, they would know, and that knowledge would destroy them.

Jenny said that Larry was innocent, and Terry Conklin's pictures would prove it. Larry Stafford would be acquitted. Then Jenny would make her choice. A free choice.

PART III

TRIAL BY JURY

1

'Nice of you to drop by,' Larry said sarcastically as soon as the guard shut the door to the private visitor's room.

'Don't, Larry,' Jennifer began. She wanted to say more, but her courage failed her. Larry started to say one thing, changed his mind, and shook his head.

'I'm sorry. It's just with the trial starting . . . I just thought you'd visit more.'

Jennifer did not answer. She turned and walked to the far end of the narrow room. Larry followed her and touched her arm.

'I said I'm sorry, kitten. I'm all wound up.'

'I know,' she said quietly. He had lost weight, and he looked sad and defeated. She did not want to hurt him any more than he had already been hurt, but she knew she would have to.

'Larry, I don't know if I can go through with it.'

Larry paled, just staring, his mouth partly open.

'What . . . what do you . . .?'

'It's no good. They'll see that I'm lying and it will make it worse for you.'

'No. No. You'll do okay,' Stafford said desperately. 'Nash believes you, right? He's a pro. If we've got him fooled, the jury will be easy.'

Jennifer tried to say something. To talk to him. But her stomach was cramped with fear and self-loathing, and she felt short of breath. Larry just stared at her, afraid to speak. The silence in the room terrified him.

'Jenny, they can't prove anything,' he said finally. 'How will they know?' He stopped. He was pleading. 'Besides, it's the truth. I told you that, didn't I? I swore to God.'

Jenny still could not speak. She could see the panic in his eyes.

'Goddammit,' he said, his voice rising, 'you can't change your story now. You'll crucify me.

'Say something. It's your fault I'm here. Do you want to bury me now?'

His voice rose in pitch and cut through her. She started to cry.

Larry grabbed her roughly by both arms. His fingers dug into her flesh, hurting her.

'Answer me, Jenny. Do you want me to die? Because that's what's happening to me here. I couldn't stand prison, locked away, I can't stand it now. The noise, the smells. This filth.'

He raised his arm like an accusing angel and pointed at the room.

'Do you hate me so much that you want me to live the rest of my life like some animal?'

She started to cry, turning her head from him, not wanting him to hold her or comfort her. He was right. She did not hate him. She was only tired of him. Disillusioned by the destruction of the love that she had once felt for him. She couldn't let him end up in a place like this. Not even if he had . . . She could not complete the thought, because if Larry had killed that woman, then she was partly to blame.

'All right,' she whispered, her voice catching in her throat. 'All right.'

Stafford let her go. He was afraid and alone, and he could see the strands of his slender lifeline unraveling before his eyes.

ORTIZ SLOUCHED DOWN in the passenger seat of the unmarked police car. He had on a heavy jacket and a sweater, and he was still cold. Beside him Jack Hennings blew into his cupped hands, then tucked them under his armpits for warmth.

'I can't believe it's this fucking cold,' he complained.

'Tell me about it,' Ortiz mumbled. He leaned forward and wiped a space on the windshield clean where it had fogged over.

'I don't see why we can't just bust in and arrest him,' Hennings said.

'I told you why. My snitch said T.V.'d have it on him. I'm not going to risk missing it in a search and have that asshole laughing at me up and down the avenue.'

'I'd rather have every nigger in the city laughing at me than have to sit out here for another hour.'

'Besides, Kermit is probably in there with him, and I want to be sure where he is when we move.'

'Monroe's a pussy,' Hennings said. Hennings was big and talked tough, but Ortiz doubted he'd be able to take Kermit Monroe one on one.

'If you think it's so easy, Lone Ranger, why don't you go over there all by yourself and call me when it's over?'

Hennings grinned. 'Don't get so nervous, Bert. I know karate.'

'Oh, Jesus, that's all I need.'

'Besides,' Hennings said, holding up the Magnum he had placed on the seat of the car, 'the man won't be doin' much wrasslin' with his balls in China. Now, if—'

Ortiz sat up. The door to Johnson's house opened, and two men were illuminated by the porch light. From where they were sitting, it was easy to make out Johnson in his ankle-length fur coat.

'Let's go,' he said, and the two policemen left the car. Johnson and Monroe talked as they walked to the curb. Ortiz and Hennings moved quickly, trying to attract as little attention as possible as they approached. Monroe turned his back to them and opened the passenger door for his boss. The howling wind muffled the sound of footsteps. Monroe turned and made a move for his gun. He stopped when he saw Hennings poised in a shooting stance.

'Freeze!' Hennings shouted.

Johnson stood with his hands half-raised and a stunned expression on his face. Then he bent his head and squinted into the dark and cold.

'Is that you, Ortiz?'

'Shut up and spread against the car.'

'What the fuck you doin', man? I'm clean.'

'I said, against the car. Both of you.'

'I ain't humiliatin' myself in no—'

Ortiz hit Johnson in the solar plexus as hard as he could, then kicked him in the crotch. The pimp looked as if he were going to be sick. He slipped to his knees. A quick look of surprise crossed Hennings's face. Monroe started to lower his hands.

'Just try it, fuck face. I'd love to waste you,' Ortiz said, swinging his weapon in Monroe's direction. The big man looked uncertain for a moment, then slowly leaned against the car as he had been told.

'Now, spread,' Ortiz commanded, pulling Johnson to his feet and shoving him against the car. Hennings kept a few paces back and Ortiz frisked Monroe. He handed a gun and a switchblade to his partner. Hennings placed them in his pocket. While Hennings's attention was distracted, Ortiz slipped the plastic baggie from his pocket and palmed it. Johnson was still doubled over and in pain, but he was doing his best to spread-eagle in order to avoid another beating. There were no wisecracks now, Ortiz thought with satisfaction. No bad-mouth.

Ortiz reached around in front of the pimp and

pretended to search inside his coat for a weapon. Suddenly, he pulled his hand out of T.V.'s pocket and waved the baggie toward Hennings.

'Bingo,' Ortiz said.

T.V. turned his head. His eyes opened wide when he saw what Ortiz was holding.

'What's that?' he asked, surprise distracting him from his pain.

'Your passport to the penitentiary, T.V. Now, move over to that police car so we can escort you downtown.'

'You planted that!' T.V. said incredulously.

'Shut up,' Ortiz said softly.

'You in on this too, pig?' T.V. asked Hennings.

'Didn't you hear Officer Ortiz tell you to shut your face?' Hennings asked.

Ortiz jerked Monroe's hands behind him and cuffed the big man. He made sure that the cuffs were too tight. He gave T.V. the same treatment.

'I'm going to read you your rights, gentlemen,' Ortiz said as the prisoners were hustled to the police car.

'You are really a sick son of a bitch, Ortiz. You plant that shit on me, then talk about rights.'

Ortiz read the Miranda rights to the prisoners, then motioned them into the back of the police car. There were no handles on the inside of the back door, and a wire screen separated the back seat from the front. Hennings drove and Ortiz leaned back. Monroe looked out the back window, accepting his fate silently. Johnson slouched beside him with a sullen expression on his face. The whole thing was unfair. He expected a beating now and then. He had seen police lie on the witness stand when an arrest was legitimate but the defendant would escape on a technicality if the truth came out. But this was different. It was . . . was . . . unfair.

Johnson looked through the mesh at the back of Ortiz's head. Ortiz wanted something. He had a feeling about it. Something he wanted bad enough to break the rules. He'd wait and see what it was. If he could, he'd do what Ortiz wanted; then he would wait for his chance.

'WHY YOU PLANT that dope, Ortiz?' T.V. asked when they were alone in the interrogation room.

'I didn't plant any dope on you, T.V. My informant said you'd have it on you and you did. Anyone who watches television knows you're a notorious pusher. Why wouldn't you be carrying narcotics?'

'My lawyer gonna tear that story apart. You got no case on me.'

'Oh, yeah? When you talk to your lawyer, ask him how he's going to do that. A court won't order me to tell you the name of an informant. It's the law, T.V.'

T.V. was silent for a moment. His eyes darted nervously from one side of the room to the other, as if looking for some way out of his predicament.

'You ain't nothin' but a crooked cop, Ortiz.'

'Try and prove that in court. You think a jury will take the word of a nigger pimp against mine? You're gonna do ten hard years on this, T.V., unless . . .'

T.V. looked up from the floor. 'Unless what?'

'Unless you tell the truth about what that white man did to your whore friend.'

'You still on that kick?' Johnson asked, surprised.

'The truth, T.V., will set you free.'

'How? How you gonna arrange for me to beat this rap?'

'I found the evidence, I can lose the evidence. You play ball with me, and this case will disappear like one of Houdini's card tricks. But you fuck with me, and I'll see you in the penitentiary doing hard time. My word.'

'Your word ain't worth shit,' Johnson said in a sudden burst of anger.

'Maybe,' Ortiz said with a broad smile, 'but it's all you've got.'

Johnson stood up and walked to the far wall. He turned his back on Ortiz. It was quiet in the soundproof room.

'And suppose I tell you what I know? Is that all?'

'No. You tell the jury. You testify.'

'I gotta . . . I don't know if I can do that.'

'Well, you better decide fast. The trial starts tomorrow and you don't have much time.'

2

A fog bank drifted across the sand, obscuring the terrain of the endless beach. Monica stopped, terrified and alone. She turned slowly, looking for a landmark, but the fog had made subtle changes and she felt lost.

The fog lifted for a moment, and a figure, half-shrouded by the mist, floated away from her. She ran after it, lifting her legs high to avoid the sand that clutched at her ankles. She must not fall or the sand would suck her down.

The fog was drifting back and her quarry was slip-ping into the shadows. She ran faster, the pounding of her heart drowning out the cadence of the incoming tide. Faster. She was losing ground. Faster. She was falling, screaming, flailing helplessly as she hurtled downward into darkness.

Then the beach was gone, and the only part of her dream that remained was the beating of her heart.

Monica looked around the room. It was her bed-room and she was sitting up in her bed, drenched in sweat. The clock read six A.M. She could try to sleep for another half hour, but she was too wound up.

Monica turned on the light and went into the

bathroom. The face she saw in the mirror was pale and had bags under the eyes. Not good, she thought, but it would not get better if she did not get a decent night's sleep.

She had been exhausted during jury selection, and her opening statement lacked the punch of David's emotional declaration of his client's innocence. Monica had watched the jurors as she outlined the evidence she would produce at trial. They had listened attentively, and she was convinced that they were responsible people who would convict Larry Stafford if they believed he was guilty. But would they believe that, or would David fool them?

Fool them. That was an odd way to describe the function of the defense bar, but Monica felt it was an accurate description. When they had lived together, David often talked of himself, self-deprecatingly, as a magician whose job it was to make people see what was not there and to conceal what was there. Monica believed that Larry Stafford killed Darlene Hersch, and she was afraid that David would make her evidence disappear with a wave of his verbal wand.

Monica opened the refrigerator and took out a container of orange juice. She put a kettle of water on the stove and tried to decide between cold cereal and frozen waffles. She settled for two pieces of whole-wheat toast.

Judge Rosenthal had been chosen to preside at the trial, and David did not object, even though

Rosenthal had issued the search warrant. Jury selection had taken longer than expected because of the difficulty in finding twelve Portland residents who had not formed an opinion about the 'Policewoman Murder.' Monica and David had agreed on a jury shortly before noon on the second day of trial. They had concluded opening statements after lunch, and she had presented the testimony of Dr. Francis R. Beauchamp, the medical examiner, before Judge Rosenthal had called a halt to the proceedings for the day.

The coffee was bitter and Monica grimaced as it went down, but she needed the caffeine. The toast was burned, too. Shit! She felt like smashing something. Not a good way to begin the most important day of the State's case. She tried to calm down.

Monica was always tense when she was in trial, but it was worse when she tried a case against David. She was a highly competitive woman who enjoyed winning. When Monica tried cases against other attorneys, she thought of them strictly in business terms. She could never think of David that way. Even after all these years she was still a little in love with him, and she knew it, so she overcompensated whenever they were matched against each other, and ended up pushing herself harder than she had to, out of fear that her feelings for him would influence her performance.

There was an added reason for her anxiety this morning: Ortiz and his surprise witness. Last night, after court recessed, she had been making notes on Beauchamp's testimony when Ortiz and Crosby came into her office. She was in a foul mood and wanted to leave, but the two policemen seemed excited.

'Beauchamp was pretty convincing, I hear,' Crosby said, settling into a chair. Dr. Beauchamp was a frustrated actor with a knack for describing fatal wounds that made them appear more revolting than a color photograph ever could.

'All Beauchamp established was that Darlene Hersch was struck in the abdomen and neck, then had her throat slit. He didn't establish who did it,' Monica replied testily.

'I don't think pinning this on Stafford is going to be a problem anymore,' Ortiz said with a confident smile.

'I'm glad to hear that, Bert. I thought we had problems.'

Ortiz's face clouded over. 'Why do you say that?' he asked.

'The case is flimsy. No offense, Bert, but all we have is your ID based on a few seconds' observation after you had been struck on the head hard enough to require hospitalization. I'm beginning to think we may have moved too fast on this one.'

'You can stop worrying, because I've got the man who is going to do it to Mr. Stafford.'

Monica put her pen down and waited for Ortiz to continue. Ortiz had a tendency to be dramatic, and he paused to heighten the tension.

'Remember Ron called you when Stafford was arraigned and asked you to oppose bail?'

'Yes,' she said, turning toward Crosby. 'You said that another officer was certain that Stafford had beaten up a prostitute and was going to try to find the police reports. I also recall being put off by you every time I've asked you about that report,' she added angrily. 'I put myself on the line at the bail hearing because of your assurances.'

'You have every right to be angry, Monica,' Crosby said sheepishly. 'Tracking down our witness just took longer than we thought.'

'You have a witness who saw Larry Stafford beat up a prostitute?'

'Exactly,' Ortiz said.

'Who is it?' Monica asked.

'Cyrus Johnson.'

'Cyrus – Jesus, Bert. I'm not going to vouch for the credibility of a known pimp and dope dealer.'

'Who else would be able to testify about Stafford's sex habits? It's the fact that he's a pimp that makes him credible.'

'Bert, you've seen David operate. Do you know what he'd do to Johnson? The man sells dope to schoolchildren, for Christ's sake.'

'If you're afraid of Nash, you shouldn't be trying this case,' Ortiz said, suddenly very angry.

Monica jumped to her feet. 'Get out of my office,' she shouted. 'I'm not going to take that shit.'

Crosby put his hand on Ortiz's elbow and Ortiz was immediately contrite.

'I'm sorry. I didn't mean . . . I think you're a hell of a good lawyer. It's just . . . well, the case means a lot to me and I want to make sure Stafford doesn't get away.'

Monica sat down and leaned back in her chair. The outburst had taken a lot out of her.

'Apology accepted. The case is getting to me, too.'

'Will you at least talk to Johnson and read this police report?' Crosby asked, placing the report in front of her.

'Yeah. I didn't really want to go home, anyway. But you two are going to stand me dinner. I'm starving.'

THE INTERVIEW WITH Johnson created more problems than it solved. The man was smooth, and she could not determine if he was telling the truth. True, the story he told her was the same story he had told the police two years ago, but he had reason to lie to the police then, and he was in trouble, and obviously anxious to deal now. Monica wanted to convict Stafford, but she would not put on testimony she believed might be perjured.

Even if the story was true, she did not know if she could get Johnson's testimony into evidence. Johnson would be testifying that Stafford had committed a prior criminal act, and the rules of evidence forbade the introduction of that type of evidence, with only a few narrowly defined exceptions. Monica was not convinced that Johnson's evidence fell under any of them. David was an expert on the rules of evidence, and she would have to research the question of admissibility thoroughly, because she knew how hard David would fight when he learned about Johnson.

Monica finished combing her hair and put on her coat. Her key witnesses, Grimes and Ortiz, were scheduled to testify today. If they survived David's cross-examination, she might not have to put on Johnson.

'AND WHAT HAPPENED then, Mr. Grimes?' Monica asked. The motel clerk had just taken the stand and had been preceded by several laboratory technicians, a supervisor from the Motor Vehicles Division who established Stafford's ownership of the Mercedes, and Detective Crosby, who testified about the search of Stafford's house.

'I gave her the key and she left. I went back to readin', and the next thing I know, I hear these screams.'

David leaned forward and began making notes about Grimes's testimony on a yellow legal pad. Larry Stafford sat beside him at counsel table, looking businesslike in a conservative dark-blue three-piece suit. David had intentionally dressed more casually than his client to give the jury an initial visual impression that Stafford, not he, was the defense attorney.

'Where were the screams coming from?' Monica asked. David heard Stafford shift nervously in his seat. He glanced at his client and caught him looking over his shoulder at the crowded courtroom. Stafford was looking for his wife, and David felt a slight pang of conscience that momentarily dampened his otherwise expansive mood. David knew where Jenny was and why she was late for court this morning. They had spent the night together, and she had returned home to change while he dressed for court.

'Did you notice Jenny this morning?' Stafford whispered, as if reading David's thoughts. There was an edge to Larry's voice, and an air of tension around him that David had noticed since the start of the trial. David expected a person on trial for murder to be nervous, but he sensed that there was something else eating at his client and that it concerned Jenny.

'She'll be along,' David whispered back. 'And don't look so down in the mouth. Take notes and concentrate on the witnesses, like I told you. I don't want the jury to see your interest lag for one second.'

'I couldn't tell who was screamin' at first,' Grimes continued, 'so I went outside in the lot. The motel rooms are behind the office, and I had to go around the corner of the building. That's when I seen this guy come bustin' out of twenty-two.'

'Did you get a good look at the person you saw running away?'

'No, ma'am, I didn't. He was runnin' too fast and there's a lot of shadow up there.'

'Go on.'

'Well, by now the screamin' had stopped, and I looked up at twenty-two to see if anyone'd come after the one that run out. I seen the door was wide-open, but no one was comin', so I started across the lot to see what's what. Just then this car came from the rear parking lot. It was the same one the girl'd come in, but she wasn't in it.'

'Who did you see in that car?'

'It was a man drivin', but I didn't get a clear look at him.'

Monica stood up and walked across to the witness box. 'Mr. Grimes, I hand you what has been marked as State's exhibit number five, and I ask you if you recognize the car in that picture.'

Grimes took the color photograph of Stafford's Mercedes and studied it carefully.

'I can't say for sure, but it's like the car that girl came in.'

'Thank you,' Monica said, returning the exhibit to the bailiff. 'After the car left the lot, what did you do?'

'To tell the truth, I wasn't too anxious to find out why there'd been all that screamin', but I got to thinkin' that someone might be hurt up there, so I went up to the room. That's when I seen 'em.'

'Who was that?'

'Well, the lights were out, so I didn't see her at first. The man was lyin' with his head against the bed. He was bleedin' and I thought he might be dead. Then I seen he was breathin', so I went to use the phone. That's when I saw her. You see a lot workin' in the hotel business, but that was terrible. I ran outa there and called the cops from my office.'

'And did the police come?'

'A few minutes later. An ambulance came too.'

'Thank you, Mr. Grimes. I have no further questions.'

'Mr. Nash,' Judge Rosenthal said, nodding in David's direction.

David took a final look at the report Detective Crosby had made of his interview with Grimes, and Terry Conklin's report of their interview. It was quiet in the courtroom, and David could hear a juror shifting in his seat and the nervous drumming of Stafford's fingers on the wooden table.

'Just a few questions, Mr. Grimes. As I understand your testimony, you did not get a good look at the man who was driving the Mercedes while Darlene Hersch was registering.'

'That's right.'

'And you did not get a good look at him when he ran out of the room where the murder was committed?'

Grimes nodded.

216

'Did you get a look at him as he drove out of the parking lot, after the murder?'

'Like I said, not a clear look.'

'Did you see his hair well enough to describe it to the jury?'

Monica had been going over her notes and listening to David's examination with half an ear. Now she lowered her pen and concentrated. She could tell from David's tone that something was up.

'Yeah, I seen his hair,' Grimes answered. 'Just for a second, but I seen it.'

'Did the driver of the Mercedes have blond curly hair like Mr. Stafford?'

Grimes leaned forward and studied Larry Stafford.

'Could he turn around?' Grimes asked, turning toward the judge. 'I only seen him from the back.'

'That's up to Mr. Nash,' Rosenthal replied.

'Certainly,' David said, and Larry stood up and turned his back to the witness stand.

'I don't remember it lookin' like that,' Grimes said decislvely.

'How would you describe the driver's hair?'

'Well, like I said, I only seen it for a second, but it looked brown-colored to me, and he had one of them cuts that came down a ways.'

'Thank you. I have nothing further.'

Monica reread the police report on Grimes rapidly. There was nothing about hair color in the report. She turned to the third page and saw why. The son of a bitch was going back on his statement to the police. This was bad, because Grimes had the appearance of an honest witness. His testimony about the hair color could be crucial in a close case.

'Mr. Grimes,' Monica asked, 'how well lit is the parking lot at the Raleigh?'

Grimes tilted his head back and furrowed his brow. 'Not too good over by the side near Tacoma Street, but there's plenty of light from that McDonald's. Bothers some of the customers sometimes.'

Monica felt her stomach tighten. Damn, she'd just made it worse. She hated surprises in trial, and this was a bad one. She decided to back off on the lighting.

'Was the murderer's car moving fast when it left the lot?'

'I'll say. It just come whippin' around that corner. He screeched his tires when he did that, and that's why I looked over.'

'So you just had a brief view of him?'

'Right. Like I said, I wasn't concentratin' on him much. I was lookin' up at the room.'

'Do you remember being interviewed by Ronald Crosby, a Portland police detective, on the evening of the murder?'

'Was that the fella that bought me coffee?'

'I wouldn't know, Mr. Grimes.'

'Nice fella. He even sprung for a doughnut. Not as tight as some a them cops I know.'

Someone laughed in the back of the courtroom,

and the judge rapped his gavel. Monica waited for the jury's attention to return to the witness stand.

'You never told Detective Crosby that the man had long brown hair, did you?'

'He never asked.'

'But he did ask you if there was anything about the man you could remember, did he not?'

'I don't recollect the whole conversation.'

'Do you remember saying that the man did not make much of an impression on you and Detective Crosby asking you if you remembered his hair, eyes, or anything else about him and your answering "No"?'

'That sounds right. Only I was talkin' about when the girl come in. He never asked about when the fella drove off.'

Monica looked as if she were going to ask another question, then thought better of it.

'Nothing further,' she said.

Judge Rosenthal looked at David, who merely smiled and shook his head.

'Nice going,' Larry whispered.

'That's what you pay me for. If I do as well with the next witness, we'll be in good shape.'

'Who's the next witness?' Stafford asked David.

'The State calls Bertram Ortiz,' Monica said.

DIRECT EXAMINATION WAS easy for Ortiz. The questions were almost identical to the direct examination during the bail hearing, and he had gone over his answers with Monica several times. First he described the stakeout and the beige Mercedes. Then he recounted his surveillance during the drive to the motel. He told the hushed courtroom of his violent encounter with the man who had murdered Darlene Hersch, his reaction when he saw Larry Stafford in the courthouse corridor, and the results of the search at Stafford's house. Then, as the jurors leaned forward, caught up in the tension of the moment, Ortiz turned toward the defense table and pointed his finger at the defendant. Direct examination was over, and Monica nodded to David.

Ortiz turned toward the defense table and waited for cross-examination to begin. His hand had been steady, and there had been no tremor in his voice when he identified Larry Stafford, because he had learned from dozens of experiences on the witness stand to control his nerves, but the fear of what David might do to him was there.

David did not rush his questions. He smiled at Ortiz and leaned back in his chair. He wanted Ortiz to wait, and he wanted to build on the tension that already permeated the courtroom.

'Officer Ortiz,' he asked finally, 'what day was Darlene Hersch killed?'

'June sixteenth,' Ortiz answered tersely. He was determined to answer only what he was asked and to volunteer nothing. The less he said, the less information Nash would have to work with.

'Thank you,' David said politely. 'And when

did you see Mr. Stafford in the courthouse hallway?'

'Early September.'

'Some three months after the murder?'

'Yes.'

David stood up and walked to an easel that the
clerk had placed between the witness stand and the
jury box. David flipped the cover page from a large
drawing pad over the top of the easel and revealed
the diagram of the motel room that Ortiz had drawn
at the bail hearing.

'During a prior hearing in this case, I asked you
to draw this sketch and to indicate your position and
the killer's position at the moment you saw his face,
did I not?'

'Yes.'

'And is this an accurate representation of those
positions?'

Ortiz studied the drawing for a moment, then
nodded.

'I believe at the hearing you stated that, at the
moment you saw the killer's face, his left arm and
leg were inside the room a bit and his body was at
a slight angle, with the right arm and leg outside the
door?'

'Yes.'

'Good. Now, you were struck immediately upon
entering the motel room, were you not?'

'Yes.'

'The lights in the room were out?'

'Yes.'

'You fell, twisted, and your head struck the bed?'

'Yes.'

'How long would you say you had a good view of the killer's face?'

'A few seconds.'

'Five to ten?'

'A little more than that.'

David picked up the transcript of the bail hearing, consulted an index card, and flipped to a page.

'At a prior hearing in this case, did you not testify as follows:

'"Q: So you saw him for a few seconds?

"A: Yes.

"Q: Less than a minute?

"A: Maybe five, ten seconds. But I saw him."'

'I think that's right.'

'So the only time you saw the killer's face was for five or ten seconds after you had been struck on the head and before you lost consciousness?'

'Yes, but I saw him clearly. It was Stafford,' Ortiz blurted out. Monica expected David to object to the unresponsive answer, but David merely smiled.

'You are certain of that?' David asked. Monica was puzzled. Why was David giving Ortiz a chance to repeat so damaging a statement?

'Positive.'

'Yes. I believe, at the prior hearing, I asked you,

"You are certain?" and you replied, "I will never forget that face."'

'Yes, I said that,' Ortiz answered nervously. He had forgotten that he had given that answer at the bail hearing.

'But the impossible happened, did it not?'

'What do you mean?'

David strolled over to the far end of the counsel table and picked up a stack of papers.

'Were you hospitalized after the blow to your head?'

'Yes.'

'Was Dr. Arthur Stewart your treating physician?'

'Yes.'

'How long were you in the hospital, Officer Ortiz?'

'About a week.'

'How long did you continue to see Dr. Stewart for problems relating to the blow to your head?'

Ortiz could feel the sweat forming on his brow. Why didn't the bastard ask the question Ortiz knew he would ask?

'I stopped two weeks ago.'

'Mid-October? Is that when he released you?'

'Yes.'

'You had a concussion, did you not?'

'Yes.'

David paused and the smile disappeared. 'And you could remember nothing about what happened inside that motel room from June sixteenth until September? Isn't that true?'

'I remembered parts of what happened. It was—'

'Mr. Ortiz . . . Pardon me. Officer Ortiz,' David said, his voice cutting like a knife, 'I have here copies of your medical records from Good Samaritan Hospital. On September third, did you visit Dr. Stewart?'

'Uh, I . . . It could have been that date. I had an appointment in early September.'

'You don't remember?' David asked with a smirk.

Ortiz felt his body tighten. He wanted to strike out at David. He felt like a butterfly pinioned on a board, waiting for dissection.

'Objection,' Monica said, standing. 'Mr. Nash is arguing with the witness.'

She could see the danger signs and had to give Ortiz a chance to collect his thoughts.

'Yes, Mr. Nash,' the judge said, 'just ask your questions.'

'Very well, Your Honor. Officer Ortiz, did you not tell Dr. Stewart during your September visit, a few short days before you arrested Larry Stafford, that you could not remember what happened inside the motel room and that you could not remember what the killer looked like?'

Ortiz did not answer immediately. He stared at David and at Stafford. Stafford stared back.

'Well, Officer?' David asked sharply.

'Yes.'

'You had amnesia, did you not?'

'Yes, if that's what you call it.'

'What do you call it?'

'I mean . . .'

Ortiz stopped. David waited a moment, watching the jury.

'Officer, if I understand your testimony, you first saw the Mercedes from a distance of one city block?'

'Yes,' Ortiz answered quickly, grateful that the subject had been changed.

'Then you followed it from a distance of approximately two city blocks?'

'Yes.'

'And, finally, you saw it briefly as you drove by the motel lot?'

'Yes.'

'Those were the only times you saw the car that evening?'

'Yes.'

'And you did not know what model and year the car was until you checked with the Motor Vehicle Division?'

'I . . . It's the car I saw,' Ortiz answered weakly.

David picked up three color photographs from his table and walked over to the witness stand. Monica drummed the tip of her pen on her desk. Ortiz was in trouble, and she did not know how much longer he would be able to stand up under

David's questioning. She had Dr. Stewart on call to testify that Ortiz, and others with amnesia caused by a concussion, could recall with complete accuracy events they had forgotten. But for the jury to believe in Ortiz's recall, they had to believe in Ortiz.

'Will you study these three photographs, please?' David asked Ortiz. The policeman shuffled the photos until he had viewed all three.

'Would you tell the jury what they are?'

'They appear to be a beige Mercedes-Benz.'

'Same type that Mr. Stafford drives?'

'Yes.'

David smiled at Ortiz and took back the pictures.

'I have no further questions.'

Monica could not believe it. She had seen David tear witnesses apart and she knew his technique. He always softened them up, as he had Ortiz, with questions that would shake their confidence. Then he progressed from point to point, ending with a series of questions that involved a major point in their testimony. The questions about Ortiz's amnesia had been expected, but she also expected more. Ortiz had been touched by David, but not badly shaken. She wanted him off the stand quickly, while he was still basically intact.

'No further questions,' Monica said.

'Call your next witness.'

'Dr. Arthur Stewart, Your Honor.'

*

ORTIZ WANTED TO discuss the case as soon as she left the courtroom, but she told him to wait until they got to her office. Dr. Stewart had been excellent and David had not scored many points. She had rested the State's case at the end of his testimony without calling Cyrus Johnson.

'But why?' Ortiz demanded when he and Monica and Crosby were alone.

'Because it wasn't necessary and I did not want to risk it.'

'You haven't shown any motive. Johnson can establish that this guy is an S-M freak.'

'Or make it look like we're trying to railroad him with perjured testimony. Look, Bert, we already have a motive. He is a member of a big law firm, but not a partner. He is married to a wealthy woman. If he is arrested for prostitution, his career and marriage could be over. What more do we need? Besides, you were terrific.'

Ortiz shook his head. 'I don't know. That business with the amnesia. Don't you think . . .?'

'I was in the courtroom, Bert,' Crosby said. 'You came off just great, and that doctor cleared that whole business up. I was surprised how easy Nash went on you.'

'Yeah. That has me worried, too. Why do you think he let up?'

'I don't know,' Monica said, 'but let's not look a gift horse in the mouth.'

'If it was a gift,' Ortiz said. 'That son of a

bitch has something he's not telling you about. I can feel it.'

Monica shrugged. 'I'm not going to worry about it now.'

'And you can still use T.V. in rebuttal, right?' Ortiz asked.

'Bert, I don't trust him. He'll do anything to get out of this dope charge.'

'I don't think so,' Ortiz said, shaking his head vigorously. 'It's too much of a coincidence.'

'Well, if the case goes as well as it has so far, it will all be academic.'

'MR. STAFFORD CALLS Patrick Walsh, Your Honor,' David said, and the clerk left the courtroom to summon the witness. David took the opportunity to collect the exhibits he would use and to review his notes on Walsh's testimony.

The defense was going well. David had started by calling several of Larry's friends and business associates, who testified to his good character. They had painted a picture of a newly wed, young professional who possessed a sense of humor and a dedication to his work. Monica, through cross-examination, brought out the fact that Larry had been passed over for partner by his firm, but Charlie Holt, the witness, had handled that line of questioning well. David thought this revelation had provoked sympathy from the jurors.

David used Barry Dietrich, the partner with whom

Larry had met on the evening of the murder, to bridge the gap between the character witnesses and those witnesses who would establish Stafford's defense. Dietrich was not enthusiastic about testifying. With the exception of Charlie Holt, the partners at Price, Winward had been reluctant to get involved in the case. However, once on the stand, Dietrich had done well.

The courtroom door opened, and a tall, angular red-headed man with a slight limp walked to the stand. David looked back toward him and noticed Jenny seated on the aisle at the rear of the courtroom. They had been together often during the last month, treating each moment alone as if it might be their last. David loved Jenny. He knew that now. Often, when they were lying together, David wondered what would happen to them when the trial ended. If Larry was free, would Jenny go back to him? David was weak and vulnerable at such moments. He would hold Jenny, afraid of what might happen if he let her go.

'Mr. Walsh, how are you employed?' David asked once the witness had been sworn.

'I'm a zone distribution manager for Mercedes-Benz of North America.'

'What does a zone distribution manager do?'

'For sales purposes Mercedes has divided the United States into zones and subzones, and I'm in charge of sales in the San Francisco zone, which covers the Pacific North-west and Northern

California. I order all the cars for the zone and distribute them to the dealers in the subzones.'

David picked up the photograph of Larry's Mercedes and handed it to the witness.

'How long have you been with Mercedes-Benz, Mr. Walsh?'

'It will be twenty-two years this April.'

'I've just handed you a photograph which has been marked as State's exhibit five, and I ask you if you can identify that car for the jury.'

'Certainly. This is our model 300SEL, 1991. It is beige in color.'

'What does 300SEL mean?'

'The 300SEL is a four-door sedan with a gas engine. Three hundred is the engine size. S means the car is one of our super-class models, the largest sedan we sell. E means the car has fuel injection. L stands for a long wheel base.'

'Do you also sell a 300SE model?'

'Yes, we do. That model looks identical, but it's four inches shorter.'

'Thank you. Now I am handing you three other photographs,' David said, handing Walsh the pictures he had shown to Ortiz on the preceding day. 'Can you identify the cars in those pictures?'

Walsh studied the photographs, then stacked them and turned toward the jury as David had instructed him to do at their pretrial meeting. He held up the top photograph.

'This photograph, which is marked defendant's exhibit seven, is a beige Mercedes-Benz.'

'Is it a 1991, 300SEL?'

'It is not. It is a 1981, 300SD.'

Several of the jurors leaned forward, and Monica cocked her head to one side, focusing her attention on the witness.

'And exhibit eight?'

Walsh held up a picture of another beige Mercedes.

'This is a 1985, 300SE model.'

There was a stir in the courtroom.

'And the final car?'

'Exhibit nine is a 1987, 420SEL.'

'If I told you that a person who had viewed those photographs had described all three cars as being the same type as the defendant's 1991, 300SEL, would you be surprised?'

'Not in the least. From 1981 to 1991 Mercedes-Benz made several models in that basic body style that were, with minor differences, very similar. From 1981 to 1983 there was a model 380SEL, a four-door long-wheel-base sedan. From 1981 to 1985 there was the model 300SD. In 1984 and 1985 there was a 500SEL and the 380SE. From 1986 through 1991 we had a model 560SEL, which was similar in appearance to the 300SEL and the 420SEL. And we had a diesel engine car in 1986 and 1987 with the same body. In 1990 and 1991 we had diesel models 350SD and 350SDL.'

'With all these cars looking so similar, how were

you able to tell that the three cars in exhibits seven, eight, and nine were not the 300SEL?'

'Exhibit seven shows a 1981, 300SD. The most obvious difference is that the 300SD is four inches shorter. If you look at the front and back doors and windows, you can see that they are roughly the same size in the 300SD, but the back door and window of the 1991, 300SEL are longer than its front door and window because of the longer wheel base. This difference is obvious to me but would not be noticeable to someone who is not familiar with Mercedes-Benz body types.

'The 1985, 380SE in exhibit eight is also shorter, and the wheel design is different. The 1991 car has a solid disk where a hubcap would normally be, but the 1985 car has a concave disk with a center hub about the size of the fuel-tank cap.'

'Mr. Walsh, what discernible difference is there between the 1991, 300SEL and the 1987, 420SEL, the car in exhibit nine?'

'Mr. Nash, there is no difference at all. Not even an expert can tell the difference between those two cars. I knew they were different only because I supplied you with the photograph.'

'Was there any difference in the number of cars sold for the four models in the four photographs?'

'No. They all sold roughly the same in all four years.'

'And what color was the most popular color for the four models we have been discussing?'

'Beige.'

David turned and smiled at Monica. To the witness he said, 'Thank you, Mr. Walsh. I have no further questions.'

'AND HOW ARE you employed, Mr. Waldheim?' David asked the distinguished-looking businessman who had just taken the witness stand. Across from David, Monica listened with one ear as she carried on a hurried conversation with Detective Crosby. Walsh's testimony had hurt, and she wanted Crosby to start looking for ways to rebut it. She was painfully ignorant about cars and had asked no questions of Walsh. That meant that, as of the moment, Ortiz's testimony about the Mercedes was virtually worthless.

'I am the vice president in charge of menswear for Sherwood Forest Sportswear.'

'Where are your headquarters located?'

'Bloomington, Illinois.'

'And that is where your office is?'

'That is correct.'

From a pile of exhibits David selected the shirt that had been seized from Stafford's house and brought it to Waldheim.

'I hand you what has been marked as State's exhibit twenty-three and ask you if you recognize this shirt.'

Waldheim took the shirt and examined it. 'Yes. This is part of last year's summer line.'

'Would you tell the jury how many of these shirts your firm distributed nationally?'

Waldheim turned slightly and addressed the jury.

'Last year was a very good year for menswear. This particular shirt was one of our most popular items. I checked our records before flying here, and I would say that we sold some five thousand dozen of this shirt nationally.'

'How many shirts are five thousand dozen, Mr. Waldheim?'

'Well, one thousand dozen equals twelve thousand shirts, so . . . let me see . . . sixty thousand shirts.'

'And that is a round figure?'

'That is correct. The actual number was in excess of five thousand dozen.'

'Mr. Waldheim, are you aware of the shirt patterns used by your competitors?'

'Certainly. We have to keep tabs on the competition.'

'To your knowledge does Sherwood Forest, or any other shirt manufacturer, make a shirt with a pattern similar to this shirt?'

'Yes. That forest pattern was so successful, especially in this area of the country, that we put out another similar line, and so did two of our competitors.'

'Thank you, Mr. Waldheim. Nothing further.'

Monica had been doing some calculations while David questioned Waldheim. There is a rule of cross-examination which holds that an attorney should never ask a witness a question unless she knows the answer. Monica had a question she wanted to ask, and Waldheim's testimony was so damaging that she decided to break the rule.

'Mr. Waldheim, your company distributes shirts nationally, doesn't it?'

'Yes.'

'How many of the shirts you were just shown were distributed in this state?'

'Uhmm, something in excess of one hundred dozen, I believe. The shirt did very well here.'

'And of those one hundred dozen, how many were distributed in Portland?'

'I'm not certain, but I would guess more than half.'

'So we are talking about approximately six hundred shirts in the metropolitan area?'

'A little more than six hundred. Yes.'

'Nothing further.'

Monica was troubled. She had softened the impact of Waldheim's testimony a little, but six hundred shirts was still a lot of shirts, and there were all those knockoffs from other companies. David was starting to cut away the basis for Ortiz's identification, and if he did that successfully . . .

There was a stir in the courtroom and Monica looked around. While she had been lost in thought, David had called his next witness – Jennifer Stafford.

*

JENNIFER WALKED TO the stand without looking at David, but she did pause momentarily by Larry's side. The look she gave him was one the jury could not see and David could not read.

Jennifer took the oath, then seated herself in the witness box. She sat erect, her hands folded primly in her lap. There was a trace of tension at the corners of her lips, and a tightness about her that betrayed her uneasiness. When David addressed her, she jerked slightly, as if she had experienced a minor electric shock.

'Mrs. Stafford, are you employed?'

'Yes,' she answered softly. The court reporter glanced at the judge, and Judge Rosenthal leaned toward the witness.

'You'll have to speak up, Mrs. Stafford,' he said gently.

'Yes, I am,' Jenny repeated.

David noticed that Larry was leaning toward Jennifer, listening to her testimony with an intensity that David had not noticed when the other witnesses were on.

'Where do you work?'

'I teach second grade at Palisades Elementary School.'

'How long have you been teaching there?'

'This will be my third year.'

'How long have you and Larry been married?'

'A little less than a year,' she answered, her voice breaking slightly from the strain. David waited for her to compose herself. He fought the urge to go to her and hold her.

'Can you remember when you first saw your husband on June sixteenth of this year?'

'Yes. We got up together and ate breakfast. Then Larry went to work.'

'Was he acting unusual in any way?'

'No.'

'When did you next see him?'

'Around eight o'clock, when he came home from work.'

'Was it unusual for Larry to work so late?'

'No. His job was . . . is very demanding. He would often keep late hours.'

'Tell the jury what happened after Larry came home.'

'We just watched some television. I can't even remember what. Then we had a snack and went to bed.'

'You and Larry sleep together?'

'Yes,' Jennifer said, blushing and looking at her lap.

'Where was Larry when you woke up the next morning?'

'In bed.'

'Do you have any reason to believe that he left your bed at any time that evening?'

'No. I'm a light sleeper, and I would have heard him if he got up.'

David paused. He had established Larry's alibi.

There was no reason to ask any more questions, and he wanted to make Jenny's ordeal as easy as possible. He turned toward Monica.

Monica acknowledged David's nod. Jennifer Stafford had been very believable, and her alibi would be difficult to break down. She did not know what to do to attack it, and she was beginning to feel helpless. She had put an investigator on the Staffords and had come up with nothing. She risked a look at David. He was chatting with the defendant, looking very sure of himself. Monica felt herself tighten with anger. She could not lose this case. She had to do something. But what?

'Mrs. Stafford, you are a wealthy woman, are you not?'

'Objection,' David said, standing.

'This goes to motive, Your Honor,' Monica replied.

'We went through this before, Mr. Nash, in chambers. You may have your objection.'

'Thank you, Your Honor,' Monica said. 'Are you a wealthy woman, Mrs. Stafford?'

'I don't know what you mean by that. I am well-off financially.'

'If neither you nor the defendant were working, could you get by?'

'Larry wouldn't accept my money. He—'

'That doesn't answer my question, Mrs. Stafford.'

'I don't need to work,' Jennifer said stiffly.

238

'But your husband does?'

'He has saved money from his job. He works very hard and—'

'Your Honor,' Monica interrupted, 'would you please instruct the witness to confine her answers to the questions?'

'Yes, Mrs. Stafford. Answer only the question put to you.'

'I'm sorry,' Jennifer answered nervously. Monica was pleased with the course of the questioning. Stafford's wife was becoming defensive, and that would help cast doubt on her credibility.

'You purchased your house for four hundred seventy-five thousand dollars, did you not?'

'Yes.'

'Mr. Stafford could not have purchased the house without your money, could he?'

'No,' Jennifer answered. She was angry and David began to worry.

'In fact, if you and he were divorced, it would seriously alter his lifestyle, wouldn't it?'

'Objection,' David said.

'Sustained. That is highly speculative, Ms. Powers.'

'I withdraw the question,' Monica said, satisfied that the jury had got the point.

'Mrs. Stafford, do you love your husband?'

David looked up. He knew that her answer would mean nothing, but he tried to read something in her eyes: a message he hoped he would see there.

Jennifer hesitated a second and Monica noticed. She wondered if the jury had, and she turned in its direction.

'Yes,' Jennifer answered softly.

'Would you lie to help him?'

'Yes,' she answered, 'but I did not lie, because I did not have to. Larry was with me, Miss Powers. He couldn't have murdered that poor woman.'

DAVID SELECTED THE Georgetown for lunch because it was dark and the individual wine-red booths provided privacy.

'I was so frightened,' Jenny said.

It was the first time they had met during the day someplace other than his office. David reached across the narrow table and touched Jenny's hand.

'You were fine.'

'And Larry?' she asked.

'He was fine, too. The trial is going very well.'

Judge Rosenthal had called a recess for lunch as soon as Larry had finished testifying. Stafford had been nervous but had handled himself well. On direct, David had limited himself to asking the defendant where he had been on the evening of the murder and filling in items of his biography that had not been provided by other witnesses. On cross, predictably, Monica had delved into Larry's feelings about not making partner and asked about his relationship with his wife. Stafford was well prepared to handle this line, as David, playing the role of district attorney, had grilled him far worse in the jail than Monica did on the stand. David enjoyed Monica's frustration as it became clear that she was making little headway. Her final questions concerned Stafford's sex life, and David felt they were sufficiently embarrassing so that the overall effect was to create sympathy for his client. When Monica asked her final question, 'Have you been with a prostitute in the past two years?' Larry's answer – 'Why would I do that, when I have a wife like Jenny, who loves me?' – had caused several of the jurors to nod their heads in approval.

'Do you . . . will you win, David?' Jenny asked.

'It's impossible to say, but I feel good about the case. I believe in Larry. I could see his sincerity when he testified. I'm a pretty good judge of people, and if I'm getting these impressions, I'm sure the jurors are, too.'

Jenny looked down at the table for a moment. She seemed troubled.

'What's the matter?' David asked.

'I've decided, David,' Jenny answered in a hushed voice. David felt his heart leap. Was she saying goodbye? Was this the end of his dream?

'No matter what happens, I'm going to ask Larry for a divorce. Then, if you want me . . .'

'Want you? God, Jenny, you don't know what this means to me. I love you so much . . . Don't cry.'

Jenny's head was lowered, but even in the dim light he could see tears coursing down her cheeks.

'I hope I'm not interrupting anything,' a voice

241

from behind David said. Jennifer looked up, startled, and David turned rapidly. Thomas Gault was standing over the table, a sly grin looking diabolical in the frame of his Chinese mustache.

'I saw you two over here and thought maybe I'd get me a scoop.'

'Gault,' David barked angrily, 'this is a private meeting.'

'But you and the lady are public people. I have my duty as an agent of the press to seek headlines wherever.'

Gault stopped suddenly when he noticed Jenny's tears. The smile disappeared.

'Say, I am sorry. I didn't realize . . . It's so dark in here.'

He whipped out a handkerchief and held it toward Jenny. She looked at David, puzzled.

'It's okay,' Gault said. 'I've been there. Had my own trial. For murder, too,' he said with a trace of pride. 'But Dave got me off and he'll clear your husband. Don't you worry.'

Jenny continued to stare at the handkerchief, which drooped from the end of Gault's hand like an ill-cared-for flag. David saved the situation by proffering his own, which Jenny took quickly.

'Look, Tom, Mrs. Stafford is upset and we would like a little privacy.'

'Sure thing. And I am sorry. Didn't mean to . . . you know.'

'Sure. And, Tom, if you want a scoop, come to court this afternoon. My last witness is going to be a doozy.'

Gault brightened.

'Now, that's the spirit. I'm givin' you great press, buddy. Sorry again, Mrs. Stafford. Your husband's got a great lawyer.'

Gault left and the couple said nothing for a moment. Then Jenny asked David, 'What's going to happen this afternoon?'

David felt a surge of excitement and smiled. 'Oh, I'm going to hammer the final nail into the State's coffin. But I don't want to talk about that now. I want to talk about us.'

'MR. CONKLIN, DURING your years as an investigator have you developed an expertise in the area of photography?'

'I have.'

'Would you tell the jury what training you have in this field?'

Terry turned toward the jury and smiled. He was an old hand at being in the witness box and appeared to be completely relaxed.

'I received my initial training in the Air Force, then studied by correspondence through the New York Institute of Photography. For a short time, after the Air Force and before I went into police work, I owned a photo studio and worked as a cameraman for KOIN-TV.

'When I was with the Lane County Police Department, I set up their photo lab, and, since going into private practice, I have done all of the accident and special photography for several law firms in town.'

'Have you ever won any prizes for your work?'

'I've won several awards over the past ten years. In fact, I won the blue ribbon in two categories at the last Multnomah County Fair.'

'Did I contact you with regard to assisting me in the investigation of the Larry Stafford case?'

'Yes, Mr. Nash, you did.'

'In this capacity, did you take any photographs at the Raleigh Motel, room twenty-two?'

'I did.'

'What was your assignment with regard to these photographs?'

'Well, as I understood it from talking to you, I was to take a photograph inside the motel room where the murder occurred that would accurately portray how a person standing where the killer stood on the evening of the crime would look to a person in the position Officer Ortiz was in when he saw the murderer.'

There was a stir in the courtroom, and several of the jurors made notes on their pads.

'How did you prepare yourself for this assignment?'

'First I visited the motel room with you and got a feel for the layout and the lighting. Then I read the police reports and sat in at a hearing when Officer Ortiz drew a diagram of the positions of everyone in the room at the time of the commission of the crime.'

David pointed to the easel. 'Is that the diagram?'

'Yes.'

'So you really got the information on the positions from Officer Ortiz?'

'That's right. His statements under oath and his written report.'

'What information did you have with regard to the lighting in the motel room on June sixteenth?'

'As I understood the testimony and the report, there were no lights on when Officer Ortiz entered the room, but there was a large globe light that illuminated the landing.'

'Where was this globe light situated?'

'To the right of the door, on the outside.'

'Were there any other lights?'

'Only those in the street. Neon signs, headlights. Things like that. The side of the motel away from the office is not well lit.'

'What did you do next?'

'A few weeks after the hearing, when I had the information about the positions of the people involved, I hired an individual who is the same height as Mr. Stafford to accompany me to the Raleigh Motel. I received permission to enter the room from the manager, Mr. Grimes, and I proceeded to set up my camera at the same height Officer Ortiz would be if he was lying in the position he described. I then put the model where the murderer was supposed to be.'

'What position was that?'

'I had him stand at the door frame, leaning into the room. His body was at a slight angle, with his right leg and arm outside the door and his left leg and arm just inside the room. The model was instructed to look down toward the camera.'

'When were these pictures taken?'

'At night, about the same time as the murder.'

David approached Conklin and handed him three photographs.

'I hand you what have been marked as defendant's exhibits number twelve, thirteen, and fourteen. Can you identify them for the jury?'

'These are three photographs taken in the motel room by me.'

'Tell the jury what they portray.'

'Okay,' Terry said, holding the first picture up to the jury. 'Exhibit twelve is a picture of a man standing in the doorway of room twenty-two. This is the model. He is standing exactly as described by Officer Ortiz at the hearing.'

'Can you see the man's face, Mr. Conklin?'

'No, sir, you cannot.'

Someone gasped and the jurors wrote furiously. Monica was straining to see the photograph.

'Your Honor, I've never seen these pictures,' she shouted. 'I object to . . .'

'Yes, Mr. Nash. The jury should not see these pictures until they have been admitted into evidence. Show them to counsel, please,' Judge Rosenthal said.

David smiled. The uproar over the improper way in which he had introduced the pictures would heighten the jury's suspense and the impact the pictures would make. He had counted on Monica's objection, and she had not let him down.

Monica scanned the pictures. She could not believe it. With the globe lamp outside and the model's head just inside the door, shadows obscured the face. It was impossible to make out the features. The other two photos were taken with the model standing straight up and leaning outside the door. In the last picture, with the head tilted back, you could make out some features, but not many, and the shadows still obscured most of the detail. Ortiz's identification had been completely impeached. She turned toward David as she began to make her legal objection to the pictures and saw the smile he hid from the jury. She felt her blood rise. Then she caught Stafford out of the corner of her eye. He too was gloating.

Judge Rosenthal was ruling in favor of the admission of the pictures into evidence, and Conklin was continuing his testimony, explaining the technique he had used to produce the photographs, but Monica only half heard it. She was seething, burning. She could not let David get away with this. She was not going to let that smug son of a bitch walk out of this courtroom scot-free. He had suckered her with those pictures, but he hadn't won yet. Monica picked up her pen and doodled the name Cyrus Johnson on her witness list.

3

David let out his belt a notch and groaned with relief. Helen Banks smiled at the compliment to her cooking and began collecting the dirty dishes.

'Why don't you and Greg get some fresh air, while I get the coffee on?' she said, stacking the dishes on a serving cart.

'Sounds like an excellent idea,' Gregory said as he pushed away from the table. It was Saturday evening and the trial was in recess for the weekend. David had rested after Terry Conklin had finished his testimony Friday afternoon. From all accounts it looked as if victory was assured. Even Rudy, the jail guard, who rarely expressed his opinion about a case, had made a comment about Stafford's being out soon.

As it did almost every year, the cold of autumn had given way to a week of false spring that fooled the flowers into opening to the October air and brought back pleasant memories of summer. Gregory lit up a cigar and the two friends strolled onto the terrace. The dark river was at peace, and so was David.

'What's on the menu for Monday?' Gregory asked.

'I don't know,' David answered as he sank into

a lawn chair. 'Monica said she might have some rebuttal, but I can't imagine what it could be.'

'Maybe she's going to have one of her investigators go out to the motel and try to get some pictures that show a face.'

'Not a chance. I had Terry's work double-checked by two other professionals before I used it. Given those lighting conditions, there's no way Ortiz could have seen the killer's face.'

Gregory leaned back and puffed on his cigar. It was quiet on the terrace. The breeze was cool, and the lights from the houseboats across the way appeared to wink on and off as the boats twisted with the current.

'What do you know about Ortiz, Dave?' Gregory asked after a while.

'Why?' David asked. He felt dreamy, fatigued by too much food and too much wine and lulled by the sounds of the river.

'I don't know. It just seems strange that he would be so certain, if those pictures are accurate.'

'The mind plays strange tricks sometimes. Don't forget, he'd just been struck on the head, and he was coming into a darkened room from the outside. There are probably a hundred explanations a psychiatrist could give you.'

'You're right. Anyway, if it helps you lock this up, I don't care what he saw.'

'Confusion to our enemies,' David toasted, taking

a sip from the wineglass he had carried with him. Gregory raised his cigar.

'If nothing else, this case has at least raised your spirits.'

'What do you mean?'

'You were a pain in the butt to have around the office for a while. I guess I can say it now, because you seem to be over your blue period.'

'I don't . . . Oh, you mean that Seals business.'

'And a few others.'

'Was I bitching and moaning that much?'

'Enough so that I was getting a little worried about you. What you need to do is settle down. Find a good woman.'

'Like Helen?'

Greg nodded.

'They don't make 'em like that anymore,' David said lightly, picturing what it would be like to see Jenny every morning when he woke up, and to kiss her every evening.

'I've gotta go to the bathroom,' Gregory said. 'Save my place, will ya?'

'My pleasure,' David said, sipping some more wine. Somewhere up the river a tanker's horn sounded. For a brief moment David felt disoriented, then recognized the unsettling feeling created by a sense of déjà vu. The night seemed to belong to two times, and he struggled with his memory to fit the past into the present. Softly, like the night breeze, it came to him. The evening he first met

Jenny had been an evening like this. A still river, night sounds, the breeze. Even the air had smelled the same. It was a vivid memory now, warm and real, as if David had been transported back in time and Jenny would soon appear on the terrace, profiled against the sky. He smiled. It was a good memory, a calming thought.

David recalled the first time he had seen Jenny on the fringe of the small group. He remembered his impressions. How beautiful she had seemed.

Then, like the last piece in a Chinese puzzle box, a new thought slipped into place, and David's inner peace shattered. Something else had happened that day. The interview with the young girl who had been the victim in the Seals case. David sat up. His heart was beating rapidly.

'Coffee's on,' Helen Banks called from the doorway.

David did not answer. He was thinking back. Trying to be sure and hoping he was wrong.

'Did you hear me, Dave?'

David stood up. He felt sick at heart.

'Is something wrong?' Helen asked.

'I just remembered something I must do. I'm afraid I'll have to skip coffee.'

'Oh, Dave. Can't you just take a day off and relax?'

David touched her shoulder and tried to gather his thoughts. He could be wrong. He prayed he was wrong.

'If I don't check on this,' he said, managing a smile, 'I won't be able to sleep tonight.'

'If you're determined . . .' Helen said with a sigh.

'Determined to what?' Gregory asked.

'I've got to leave, Greg. Something I just remembered, and it can't wait.'

Gregory looked at him hard. He discerned the lines of worry on his young friend's face and knew that whatever was bothering David was serious.

'Can I help?'

'No. Thanks. This is something I have to do alone.'

And he was alone. More alone than he had ever been.

THE SECURITY GUARD in the lobby signed him in, and David took the only working elevator to the thirty-second floor. He used his key to unlock the door to the firm offices and walked rapidly down the corridor to the file room, flicking light switches as he went. Darkened corridors were suddenly bathed in light as he advanced.

The file was in the Closed section. It was thick and intact. The audiocassette was tucked into a small manila envelope that had been taped to the inside of the folder. David carried the file to his office and closed the door. He took a tape recorder from his bottom drawer and fitted the cassette into it. He pushed a button and the tape began to unwind. David leaned back and listened, praying that he was wrong. Hoping that he would not hear what he knew he would.

It was there. The very first thing on the tape. He pushed the Stop button, then Rewind, and played it again to be sure.

'This is Detective Leon Stahlheimer,' the voice on the tape said. 'It's Thursday, June sixteenth . . .'

David switched off the recorder.

All lies. She had lied on the stand and she had lied to him. Used him. Had it all been a play to her? A carefully rehearsed role? Had any of the emotions been real? What did it matter? How could he ever love her again?

David switched off the office lights. It was better in the dark. Not seeing enabled him to direct himself inward. What should he do? What could he do? He felt powerless, defeated. He had built a dream on Jennifer's love and Larry Stafford's innocence, and the dream had crumbled, breaking him under the debris.

All the despair he had felt months before flooded back, drowning him in a sea of self-pity and disgust. The dead feeling he thought he had conquered returned to gnaw at him, leaving only the bones of a sorry, tired, and aging man.

David looked at the desk clock. It was midnight. Not too late for a confrontation. Not too late to put an end to something that had been so good.

DAVID REMEMBERED LITTLE of the mad drive to Newgate Terrace. There were occasional lights on the early-morning freeway, then a winding country road and the crunch of gravel under his tires. House lights came on after his second knock, and the first thing he recalled clearly was Jenny's face, pale from sleep.

'You lied,' he said, forcing her back into the hallway. The darkened surrounding rooms gave him the feeling of being in a miniature theater.

'What?' she asked, still groggy from sleep. He grasped her shoulders and made her look at his eyes, fierce now with the pain of knowing.

'I want the truth. Now. Everything.'

'I don't—' she started, then twisted painfully in his grasp as his strong fingers dug into the soft flesh of her shoulders.

'I'll make it easy for you, Jenny,' he said, making the name he had once loved to hear sound like a curse. 'We met that evening at Greg's house. Senator Bauer's fund-raiser. You remember? The first night we made love.'

She flinched. The way he had said 'love' made it sound sordid, like copulation with a whore in a wino hotel room.

'I interviewed a girl that morning at the juvenile home. We recorded the conversation. The date was on the tape. June sixteenth. The day Darlene Hersch was murdered. You couldn't have been with Larry that evening, Jenny. You were fucking me. Remember?'

Her head snapped sideways as if she had been slapped. He shook her to make her look at him.

'Don't,' she cried.

'You lied to me.'

'No!'

'Knowing all the time . . .' he screamed at her.

'I didn't . . . I . . . Please, David, I love—'

'Love,' he shouted, bringing the back of his hand sharply against her cheek. Her eyes widened in shock and she crumpled at his feet.

'So help me, if you ever use that word again, I'll kill you. You know nothing about love,' he said between clenched teeth.

She reached out blindly, trying to touch him.

'It wasn't . . . I . . . Let me talk to you. Don't just go like this. Please.'

He watched her, huddled like a child at his feet, her long golden hair cascading over shoulders that jerked with each wretched sob.

'I'm sorry, David. I really am,' she wept, 'but there wasn't any other way. I couldn't think of anything else to do.'

'Not even telling the truth?'

'I was afraid you wouldn't defend Larry. I thought . . . It looked so bad. And I still believe he is innocent. But no one else would have.'

David looked at her hard, trying to see behind her ravaged, tear-stained face.

'Innocent?'

'Larry swears he is. I don't know if . . . I don't think he's lying.'

'But he lied to me about being with you on the evening of the murder.'

'Yes. I told you, that day in your office. We fought. He had dinner with Barry Dietrich, then went back to his office to work. I was sick of it. I never saw him anymore. It was that damn job. Making partner was all that counted. I called him and told him that I was going to leave him.'

As David listened to Jenny, he could hear echoes of his fights with Monica. David sagged and sat down on the bottom of the staircase. Jenny looked spent. She had stopped crying.

'The marriage was a mistake from the beginning. Larry is like a child, self-centered, domineering. Everything had to be what he wanted. That night he came home in a rage. He shouted at me, called me names. "I didn't understood him." "I didn't want him to succeed." After a while I didn't even hear what he said. I went upstairs and slammed the door to my room.'

'Your room?' David interrupted.

'Yes. You didn't know? Of course you didn't. No, we hadn't slept together for a month. I told you, things had been bad.

'I heard Larry's bedroom door slam and it was quiet. I don't know why I remembered about the fund-raiser. I think the invitation was on my dresser on top of some other mail. I just needed to get out, so I took it and left.'

'And Larry?'

'He was still at home when I drove away. Don't you see how hard it was for me? I felt so guilty. When I met you, when you made love to me, it was so different. I felt as if you were giving something, not taking, like Larry. I didn't know what to do. At first I thought I would just leave him. Then I didn't have the courage. And I still loved him in a way. It was all so mixed up. And it got a little better after that evening. He tried. He cut down on his work a little. Stayed home more. It wasn't much, but it was an effort, and I was still guilt-ridden because I had cheated on him. I didn't feel as if I'd cheated. It had all been so good. But a part of me felt as if I had betrayed a trust.'

She stopped and he moved over to her, sitting on the floor, letting her rest against him.

'Then Larry was arrested and I realized what night the murder occurred. The evidence looked so convincing. His shirt, our car. That policeman saying it was him. But Larry said he was innocent. That he had stayed home after I left. He swore it to me.'

'Why didn't you tell me the truth?'

'I was afraid. I wanted you to represent Larry, because I believed in you. I knew you could clear him. If I told you the truth . . . reminded you that the murder occurred on the night we met . . . you would have been a witness against Larry.'

'And now, as his lawyer, I can't be.'

She looked away from him again and said, 'Yes,' in a very small voice.

'So what do we do now, Jenny?' David asked.

'What do you mean?'

'I mean that you committed a crime yesterday. You perjured yourself. And so did Larry. And I know about that. Do you know what my duty is under the Canons of Ethics? As an attorney, an officer of the court, I have a duty to tell the judge what you did and a duty to get off the case if Larry won't recant his testimony. I'm committing a crime and subjecting myself to possible disbarment if I don't tell Judge Rosenthal about this.'

'You wouldn't—' Jenny started.

'I don't know what I'm going to do. I'm so mixed up I can't think.'

David stood up and walked to the door. His feet felt leaden, and he had no heart for anything anymore. The trial, his practice, this woman, his life. Nothing seemed to mean anything. There were no values, no goals.

'David,' she said when he reached the door, 'I love you. You know that, don't you? Tell me you know that I never lied about that.'

David turned to face her. He was not angry at her, just dead inside.

'I know you used me, Jenny. I know you played on my emotions. I know I still love you, but I don't know if I can ever trust you again.'

259

'Oh, God, David,' she called after him. 'Don't cut me off like this. Don't you see? I don't know if Larry killed that woman or not, but if he's innocent, you must help him, and if he's guilty . . . I couldn't let him go to prison thinking that he'd gone after that woman because of me.'

THE ROADSIDE FLASHED by and car horns occasionally broke the stillness. It would be easy to end everything by simply closing his eyes and letting the car take control. When the road began to waver, David shook his head to clear it. He did not want to die. He was certain of that. But life at the moment was confused and a torment.

He had several choices. He could make Jennifer retake the stand and recant her perjured testimony; he could go to the judge if she refused; or he could do nothing. If Jenny recanted, Larry would surely be convicted.

Would that be so bad? Yes, if he was innocent. There was still that possibility. Until tonight David had been convinced of Stafford's innocence. The pictures discredited Ortiz. Larry's story was so believably told. But what if he was wrong and Stafford was guilty?

David thought about Ashmore and Tony Seals. He felt sick. Once more he saw the autopsy photographs of the little girls that Ashmore had molested, then killed, and once again he heard Jessie Garza describe crawling down the mountain. What was he doing

260

defending these people?

And Larry Stafford, where did he fit in? David could see the gash in Darlene Hersch's throat. That was why any lawyer worth his salt fought so hard to keep out pictures of the victims in death. Death could be handled and sweet-talked in the abstract, but pictures made it real for a jury. Made the jury feel and smell and taste the horror that is violent death. David could touch that reality now. The steel shell he had built around his sensibilities had started to crumble with Ashmore, and all his defenses were now down. But his fear of being responsible for setting loose another killer was still at odds with his feelings of love for Jenny. He felt used, he felt a fool, but he still loved her. In the end he no more knew what he would do than he had when he'd left her.

4

'I know everything,' David told Larry Stafford. They were seated in a vacant jury room that Judge Rosenthal permitted them to use for conferences. Stafford was dressed in navy blue with a light-blue shirt and navy-and-red-striped tie. Just the right amount of cuff showed, and his shoes were polished. Only his complexion, turned pasty from too much jail time, did not fit his young-lawyer image.

'I don't understand,' Stafford said nervously.

'Jenny told me. Oh, you don't have to worry about her. I figured it out. She didn't volunteer anything.'

'I'm still not sure what you mean.' Larry answered warily.

David was tired of the games, and just plain tired. He had not slept last night, and he was having trouble handling even the simplest thoughts. He came to the point.

'I know that you and Jenny lied when you testified that you were together on the evening of the murder. I know you had a fight and she left the house. You have no alibi and you both committed perjury.'

Stafford said nothing. He looked like a little boy who was about to cry.

'Did you kill her, Larry?' David asked.

'What does it matter? Would you believe me if I said I didn't?'

'I'm still your attorney.'

'It's been like this my whole fucking life,' Stafford said bitterly. 'So close. Then, bam, the door snaps shut. I marry this dream girl. She's beautiful, wealthy. And she turns out to be a bitch who thinks only of herself.

'I kill myself to get through law school, get into the best firm, and the bastards won't make me a partner, because I don't have the right breeding.

'But this is the biggest joke of all, and I'll probably end up in prison.'

'I asked you if you killed her.'

'You won't believe what I say any more than Jenny did.'

'Then why do you suppose she lied for you?' David asked, angered by Stafford's display of self-pity.

'How would it look? Jennifer Dodge of the Portland Dodges, who already married below her station, married to a murderer. How could she hold her head up at the horse show?'

'You're a fool, Stafford. You're so self-centered, you can't recognize—'

'I recognize when I'm getting the shaft. I know what that little bitch wanted out of this. I was one of her charity projects, like that school she teaches at. Take a poor boy to lunch – or, to tell it like it was, to bed. She was slumming, Nash. But as soon as I wanted to make something of myself, she started in. She never understood me. That I didn't want to owe her anything.'

'But it didn't bother you when she perjured herself and risked prison for you?'

'If she hadn't run out on me that night, none of this would have happened.'

'None of what?' David demanded. Stafford stopped, confused.

'None of . . . my arrest. Look, it's obvious I didn't do it. You proved that. I mean, Grimes already said that the killer had long brown hair, and what about those pictures and what Walsh said about the car?'

'What are you trying to do, Larry? Convince me you're innocent? Let's look at the facts the way I would, with my information, if I was prosecuting this case.

'The killer wears a shirt identical to a shirt that you own and wears pants similar to pants you own. He drives the same make and color car. He has the same build. And a trained police officer swears under oath that he is you. What do you think the statistical odds are that two people in Portland would own the same pants, shirt, and expensive car?

'You had the opportunity. No alibi. And it would be natural for a man who has just had

264

a fight with a woman who has cut him off sexually . . .'

Stafford's head snapped up.

'Yes, I know about that, too. It would be natural for such a man to go out looking for a woman.

'Then there's motive. If you had been arrested for prostitution, your marriage would have been endangered and your tenuous chance to make partner destroyed.

'Arrayed against these motives and amazing coincidences in dress and physique, we have the word of one old man that the killer did not have curly blond hair, some fancy statistical footwork that probably won't get by any halfway intelligent juror who starts thinking about the sheer number of those coincidences, and a few trick photographs.

'What would your verdict be, if you were a juror?'

Stafford hung his head. 'What do you want me to say?' he asked.

'What do I want . . .? Goddammit, you're lucky I talked to you at all. I should have dragged your wife in front of Judge Rosenthal and made her recant on the stand. But I'm still your lawyer and I want it from you. Did you kill Darlene Hersch?'

Stafford wagged his still-bowed head from side to side but did not look David in the eye.

'I don't care anymore,' he said. 'And once the jury hears what we did . . .'

'If,' David said.

Stafford looked up at him, like a dog begging for food.

'You're not going to—?'

'You aren't the only one involved in this. I don't know if you killed that woman or not, but I'm not going to let you drag your wife down with you, by making her admit that she perjured herself.

'And if you are innocent, there isn't a chance that a jury would find you innocent if it learned about what you two did.'

Stafford started to cry, but David did nothing to comfort him.

'Just one more thing, Stafford. Are there any other little goodies that I should know about? And I mean anything.'

'No, no. I swear.'

David stood and walked to the door. Stafford seemed to lack the energy to move. He sat hunched over, staring at the floor.

'Pull yourself together,' David ordered in a cold, flat monotone. 'We have to go to court.'

DAVID TOOK HIS place at counsel table and watched the events of the day unfold like a dream. The jury was seated in slow motion and Monica appeared, her arms loaded with law books. If he had been concentrating, this would have struck him as odd on a day set aside for closing argument, but nothing was registering for David. He just wanted the case to end, so he could decide what to do with his life without the pressure of having to care about the lives of other people.

Stafford had been brought in by the guard before the jury appeared, but he exchanged no words with his attorney. The judge came in last, and the final day of the trial commenced.

'Are you prepared to argue, Ms. Powers?' Judge Rosenthal asked.

'No, Your Honor,' Monica replied. 'The State has one rebuttal witness it would like to call.'

'Very well.'

Monica signaled toward the back of the room, and Cyrus Johnson swaggered in, dressed in a white shirt, crew-neck sweater, and brown slacks. David watched Johnson walk to the witness stand, trying to place the face. It was only when the witness stated his name that David began to feel uneasy.

'Do you know that man?' David demanded. Stafford paled and said nothing, unable to take his eyes off the witness.

'Are you also known as T.V., Mr. Johnson?' Monica asked.

'You'd better tell me what this is all about,' David said, his voice low and threatening. Stafford did not reply, but his face had the look of a person who knows that his death is imminent.

'And would you tell the jury what your occupation was on June sixteenth of this year?' Monica asked, swiveling her chair to watch David and Stafford react.

'Uh, well, uh,' Johnson started uneasily, 'I guess you could say I managed some women.'

'You mean you were a pimp?' Monica asked.

There was a commotion in the courtroom and the judge pounded his gavel for quiet.

'Ms. Powers, you are asking this man to admit to criminal activity. Has he been warned of his rights?'

'Mr. Johnson is testifying under a grant of full immunity, Your Honor,' Monica replied, handing a notarized document to the Court and a copy to David. The judge studied it.

'Very well,' he said when he was finished. 'You may proceed.'

'Mr. Johnson, have you ever seen Larry Stafford, the defendant in this case, before?'

Johnson stared at Stafford for a moment, then turned back to Monica.

'Yes, I have.'

'Would you tell the jury the circumstances of that meeting?' Monica asked.

Johnson shifted in the witness box and Monica tensed, waiting for David's objection. When it did not come, she glanced tentatively at her former husband. She was startled by what she saw. David, who was usually so intense, was slumped down in his chair. He looked sad and uncaring. Monica had sprung surprises on David before and had seen him handle other lawyers' challenges. Thinking on his feet was where David excelled. The David she saw now looked defeated.

'It was a couple of years ago. I would say in September. This dude, uh, the defendant, come up to one of my women in the Regency Bar, and they split a few minutes later. Now, I don't make it a practice to bother my girls when they're workin', but somethin' about this dude bothered me, so I followed them.'

Judge Rosenthal looked over at David. He, too, was waiting for an objection. When David said nothing, the judge toyed with the idea of calling the lawyers to the bench to discuss the direction the testimony was taking, but Nash was an experienced attorney, and he had conducted an excellent trial so far. The judge decided to let David try his case his way.

'We was usin' a motel on the strip then, so I knew right where they was goin'. I parked in the lot near the room and waited. About ten minutes later I heard a scream, so I went up to the room.

'Mordessa is naked and scramblin' across the bed, and this dude,' Johnson said, pointing at Stafford, 'is right on top of her, beatin' her good. She got blood comin' out of her mouth and her eye looked real bad.

'I was carryin' a piece which I pulled and told him to freeze. He does. Then I asked what happened. Mordessa says Stafford wanted her to do some real kinky stuff, like tyin' her up and whipping her. She tells him it's extra and he says that's cool. Then somethin' about him scared her and she changed her mind. And that's when he starts beatin' on her.'

'What happened then?'

'The cops, uh, police arrived. I guess someone heard Mordessa screamin' and called 'em. Anyway, this white cop asks Stafford what happened and he don't even speak to me. Stafford says we tried to roll him and the next thing I know, we're down the station house charged with prostitution and attempted robbery.'

'Did you tell the police your story?'

'Sure, but they wasn't too interested in our version.'

'What finally happened to the charges against you?'

'Nothin'. They was dropped.'

'And why was that?'

T.V. smiled and pointed at Stafford. 'He wouldn't prosecute. Said he never said no such thing to the police.'

'Is there any question in your mind that the man who beat up Mordessa is the defendant, Lawrence Dean Stafford?'

Johnson stared at Stafford and shook his head.

'No, ma'am.'

Monica paused for effect, then said, 'Your witness, counselor.'

The courtroom was hushed and all eyes turned toward David. Stafford's head was bent and he stared at the blank legal pad that lay before him.

He had not moved during Johnson's testimony.

David also sat motionless. As Johnson had testified, the lawyer in him had seen the numerous objections and legal motions he could have made to keep Johnson's testimony out, but he had made none of them, because there was another, more human, part that would not let him.

Each time he thought about objecting, he thought about Tony Seals and Ashmore. He was tired of letting the animals out of their cages and tired of justifying his actions by the use of philosophical arguments he no longer believed in. Stafford was guilty. He had murdered Darlene Hersch. There was no longer any doubt in David's mind. David had to protect future victims from a man like Stafford, not use his skills to endanger others. Stafford had taken a life and he would pay for it.

The judge was calling his name for a second time. The jurors were staring at him. A low rumble of voices was beginning to build among the spectators. David shook his head slowly from side to side.

'No questions,' he said.

And Stafford never said a word in protest.

PART IV

TRIAL BY FIRE

1

The visitor's room at the state penitentiary was a large, open space filled with couches and chairs upholstered in red vinyl and outfitted with chrome armrests. Three vending machines stood against one wall. There was an occasional low wooden table with an ashtray on it.

Jenny had never been in a place like this before, and the visits depressed her. The other prisoners seemed strange and threatening and not like anyone she had ever met. Whenever she entered the prison, she felt like a visitor to a foreign country.

Larry did not understand her reluctance to touch him. All around them wives, lovers, and relatives embraced the other prisoners. She tried to explain how she felt to Larry, but he saw her reticence as another betrayal.

'I talked to Mr. Bloch,' Jenny said. 'He says he'll have your brief filed at the court of appeals this week. He sounded hopeful, Larry.'

Stafford shook his head. He had fired David as soon as Judge Rosenthal had imposed the mandatory life sentence on him. Jerry Bloch, an experienced appellate attorney, was representing him now. They had talked about the appeal last week.

'I'm not going to get out. That bastard Nash saw to that when he railroaded me at the trial.'

'But Mr. Bloch—'

'I talked to Bloch. Don't forget, I'm a lawyer. There aren't any errors Bloch can work with, because Nash never objected when they put that pimp on the stand. That son of a bitch socked me in here but good.'

Jenny said nothing. She had been through this before. Once Larry got started, he would stay in a rage during the entire visit.

'If he'd cross-examined Johnson or kept him off . . . Jenny, there were a thousand ways he could have kept that pimp off the stand.'

He could also have told the judge that you and I lied, she thought to herself, but he didn't. He didn't do anything. An image of the last day of Larry's trial slipped unbidden into her consciousness. Once again she saw T.V. Johnson walk from the hushed courtroom. The jury filing out. The judge and prosecutor following. But David and Larry had not moved. And when the guard finally led Larry away, David still remained seated. She had waited for him in the back of the room, wanting to talk to him, to hold him.

When everyone else had left, David got to his feet slowly, as if he were climbing the last section of a steep mountain grade. When he turned, he looked exhausted and his eyes had lost their focus. He packed his papers away and walked toward the door, up the aisle in Jenny's direction. When he reached her, he paused for barely a moment and looked down at her. Where she had expected hate, she saw only despair. The look of a man who had given up everything without a fight.

That evening, after short deliberation, the jury returned a verdict of guilty. She had not seen David since. He never answered her calls and never seemed to be at home. After a while she stopped trying.

'Bloch says if we lose the appeal in the supreme court, I can go into federal court and allege incompetence of counsel. But I have to wait and exhaust my state appeals first.'

'We can do that, if you want to.'

'You bet I want to.'

'Won't it come out that . . . about my not being with you that night?'

'I don't care, Jenny. That's only perjury. I'm in here for life for a murder I didn't commit.'

And what about me? she wanted to ask, but she couldn't. If she had to be punished in order for Larry to get out, she would be getting what she deserved. If she hadn't betrayed David, he would never have collapsed the way he had. Larry was in prison because she had destroyed David with her lies.

David. How she loved him. More so now that he was lost to her forever. She remembered the night they had first met. It had taken all her control to refrain from calling him. And why hadn't she? Guilt. It was always the same answer. Guilt had prevented her from asking Larry for a divorce long before Darlene Hersch was murdered. Guilt prevented her from telling David the truth. And guilt was keeping her shackled to a man who would probably spend the rest of his life in prison.

THE UPTURNED COLLAR of Thomas Gault's jacket blocked the icy wind and sent it skittering through the drunken sailors and carousing longshoremen who crowded the sidewalk. Gault pushed open the door of The Dutchman, a noisy workingmen's bar that took its trade from the docks. A gust of wind chilled two men who were sitting at the bar, and they looked Gault's way when he entered. The bar lined the wall to Gault's right, and a row of booths occupied the wall on the left. Most of the room was filled with Formica-topped tables. Two pool tables stood in a cleared space near the gents' room.

'Shut the door,' one of the men at the bar commanded. Gault smiled to himself. He didn't come to the docks for the atmosphere. He came for the action. And it looked as if tonight the action might start sooner than he'd expected. He had planned on shutting the door, but now he let it stay open.

'Shut it yourself, asshole,' he said, and walked down the bar without another glance in the man's direction. He heard an angry murmur behind him, and a few seconds later the door slammed shut.

278

Gault positioned himself with his back to the wall at an unoccupied table by the jukebox where he could view the room. A waitress brought him a beer and he took a sip, watching the man he had insulted over the rim of the glass. He was a little over six feet. A thick roll of fat slopped over his belt at the waistline, and his shirt was partially out of his pants, exposing a sweat-stained undershirt. His movements were slow and jerky. It was obvious that he had been drinking for some time.

The fat man's companion was Gault's size. His figure was trim and he seemed sober. The fat man seemed to have forgotten about the incident at the door and was back in his cups. Too bad, Gault thought. He let his eyes drift over the rest of the room. A sailor and a heavyset woman with teased blond hair were shooting pool against two boys in work shirts and jeans. The woman sank her shot. One of the boys swore. The sailor laughed and smacked the woman's ass.

Three men a few tables from Gault were arguing about an upcoming heavyweight fight. When Gault's eyes moved back to the bar, they met the fat man's by accident and stayed there. The staring match was no contest. The fat man folded in less than a minute and gave Gault the finger to save face. Gault blew the fat man a kiss. The man got off his stool and started up the bar. His friend grabbed his elbow in an attempt to restrain him, but he lurched free, stumbling against the bar as he broke the shorter man's grip. He staggered in Gault's direction, and his friend followed after a moment's hesitation.

'Were you lookin' at me, dog turd?' the fat man demanded when he reached Gault's table.

'Leave it be, Harvey,' the shorter man said.

'He blew a kiss at me, Al,' Harvey said without taking his eyes off Gault. 'You seen that. Fags kiss boys. You a fag skinhead?'

'You're so cute, I'd let you find out,' Gault lisped effeminately.

'I think you'd better split, buddy,' Harvey's friend said, suddenly angry at Gault.

'I thought you had more sense than your friend,' Gault said sharply, pushing his chair back and slowly getting to his feet.

'I don't like a smart-mouth any better than Harv, so why don't you leave while you still can.'

'Can't I finish my drink?' Gault asked in a mocking tone. Harvey stared at Gault for a second, then swept the beer off the table. The glass shattered on the floor and the noise in the bar stopped. Gault felt a rush of adrenaline. His whole body seemed in movement.

'It's finished—' Harvey started, his wind suddenly cut off by the foot that Gault snapped into his groin. Gault's left foot connected with the fat man's temple. Harvey's head snapped to one side and he sat down hard.

Gault pivoted, blocking Al's first wild punch with his forearm. He aimed a side kick at his opponent's kneecap. It was off, striking with only enough force to jostle him off balance. The follow-up left only grazed Al's eye.

The advantage of surprise was lost and Al had good reflexes. He charged into Gault, wrestling him backward into the wall. Gault grunted from the impact, momentarily stunned.

Harvey was on one knee, struggling to get up. Gault brought his forehead down fast. Al's nose cracked. Blood spattered across Gault's shirt. He boosted his knee and felt it make hard contact with Al's groin. There was a gasp and the grip on his arm relaxed. Gault drove a right to the solar plexus and shot his fingers into the man's eyes. Al screamed and sagged. Gault snapped the side of his hand against the man's neck, and he sank to the floor, his face covered with blood.

Glass shattered and Gault set himself as Harvey moved toward him, a broken bottle held tightly in his hand. Gault circled warily, keeping distance between them. Harvey feinted and Gault moved back. He felt the edge of the bar cut into his back. There was a flash of movement behind him and he shifted slightly, but not enough to avoid being hit across the back of the head by the sawed-off pool cue the bartender kept for just such occasions.

THE PHONE WAS ringing. David opened his eyes slowly and struggled to bring his other senses into focus. He became aware of a sour, phlegmy taste

281

in his mouth and a dull ache behind his eyes. The phone rang again and he flinched. It was still dark outside. According to the digital clock, it was two in the morning.

David picked up the receiver to stop the ringing.

'Dave,' a voice at the other end called out.

'Who is this?'

'It's Tom. Tom Gault. I'm in jail, old buddy, and you gotta come down here and bail me out.'

'Who?' David asked. The words had not registered.

'Tom Gault. Bring your checkbook. I'll pay you back when I get home.'

David sat up and tried to concentrate. 'What did you do?'

'I was in a fight. These clowns have charged *me* with assault. I'll explain it all to you once I'm out.'

David didn't want to go to the jail at two in the morning. He didn't have any great urge to see Thomas Gault, either. But he was too tired to refuse Gault's request.

'I'll be down as soon as I can get dressed,' he said, turning on the lamp on his night table.

'I knew I could count on you,' Gault said. After a few more words, they hung up.

David's head was ringing. He'd had too much to drink, but that was becoming routine. He took a deep breath and made his way to the bathroom. The glare from the lightbulbs hurt his eyes, and his image in the mirror caused a different type of pain. His complexion was pale and his flesh doughy. The features were beginning to run together. When he removed his pajamas, he saw the erosion of clear lines on the other parts of his body.

David had not exercised, or done much else that humans do, since Larry Stafford's conviction three months before. The day after the trial he had backpacked into the wilderness to try to sort out the events of the preceding days, but the silence of the shadowy woods had trapped him alone with thoughts he did not want to encounter. He had scurried home.

Jenny had phoned while he was away, but he did not return the calls. He tried to work but could not concentrate. Once, in the solitude of his office, he broke into tears. In the course of representing Larry Stafford, he had betrayed the trust of the court, sold out his principles, and given up on himself. In the ruins of the case he saw the wreckage of his career and the destruction of the carefully constructed fictions concerning truth and justice he had erected to hide from view the emptiness of the profession he had so zealously followed. Life was intolerable. He moved through the days like an automaton, eating little and drinking a great deal.

Gregory Banks had sensed his friend's despair and had ordered him to spend two weeks away. The bright Hawaiian sun and the gaiety of the tourists at the small resort hotel where he had stayed only heightened David's anguish. He tried to take part in conversations but lost interest. His one attempt at an affair had ended with humiliating impotence. Only drinking helped, but the surcease from pain was temporary, and the horrors were twice as vivid once the effects of the alcohol wore off.

David returned to Portland early and without notice. He stayed home, unwashed and unshaven, letting himself become as gross and disgusting physically as he felt he had become spiritually. In the silent ruin of his home, it became clear to David that he was breaking down. He did nothing to stop the process. Instead, he lay about drunkenly, like a spectator at his own funeral.

In the end it was the smell of his body that saved him. One morning he awoke sober enough to whiff the odor of his sheets and the stench from his underarms and crotch. He was overpowered and driven to the shower. A shave and a decent breakfast followed. The crisis had passed, but David was far from well.

Back at the office David appeared to be in control. Except that he was more likely to miss appointments and appear late for court. The effort it took to put up a front was taking its toll in stomach pains and sleepless nights. And there was the frequent lunchtime martini or two. And Monday began to run into Wednesday and feel like Friday, while David, stabilized in a state of functioning disrepair, ceased to see the meaning in anything anymore.

*

'WHAT WERE YOU doing down there, anyway?' David asked. He was driving Gault home from the county jail.

Gault smiled, then winced. He was a mess. Harvey had taken his revenge on the unconscious writer before any of the patrons of The Dutchman had thought to stop him. A cut that had taken several stitches to close ran across the top of his right eyebrow, and his nose and a rib had been broken.

'I was lookin' for a fight, old buddy,' Gault answered in a tired voice.

'What?'

'I like to fight, and bars are as good a place as any to find one.'

'Are you crazy?'

'Sometimes. But life's crazy. Don't you read my books?'

They drove in silence for a while, which Gault appreciated. He was exhausted, but pleased with the night's outing, even if he'd taken a few lumps. As they drove along the empty highway, he thought back over the fight and savored its good moments.

'Do you do this often?' David asked after a while.

'Curious, aren't you?' Gault laughed. 'Yeah, Dave, I do it often, only I usually don't get suckered like I did tonight.

'It's a good feeling when you fight. Even when you get hit. The pain makes you feel alive, and the hitting ... there's nothing like a solid punch. The feeling moves up your arm and through your body like electricity. No, there's nothing like it, except maybe a kill.'

David stared at Gault in disbelief.

'You're serious, aren't you?'

'Completely. I'm too tired and sore to joke, old buddy.'

'You actually enjoy hurting people?'

'It's not the hurting, it's the not knowing how it will turn out. The fear when you start and the satisfaction when you win.'

'But, my God, you could get killed in one of those places.'

'Sure. And that makes it better. There's no Marquis of Queensberry rules in the jungle. You play for keeps. We did that in the bush, old buddy. Played for keeps. So did the niggers. Hand to hand with no referee. It makes you feel alive, because when you're near death or when you end someone else's life, you realize the value of your own and how fragile that gift is.'

David was shaken. He knew from his association with Gault how volatile the writer's personality was. And, of course, he knew about Gault's soldiering. But he had never thought about the writer as a professional killer. He remembered the time when Gault had strung him along about killing his wife. Was this another joke, or had his confession been the truth, after all?

'Life is experience, Dave. Without adventure we die. War makes you alive. Fear makes you alive. You must know that. Why else do you handle murder cases? Come on. Admit it. There's a vicarious thrill being that close to death and the person who caused it. Doesn't a little bit of secret admiration ever worm its way into your heart, old buddy, when you sit next to a man who has had the courage to take another human's life?'

'No, Tom. I've never felt that way,' David said.

'Yeah?' Gault answered skeptically. 'Well, different strokes for different folks. Right, old buddy?'

David didn't answer, and Gault closed his eyes. The darkened countryside swept by in a blur. Neither man spoke again until they arrived at the lake.

A STONE WALL with an iron gate marked the boundaries of Gault's property. A half-mile driveway led from the gate, through the woods, to an isolated hilltop overlooking a small lake. Gault's home, with its wood-gabled roof and porous-stone exterior, was modeled after a French country house. David stopped in front and nudged Gault awake.

'Sorry I fell asleep on you,' Gault said. He sat up and stretched. 'Why don't you come on in and I'll fix you a drink?'

'It's almost four A.M., Tom. I've got to get some sleep.'

'You can sack out here. It'll save you the trip home.'

'Thanks anyway.'

'Actually, there was a little legal matter I wanted to discuss with you.'

'Can't it keep? I'm out on my feet.'

'I'll get you some coffee. Besides, I think you'll be interested in what I have to say.'

The house was dark inside and Gault turned on a few lights. He left David in a small study and went for the coffee. The oak woodwork and floors gave the room a Gothic quality that unsettled David. A grotesque mask, which Gault had collected in Africa, hung from the wall across from him, and a gray stone fireplace sat in the shadows to his rear.

'What's new with Larry Stafford's case?' Gault asked innocently the moment he entered the room. David felt his heart skip.

'I don't know,' David answered. 'Jerry Bloch is handling the appeal.'

'That was a tough break for you,' Gault said as he sat down across from David. 'I thought you had that one, then that pimp testified.'

Gault paused; then a small smile turned up the corners of his lips.

'Just between us boys, Dave, did he do it?'

'I can't talk about that, Tom,' David said, hoping Gault would change the subject. 'That's privileged information.'

'Sure, I forgot. Say, what would happen if someone popped up and confessed? You know, said he

288

did it. Would that guy get off because Stafford's been found guilty?'

'Not if the person who confessed was the killer. They'd let Stafford out and put the real murderer on trial.'

'That makes sense.'

For a moment Gault appeared to be deep in thought. David was very tired and he wanted to get on with Gault's problem. He was about to speak when Gault said, 'I've got one for you, old buddy. What if some guy came to you as a client and told you he did it, but he says he doesn't want you to tell anyone. What happens then?'

'What do you mean?'

'Well, you can't repeat anything a client tells you, right? I mean, there's that privilege, right?'

'I see what you're getting at. I'd have to do some research, but I guess I couldn't tell anyone about the confession.'

A wry smile played on Gault's lips.

'And an innocent man would stay in prison.'

There was a wistfulness in Gault's tone that alarmed David.

'Yes,' he answered uneasily.

'That would put you in a tough position, wouldn't it, old buddy?'

'Look, Tom, I really am tired. What's this legal problem that's so urgent?'

'Don't want to discuss the murder of that police lady, huh?'

'Not really.'

'Don't you want to know who did it?' Gault asked in a voice so low that David wasn't sure he'd heard him correctly.

'Got your interest now, don't I? But, hell, if you're really tired, we can talk some other time.'

David didn't move and he didn't answer. He was suddenly very aware of how isolated Gault's house was. The writer's eyes twinkled, giving a devilish cast to his handsome features.

'You know, I really felt bad when Larry was convicted. I thought for sure you'd get him off. And there's another thing. I don't think it's fair, his getting all the credit when I did all the work. It's sort of like someone getting a Pulitzer for a book I ghosted.'

'Are you telling me that you killed Darlene Hersch?'

'That's right, old buddy. I did it.'

'If this is another joke like that confession to Julie's murder, it's in bad taste.'

Gault's smile widened.

'I killed Julie, too. I want you to know that. And there have been others.'

'Ortiz said the killer had curly blond hair,' David said, trying to keep his voice steady.

'He did.'

Gault stood up and walked over to a desk near the doorway. He pulled a blond wig from the bottom drawer and showed it to David.

290

'I was so damn famous after that trial, I had to disguise myself every time I wanted a little action.

'You know, Dave, there are some girls that like to get laid by the criminal element, but you'd be surprised at the number that are turned off by the prospect of winding up the evening dead. Actually, I don't look half-bad as a blond.'

'Why did you kill Darlene Hersch?'

'I'm a little ashamed about that. The truth is, I panicked. I'd been out at a few bars and couldn't score. Then, what do I behold, but a vision of loveliness standing on the corner.'

Gault shook his head sadly at the memory.

'I had terrific plans for Darlene, but she went ahead and spoiled everything by trying to arrest me.' He shrugged his shoulders. 'Like I said, I panicked. Hit her quick. Then I realized I'd have to finish her. I'd had enough of the law after my murder trial, and I didn't relish another trial for assaulting a police officer.'

'And the others you mentioned?'

A wistful expression replaced Gault's smile.

'You know, you'd think I would have been happiest after I made all that money from the books and the movies, but the years as a mercenary were the best times. I felt alive then.

'Life is dull, Dave, deadly dull. One boring, repetitive act after another, until you die. But a creative person can create experiences. Being rich was an experience. And marrying that bitch movie star. It's something most people only read about, but I made it happen. Only that gets boring, too, so you have to move on.

'All experiences become boring after a while, Dave, except one. Killing never gets boring.'

'Why are you telling me this?' David asked.

'I trust you, Dave. Especially after the way you worked so hard to defend me when, in your heart, you thought I was guilty. I still remember your closing argument. So forceful. So sincere. And all the time you thought I was guilty as sin. A man who can lie like that can be trusted.

'I've wanted to discuss, I guess you'd call it my philosophy, for a long time, but until I learned about this attorney-client privilege, I couldn't take the risk. Now I feel a lot better, knowing that anything I tell you is confidential.'

David couldn't move or speak. He felt wasted. Gault studied him, then burst out laughing. David half expected, hoped, that Gault would say this was all a joke.

'Puts you in a predicament, don't it? Stafford rots in prison because you folded at trial . . .'

David's head jerked up and he started to say something, but Gault raised his hand.

'Hey, old buddy, I'm not being critical. It's just the word goin' around. I do a little reporting, remember. That means interviewing. There are a lot of lawyers who figured that you could have kept Johnson off the stand if you wanted to. But you didn't, did you? And we both know why, don't we?'

Gault winked and David felt his heartbeat quicken. 'What do . . .?'

'It's okay, old buddy. We all have our little secrets. And yours is safe with me. I got a tad suspicious when I ran into you and Stafford's old lady in that cozy dinner spot, so, in the interests of good journalism, I decided to follow you. It turned out to be pretty easy, especially at night.

'Hey, don't get uptight. I'm nonjudgmental. Shit, a guy who's murdered a couple of people can't go around throwing stones at someone for dickin' a married woman, can he?'

'You son of a bitch,' David said hoarsely.

'Hell, I'm worse than that. But there's no reason to take this personally, and as I said, your secret is safe with me, just like I know mine is safe with you.'

'You'd let an innocent man stay in prison for something you did?' David said, immediately feeling ridiculous for asking the question of a man like Gault.

'What choice have I got? To get him out, I'd have to put me in.'

Gault walked back to the desk and replaced the wig.

'Tom,' David said cautiously, 'I think you need help. It's a good sign that you've decided to talk to me and—'

Gault shook his head, amused.

'None of that psychiatric horseshit, please,' he said, wandering out of David's line of vision. 'I'm not crazy, old buddy. I'm a sociopath. Read your textbooks more carefully. See, I know what I'm doing, I just don't give a shit, because I don't have the same moral structure you have.' Gault was directly behind David and the writer's voice was low, soft, and vaguely menacing. 'In fact, Dave, I don't have any moral structure at all.'

Gault stopped speaking. It was completely quiet in the house. David's heart was racing with fear. He wanted to run, but he couldn't move.

'A sociopath operates on a pleasure-pain principle,' Gault continued. 'If you and a sociopath were all alone in a dark house with no one around for miles, a sociopath is the type of person who could kill you, just for kicks, if he thought he could get away with it.'

David heard a click near his ear, and he remembered the jagged slash that seemed to divide Darlene Hersch's neck in two. He dived forward, putting as much distance between himself and Gault as he could. There was a chair across from him and he crashed into it, twisting to face Gault and bringing his hands up to fend off an attack.

Gault watched motionless from the fireplace. He had a switchblade in his hand and he was smiling.

'Not a bad move for a fella who's not in tip-top

shape. Of course, you should never have let me get behind you in the first place.'

David stood up. He was looking around desperately for a weapon.

'I know what you're thinking,' Gault said, 'but a weapon wouldn't do you any good. If I wanted to, I could kill you anyway.'

Gault paused, and David knew it was true. He felt defeated and strangely calm, now that he knew he was going to die.

'But I don't want to kill you, old buddy,' Gault said, his grin back in place. 'Hell, you're my friend and my lawyer. Why, you saved my life, and it would be plumb ungrateful of me to carve you up the way I did Darlene.'

Gault pocketed the knife and David started to shake all over.

'Being egotistical,' Gault continued, 'I have great faith in my ability to judge people, and I made a little bet with myself. Tom, I said, Dave is your pal and an honorable man. If you tell him something in confidence, you can count on Dave's sense of professional ethics and his friendship to keep your secret. You can trust a man like Dave to die rather than reveal a client's confidence. Even if it means that an innocent man has to spend the rest of his life in prison. That's what I said to myself. Now, am I right?'

David wanted to answer Gault, but he couldn't speak.

'Am I right?' Gault asked again, his mouth a grim line and his eyes hard and cold.

'Why are you doing this to me?' David asked.

'Maybe I'm just a modern-day Diogenes, looking for an honest man. Or maybe I just want to see you squirm.'

'You bastard,' David said, his anger momentarily conquering his fear.

'Now, that's the wrong attitude, Dave. Getting angry isn't going to help you out of your predicament. Look at this as if it were a chess problem. White to move and win. Maybe there's a mate, maybe there's only a gain of material, or' – and Gault paused – 'maybe the person who constructed the problem cheated and there's no way white can win.

'Now, why don't you go home and get some sleep? You look worse than I do.'

2

Ortiz sat in the back row of the courtroom listening to Judge McIntyre decide the motion to suppress evidence that had been filed by Cyrus Johnson's attorney. The law was clear, the judge said, that in order to search a person without a search warrant, a police officer had to have probable cause to believe that a search would turn up evidence of a crime, and no time to get a warrant. When Cyrus Johnson was searched, the judge continued, Officer Ortiz did have time to get a warrant, and he did not have probable cause to believe that Johnson would have narcotics on his person. Regretfully, he concluded, he had no choice but to forbid the State to introduce evidence in a trial where the seizure of that evidence violated the mandate of the United States Constitution.

Johnson's attorney smiled and shook his client's hand. Johnson did not return the smile. Instead, he looked toward the back of the courtroom at Ortiz. Ortiz was standing to leave. The narcotics officer had known all along what the result of the hearing would be. He had tailored his testimony to fit the latest Supreme Court opinions, so that the evidence against Johnson would have to be thrown out. He had also contacted the district attorney in charge of the case and told him that he had probably acted too hastily in searching Johnson. In light of Johnson's testimony at Stafford's trial, he and the DA had both agreed that the drug case should not be that vigorously pursued.

'Hey, Ortiz,' a deep voice called. Ortiz turned and saw Kermit Monroe sitting on a bench by the courtroom door.

'What can I do for you, Kermit?' he asked.

'T.V. wants to see you. He asked me to make sure you didn't go nowhere before he had the chance to talk.'

'Tell T.V. some other day. I'm busy.'

'Hey, man,' Kermit said, getting slowly to his feet, 'why you always have to make things difficult? T.V. said this was important and for you to wait. He got some kind of tip for you. So why bust my balls when he wants to do you a favor?'

Ortiz was about to answer when Johnson walked out of the courtroom.

'You want to see me?' Ortiz asked.

Johnson grinned. 'Yeah, I want to see you.'

T.V. shook hands with his lawyer and they parted.

'Let's go down to my car where I know there's no bugs,' Johnson said, still grinning. Ortiz shrugged. Maybe Johnson had decided to turn informant. It wouldn't be the first time a big operator had got scared after some real heat.

They took the elevator downstairs, then walked to the parking structure across from the courthouse. T.V.'s car was parked on the fifth floor, and Monroe slid into the driver's seat while Ortiz and Johnson got into the leather-covered rear seat.

'Now, what's so important?' Ortiz demanded.

'You fucked me up, Ortiz. You planted shit on me, then made me stool to get rid of the rap. You made me sit through that court case and spend a lot of money on a lawyer. And you perjured yourself and broke the law. Why did you do all that shit? One reason, right? To get that poor honky Stafford. To nail his butt to the jailhouse door. Am I right?'

'Go on, T.V. You either have something to say or you don't. I don't have all day.'

'Oh, this won't be no waste of your time, Ortiz. See, I wanted you to know that I lied. That bullshit I testified to was just that – bullshit.'

He stopped to let what he had said sink in. Ortiz looked puzzled.

'Oh, Stafford tried to buy a little action and he hit Mordessa, but it didn't happen the way I said. That white boy wanted some dark meat, but he didn't ask for nothing kinky. When he got up in the room, Mordessa, that dumb cunt, tried to boost his wallet. He caught her and she started wailin' on him.

'Mordessa is one mean bitch and she packs a wallop. Stafford had to hit her a good shot just to keep her off him.'

'What about the story you told the police?'

'Hey, I had to think quick when the pigs arrived. I decided to tell them the dude had done somethin' that would really embarrass him so he wouldn't press charges. I just said the weirdest shit I could think of. But that Stafford ain't no sado-what-you-call-it. Shit, he wouldn't a done nothin' if Mordessa hadn't hit him so hard.

'So you see, my man, the very words which you solicited by illegal means and forced me to say was lies. And you know that jury would have acquitted Stafford if it wasn't for me. But you can't tell nobody that I lied without gettin' yo'self in trouble, can you? Which means you got to live the rest of your life with what you done, while Stafford spends the rest of his life at the state pen.'

Ortiz leaned back in his seat, trying to think. What did it matter if Johnson had lied? Stafford lied, too. He had sworn under oath that he had never gone with a prostitute. Ortiz knew who he had seen in the doorway of that motel room. Larry Stafford killed Darlene Hersch.

'You know somethin', Ortiz. You white boys are real sick. That's what I come to learn, bein' in this business. You plantin' that dope on me, Stafford havin' to buy pussy, and that writer . . .'

Johnson shook his head and Ortiz looked up at the pimp.

'What writer?'

'The one that beat up Mordessa and wanted her to do all that kinky stuff. Shit, he already got away with murder. Mordessa's lucky she ain't the one that got killed.'

'What are you talking about?'

'Mordessa seen him in the papers when he got off. Didn't recognize him at first, 'cause he was wearin' this wig when he beat on her. That's where I got the story from. She was a sight. Said he wanted to tie her up. When she said no, he started kickin' her and hittin' her till she cried. And it takes plenty to make that woman cry. He hurt her bad. Then he kills his wife.'

'Who are you talking about?' Ortiz asked slowly.

'I can't remember the name. His wife was rich, though, and she was beat to death in that mansion by the lake.'

'Thomas Gault?'

'That's the one.'

Ortiz stared at Johnson. 'You mean that story you told on the witness stand did happen, only it was Thomas Gault that beat up your whore?'

'That's what I been sayin'.'

'What kind of wig did he wear?'

'I ain't got no idea.'

Ortiz opened the car door and got out. He felt as if he were drowning.

'Where you goin', Ortiz?' T.V. asked with a laugh. 'You goin' to church or you goin' to tell the law that that Stafford boy is in jail, only he ain't guilty? Only you can't do that, can you, 'cause you'd have to tell on yo'self.'

Ortiz walked away from the car. The motor started, and Monroe drove as close to Ortiz as he could, squealing his tires as he headed down the ramp. Ortiz didn't notice.

Just because Johnson lied, it didn't necessarily follow that Stafford was innocent. But the wig . . . Gault and Stafford had similar builds. With a blond wig . . .

Then Ortiz remembered the mystery man that Gault swore murdered his wife. He had been described as being athletically built, of average height, with curly blond hair. A description that would fit Gault if Gault's hair was curly, blond. And Stafford.

Ortiz remembered something else. Grimes, the night clerk at the Raleigh Motel, testified that the man he saw driving away from the motel had brown hair that was a bit long. Gault had brown hair, which he had worn long at his trial. If he had removed a wig after killing Darlene, that would explain how Grimes could see a man with brown hair, and he, a man with blond.

Could he have been wrong about Stafford? It seemed impossible for two men to have the same build, shirt, pants, and car. Yet Gault and Stafford were built alike and the pants were common enough.

The shirt? While it wasn't the most common type, there had certainly been enough of them in Portland.

And the car? That was simple enough to check on. Too simple. Ortiz felt his gut tighten. He was afraid. Afraid he had made a terrible mistake. If Gault owned a beige Mercedes, then Larry Stafford might very well be innocent.

GREGORY WAS FINISHING some dictation when David entered.

'You're on the bar ethics committee, right?' David asked, sinking into a chair.

'Yes. Why? You haven't done anything unethical lately, have you?' he asked, half joking.

'Let me give you a hypothetical and tell me what you think.'

Gregory turned off his dictation equipment and leaned back. His eyes narrowed with concentration and he cocked his head slightly to one side.

'Assume that a lawyer represents A in a bank-robbery case and A is convicted. Later B hires the lawyer to represent him in an unrelated legal matter. While the lawyer's client, B tells the lawyer, in confidence, that he committed the bank robbery for which A has been convicted, as well as several other robberies. When the lawyer suggests that B confess to the authorities so that A can be released from prison, B refuses. What can the lawyer do to help A?'

Gregory sat thinking for a moment, then took a book from the credenza behind his desk. He rifled the pages until he found what he was looking for.

He read for a few more moments. David sat quietly, staring past Banks through the window toward the foothills. He felt a wave of pain in his stomach and placed his hand over his belt line, gently massaging where it hurt.

'I'd say your lawyer has a problem,' Banks said. 'According to *Wigmore on Evidence* and the Canons of Ethics, a client's confidential communications can be revealed only if the client sues the attorney, in which case the attorney can reveal those confidences that bear on his defense of the client's charges, or if the client tells the attorney that he is planning a future crime, in which case the attorney can make those disclosures necessary to prevent the future crime or protect those against whom it is threatened. If the communication is in confidence and made while the client is seeking legal advice, the confidence is permanently protected.

'I'm afraid that the lawyer can't help A in your hypothetical.'

David sat quietly, thinking. Gregory had confirmed what he had believed all along.

'What if the lawyer decided to violate the Canons of Ethics and breach the confidence?'

'He could be prevented from revealing it in court, and the client could successfully resist being forced to corroborate it. You'd have a tough time convincing the authorities to let A out of prison under those circumstances.'

The pain in David's stomach grew worse. David

took a deep breath and hoped that Gregory would not notice his discomfort.

'Is there anything I can help you with?' Gregory asked.

David desperately wanted his friend's help but knew he could not ask for it. How could he reveal what he had done and still maintain Gregory's respect?

'No, Greg. It was just a hypothetical question.'

Gregory wanted to pursue the matter, but, instead, he asked, 'Shall we go to lunch, then?'

'I'm sorry, Greg, but I'm going home. I don't feel well.'

'Dave, are you sure I can't help you?' Gregory asked. 'If there's anything bothering you . . .'

David shook his head. He smiled weakly. 'No problem. Just an upset stomach.'

He stood up.

'See you in the morning.'

'Yeah,' Banks replied. His brow furrowed, and he did not move for several minutes after David left the office.

'WHY ARE YOU interested in Thomas Gault?' Norman Capers asked.

'I'd rather not say, Norm,' Ortiz answered.

Capers shrugged.

'Hell, what do I care? If it will help put that bastard away, I don't care if I never find out.'

Ortiz was surprised by Capers's reaction. Norm

305

was an experienced, professional prosecutor who had been in the DA's office a long time. He rarely let himself get emotional about a case.

'You don't like his writing style?' Ortiz inquired lightly, hoping to egg Capers on.

'I don't like that bastard, period. I've prosecuted a lot of people, but he . . . I don't know how to put this. Julie Gault . . . Whoever did that really enjoyed his work.'

Capers paused and examined a thumbnail.

'You know, he was cracking jokes all through that trial,' he continued. 'Treated the whole thing like it was a comedy put on for his amusement. Oh, not when the jury was around. Shit, as soon as they filed in, he'd sit up straight and put on this sad look. And on the stand . . . You know, he actually broke down and cried.

'It was all phony. After the jury went out, he turned to me and winked. But he was terrific on the stand and that's all those people saw.'

'You think he's capable of killing someone?'

'Gault? He's some sort of whiz at unarmed combat. Don't you know his background?'

Ortiz shook his head. 'I wasn't involved in the case, so I didn't pay that much attention to it. Just scuttlebutt around the station house and the articles in the papers.'

'Our Tom is a killer, all right. You know he was a mercenary in Africa all those years. There's a screw loose there. A big one. When he was living in Hollywood, he got into some pretty nasty fights, and I hear he's been in a few here.'

'Is he a womanizer?'

'Gault? If it moves, he'll fuck it. And he's mean there, too. We spoke to a couple of ex-girl friends during our investigation. He's beaten up more than one. Very vicious and with a smile, like he was really enjoying himself. That boy is very sick and very clever.'

And, Ortiz thought, Motor Vehicles lists him as the owner of a beige Mercedes.

3

David drove aimlessly for an hour, then went home. He was exhausted, and the pain in his stomach had increased. As soon as he was through the doorway, he poured himself a drink. He knew alcohol would aggravate his stomach, but the pain from self-accusation and self-pity was far worse than physical discomfort.

The first drink helped very little, so he poured another. His conversation with Gregory Banks made him realize how alone he was. He recalled a scene from George Orwell's *1984*. The State had devised a torture. A helmet was fastened over a man's head. The front of the helmet contained a small cage, even with the prisoner's eyes. In the cage was a rat, and separating the rat from the man was a movable partition. The privilege between attorney and client, like that ghastly helmet, locked David in with Gault's secret, where it could gnaw at him, torturing his every waking moment.

Even if there was no privilege, David would be helpless. He had no proof, other than Gault's confession, that Gault had killed Darlene Hersch. If Gault denied that he had confessed, how could

David prove him a liar? David wasn't completely convinced himself that Gault wasn't playing with him. David had learned enough about Gault while he was representing him to know that the man had a very wide streak of sadism in him. David remembered how he had felt during that moment when Gault had stood behind him with the open switchblade. Every moment of his life would be like that if he betrayed Gault's trust.

And there was something else that tortured David. He had always had his pride. Now he had lost his pride, but only he and Jennifer Stafford knew why. If he went to the authorities, Gault would make David's affair with Jenny public. Everyone would think that David had thrown Larry Stafford's case to get Larry out of the way so he could continue as Jenny's lover. He would be disbarred, disgraced, and no one would believe his accusations against Gault.

David finished his drink. He wanted another one, but he didn't have the energy to get it. The lights of the city distracted him from his thoughts for a moment. It had been light when he'd left his office, but it was dark now. He hadn't noticed the transition. He was very tired. The thought of curling up and sleeping on the floor appealed to him. He tried it. The carpet was soft, and there was nothing but dark velvet when he closed his eyes. And Jenny. Her face and form slipped into his thoughts unbidden. He opened his eyes and stared up at the ceiling. Jenny would understand his torment, because she was part of it. If he could talk to Jenny . . . But would she see him?

A wave of self-doubt washed over David and his hand began to tremble. He wanted to stand up, but fear immobilized him. How could he face her? What would she say to him? He had stayed away from Jenny because he felt that she had betrayed him, but now he saw that he was the betrayer. Jenny had lied for Larry out of a sense of loyalty and because she believed he was innocent. There had been no purity in David's motives. He had rationalized his actions in court by telling himself that he did not want to free a killer, but he knew that was not the real reason. He wanted Jenny, and he had betrayed Larry to hurt them because he felt that they had deceived him. Did Jenny despise him? She must know what he had done. It didn't matter. She was the only one he could turn to.

HALFWAY TO THE Stafford house, David almost turned back. He secretly hoped that Jenny would not be home so he would not have to face her, and it was with a mixture of hope and dread that he saw the lights shining in the living room when he pulled into the driveway.

Jenny answered the door after the first ring. She was barefoot and wore a yellow shirt over a pair of faded jeans. The strain of the past months made her seem older, but no less beautiful.

'Can I come in?' David asked hesitantly, almost apologetically.

Jenny was stunned by his appearance. He was heavier, unkempt, and washed-out. There was no sign of the energy that had been such a vital part of him.

'I don't know,' she answered. Her voice trembled. She felt crazy inside, pulled in so many directions she thought she would come apart.

'You have every right . . .' David started. 'Jenny, I have to see you. It's about Larry.'

She drew back a step and studied David's face for clues. The odor of alcohol was strong. He looked destroyed.

'What about Larry?'

'Can I come in?' he repeated.

Jenny paused for a second, then led the way to the living room. David watched her walk. Her back was rigid, her steps precise, as if she were prepared to flee. Her reticence depressed him, but he should have expected it. Once during the ride over he had fantasized a tear-stained reunion, with Jenny throwing herself into his arms. He had been a fool even to think of such a thing. He was grateful she would so much as talk to him.

'What about Larry?' she asked again when they were seated on one of the living-room sofas.

'Jenny, he may be innocent.'

Jenny looked bewildered.

'I have a client, a man I am representing on

311

another matter. He has confessed to killing Darlene Hersch.'

Jenny shook her head as if to clear it. She was off balance. She had always believed that Larry was innocent, but what would this all mean for her?

'I don't understand. Someone else confessed to killing that woman?'

'Yes.'

'Why are you telling me this? Why haven't you gone to the police?'

'It's very complicated. The confession, it was told to me in confidence. It's a privileged communication. By law I can't reveal it to anyone without my client's permission.'

'Will Larry . . .? Does this mean he'll go free?'

'Not unless my client allows me to tell the police.'

'But surely . . . he wouldn't let an innocent man stay in prison.'

'You have to understand. This man . . . it's a game to him. He gets pleasure out of hurting people. He confessed to me because he knows I can't tell the authorities. He told me to torment me. I'm not even certain that he's telling me the truth.'

'Wait a minute. What do you mean it might not be the truth?'

'He did this once before. Confessed to committing a crime. That time he retracted the confession. It could all be a practical joke.'

David saw the confusion on Jenny's face. He

looked away and caught his reflection in the window glass. It startled him. He looked weak and pathetic. The type of person who would be susceptible to the meanest practical joke.

'If this is all some kind of joke, why did you come here? Why are you telling me this?'

'Don't, Jenny. I had to talk to someone. I couldn't keep it inside any longer. And I don't think it is a joke. There's something about this man. I know he's capable of killing.'

'But why me, David? Why did you come to me?'

She was watching him intently, searching with her question for far more than she had asked. David tried to read her eyes. He was afraid to say what was in his heart. Afraid of making a fool of himself. Afraid he had already lost her. But he knew that this was the moment to speak, not evade, and he gathered his courage.

'I came to you because I still love you. I never stopped.'

David paused and Jenny saw that he was crying.

'Jenny, I've been a mess since the trial. I've lost my self-respect, and I've lost interest in everything that ever meant anything to me. But not my love for you. I just couldn't face you.'

David looked away. Jenny felt as if a dam had broken inside her, setting free emotions she had thought she would never feel again. She reached up and touched David's cheek.

'God, Jenny,' he sobbed. She held him tight.

'It's all right,' she whispered, rocking him back and forth.

'I didn't know what to do and I had no one I could go to.'

'You always had me, David. Always.'

'I couldn't come to you. Not after what I did to Larry.'

'You didn't do anything to Larry. Larry and I did something to you. We lied to you and used you.'

David sat up and held her by the shoulders. 'It was wrong. What I did was wrong. We both know that. I should never have represented Larry feeling the way I do about you. Now we have to get him out of prison.'

'I still think you should tell the police,' Jenny said firmly.

David shook his head. 'You don't understand. Since the confession was made in confidence, nothing I reveal could ever be used in court. He could deny he ever made a confession, and there would be nothing we could do.'

'Who is this man? Who killed Darlene Hersch?'

David hesitated. Even now his legal training made him rebel at the thought of violating the code of ethics.

'Thomas Gault,' he said finally.

'Oh, my God. I knew Julie Webster. That was horrible.'

'I know, Jenny. And I'm the man responsible for

314

putting Gault back on the street so he could kill again.'

'There must be something we can do.'

'I've thought about it and thought about it. I can't find any way out. Anything I initiate will . . .'

David paused. The germ of an idea came to him. What if . . .? David started pacing back and forth. Jenny watched him. There was a fire in his eyes that had burned constantly in the old David. It made her feel good to see it again and to think that she may have had something to do with rekindling it.

TERRY CONKLIN SCANNED the diners in the all-night restaurant and spotted David in a booth toward the back. David was sipping from his second cup of coffee when Conklin reached him.

'This better be good,' the investigator said. 'I was sound asleep. Rose is really pissed.'

'I'm sorry.'

Conklin was going to say something else, but one look at David stopped him. He had not seen the lawyer since Stafford's trial, and the change in his friend's appearance was startling. David's face was puffy, his eyes were bloodshot, and his suit was creased and stained.

A waitress appeared and Conklin ordered coffee. As soon as she walked off, David said,

'I want to hire you.'

'I'm pretty busy, Dave.'

'I know, but I'm desperate. I'm willing to pay

twice your regular rate and cover the cost of anyone you hire to take up the slack on your cases.'

'This is that important?'

David nodded.

'Who's the client?'

'Me.'

'What's this about?' Conklin asked cautiously. If David was in some kind of trouble, it would explain his appearance, but Conklin could not imagine David's doing anything illegal or unethical.

'A client of mine told me some information in confidence. I have to know if he was telling me the truth or if he's lying to me.'

'Who's the client?'

'Thomas Gault.'

'I thought that case was over.'

'It is.'

'So this is something new.'

'Yes.'

'What did he tell you?'

'I can't disclose that. I'm afraid anything you find may be tainted if I break the confidence.'

'Tainted? How?'

'If a lawyer reveals an attorney confidence and the police use the information to solve a crime, I believe the courts would prevent the district attorney from using the evidence at trial.'

'So you can't tell me what Gault said?' Conklin asked incredulously.

'That's right.'

316

'How am I supposed to conduct an investigation if I don't know what I'm investigating?'

'I can tell you information that doesn't violate the confidence, and I'll answer any questions I can.'

Conklin started to make a sarcastic remark, but he saw the pain on David's face.

'Okay. I'll play it your way. What can you tell me?'

'I'm upset because Larry Stafford was convicted.'

Conklin's brow furrowed. 'This is about the Stafford case?'

'I can't answer that.'

'So Gault told you something about the Stafford case and you think he might be lying.'

David did not respond.

'I feel like I'm playing twenty questions.'

'Don't stop. I feel as ridiculous as you do, but this is too important to screw up. I want you to be able to pass a polygraph test if a defense lawyer asks if I broke Gault's confidence with you. Now, think about what you know.'

'You told me that you're upset because Stafford was convicted, you want to know if Gault lied to you about something that probably concerns the Stafford case. I don't get . . .'

Conklin paused. He studied David. In all the time he'd known Nash, he had never seen him looking like this. It would take something monumental to destroy his friend's self-confidence. Conklin leaned forward and stared directly into David's eyes.

317

'Gault told you he killed Darlene Hersch, and you want me to find out if he lied,' Conklin said. David did not move. Conklin slumped against the back of the booth.

'Have your secretary send me a retainer agreement setting out the terms of your employment,' David said.

4

Terry Conklin's investigation started in the public library. There were numerous articles about Thomas Gault, because he was a famous writer. After Gault won the Pulitzer, *The New York Times Magazine* featured a cover story that gave a detailed account of his service as a mercenary in South Africa, Liberia, and several other African nations and included interviews with soldiers of fortune who had served with him. If Gault killed his wife, it would not have been the first time he had done in someone with his bare hands.

After the library Terry went to police headquarters, where he obtained copies of police reports of incidents involving Gault. Conklin expected the domestic-violence complaints filed by Julie Webster Gault, but he was surprised by several reports of assaults committed by Gault in bars, including a recent account of a fight at a dockside bar called The Dutchman. Terry noted with interest that the incident had occurred only days before his meeting with David. He also noted that the person who posted bail for Gault was none other than his new client, David Nash.

Conklin interviewed the bartender and another witness, who recounted Gault's fighting skills and the impersonal way he had provoked the fight. Conklin ran down an ex-girl friend who was still afraid of Gault, even though she had not seen him in over two years. Two other women refused to talk to Terry.

Conklin was initially troubled by Detective Ortiz's description of Hersch's killer as having curly blond hair, but he remembered that Merton Grimes's description of the killer's hair would fit the way Gault had worn his hair when he was tried for Julie Gault's murder. If Gault used a wig to disguise himself because of all the publicity his trial engendered, it would explain the differences in the descriptions of Hersch's killer. Conklin also learned that Gault owned a beige Mercedes.

At the end of a week Terry Conklin was convinced that Thomas Gault could easily have killed Darlene Hersch, but he had absolutely no proof Gault even knew who the dead policewoman was. Conklin was reduced to following Gault in the hopes that his quarry would lead him to a witness or evidence that would help him solve David's dilemma.

Each morning Conklin parked his car on a side road near Gault's property and climbed a small hill, where he watched the house from a copse of trees. Conklin rarely observed any activity before ten, when Gault would leave the house for an hour-long run. Gault always looked as if he had broken a sweat before the run, and Conklin guessed the writer performed some kind of physical exercise before leaving the house.

Three times a week Gault worked out at a local dojo, where he received private lessons from the owner, a former instructor of unarmed combat for the South Korean Army. On the days he did not go to the dojo, Gault did not leave his house before midafternoon.

If Gault's activities during the daytime were dull, his nights were anything but. Gault spent almost every evening in a bar or nightclub. On one occasion Gault returned home with a woman, who left by cab shortly before Gault's run. Toward the beginning of the second week, Gault's evening routine changed. Instead of going directly home from the bar or nightclub, Gault drove to Portland's industrial area. He always parked near a deserted warehouse that backed on the Columbia River. The warehouse had 'Wexler Electronics' written on the side in peeling red paint. Conklin checked the corporate records. The company had gone under a year ago, and the property was tied up in litigation.

The first time Gault drove to the warehouse, Conklin waited in his car. A high chain-link fence separated the warehouse from a strip of sandy land that sloped down to the river. Conklin watched Gault take a large rug and a flashlight from the trunk of his car and disappear around the side of the warehouse that abutted the fence. Half an hour later Gault reappeared. He seemed winded. Conklin saw him wipe his forehead with his shirtsleeve, then drop the flashlight into his trunk and drive off.

The second night Gault took the flashlight and a large toolbox from the car, returning an hour later with both items.

On the third night Conklin did not follow Gault when he left the warehouse. As soon as Gault's car was out of sight, Conklin took a flashlight out of his glove compartment and walked to the fence. The wind from the river chilled him. He hunched against it and played the light beam over the ground, then along the warehouse wall. Nothing.

Conklin heard a sharp tapping in front of him. He raised the beam. A door was snapping against the side of the building. Conklin approached it cautiously. He looked around, then entered the warehouse. The high roof shut out the moon and stars, leaving the flashlight beam as the only source of light. Conklin was overcome by a sense of dread. He felt enveloped by the darkness, as if he were fathoms deep in the ocean at the point where light is completely absorbed by the water.

The flashlight showed Conklin rusted girders, an abandoned wooden pallet on which an open and empty packing crate rested, and random stacks of two-by-fours covered by cobwebs and dust. He took a few steps forward and picked out a section of the floor that was covered by the rug Gault had taken from the car on the first evening. Conklin walked over to the rug. It was cheap and dull green. He shone the light around the area and saw nothing else that would help explain why Gault had left it in the warehouse or why Gault had returned to this place on three successive evenings.

'I hope you like the rug.'

Conklin jumped and almost dropped the light.

'I bought it for you.'

Conklin turned in a circle, but there was no one there.

'Before I give you your gift, you will have to answer some questions, Mr. Conklin.'

'Gault?'

'Who else have you been following for the past two weeks?'

'We can talk. Why don't we go outside?' Conklin said, turning slowly so as to face the place where Gault's voice had been.

'No, thank you. Here will be just fine. Sound won't carry as far. Lowers the risk of someone hearing you scream.'

5

'Mr. Nash,' David's secretary said, 'it's Mr. Gault again.'

David felt a flush of fear, then anger.

'Tell him I'm in conference.'

'He says he'll come down and cause a scene if you try to put him off.'

'Jesus.' David looked out the window. 'Okay. Put him through.'

'Hey, old buddy,' Gault said as soon as David picked up the phone, 'I need your help.'

'Look, Tom, let me make this clear. I don't want anything to do with you. Not now. Not ever.'

'Hey, no need to be so hostile.'

'Listen . . .'

'No, you listen,' Gault said. There was an unmistakable edge to his voice. 'If you hang up this phone, I might have to call the *Oregonian* with an interesting item about Mrs. Stafford. You remember her, don't you?'

David sucked in a breath. 'All right. What do you want?'

'Just some advice. What say we meet for lunch? My treat.'

GAULT HAD CHOSEN a small French restaurant in north-west Portland. The lunch crowd was made up of a round table of older women, several businessmen on expense accounts, and a few young lovers. The maître d' showed David to Gault's table, and the writer greeted him with a relaxed smile.

'Some Reisling?' Gault suggested, taking a tall bottle of wine from the ice bucket at the side of the table.

'Let's just cut to the chase, Tom. I'm tired of games.'

'Oh? That wasn't my impression. Nonetheless, I agree. Let's get down to business. I'm working on a new book and I'm stuck for an ending. I hoped you could help me out. The book is about a writer. Someone like me, actually. Now, this writer is minding his own business when he gets the funny feeling that he's being followed. Sure enough, he is.

'At first the writer thinks it's just some literary groupie, but the fellow never approaches him. The writer begins to get nervous, so he lays a little trap.'

Gault paused to watch David's reaction.

'It must be a pretty good plot,' Gault said. 'I see I've got you on the edge of your seat already. Now, where was I? Oh, yes. The trap. The writer has heard that old saw "Curiosity killed the cat" and sets out to pique his tail's curiosity. Each evening he goes to an out-of-the-way, deserted location and does something mysterious, hoping that the mystery man will follow him inside, where it is nice and quiet and the writer can ask a few questions without having to worry about being disturbed.

'After three nights our little pussy takes the bait. Guess what happens next?'

David sat in stunned silence.

'No guesses? Well, you see, the writer loves his privacy and he certainly doesn't appreciate anyone violating it. Do you know what my character does to this intruder?'

Gault smiled. The blood had drained from David's face.

'In my story the writer tortures this fellow, who answers every question he is asked. It's quite a violent scene. Blood spraying all over, bones cracking. I may have to tone it down before submitting it to my editor. She has a weak stomach, and I don't know if she'll be able to take this much graphic violence.

'Anyway, the writer has just had some trouble with the law, so he has to keep this little incident hush-hush. All this torture has taken place on a large rug that does an admirable job of absorbing the blood. The writer rolls up the dead man in the rug, cleans up the mess, and gets rid of the body, leaving no clues for a sleuth to find. But that's where I'm stuck. What happens next? For the life of me, I can't figure it out.

'My character knows the identity of the dastardly coward who hired the victim. I guess the writer could confront him. But I don't know . . . That seems like such a cliché, and the critics have been so lavish in praising my originality.' Gault shrugged. 'I'll admit I'm stumped. That's why I called. You have a fertile imagination. I hoped you could help me.'

David stood up so quickly, he knocked over his chair. Gault watched, greatly amused. The sound of the chair crashing to the floor brought on a sudden hush in the restaurant. The diners turned toward David as he staggered away. Gault threw his head back, and his laughter followed David out onto the street.

6

Monica Powers was getting ready for bed when the doorbell rang. She put a bathrobe on over her nightgown and went to the door. David had never been to her apartment and she was surprised to see him. She was more surprised by his appearance. Since the Stafford trial she had heard disturbing rumors about David, and his disheveled clothes, bloodshot eyes, and uncombed hair seemed to bear them out.

'I need your help, Monica,' David said. His shoulders were hunched, and he could not look directly at her when he spoke. Monica stood aside and let David into the apartment.

'You look awful. What's going on?'

David wandered into the living room and slumped down onto the couch. Monica sat opposite the couch on a straight-back chair. Suddenly David's shoulders shook and he began to cry. He hid his face in his hands. Monica rushed to the couch.

'I didn't know where else to go,' David sobbed.

Monica held him tight and rocked him. David clung to her. After a few minutes she could feel him relax and she let go. David ran his coat sleeve across his eyes.

'I'm sorry,' he managed.

'What's wrong? Talk to me.'

David rested his head against the back of the couch and closed his eyes.

'It's Terry Conklin. He's dead and I'm responsible.'

'What?!'

'Thomas Gault tortured him and buried the body.'

'I don't understand . . .'

David sat up and leaned forward. He looked straight down, his head bowed.

'Gault told me something in confidence. I couldn't go to the police. What Gault said was protected by the attorney-client privilege. Gault is a sadist. He'd confessed to killing someone before to unnerve me. Then he told me it was a joke. He had me so confused. When he . . . when he told me this new information . . . I believed him, but he's such a convincing liar . . .'

David paused. His lips were dry and his throat was raw from crying.

'I . . . I thought I'd be clever, so I hired Terry to check out Gault's story. Then, yesterday, I met with Gault. He told me he tortured Terry to death and disposed of the body.'

'He confessed to murder?' Monica asked, as if she were not certain she had heard David correctly.

'Not directly.'

David recounted his lunch conversation with Gault.

329

'How do you know Gault isn't playing another sadistic game with you?' Monica asked when he was done.

'Terry is missing. I called his wife as soon as I got back to my office. Rose doesn't know where he is. He always comes home or checks in with her. She hasn't heard from him since the day before yesterday.'

'What did Gault say that prompted you to hire Terry Conklin?' Monica asked.

David hesitated. Then he said,

'He told me he murdered Darlene Hersch.'

'Larry Stafford killed Darlene Hersch.'

'Gault has a build similar to Larry Stafford's, he drives a beige Mercedes, and he showed me the curly blond wig he wore when he murdered Darlene Hersch. He also confessed to other killings, including Julie Gault's.

'Remember Grimes's testimony about the killer having brown hair? Gault has brown hair. If Gault wore a curly blond wig, then took it off in his car, Ortiz would have seen a man with curly blond hair and Grimes would have seen a man with brown hair.'

'Ortiz is still certain he saw Stafford.'

'You know what the lighting conditions were like that night. You saw Terry Conklin's pictures.'

'Very skillfully taken pictures, I must admit,' Monica said sarcastically.

'No, Monica, those pictures weren't doctored. I had other professional photographers duplicate Terry's work. They weren't phonies.'

'I know,' Monica said with a sigh. 'I sent a police photographer to the motel, and he got similar results.'

David spent the next half hour going over his relationship with Gault from their first contact to the meeting at the restaurant. He omitted only reference to Jenny and their affair. He knew it would be better to tell Monica everything, but he couldn't bring himself to reveal their relationship.

'I don't know,' Monica said when he was finished. 'Gault obviously has mental problems or else he wouldn't be playing this kind of game with you, whether the confession is true or false. But he did retract his first confession, and as you pointed out, there isn't a shred of evidence that connects him to the murder of Darlene Hersch. As for Terry Conklin, we don't even have a body.'

'He did it, Monica. If you'd been there and heard him . . .'

'I wasn't, though.'

'Does that mean you won't do anything?'

'No, David. You wouldn't have come to see me if you didn't think Gault murdered Darlene Hersch and Terry Conklin.'

Monica paused. She seemed uncertain whether to continue with what she was going to say.

'David,' she asked hesitantly, 'what happened

to you during Stafford's trial? You seemed to fold up and die when I put Johnson on. You must know that you had a good chance to keep him from testifying.'

David looked at the tabletop to avoid looking at Monica.

'I won't discuss the Stafford trial. You'll have to respect my wishes.'

Monica wanted to pursue the matter, but she sensed David's pain. She had too much respect for him to go any further.

'I think I should bring Bert Ortiz in on this,' she said. 'He's the one you have to convince. If he doesn't change his mind, you have no case.'

'You're right,' David agreed. 'Can he be trusted to keep this quiet?'

'I think so.'

'Then call him.'

'DAVID GAVE ME some very unsettling information about the Darlene Hersch murder tonight. I want you to hear it, but you have to agree to keep this meeting confidential.'

Ortiz was confused. When Monica had called, she had told him she wanted to discuss the Stafford case, but she had refused to be more specific. His first thought was that she had found out about his arrangement with T.V. Johnson, and he had given a great deal of thought to what he would say if Monica accused him of setting up the pimp. Then, when he'd arrived, he was surprised to see David.

'I'll keep what he says secret,' Ortiz agreed. He sat in an armchair opposite David, and Monica sat beside David on the couch.

Ortiz listened as David repeated what he had told Monica.

'What do you think?' Monica asked when David finished.

'I don't know,' Ortiz answered cautiously. He couldn't believe his luck, but he did not want to appear overexcited. 'This is all so sudden. I'm pretty positive about Stafford, but . . . What do you think, Monica?'

'I don't know either, Bert. But I think you should look into the possibility that we were mistaken.'

'How do we know this isn't another one of Gault's pranks? After all, you're the guy who says he's unbalanced,' Ortiz asked.

David shook his head. 'It could be, but I think we have to operate on the assumption that it isn't.'

'Okay. That leaves us with the problem of proving Gault killed Darlene and Conklin. How do we do that?'

David shook his head. 'I don't know. I've been trying to figure out the answer to that question all day.'

'We can try to establish where he was the night Darlene died,' Monica said. She turned toward David.

'Didn't he tell you he tried to get some action at a few bars earlier in the evening?'

'He did,' David answered. 'We could circulate a picture and see if anyone recognizes him.'

'That was months ago,' Ortiz said. 'No one is going to remember Gault after all this time, especially if he was in disguise. And we don't even know what bars he went to. It could be any bar in Portland.'

'You're right,' Monica agreed.

'What about the wig?' Ortiz asked David suddenly. 'You said he showed you the wig. That means he kept it all this time, even though it could tie him into the murder.'

'That's right,' David said. 'He probably still has it.'

'Monica, let's write out an affidavit for a warrant to search Gault's house,' Ortiz said, excited by the prospect.

'We can't, Bert. That wig was shown to David as part of a confidential communication. He's the only one who's seen it, and he can't violate the confidence.'

'Shit.'

Ortiz stood up and began pacing.

'How about putting a tap on his phone or wiring David, then putting the two in contact?' he suggested.

'We have the same problem. It would be an invasion of the attorney-client privilege,' David said. 'Besides, I doubt that Gault will discuss this over the phone. He's too smart. He'd suspect something was up.'

The three were silent for several minutes. Finally, Monica said, 'Look, I have a trial tomorrow, and I have to get some sleep. Why don't we think about the problem and get back in touch after five?'

'I agree,' David said. 'I'm exhausted. We might get some ideas after a night's sleep. I'll call in the late afternoon, Monica, and we can arrange a place to meet.'

'How DOES IT feel to be working for the good guys?' Ortiz asked when they were alone in the elevator.

David blushed. He hadn't quite thought of it in those terms, but there was a good feeling in trying to keep someone from hurting others, instead of trying to make a shambles of conscientious police work.

'I never felt I was working for the bad guys,' David answered defensively.

'Yeah, well,' Ortiz answered with a grin.

As it turned out, Stafford had been a 'good guy,' David thought. Gregory had been right, after all. You couldn't have one system of justice for the guilty and one for the innocent. If David had defended Stafford instead of judging him, Stafford might be free now.

ORTIZ WAS THINKING about Thomas Gault as he walked to his car. How could they trap him? There had to be a way. He heard David's car door open and shut. His car was nearby in the apartment parking lot. He unlocked the door and sat behind the wheel.

David drove by and Ortiz lit up a cigarette. He felt sorry for Nash. The guy looked awful. He wondered how he would feel carrying around the burden of Gault's confession and not being able to do anything about it. Then he realized that that was exactly what he was doing.

Ortiz started his car. He was bushed. He'd sleep tonight. No alarms, either. He glanced out the window at nothing in particular as he neared the exit to the street. David's car was half a block away, headed east. Across the street, to the west, a car turned on its lights and attracted Ortiz's attention. His heart stopped. He slowed and pulled into an empty parking space after shutting off his lights. The car across the street pulled into traffic, keeping some distance behind David's car. Ortiz backed out of the space and started to follow. The car was a beige Mercedes.

7

David noticed the headlights in his rearview mirror as soon as he turned off the highway, but he was too lost in thought to pay any attention to them until he saw them follow him up Jennifer's driveway. He parked and stared back at the car behind him, trying to see who was driving. The glare of the headlights made him shade his eyes. Then the car stopped, and he saw that it was Gault's Mercedes.

'What are you doing here?' he demanded when Gault got out of the car.

'Hi, Dave,' Gault replied cheerfully. He had a gun in his hand. 'Why don't you shut up and ring the doorbell? It looks like your lady friend is waiting up for you.'

'What is this?' David asked, frightened by the contrast between Gault's nonchalance and the gun he was holding.

'The denouement, old buddy,' Gault replied. 'Now, do as I say and ring for your honey.'

As soon as the door opened, Gault pushed David into the entranceway.

'Good evening, Mrs. Stafford,' Gault said, shutting the door behind him.

'What's going on, David?' Jenny asked, looking from the gun in Gault's hand to her lover.

'I don't know what he wants, Jenny,' David answered.

David moved beside Jenny and took her hand. Gault looked around the entrance hall and into the living room.

'I'm going to ask you some questions, sweets,' Gault told Jenny, 'and I want straight answers. If I don't get them, I'm going to shoot your kneecap off, and, believe me, that is the most painful injury you can imagine. Do you understand me?'

'Yes,' Jenny answered, her voice trembling.

'Is there anyone else in this house?'

'No,' Jenny answered quickly.

'Good. Now here's question number two: are you expecting anyone besides David to visit tonight?'

'No.'

Gault smiled. 'That makes it cozy, then, doesn't it? Just our little ménage à trois and no one to disturb us. Why don't we step into the living room,' Gault said, motioning with the gun. He followed David and Jenny.

David knew he had to stall for time. Gault was crazy, and if he didn't keep him talking, the writer might shoot them where they stood.

'If this is another practical joke,' he said, trying to sound calm, 'why don't you drop it? You're scaring the hell out of Jenny – and me, too.'

'Not trying to humor me, are you, old buddy?

338

Fess up, now. You know this isn't a joke, don't ya?'

David didn't answer and Gault shook his head sadly from side to side.

'You let me down, Dave. You really destroyed my faith in human nature.'

'What do you mean?'

'You broke your oath, didn't you?' Gault teased. 'Went yappity-yapping to your ex about our little secret.'

David's stomach turned over.

'Nothing to say to me? No denials?'

David's throat was dry and his voice caught when he tried to speak. Gault watched him, amused. He seemed to have all the time in the world.

'Want to know something, old buddy?' Gault said. 'I'm not mad at you. You're still my pal. See, I counted on your going to the police.'

David was confused.

'You thought I'd tell them you killed Darlene Hersch and Conklin?'

'It was a sure thing. Hell, Dave, you're a bowl of mush. You're drunk half the time and not worth a shit as a lawyer anymore. I knew you'd never stand up under the kind of pressure I put on you.'

'I don't understand,' David said. 'If you hadn't told me, no one would ever have guessed you killed either one. You'd have been perfectly safe.'

'I don't want to be safe, old buddy. You know, I lied to you a little, the other day, when I said that killing never gets boring. Even that loses its edge after a while, if there's no variety. Think of how interesting it will be for me to outwit the police when they investigate your and Mrs. Stafford's murders.'

Jenny's eyes widened and she gripped David's hand tightly.

'Yeah, Mrs. Stafford, I'm sorry about that, but it's got to be. See, the cops and the DA will know I killed Julie, because Dave told Ms. Powers I confessed, right?'

Neither Jennifer nor David answered, and Gault went on.

'But they can't do anything about that, because I can't be retried once I've been acquitted. Score one for the bad guys.

'Now they know I killed Darlene Hersch and the investigator, but there's no way they can prove it. I destroyed all the evidence, including the wig and the knife, and who would believe Ortiz if he said I killed Hersch, after he was so positive about his identification of Stafford?

'Then, there's my confession to you. Only you'll be dead. So the cops will only have one case left. Monica Powers will know I killed you, because I have the motive: my confession to you. I'll be the number-one suspect. The only problem is, they'll never be able to tell a jury about my confessions, right?'

'Why won't they?' Jenny asked David.

'You tell her, counselor,' Gault said with a satisfied smile.

'Gault can object to Monica's telling the jury about anything he told me in confidence as a client,' David said.

'And don't forget hearsay, old buddy. A witness can't tell the jury what someone told her outside of court, right? See, I've been doing a little legal research on the side. Say, do you think I should go to law school? After you're gone, someone will have to take over the criminal practice in this town.'

'You think you're so smart,' Jenny said. 'You'll slip up. They'll get you.'

Gault shrugged. 'It's possible. Hell, I'm not perfect. But what's a game without a little risk? Now, why don't you two shut up, so I can decide how I want you to die.'

ORTIZ SUSPECTED WHERE David was headed when the lawyer turned off the highway. If he stayed too close on the deserted country road, Gault might spot him. If he guessed wrong, and David was not headed for the Stafford house, he was sure to lose both of them. He decided to take a chance and hang back.

The gamble paid off. Ortiz parked his car some distance from the entrance to the Staffords' driveway and moved onto the grounds through a gap in the hedges. He crouched down. From his position in the shadows, he could see David and Thomas Gault talking in front of Gault's car. Gault's back was toward him, and he did not see the gun until Gault moved aside, pressing himself against the wall to the left of the front door.

The front door opened and Gault shoved David forward. The door closed. Ortiz waited for a count of ten; then, still keeping to the shadows, he ran to a position to the right of the front door. He knew, from the day they had searched the house, that the living room was to the left of the door as you entered. There was a light on in that room, but the curtains were drawn. The room to the right – the dining room – was dark.

Ortiz remembered that there was also a side window in the living room. He ran quietly to it and peered into the room. Gault was herding David and Jennifer Stafford toward him. He ducked down quickly and moved away from the window. Gault still had his gun out. Ortiz had to figure out how to disarm him without endangering the two prisoners. Coming in the front door was out. It was probably locked, but even if it wasn't, the door's movement would be visible from the living room. Ortiz would have no way of knowing where Gault was when he made his move.

What other way was there to get into the house? Ortiz raced around back. The rear door was locked, and he couldn't see any other entrance at the back of the house. He glanced upward. The balcony to Larry Stafford's room hung over him. Ortiz remembered noticing, when he had searched the room, that it had sliding glass doors.

He looked around for something to stand on, to boost himself up. There was a garbage can outside the kitchen door. He took the top off quietly, setting it down on the grass. The can was half-full. He carried it to the balcony and turned it over slowly. An empty bottle rattled against the aluminum side, and Ortiz swore under his breath. He froze, pressing against the side of the house. After a short period he moved over to the can and stepped on top of it. The ground was muddy and the can swayed under his weight. For a second Ortiz thought he was going to fall, but he maintained his balance and the can stayed upright. Now the trick was to catch hold of the bottom of the balcony and pull himself up without overturning the can. He put his gun in his waistband and extended his arms upward, slowly. He grasped the metal railing that ringed the balcony. He pulled himself up, chinning the way he'd done as a boy in gym class. The can stayed still, but Ortiz had not chinned himself in a while. His arms began to shake and his wrists hurt. He clenched his teeth and strained upward, dragging his body up high enough so he could swing his left foot over the bottom of the balcony. The rest was easy. He was soon standing outside the darkened bedroom.

Ortiz tried the glass door. It was unlocked. He slid it open and moved quickly to the bedroom door. He crouched low and to the left side and eased the door open. There was no one in the hall, and he could hear muffled voices coming from downstairs.

The hallway and stairs were carpeted, and Ortiz made no sound as he began his descent. The top part of the staircase could not be seen from the living room, but the bottom half was even with the entrance to that room. Halfway down, Ortiz could see a section of the room. The voices were coming from the part he couldn't see. A woman was pleading and a man was talking in a low, soft voice. The woman had to be Jennifer Stafford, and Ortiz prayed that she would hold Gault's attention long enough for him to make his move.

Ortiz crept down a few more stairs. As soon as he saw any part of a person, he would vault the banister and hope he could pick out Gault before Gault could get a bead on him.

He moved down to the next stair. He could see a third of the living room. There were a long couch and a coffee table and the front window in his line of vision. With the curtains closed, there was no reflection to show him the positions of the people in the room.

One more step. This time he could see half of a mantelpiece and part of a modern painting. There was movement, and a man's back blocked out part of the mantel. Ortiz vaulted the banister, landing and aiming at the same time. Nash had worn a suitcoat and white shirt. He was aiming at a black pullover.

David saw Ortiz just before he moved. He and Jenny were standing behind a second sofa that faced the front of the house. Ortiz yelled, 'Freeze!' Gault turned his head for an instant. David crashed sideways, throwing Jenny to the floor behind the sofa. Gault realized he had lost his hostages. He kept himself outwardly rigid, but inwardly loose and ready to move. Ortiz moved forward slowly in a shooting crouch, his gun held straight out in front of him.

'Raise your hands very slowly and drop the gun,' Ortiz commanded.

Gault knew he had only one chance. He could see Ortiz moving in behind him in the reflection from the window at the side of the house. If he tried to turn and fire, he would be dead. He waited until Ortiz took another step and raised his hands, still holding the gun.

'Drop it, Gault,' Ortiz ordered, his eyes fixed on the gun hand as it rose upward.

Gault had counted on that. He raised his left knee waist high and snapped the heel of his left foot backward into Ortiz's solar plexus. Ortiz felt as if he had been hit by a hammer. All the air rushed out of him. He fell.

Gault retracted the leg, turned, and fired in one motion. Ortiz was sitting when the bullet smashed into his brain, but his finger squeezed the trigger of his gun before Gault's bullet connected. Ortiz's bullet shattered Gault's right shoulder. Gault's arm jerked upward, the gun flew backward over the sofa, and Gault crashed to the floor.

David watched the gun sail through the air. He was too stunned to move. Even as he was hit, Gault called on his reserves. He was conditioned for moments such as these. He knew he had to get the gun. But he couldn't move. When he tried to pull himself up, his body wouldn't respond. He toppled sideways and clawed the sofa for support.

David looked at Jennifer. She was screaming. He saw Gault's hand grip the carpet. Gault was trying to drag himself to the gun. David scrambled over Jenny. He felt a hand close on his leg and he dived outward, stretching toward the weapon. His hand closed on it, and tremendous pain flashed through his leg where Gault had struck it with a karate blow. David gasped and rolled to his back. Gault was kneeling, one knee and one arm supporting his body. Gault's right side was covered with blood. He was looking at David, but his face was expressionless. David was in agony. He pointed the gun.

'Get back,' David said, but there was no confidence in his voice. Gault lurched toward him and David swung the gun wildly. The barrel smashed into Gault's eye and he crashed to the floor, landing on his damaged shoulder and rolling to his back. David lay where he was, shaking.

THE NEXT FEW minutes were a blur for David. Somehow he got to the couch. He remembered Jenny holding him there and shaking as badly as he was. He remembered thinking how surprisingly untouched the living-room furniture seemed: a ridiculous thought under the circumstances. And he remembered fighting to keep from vomiting as the events of the preceding minutes came back into focus. Gault moaned and Jenny's head jerked toward him. The writer's eyes opened. Neither David nor Jenny moved. Suddenly, Gault smiled.

'Looks like you got me, old buddy,' Gault started. Then his face contorted in pain.

'Whew,' he said when the pain passed. 'That was pretty bad. You callin' an ambulance?'

'Why should I?' David asked.

'You wouldn't let a client bleed to death on your girlfriend's rug, would you?'

'You were going to kill us,' David said.

'Sure, but I'm crazy, not a man of the law like yourself.'

'You're not crazy, Gault, just bored. Remember? You said so yourself.'

'Shit, Dave, you can't believe what a crazy man says. And I am crazy. Make no mistake. My new lawyer will prove it beyond a reasonable doubt,' Gault said with a smirk. 'Unless, of course, you want the case. Say, wouldn't that be a twist? We'd really make headlines with that one. "Lawyer Defends Man Who Tried To Kill Him."'

Gault started to laugh, then winced with pain. The laugh turned into a cough. Jenny stood up and started to walk across the room toward the phone.

347

'Where are you going?' David asked.

'To call the police,' she said.

'I don't think we should call them just yet,' David said softly. He was sitting on the edge of the couch, his eyes on Gault.

'But . . .' Jenny started.

'He's right,' David said. 'Gault will hire the best lawyers and a raft of psychiatrists, and the jury will find him not guilty by reason of insanity. He'll spend a few years in a mental hospital, then have a remarkable recovery. Won't you, Tom?'

Gault just smiled.

'And Larry will still be in prison, won't he?'

Gault's smile broadened. David picked up the gun he had laid on the couch.

'David, don't,' Jenny said, suddenly realizing what David intended to do.

'Don't worry, sweets,' Gault said. 'Dave doesn't have the guts. He couldn't shoot me before and he won't do it now.'

David raised the gun.

'Please, David,' Jenny begged. 'He's playing with you. Making you follow his rules. Making you fit into his idea of what people are.'

David looked at Jenny. His hand was trembling and he looked desperate.

'That's why I have to kill him, Jenny. I know what I'll be if I do, but I lose either way. Gault's different from other people. I could never win against him,

348

but I can stop him from destroying other people, the way he's destroyed me.'

'Well, well,' Gault said in a mocking tone. 'You can feel it, Dave, can't you?'

'Feel what?' David answered, less sure of himself.

'The power. Like God's. You can see I was right, can't you?'

'I'm not like you,' David said, his voice wavering.

'But you will be, as soon as you pull the trigger.'

'He's right, David,' Jenny pleaded. 'Please don't kill him.'

'Do you want me to pray to you first, old buddy? You might find that satisfying.'

'Don't you see what he's like, Jenny?' David said, his voice filled with loathing for the thing on the floor.

'David is my shepherd,' Gault chanted, 'I shall not want.'

'Shut up.'

'Even though I walk in the valley of the shadow of death . . .'

'Shut up,' David screamed, pointing the gun.

'. . . I shall fear no evil . . .'

David looked over toward Jenny. She was wide-eyed, staring at Gault with complete revulsion, as if she were really seeing him for the first time.

'. . . for David is with me.'

349

The gun exploded. There was no sign of remorse or fear on Gault's face when David pulled the trigger. Only contempt. That was when David knew he had done the right thing.

8

David stacked the last of his framed diplomas in the cardboard carton at his feet and sealed the top with masking tape. He stood up and looked around the office. The walls were bare. The desk drawers had been cleaned out. It had ceased to be David Nash's office.

'Got everything packed away?' Gregory Banks asked from the doorway. David hadn't heard him come in. He had been thinking about the office.

'Yeah. It's all taken care of. There wasn't much, anyway. These diplomas,' he said, indicating the box, 'some personal stuff from the desk.'

David shrugged.

'Yeah, well,' Gregory said. They stood in the room without speaking for a moment.

'Damn, I'm gonna miss you, Dave,' Gregory said finally, his voice catching. David was embarrassed by Gregory's unusual emotional display.

'Hey,' he said, 'I'm just going on a vacation. I'll be back. Maybe not as a lawyer, but I'm not leaving town forever.'

Larry Stafford was out of prison, and Jenny had reinstituted the divorce proceedings. David and Jenny

351

were going to disappear for a while. David wanted to catch up on all the things he had missed while building his career. There was Abu Simbel to see and the Great Wall of China. They would travel together for a year. Maybe longer. When they returned, Jenny's divorce would be final. Then they would decide about their future together. Maybe it would work out. Maybe it wouldn't. They would see.

'What will you do if you don't practice law?' Gregory asked.

'That's something I don't want to think about now. Don't be so maudlin. Hell, you're making me feel worse than I feel already.'

Gregory blushed. 'You're right. Shit, I never used to get so sloppy. It must be old age.'

David smiled, and so did Greg.

'That's the boy,' David said.

He looked away from Gregory and looked at the room once more. The desk was big and old. He'd had it since he'd started practicing. He tried to remember how much he'd paid for it secondhand, but the price escaped him.

David reached out absentmindedly and ran his hand over the corner of the desk. He thought about the framed clippings he had just packed away. Some of the most exciting moments in his life had started in this room.

David had loved the law and he had been a good lawyer. Maybe one of the best. But that part of his life was over forever, once he'd pulled the trigger and ended Thomas Gault's life. No matter what the justification for the act, it had made it impossible for David to continue to practice his profession. The killing of Thomas Gault had made him an outlaw, even if no one other than Jenny knew.

'You'll come to dinner tomorrow night?' Greg asked.

'Of course.'

The plans had already been made. He was leaving the country in two days. Jenny would meet him in London in two weeks. No one knew about their affair and they felt it best to keep it that way. The Gault case was closed and they saw no reason to stir up any suspicions.

No one had questioned the story he and Jenny had agreed on. David had told the police about Gault's confessions and his meeting with Monica and Ortiz. He had recounted the incident at the house truthfully, except for one detail. David had said that Ortiz had fired, wounding Gault, who had fired simultaneously, killing Ortiz. The shot that killed Gault had been squeezed off by Ortiz just before the policeman died.

David apologized for handling Ortiz's weapon and for moving the bodies. He should have known better, but he was pretty shaken up. No one had been critical. After all, he and Jenny had gone through an ordeal. And no one really cared that an insane cop killer had been shot to death.

'I've got to get going, Greg,' David said, hefting the carton and heading for the door.

'Sure,' Gregory said.

They both paused in the doorway for one last look at the bare room.

'You'll be back,' Gregory said firmly.

'Maybe,' David said.

But he really didn't think so.